The Eyes Have No Soul

The Eyes Have No Soul

Matthew W Harrill

Copyright (C) 2018 Matthew W Harrill
Layout design and Copyright (C) 2018 Creativia
Published 2018 by Creativia
Cover art by Inkubus Design
This book is a work of fiction. Names, characters, places, and incidents are the product of the author's imagination or are used fictitiously. Any resemblance to actual events, locales, or persons, living or dead, is purely coincidental.
All rights reserved. No part of this book may be reproduced or transmitted in any form or by any means, electronic or mechanical, including photocopying, recording, or by any information storage and retrieval system, without the author's permission.

For Scott
Nothing in the world can stop you taking it on and prevailing. Diabetes isn't an end. It's a beginning.

Prologue

No matter how hard Clare Rosser tried to escape the house of her birth in the sleepy forest town of Holden, Massachusetts, life kicked her in the guts by drawing her back. It had only been eighteen months. Freedom had been hers at last. Clare, with all her determination and drive, had sworn that she would get out of Dodge. Yet here she was, in her sophomore year, being dragged home in order to mitigate another disaster. She just could not escape.

The trouble was she had no idea exactly what she was returning to this time round. Only hours before, Clare had been watching an old John Wayne flick with her friends and boyfriend. One phone call later, she had hurtled down route 90 from her rented house in Brookline, Boston, to deal with the latest drama. Was Mom ill? Had Dad drunk himself senseless again? Nobody would say.

Clare gazed at her blue-eyed reflection in the rear-view mirror of her Mini Cooper, a car given to her by her parents as a sweet sixteen present, and four years later the only item from them she treasured. Dad had imported the shell and restored the car to perfect working order, painted it red with twin white stripes on the hood and delivered it to her with a bank of blinding headlights attached to the front and a full tank of diesel. Never mind that it was a petrol engine and had to be fully drained and cleaned before she could take it out.

One of many mistakes her dad had made with the best intentions, like the time he had chased off a would-be boyfriend who just wanted to play her a song with his guitar. He wanted his daughter homebound. It only drove her further away. Her cell began to ring from its place on the passenger seat; Clare picked the phone up, wedging it between shoulder and ear. "Hello?"

"Clare? Clare Rosser? Is that you?"

"Yes. This is Clare."

"Hello dear, it's Dr. Julian Strange. I am your family —"

"Yes, I know perfectly well who you are, Julian. What's going on?" Julian Strange had been the Rosser family physician for as long as Clare could remember. He had dealt with the fallout of her parents' bouts of alcoholism with good grace, patient and informative. He was professional to the core when Clare had needed a father figure, sometimes impersonal, like he didn't want to get too close.

"Are you on your way?"

Clare glanced out of the window. In the growing dusk, the woodland of southernmost Holden thrust up like a series of fingers clawing out of the hillside ahead. The police roadblock, comprised of three cars parked at random angles on the nearside of the railway crossing, lay between her and her house beyond. "I'm nearby. Julian, what's going on?"

There was a pause. "Just… Just get here as soon as you can, Clare."

"What do you mean 'get here as soon as you can'?" Clare shouted down the phone in response. "Why can't you just tell me what's going on?"

There was no reply. Clare glared at the screen. The call had been disconnected. This left her even more frustrated. Resisting the urge to scream and throw her phone, Clare set it down on the black vinyl of the passenger seat and concentrated on the roadblock. It would do no good for her to end up another footnote in the Rosser family casualty dossier. She gripped the steering wheel so hard the molded plastic creaked and turned the car around. There was another way in.

Holden's outskirts flashed by in a blur of buildings and streetlights, the traffic for once accommodating Clare as she traversed the town.

By the time she turned into the far end of Pleasant Street, the sky was almost completely black, only the slightest impression of darkest blue giving hint that beyond the hills of central Massachusetts, it was not yet fully night.

The bank of headlights on her Mini Cooper made Clare feel as though she was burrowing through a tunnel of light into the forest leaning over the highway. So intent was she on getting to her parents' house that she jumped with a small yelp when her phone rang once more, the 'Star Trek' theme blaring loud. Her brothers' name was on the screen.

A deer jumped out of the forest. Clare slammed on her brakes. In an instant, it leapt away, another ghost in the dark, a memory to be retained on this bizarre night. Once the shock passed, Clare took a deep breath, willing her body to calmness. She only had one goal: Reaching her brother.

"Jeff, tell me that you're home."

There was a pause, as if the person on the end of the line were confused by her response.

"Clare?" It was her brother.

"Jeff? Where are you?"

"I was away hunting with Bo and his dad. I just got back. What's going on? There's police all round our house."

In one of those strange moments of lucidity, insight hit Clare. "Jeff, have the police seen you?"

"Not yet. I'm standing by the big tree in the McCade's garden." The treehouse was now rotten, timbers uncared for and disused. Clare remembered it well, three houses away from her own. Good memories from childhood, like that old tree, were rare.

"Jeff, I want you to stay right there. Stay out of sight."

"What's going on?"

"I… I don't know. They won't tell me. Hold on, I'm coming."

The road plunged back into woodland as Clare navigated Sunnyside Avenue, an ironic name if any given the manner of her visit. Up ahead, she could see the flashing blues and reds of a fleet of police vehicles, packed onto the gravel driveway. This was not just the local sheriff come to visit.

An ambulance had just pulled away, speeding off in the opposite direction past the first roadblock. Clare resisted the urge to follow it and parked on the street, out of sight of the flashing lights. The earthy scent of woodland was normally a balm to her, but there was nothing calming about what was going on here.

As soon as she jumped out, intent on finding Jeff, a figure stepped out of the shadow of the garden.

"It's you," Jeff said. With a slight height advantage, Jeff Rosser made an imposing shadow backlit as he was by blue and red strobes.

Clare grabbed her younger brother in a brief embrace. He was ice-cold. "What's been going on here?"

He turned to the scene of whatever crime had been committed. "I don't know. They carried… something out just now. Evidence zipped up in two black bags. It didn't look heavy enough to be bodies. Clare, did Dad finally snap for good?"

"You think he'd kill Mom?"

Jeff nodded, unable to utter the words they were both scared to say, lest they be true.

"He couldn't."

"Clare, you haven't been here. Dad's been all over the place. He looked thin, like he wasn't eating right. So did Mom. All they did was drink all day. Anything they could get their hands on. I stayed out of the way. I've been away over the weekend."

Clare held on to him for a moment. His body was cold, tired. He shivered in her grasp despite his muscular body. "Get in my car and stay there. There's a blanket in the back. Wrap yourself in it. No arguments. I'll go take a look around and come get you when I know something."

Clare left her brother by the Mini, every step taking her closer to uncertainty. Her home should have been a refuge, *the* sanctuary to which she could retreat in times of crisis. Yet here it was, the nexus of chaos it had always been. She passed several vehicles, all unattended, engines still hot, reaching the yellow tape that read: 'Crime scene – do not cross'. It was her house. She cared not for such barriers.

"Miss," warned a deep voice from beside the front door, "step back please. You can't come in here."

"The hell I can't," Clare shot back. "My parents live here, and you guys called me. I didn't drive all the way from Boston to be turned away."

The cop appeared confused. He turned to another cop. "Who called her?"

Clare pounced on this moment of hesitancy to lift the tape and push the front door wide open. Intuition told Clare the face she looked upon now would become one that would corner her at every turn from this point forward in her life.

"Hello, I'm Detective Andrew Harley. Can I help you, young lady?"

Clare stared, silent. There were people in her kitchen, beyond the hallway, two men wearing FBI accreditation glanced up at her and closed the door. The detective attempted to block her view with his considerable frame.

"Miss, are you Clare Rosser?"

Her attention turned from the intruders in the kitchen. "Yes, I am Clare. What are you doing here? What happened?"

Harley frowned. The crease in his brow was made all the more severe by the iron-gray hair cut short, military style. Clearly, he was not used to being addressed in such a manner. His bulk was muscle turned to fat judging by the lack of definition around his midriff. This was a man used to giving orders from an office, not pounding the beat.

"If you would sit down—" Harley indicated with one greasy hand that she move to the couch in the living room. His breath reeked of beer. This was a man who, until very recently, had been out enjoying himself at some cheap diner.

The Eyes Have No Soul

"No, dammit, I won't sit down. I've just driven from Boston and nobody will give me any answers. Why are Federal Agents in my kitchen? Where are my parents?"

Harley attempted to guide her to the lounge. Clare dodged round him and ran up the stairs to her mother's bedroom; her parents had slept apart for years in an attempt to maintain the fiction of family. They were ultimately too cowardly to separate for good. They had always felt the need to suffer in silence, the pretence enough to fool outsiders.

"Wait," called Harley's croaky cigarette-scarred voice from behind her. "You can't go in there."

"Mom?" Clare called. "Dad?" She threw open her mother's bedroom door and froze.

The room had been scoured clean. A man in a boiler suit was scrubbing the floor. The room reeked of disinfectant. In a moment, Harley was upon her, yanking her out by the arm. "This is a crime scene, girl."

"Where exactly is your crime scene? You can't have been here much more than an hour."

He pulled her to the landing, knocking into a side table. A lamp tipped over, rolling to hang by its cable.

"Where is all the equipment? Who's leading the walk-through? Where are all your analysts?"

Clare tugged against him, standing her ground as he attempted to pull her down the stairs.

"How can you have taken trace evidence if the room is clean? Where are the photographers? Sketch artists? Where is your evidence log?"

She snatched her arm away from the detective. "Where. Are. My. Parents?"

Harley's skin had begun to mottle with suppressed rage. His voice was strained. "I'm sorry, Miss Rosser, your parents were found deceased earlier. There was no sign of a struggle. The bodies have to go off for post mortem…"

The words hit her, but did not register beyond the word 'deceased'. Her parents were gone. All sound became muted, as she looked inward, seeking a logical explanation. Her parents were dead? They were dysfunctional, but they wouldn't just lie down and die. The taste of iron spread around her mouth and Clare realized that she had bitten her bottom lip.

Harley was still speaking to her. "...social services will be contacted."

"What? No. I don't need social services. I'm twenty; Jeff is nearly eighteen. We will manage just fine. When will the police and lab reports be available?"

Harley appeared caught off-guard by her straightforward, dispassionate approach. "I don't know what you think you will glean from that, young lady."

His tone just made her mad. How dare he talk down to her?

"Don't be so condescending. I'm majoring in Criminal Justice at Boston. I know what's supposed to be going on here. You don't clean up a crime scene after an hour."

"Unfortunately for you, we are not in Boston."

So this is how it was. Clare pushed past Harley and started down the stairs. "Fine, I'll just ask those Feds."

"What Feds?" came Harley's seemingly innocent reply.

Clare turned at the bottom of the stairs to glare at the man then ran to the kitchen, finding it now devoid of any life. She stood there for a moment, confused, before Harley closed in behind her, the front of his belly touching against her back.

"Thank you for your cooperation, miss. It has made our conclusion to this investigation much more thorough. If you need anything else..." Harley ran his hand down her arm. "You have but to call the precinct in Worcester and ask for me."

Clare remained motionless. Evidently deprived of more sport by lack of reaction, Harley moved off, his heavy footsteps making the floorboards creak as he left the house, the door wide open. What police cars were left pulled out of the driveway and onto the road, vanishing in a cloud of grit-filled dust.

The Eyes Have No Soul

The house was empty, soulless. The pines that leaned over accentuated the gloom. The heart of Clare's home had been ripped out, leaving a gaping hole that could never again be filled.

At length, Clare felt a familiar presence. "They've gone, Jeff."

"The cops? Yeah, I watched them. That last one looked nasty."

"No Jeff. Mom and Dad. The cops took their bodies, and I think we won't ever find out why."

Jeff put his arm around her shoulder in an attempt to comfort her. Clare took hold of his hand. Jeff had always cared for others over himself. He had a huge heart.

"Are you gonna be all right?" she asked, still stunned by the turn of events.

Jeff squeezed her tight. "I'll be okay. I've pretty much avoided them since you left. I'll be joining you in October at Boston. I got in."

This at least brought a smile to Clare's lips. He hadn't mentioned anything until now. "Jeff, that's fantastic. I'm so proud."

He shrugged. "I might make something of myself yet. What about you?"

Clare turned to her younger brother. "I'm gonna find out what that cop wouldn't tell me."

Chapter One

"You can do this."

Clare Rosser studied her reflection as she leaned over the sink in the Worcester P.D. restroom. It was a room designed by men, for men: Functional and faded yellow, reeking of cheap pine cleaner. It cried out 'no women allowed'. After ten years of being stuck in forensic analysis, she would change that.

Her hands gripped the side of the sink, nails trimmed back in a fit of haste, skin taut and lifeless, the skeletal nature of her narrow frame betraying the bone and tendons beneath with far too much ease. She attempted a smile, but it came off as more of a grimace. Blue eyes stared back at her from behind horn-rimmed glasses, the lenses perfectly clear but far too thick for her preference. It was a legacy of reading in dim light or at night with flashlights.

Clare considered her face. It was not unattractive, with high cheekbones and pursed lips. Her small ears were hidden behind honey-blonde hair that hung limp in a style that might have been called a bob were it not just too long, descending lifeless over the top of her shoulders. She brushed the hair back past her right ear, a habit from childhood she had never managed to break.

She leaned forward, reassessing her previous motivation. "This is what you have been working toward. You. Will. Do. This."

Her voice was determined; some might say harsh. Years of mothering Jeff following the death of her parents twelve years ago had lent an air of authority to what she was convinced were flowery enough tones. It was a voice others used to tell her 'put people at ease'. Perhaps that was their way of saying she sounded boring. She was not the girl she had been when this had all started. Seasoned, some might call her now. Jaded was perhaps a better term.

Clare sighed. It was her whole demeanor, she decided. With the lace-cuffed silk blouse and the light-green woollen cardigan done up with mottled-brown buttons she favored atop the calf-length heavy tweed skirt, she looked quite the schoolmistress, a good decade older than her thirty-two years.

Her only concession was her footwear. She glanced down at the pair of khaki walking shoes she wore everywhere, the word 'Berghaus' emblazoned on the side in black stitching. Dried mud crept up the sides of the soles, evidence of her walk through the gorgeous autumn woodland on her way to the bus, the golden leaves of the American Linden mixed with the reds and greens of fading oak. Clare preferred the outdoors. It was the unexplained circumstance of her parents' death that had led her from the woods and into the forensics labs, via a degree from Boston in Criminal Justice.

Only half an hour before, she had been in the lab, white-coated and studious, working her way through the backlog of rape kits that had been pouring into the department. This particular kit had been proving most elusive. Despite the extensive set of swabs and clothing, all results appeared to just fade away before her, the analysis always proving inconclusive. Clare was a firm believer in logic and ran her finger over the small golden badge on the lapel of her blouse as if to remind herself why she was doing this.

The call had come out of the blue. Captain Latchford wanted to see her. This could mean only one thing. Her test results were in, and she had an interview for patrol. At long last, she would be one step closer to a place that would make a difference, a place she could use her skills to find the answers both she and Jeff had sought for the last dozen years. She had never wanted anything more for herself than closure.

Turning away from the mirror, Clare pulled on the handle of the restroom door. Her hand slipped, slick with sweat. She really was nervous now. Wiping her hand on the ridged fabric of her skirt, she tried again and made it into the hallway. The door slammed shut behind her, and she jumped. Clenching her jaw, she thrust her hands down by her sides, taking a deep breath and ignoring the chuckles of a couple of passing beat-cops.

The hallways of the precinct were much the same in nature to that of the restroom. Clare felt, as she often did, that she might well be walking the set of *Hill Street Blues* with the crowded bulletin boards dripping leaflets of rule and instruction, missing people, out-of-date social events. The cops that held sway here didn't realize they were in the twenty-first century. The musty scent of old, curled paper stuck in the back of her mouth. The hallways were cloying in the early autumn and unbearable in the summer. At least, her labs were clean and air-conditioned.

Polished floor tiles gleamed as the over-bright panelled ceiling illumination shone back up at her, causing Clare to squint. As she reached the conference room, the location of her interview, the notices were replaced with framed scenes of faded old Worcester and the officers, men with integrity, who had founded this station. It gave her pride to know that at one time, there had been people interested in the actual job of policing.

Clare took a deep breath and closed her eyes, steadying her nerves. Inside this room lay her future. Beyond this door were the answers she sought and had worked so hard for, how her parents had died. She knocked once, the sound echoing down the empty hallway behind her, and entered.

The centerpiece of the conference room was a flag that hung from the ceiling. The dark blue background hosted the shield she had strived to earn, with the words 'Worcester Police Department' emblazoned in gold beneath it. This symbol had always given Clare hope, and more than a little longing for resolution. Yet today, the flag went unnoticed as Clare stared in disbelief at the people gathered around the table beneath it. All men. The scene looked like the parole hearings in The Shawshank Redemption, and her stomach began to tighten.

Two of the group Clare did not know, but she recognized Detective Paul Barton and his cohort, Lieutenant Nick Morgan in an instant, sneers on the faces of both. There was no sign of Captain Latchford. This did not bode well. She approached and took her seat.

One of the unknown men, bordering on elderly with sagging jowls and a belly that threatened to burst his uniform asked, "And you are?"

"Clare Rosser, sir." He had rank over her whether he displayed it or not. "Be polite," Mom had said in one of her last lucid moments before Boston. The memory had stuck.

In response, the old man turned to his colleagues. "Looks like they'll let anyone apply for patrol now." He proceeded to wheeze a laugh at his own joke.

Clare let it slide. This was too important. Her entire life had built to this moment. "If I may, I was called here by Captain Latchford. Is he not part of the interview panel?"

Barton, a thug with tiny, suspicious eyes, squinted at her beneath a crop of curly brown hair and shuffled papers on the table in front of him. "I'm afraid Devin had to step out. A case of… what did he call it?"

"Boiling, twisted guts is how he described the feeling," supplied Morgan, a short, suave man but known to contain a ferocious temper behind his dark looks. "As it stands, you're double-booked. Please go to room forty-two, where your interview will take place. Thank you."

And that was it. Struggling to breathe amidst the testosterone wafting from this collection of alpha males, Clare turned with as much dignity as she could muster and left.

Her destination was only a few doors down. The wooden door was painted white with frosted glass, the kind that looked like it had a grid of metal wiring going through. It was a typical soulless representation of the entire precinct in Clare's opinion. The polished brass nameplate read 'Captain Andrew Harley' in black letters. This meant a rejection. To Clare, it was the worst kind of no. Yet, she persisted.

Clare knocked three times on the door and waited. Patience was a virtue. There were voices within, jovial in nature. The glass darkened, and the door opened after a brief pause. Wearing his trademark oversized blue suit trousers and a beige shirt with the sleeves rolled up, the aging detective Mike Caruso finished a joke, walking past her without acknowledgement. Clare was left in the hallway, an open door between her and the captain's desk.

A few awkward moments passed before Harley glanced up. "Ah Clare, there you are. Come in and take a seat."

On his deathbed, Harley will be perfunctory. Doing as bidden, Clare shut the door behind her, sitting opposite the captain, arranging her skirt to her satisfaction, and brushing her hair back. The room was soundproofed. Despite its age, there was an utter lack of noise anywhere, now that she sat still. It was unnerving. Resting her hands in her lap, Clare waited for the Captain to finish reading through his documentation. It gave her a chance to study his face. With a granite jaw and receding grey hair, he was every bit the aging commander, safe in the knowledge that he would end his career exactly where he had started it. The yellowed tips of his agitated fingers and slight wheeze when he breathed told a different story. Harley was a well-known chain-smoker who no doubt wanted nothing better than to be outside puffing away. The room stank of stale smoke, more than should be from an outside smoker, testament to the fact that he didn't always obey office rules. Clare suspected that with the stress of the job he wouldn't make retirement.

"So then. Clare. Clarey-Clare. Let's see." His voice, while deep, had traces of his addiction in it, the graveled tones he used to end sentences, the slight breathlessness.

"What do we have here? Born, Worcester, nineteen eighty-two." He paused and glanced up at her as if he couldn't quite believe the fact. "You attended Davis Hill Elementary School, Holden. You then moved on to Wachusett Regional High School, Holden. Not one for adventure, are we? Ah, here we have it. You graduated with a Degree in Criminal Justice, Boston. Then straight back here, enrolling in the department as an analyst, exceling in forensic science ever since." The unspoken question was left hanging.

"Why do you care why I stayed? Most people stay near where they're born and raised. My brother was here, as you well know. I felt obliged to look after him. As it was, I was home every weekend until he joined me in Boston. You know all of this. This isn't a real job interview. Why persist with the charade?"

Harley shuffled through his documents, ignoring her question, the noise of sheet scraping sheet irritating her. "Ah yes Jeff, your younger half-brother, the only other occupant of your house other than Steve the cat."

The mention of the tortoiseshell stray she had fostered brought a small smile to Clare's mouth.

"You brought up your brother alone?"

"I had no choice. It was that or the foster care system, which was pointless since he was almost eighteen. After my parents..."

"Ched and Patricia Rosser," Harley supplied as if their names weren't already burned into her soul.

"Found dead October twenty-second, two thousand and two. Cause of death?" He looked up, his face unreadable. "It appears this was inconclusive."

"There was more to it than an inconclusive result, and you know it," Clare argued. "You were there, in my house when I arrived, with no crime scene left to analyze, after an hour of examination!"

"There were suspicious circumstances with no evidence. I know this, Miss Rosser. My report is still perfectly legible."

"There were stains on the floor..."

"No evidence. It says so in this report. This signed and authenticated report."

Harley pushed a folder yellowed with age across his desk toward her, opening it so she could read. The words 'death by natural cause' burned into her mind. There was no such thing. Not with so many police there, and Feds to boot.

Harley stared at her. Unbowed, Clare stared straight back, only averting her gaze to brush her hair back once more.

Harley grunted at her evident admission of subservience and continued to read. "All right then. Written test scores came back as ninety-eight percent. That's quite exceptional. Your use of logic is without flaw, just about."

Clare was stunned, blinking a couple of times; she caught her breath. "Does that mean I get the job?"

"In a word, no."

Clare's heart sank. She had expected this result given the turn of events, yet she had fostered a glimmer of hope in her heart. Harley had done this on purpose, baiting her. He had never liked her, not since the first time they had met, her as a student challenging his sloppy methods at the scene of her parents' death. If he were to have a motto, she was sure it would read, 'never question the alpha-male'.

"Logic is not the only way to solve a crime. We were looking for a demonstration of insight, of gut instinct in your written test. You failed to think outside of the box, and in our patrolmen, especially those who have aspirations to detective, we want those that see the trees and notice more than a collection of wood and leaves."

"Those test scores must without any doubt put me ahead of anybody else who has taken them." Clare was growing incensed. The decision had been made, against all logical reasoning.

"That's not your problem. You are a great forensic expert. You use facts and rules and apply them to the job. That is enough for what you do in analysis. It is not the only required skill to make detective. We both know why you want the job, and it is not to solve any other crime but that which you perceive has been committed on your parents. Let me be as clear as I can to you." Harley leaned forward, his eyes piercing. "That. Case. Is. Closed. If you keep persisting in trying to find answers that are not there, you will find yourself out of a job in this department and, without a doubt, on the wrong side of a jail cell. Give it up. Keep doing what you do best. Good morning."

The Eyes Have No Soul

    The dismissal brooked no argument. Captain Harley turned away, picking up his cell phone. Soon, he was chortling to another colleague, the topic of discussion sexist and ribald.
    Clare remained seated, glaring at her nemesis. She wouldn't be dismissed this way. At least not until Harley noticed her still present and flicked his hand toward the door, dismissing her without even looking. Maintaining her dignity, Clare left without looking back, though inwardly she was seething. Her dream was shattered.

Chapter Two

This wasn't over. Clare stood staring at Harley's door, trying to imagine how that conversation could have taken any other direction. Her dreams dashed again.

"For now," Clare growled at the office, the scent of defeat only a whiff in her nostrils.

"What's for now?" A voice, polite and very familiar, enquired. Versace perfume confirmed the presence of a friend.

Clare turned away from hurling imaginary insults at her nemesis, to find the diminutive Tina Svinsky, all bubbles and cheer, smiling up at her. "Walk with me."

Tina fell in beside her, the frenetic movement of a shorter person attempting to keep up with her taller companion comedic in nature. Clare produced a rueful smile. Tina Svinsky was ten years her senior and at an inch over five feet in height, five inches shorter. During Clare's tenure in forensics, Tina had become the darling of the precinct. She made detective younger than anybody in the history of Worcester P.D., served on several multi-jurisdictional federal task-forces combating organized crime, and had earned the nickname 'The Golden Sweeper' for her insight and seemingly preternatural ability to clean up an ever-growing list of murder-one cases. The world was going straight to hell, except for Tina's aptitude for solving crime. She had become everything Clare wanted to be.

"So do you want to tell me what happened back there?" Tina said this without looking at her as they traversed the hallways of the precinct. Fortunately for Clare, the station was a large enough hub that she could avoid Harley should she so desire.

"He stiffed me," Clare muttered. "I didn't make patrol again. That's the third time in six years. The promotion panel was full of his cronies and they sent me to him for my own personal interview." She snorted a laugh of derision. "Apparently, I am one hell of an analyst but will never be detective material so I'm not even going on the beat." Her comment was ladled in sarcasm.

"Where was Captain Latchford? Isn't he responsible for promotions in his department?"

"They said he was taken ill. Right before I went in. I had the call from him not thirty minutes before the interview."

A janitor bustled past, pushing a bucket on wheels with the handle of his mop. He kept his head down as he passed the two women, but Clare watched him as he moved to the far side of the hallway. The janitor stole a glance at her as he slunk around a corner on his way to what she presumed was his lair in some distant part of the building. He looked at her as though he knew her, his face somewhat familiar; it creeped Clare out.

Tina followed Clare's gaze. "Everything all right?"

"I feel like I know that guy."

"The janitor?"

Clare brushed her hair back with a finger. "I don't know. It's one of those days, I guess."

Tina reached round with an arm, constricting Clare with a tight squeeze. Small definitely did not mean weak. "I'm sorry, sweetie. I wish there was something I could do."

"Can't you speak to your bosses? I can do this, Tina."

"Sorry, hun. They are out of town. That's the thing about working for multiple jurisdictions. Nobody knows from one day to the next where they might end up. Besides, you know they keep their own counsel on who they choose to join their ranks. Until you are noticed, or I join the ranking officers of the task force, your job is here. Your best chance is doing something unprecedented." Tina stopped at a gray door, very nondescript and unassuming. She placed her hand on Clare's arm. "Look, I'm here for a week or so. I'm babysitting some junior detectives who're looking into thefts at the unopened wing of St Vincent's hospital. I've got to head out now to that half-staffed county jail for a couple hours. That's where they're holding the suspects. When I get back, let's get together to work on highlighting your transferable skills and honing the instinct you don't appear to need. In time, maybe you will get that chance."

"My analysis of the situation concludes you are correct."

Tina grinned impudently in return, evidently pleased that she had gotten through, and with a quick bob of the head, disappeared into the dark room beyond the gray door.

Clare signed and resumed her trudging march to the forensics lab.

Two flights of stairs and several sterile hallways later, Clare was still wondering what her purpose in life really was as she entered her home away from home, the Worcester Police Department's forensic analysis labs. She took a deep breath, leaning forward until her forehead touched the rough surface of the doorframe where varnish had long peeled away. They were going to want to know what went on upstairs. She pulled on the cool stainless steel handle, breaching the divide between the archaic past and the scientific future of policing.

The forensics lab was one of the few parts of the precinct to have been upgraded. Along with the morgue, which would once not have looked out of place in a fifties horror flick, Clare's lab had been granted funds by a state committee who were attempting to bring policing into the twenty-first century. Naturally, the upgrade had been resisted by Harley and his troop of eighties throwbacks. In a rare move, the District Attorney had thrown out their objections and forced them to embrace the technological advances of the new world. Everybody had an agenda.

Clare pulled the door closed with a little too much force. The slam caused all three of her colleagues to stop and look up from their respective niches in amongst shelves bearing reference books, ultra-modern spectrometers and other assorted gadgetry. She took a moment to breathe in the scents. Ancient knowledge, passed down in writing since the first great scientists realized that evidence could solve cases with irrefutable proof, mixed with newly polished wood and modern fabrics. It calmed her. The lab was bright with fake lighting, but this was new; the aim was to simulate day. No wonder the team had the reputation of living in another world from the rest of the precinct.

"Here to pick up your junk?" asked Sunny Chen, a second generation Chinese American, without looking up from the mass spectrometer. His words were blunt, but he meant well.

"Not this time." Clare attempted to put a brave face on, but her voice was full of frustration.

The youngest member of the team, Alison, who was twenty-five and had only joined the previous year, approached still clad in lab coat and blue rubber gloves. She wrapped her arms around Clare, who was grateful for the contact.

"I'm sorry," she said, a few wisps of red hair coming loose across her face. "At least you still have us."

Alison's innocent comment made Clare smile. The warmth she radiated was infectious. "That's true. What would I do without my little family?"

"So there was no chance at all?"

Clare shrugged, moving across the room to her desk, where a row of folders sat on a shelf above a gray desk, bare but for a laptop and a small framed photo of her tortoiseshell cat, Steve. Clare always kept her office space logical and tidy. She flicked on the laptop, seeing an email waiting in her inbox: confirmation that she had been unsuccessful. She deleted the message without reading it and slapped the laptop closed, causing Sunny to jump. "There's only one way to advance in this place: Work with Harley."

"Good. You aren't busy," said a voice from the other end of the lab where Helen, the boss, presided over the team. "Clare, come join me in my office please."

The door to Helen's office was open; Helen Cook, the detective in charge of the various Crime Lab teams had witnessed all of Clare's conversation. Her face without expression, Clare crossed the intervening space and shut the door behind her.

"Take a seat," Helen invited, pointing at the chair opposite her own at a small round table.

Clare did as bidden. She had always loved this office. Floor to ceiling shelving held a wealth of literature, medical and otherwise. The grand, white L-shaped desk that was Helen's center of power stood unused for now. Helen only sat there on official business, so this was to be informal.

"Water?" Helen offered.

"Please. I've been parched lately." Clare drained the proffered glass in one go upon receipt.

Helen watched her for a moment before continuing. "Are you all right?"

"What do you mean? Has my work not been up to standard?"

"No, that's never been a problem. You just appear a bit… underfed is probably the most accurate word. I need to make sure you are all performing as best you can. Beyond that, I care."

Again Clare examined her hands. "Maybe I could eat a bit more. It doesn't seem that important lately."

Helen leaned forward. "See that you do. You can't function if you don't eat properly. Now, tell me what happened."

Clare attempted to calm the turmoil within her thoughts. "Would it really be any surprise to you? We all knew Captain Latchford was a man of fairly progressive views. He was taken ill between the phone call and my getting to the interview. Harley staged the whole event to show me up."

"That's a pretty strong accusation," Helen warned.

"You know the story as well as anybody. He's blocked me from the very first time we met. There are files out there with information about what happened to my parents, I'm convinced of this."

"Have you considered that this fact might be the very reason you are blocked from joining the squad of the very man you are trying your best to bring down? You have aptitude and intelligence but you fight him every step of the way. It's professional suicide or at the least strongly masochistic."

Clare frowned. "I wasn't applying to his squad. I was applying to Latchford's. I'm not afraid of him."

"That is evident. But fear is not the issue. Andrew Harley is old world, with a network of like-minded thinkers. There is no place in his division for a woman, especially one with guts."

"Tina?"

"Detective Svinsky isn't subject to Harley's influence in her task force, Clare. That is not the case for Worcester-based cops. I just got off the phone with an old friend. One who knows more about this precinct than most of the other officers; Devin, Captain Latchford, was causing waves among his fellows. They don't like his progressive thinking. He is seriously ill, in the ICU at UMASS. They aren't confidant he will make it. I'll tell you what that means. Harley is in charge of the detective bureau. However, he has his fingers in all sorts of pies. If the legal system didn't prevent it, he would send forensics back to the dark ages. He is a dinosaur, but one with clout."

Clare's eyes narrowed. "You agree with me."

"I do. However, you have to remember I can't afford to have idealism expressed in such an obvious way. You haven't been exposed to the management in such a profound manner before. You do not want to make enemies out of people who are already not fond of you."

Clare's heart began to thump hard in her chest. Support unlooked for was always welcome and the adrenaline surged through her body. A bead of sweat began to wind its way down her neck. "You agree with me; yet, you want me to stay quiet?"

"I want you to consider what impact your actions might have if you try to cause a stir. You won't just be exposing yourself to them, but this entire department, and the advancements that benefit us."

"Harley has bigger ambitions." Clare mulled this over for a few moments. Corruption. How deep did it run? The promotion panel, certainly. Any appeal was out of the question in the state of Massachusetts without obvious discrimination. Were her colleagues corrupt? Clare glanced out at the lab through the window beside the door, and then back at Helen.

"He wants to be Chief. That's it, right?"

Helen crossed the room, pausing to glance at the team before she drew the blinds. "He could well end up in that position. Chief Goldsmith is far past retirement age. Promotion is likely to come from within given the network Harley has."

"Chief Harley," Clare spat. "That sounds like a bad joke."

"It's been years in the making. You are on his side, or you don't have a side. That's really all there is to it."

Clare stared in a moment of silence at her boss, a woman she had always trusted to lead the team forward, full of sensible decisions. She played the game just like the rest of them.

"I never stood a chance did I?"

"Let me give you some advice, Clare. If you continue to seek the answers here in this manner, you will find life very difficult. I only offer this to you because I am fond of you. I have protected you more than you know. However, with this turn of events, it won't be enough. Keep your head down."

Taking a deep breath, Clare stood. "You won't want me to say anything, I presume?"

"Best not."

"Look, it's been a hell of a day so far. I'm gonna take some time to assess my situation. I just can't stay in here right now."

Helen didn't move. "I think that would be preferable. Don't do anything precipitous."

The Eyes Have No Soul

Clare pushed her way out of the office. In the lab, Sunny and Alison had again stopped working, watching her.

Stopping only to grab her bag, Clare said, "I'll be back." She refused to look them in the eye, focusing on the door to the lab. She passed through, letting the door swing shut behind her. Outside, those in the hallways scrambled to get out of her way, or stopped and stared, mocking smiles on their faces. Did everybody here know about her? There was a nervous aroma in the air, as if everybody were reluctant to be seen even standing next to her.

Clare ignored them all and walked out of the precinct, heading for her car. She glanced back. In a window near the entrance stood the janitor, watching her without moving.

Chapter Three

Still ranting under her breath Clare hunted down her car, now a scarlet '69 Chevy Impala, and wrenched the door open. Turning the engine with a harsh twist of the key, she gunned the throttle, gripping the cracked cover of the steering wheel so tight the jagged edges of the painted chrome rim threatened to cut her hands. The town of Holden was the perfect antidote to the bustle of Worcester. Twenty miles out from the city center, it was an easy commute, no more than an hour on a day of heavy traffic, half that if Clare felt liberal with the gas.

Only six miles from end to end, Holden lay north-west of the city. It lay in a gentle bowl amid the rolling hills of central Massachusetts, the peaks crowned with groves of oak and beech in the early stages of the riot of fall colours. It made living in Massachusetts a blessing.

The traffic was light at this time of day, before rush hour commenced and gridlock ensued. Clare missed her nimble Mini Cooper. It had been logical to appropriate Dad's much larger car when her favorite toy had finally broken down for good. She loved it but it had become a money pit.

Half way home, Clare decided to stop at one of her favorite spots. Just south of Holden lay Chaffin Pond, a beautiful fishing lake. It had been a favorite haunt of her father when she was young. Throughout her childhood he would drag her along to fish for large-mouth bass and each time she'd always make a bigger catch.

Taking a left onto Gail Drive by a miniscule green road sign, Clare enjoyed the homey nature of the place: Single-story houses with ornate mailboxes and sculptured gardens. Pylons and overhead wiring jumped from side to side, somehow not looking out of place amidst the assorted conifers and pines scattered about the place.

She shifted into neutral and let the engine idle as the car rolled down the slight incline. At the end of the road, speckled with shade, Clare brought the car to a halt on the side of a turning point. Trees blocked the view of the lake. Since Clare had no need to be anywhere, she left the Impala where it was and crept through the trees to the edge of the lake.

The sight was worth the wait. Green-blue water reflected the sunlight as if trying to impress the heavens. A slight breeze caused the merest ripples atop the surface. Clare stopped for a moment, closing her eyes and breathing in the clean air. Despite the proximity to development, it was a world away from the pollution-filled Worcester streets. In the distance off to her right, Clare noted the squeaky chirrup of a small flock of bluebirds. Nearby, an insistent tapping betrayed the presence of a nuthatch as it tried to jimmy open an early-fallen acorn.

"Beautiful sight, isn't it?" said an elderly voice from off to her right.

Startled, Clare turned toward the source of the voice, finding instead the madcap nuthatch scampering headfirst down the trunk of a gnarled old oak to where an acorn was wedged in a crack. Beyond the tree, an old man waited, rod in his right hand, the forefinger of his left across his lips. They watched in silence as the bird attempted to crack the nut, before sensing an audience and flying up to perch in another branch, where, in safety, it could berate them in high-pitched and nasal tones.

Clare smiled. "It is indeed. Just the break from reality I needed. How goes the hunt?"

The old man shrugged, a flat cap full of decorated fishhooks slipping to one side of his head. He grabbed the hat before it fell to the ground. It looked as old as him. "So so. Not a lot biting in this sun."

"Is it full of weed down here? Large-Mouth Bass don't grow so big when there's a lot of weed. It stunts their growth and makes them harder to catch."

The old man blinked in surprise. "Local gal, are ya?"

"My dad used to bring me here," Clare didn't want to answer his question directly.

He accepted her response with good grace. "You'd be surprised how they take if you use the right lure, cast in the right place."

With that, the old man jerked his rod away from her, the bend indicating that he had struck.

"Fish on!" he chortled with glee and began to spar with his unseen aquatic foe. The fish was strong; several times the old man had to let line out just to prevent the tension from snapping his rod.

"The damn bugger's headed for the weeds," he cursed and began to pull the rod up and down, winding in the line as he did so.

"Hand me that net, would you, girl?"

Clare did as bidden. Clearly used to fishing alone, he manipulated the net with one hand while holding the rod high with the other. Crouching at the edge of the lake, he reached into the net, freeing his catch from the hook. Lifting the fish up with expertise, he showed off his trophy.

"Little beauty," he glowed. The fish was white underneath, becoming a very healthy olive green with dark speckles up higher. What stood out was the cavernous mouth, used for swallowing smaller fish, the feature that gave this species its name.

Clare reached over to stroke the smooth underbelly, the ridges of scales bumping under her fingers as she trailed her hand up along the side of the fish. "What are you going to do with it?"

He smiled, placing the fish in a larger net with care, a holding cell in which several other fish were swimming. "Dun know. Might cook some. Release the females. They're invasive, but a great fightin' fish. Smaller ones tend to taste better.

Clare leaned forward to get a better look at the haul, and the old man squinted at her. "I know you, gal. I recognize your face."

"You do, yeah?"

"You're Ched Rosser's girl. Clara."

"Clare," she smiled.

He shrugged. "Meh, close enough. Don't expect you to remember me. My name's Jim. Jim Bridger."

"Like the mountain man? I wrote a paper on him at school." Clare referred to the legendary pioneer explorer who traversed the Rockies in the nineteenth century.

This set Jim off in a fit of laughter, a wheeze that betrayed some kind of respiratory condition. "Wish I had his constitution. I worked with your pa at Alden Research, just up the way there."

"Retired now?"

Jim leaned back against the oak. "Only on account of my health. Knew your pa well, I did. Shame he took ill the way he did and your ma too. Lovely couple."

On the outside they were. Clare decided to go for broke. "I'm still looking into why they died. Did you ever hear anything?"

Jim looked lost for a moment as he thought about this. "Nah. Ched looked like he lost a bit of weight before he left work, but then that's no crime." He patted his rather ample belly. "We could all do with a bit o' that."

Clare turned her hands over, examining them for the umpteenth time that day. "Perhaps we could."

"You should go visit the lab. There was a whole bunch of your pa's stuff that they never got rid of. Stored it in a box somewhere, so I heard."

"Really? I never knew. Nobody ever got in touch."

Jim was about to elaborate when a shrieking voice pierced the serenity of the day.

"Hey, you wanna move that monstrosity from off my property? Goddamned Chevy beast parked up there like you own the place."

Jim frowned. "Marie Small, you cease your shrieking..."

"No, no. It's all right. I'll move. Jim, thanks for the memories."

"Be sure and stop by again sometime, girl. Maybe you and I'll have a fish-off."

"I'd like that."

Clare made her way back through the trees to find a rather petite old lady, silver-haired with dark eyebrows, glaring at her.

"You get gone now girl, else I'll call the cops."

The idiocy of some people astounded her. Clare wanted to argue that she was nowhere near the woman's property, which she was not. Yet, the prospect of any of this getting back to Harley was too risky. Clare glared at the woman, got into her car, revved the engine too loud, which wasn't good for it, and drove off.

Trying to keep a lid on her temper, Clare rolled down the window of her Impala, the antique chrome handle creaking in protest at the force applied. The late September air poured in, still warm in the middle of the afternoon, overlain with the pungent scent of woodland resins. The people of Holden were proud of their town, the pride reflected in the almost-clinical approach to horticulture. Clare appreciated this; the sense of order appealed to her fastidious nature. She waved to Geraldine and Tony, the sweet elderly couple who were content to enjoy their twilight years sitting together on their sheltered porch, watching the coming and goings of the town. Such simple pleasures were so hard for Clare to come by.

Turning off the highway, she slowed to a crawl as she passed through the shady oak grove that was the beginning of Pleasant Street, one of the less-populated streets in Holden and home to half a dozen of the oldest houses in town. In this heavily forested area, it was easy to lose track of just how close one was to civilization; the main road disappeared from view as she eased the car around the bend to the right. In a moment, she was alone in the woods.

Clare paused as she reached the railroad crossing. Known as the BB&G, the line stretched from Worcester up to nearby Gardner. The town had sprung up around a natural crossroads back in the eighteenth century, and the railroad had followed suit. No train approached from either direction, and she crept across the tracks, keeping a wary eye out just in case. An unused spur of the line extended from the mainline into the trees, partly covered with asphalt, partly overgrown with foot-long ferns that rustled against the side of the Impala as she pushed past. The track ended in a brick-walled tunnel, partially drilled into the hill behind her house, an abandoned relic of an older line, long since forgotten. Thick timber boards had slowly rotted over the years so that there were ways for the young and adventurous to gain access. She had only been in there a few times. The darkness was absolute.

Clare encouraged her car with a little gas, and it edged off the road, pushing through low-hanging branches until she reached an opening to the mulch-covered track to her cottage. A route ignored by her parents, the track had been the playground for Clare, Jeff and their friends through their childhood. Quests had been adventured, foes vanquished, all under the ancient oaks and in the shadow of the whitewashed walls of the fortress behind. The blackened timbers were strangled with twisting ropes of wisteria, the wealth of pale green leaves hiding most of the original surface. The whitewash beneath had long since faded to a dirty yellow. Clare inhaled the fresh air, seeking a trace of the scent. No perfume, just the heavy tang of earth and wood.

The track ended at a large pile of rubble, the remains of an outhouse left to gather moss over the decades. At its base lay a shallow pond, barely more than a puddle. Clare intended to bypass this as she headed toward the house, but an object at the edge of the water drew her attention. A small plastic ship rested at anchor, the white funnel atop a blue hull was wedged between two rocks. The neighbor's kids must have been playing again. Clare approved of the fact that the adventures continued even though she was now grown. A new generation worked their magic. In the distance, from beyond the impenetrable pine-covered ridge behind her house, the noise of kids playing sports filtered through, rising in volume as the sound traveled on the wind. Wachusett Regional High School lay so close, yet seemed a world away from this tiny, forested community.

Her garden glowed in the warm afternoon sunshine, the lawn a verdant green, beads of moisture from the morning dew refracting the light as they resisted the warmth of the day. Minuscule insects flitted in and out of the sunbeams, a myriad of microscopic golden motes. In stark contrast to the random nature of the grasping wisteria vine, the garden was well manicured, simple, and logical. One could have described it as perfunctory.

Taking one final deep scented breath from her private glade, Clare turned to the house and stopped. The front door had been left open. Clare looked about. The day grew suddenly cold. The hairs on her arms stood on end. She was not alone.

Chapter Four

Cautious but intrigued and made brave by anger, Clare pushed the door all the way open. How dare someone come into her home uninvited? She took a step into the hallway, being careful to muffle her footsteps on one of the rugs. A noise came from the kitchen, a muffled bump. She paused.

Careful here. Grab a weapon. Anything.

Clare reached for a small statue her brother Jeff had been awarded. A gold column mounted with an elongated star that looked more like the Starfleet symbol from *Star Trek*, would serve well to stab or bludgeon with if the situation came to such. It was compact and heavy.

Cautious moves. One foot placed with care in front of the other. Silent. Focused. Ready to act. Today was not a day to test Clare Rosser. Brushing her hair back over her ear with her free hand, she took the step that brought her within reach of the kitchen door. Sturdy bleached oak, the door was a couple of inches ajar, allowing for a partial view of the kitchen. The intruder could be hidden anywhere beyond, but there was no sign of disturbance.

Clare pushed the door on silent hinges, making the gap large enough for her to squeeze through while maintaining the maximum level of protection. Taking a breath to calm her nerves, she moved forward, trophy held chest high before her. She turned several times, attempting to assess the nature of the intruder. Nothing stood out. The kitchen was empty. She let out a slow breath, leaning against a cabinet, willing the tension away. Something touched her hand, and she yelped.

Turning to face her attacker, Clare was met with a small furry face turned at a slight angle. A brief 'meow' came from the tiny mouth.

"Steve!" Clare exclaimed, withdrawing her weapon and reaching her other hand out.

The tortoiseshell cat, a rescue animal, stuck his head up. Clare leaned forward, her face next to the shelf on which he stood.

In response, Steve pawed at her nose in greeting and nuzzled her head, purring.

"Ah good, you're back," said a voice from behind her.

Without thinking, Clare swung her arm, letting fly with the trophy. The pointed star embedded in the soft plaster of the kitchen wall with an audible 'thunk', three inches to the side of a very startled Jeff Rosser.

"Whoa! Steady on there, sis."

Clare put one hand to her forehead, feeling the sweat present. "Jeff. You imbecile! What are you doing?"

Clad in his dark-gray Armani business suit, with a pinstripe shirt and black tie, Jeff cut an imposing figure. That was even despite the red corkscrew curls erupting from his head, which would have made most people look comical. It was his badge of honor, marking him as the firebrand businessman people had come to fear. He was cutthroat.

"Visiting," he replied, "and making lunch. You know you really need to keep the fridge stocked. I'm almost forced to eat healthy." He placed a plate of egg salad sandwiches on the table and pulled the trophy out of the wall in one smooth move, admiring it as it came free. "Why do you keep all this crap, Clare? It looks like one huge antique store in here."

Clare shifted the chairs around the table so they remained exactly where they had been the night she came home to find her world had changed. "It reminds me of Mom and Dad, that there are answers out there still to be found."

"Yeah but this is a museum of a miserable childhood. Move on, already."

"No Jeff. It's my choice to live this way. I have my space. There was something that went on here, sinister in nature. Everything stays the way it was, no matter how long, until I can work out what it means."

Jeff shook his head. "This is obsession, sis. You're a damned-good forensic scientist. You know better than anybody that this won't solve anything."

Clare ran her hand along Steve's back, causing the cat to arch in pleasure. Steve was the only one she would allow to knock objects out of place.

"Perhaps it won't. Yet I believe there must be something I've missed."

"You just have to assume that you won't."

"No, I can't accept that." A wave of weariness came over her. Clare pulled out an ornate wooden chair and collapsed into the seat.

"Are you all right? You look like you're losing weight, sis. That's no good. There's nothing to you as it is."

Clare shrugged. "I'm fine. Not eating as much as I'd like, but that's always a good thing, isn't it? I'm just a bit tired and thirsty."

Without passing further comment, Jeff found a glass in the cabinet above the sink, filled it with water, and handed it to her.

Clare smiled her thanks and took a sip, which became a series of gulps. In no time at all, the glass was empty, yet she felt strangely dissatisfied. "Why are you here? It can't be just for food."

Jeff trailed his hand along the painted kitchen wall. "It's strange. My apartment in Boston is being renovated, and I took some time off. Just felt a longing to hang out here, see my big sis, her strange puritan idiosyncrasies and all."

"Well you could at least shut the front door when you come in."

Jeff's face frowned in confusion. "I came in through the back. The same way I always have. You're the only one that ever uses the front. I didn't even realize it was open."

It was true. Ever since childhood, Jeff had preferred to skulk in the back entrance. That way there was a better chance of avoiding the parents if they were in one of their collective 'moods.'

"It was open when I got here. Someone's been inside."

Jeff peered into the hallway. "Nobody's here now."

"How did you get here? I didn't see the Porsche."

"I walked. Car's being detailed over at Dick's Auto Body. It's a nice day, and I felt like stretching my legs. Why the sudden inquisition?"

Clare drew a slow breath. Unexplained events never happened in Holden. Not since their parents. "Just a bit tightly strung today I guess. I had a bad day at the office."

Jeff grinned. "That's why you're home early. Walked out, eh? Quit?"

"No, it's nothing like that. Just an ongoing disagreement that led to me requesting a bit of cooling-off time before I said something I really would regret."

Around a mouthful of sandwich, Jeff mumbled, "Well, this is gonna top your day right off. Roger Bartow came back yesterday."

Clare nearly dropped the empty glass. "You serious?" The long-time absentee father of one of her neighbor's kids had often been a topic of discussion in the area, especially with him disappearing around the time of her parents' death. Some locals had tried to lay the deaths at his feet purely on opinion and hearsay. It had never gotten anywhere.

Jeff nodded. "Annette Cameron gave me a call when she couldn't get hold of you. Lucky I was on my way, eh?"

Clare was already on her way out the door. "You staying here?" she called back.

"And remain alone in this relic? Fat chance." Jeff dropped his plate for an inquisitive Steve to sniff over and hurried after her, leaving the door swinging.

Clare was outside and hopping up onto the raised gravel drive of the Cameron house in moments. An abandoned old trailer for a boat sat on the track, wheels wedged into immobility with wooden chocks. She dodged around this. The house, with its newly finished brown siding and white window frames, gleamed at her in the afternoon sun, fitting perfectly with the early autumn colors in the surrounding trees. The house inside would be nowhere near as beatific.

Clare knocked. Not waiting for an answer, she opened the porch door. "Anne?"

"In here, honey," called Anne's mother, Annette.

Clare picked her steps carefully as she wound her way through the hall. Cardboard boxes were stacked with magazines, as if their location were death row and the weekly recycling the sentence that would never come to pass. Random plastic toys, many faded and broken, scattered in shady patches threatened to trip her. Marbles, dolls, heaps of sneakers discarded for a trip to the refuse tip that was beyond reach. Why they couldn't see it as mess was beyond Clare's logical mind.

She winced as she passed through the kitchen. Plates were piled up high, discarded and stained to a permanent state of filth. A random gathering of elegant crystal goblets stood majestic but for the wine staining the sides where it had evaporated. A sink was piled with saucepans. A putrid smell emanated from this room. It turned Clare's stomach, and she tried to take shallow breaths so as not to inhale too much. Jeff followed close. Clare felt him about to comment; she knew her brother would find this hard to bear, and she shook her head with a warning glance to keep his thoughts private.

Finally, the filthy obstacle course ended with the entrance to the living room, a relative sanctuary of order in the midst of the mess.

On a couch, Anne Bartow sat, face pale, straw yellow hair pulled back in a bun. She didn't even glance up. Her parents, Ted and Annette Cameron, flanked her as if to protect her from the world. Off to one side, Roger Bartow's son, Dean, sat bored in a shirt and tie as if awaiting a trip to church. Anne's two younger children from a subsequent tempestuous and ultimately failed relationship, Grace and Bo, played on the floor with whatever detritus could be found to amuse them.

"Is it true?" Clare asked without any preamble.

"Yes, dear," Ted replied. His green plaid shirt was creased and worn, his eyes overtired beneath thick-lensed glasses that appeared to support his mass of white hair as much as it kept it out of his eyes. "When we woke up this morning, he was already down here with her. I can only imagine Roger gave Anne the shock of her life."

"You'll be fine, hun," Annette reassured her daughter. Anne just stared straight ahead, as if focused on a vision only she could behold.

Jeff leaned down and wiggled his fingers in front of her eyes. "There's nobody home."

This earned him a glare from Annette. "Well, of course there ain't. Poor thing was probably shocked dumb at him being here."

"Well, where did he come from? How did he get in?"

Ted barked a laugh. "That door's never locked, you know that. If Holden weren't so goddamned friendly, maybe we'd have decent locks and a bit of security. How many times have you just wandered in off the street?" He was angry and upset at seeing his daughter sitting there helpless. Clare understood this; his lashing out was his only method of expressing his feelings.

"Seems to be catching, that," Jeff observed.

"My front door was open when I arrived home," Clare elaborated. "It wasn't either of us."

"Maybe it was the boogeyman," muttered Dean.

"Dean Bartow, that's enough out of you," admonished his grandmother. "Kid's a chip off the old block, all right."

Dean sat glowering under a mop of black hair but said no more.

"And nobody heard what was said? He never spoke to any of the kids?"

"The kids were all in bed," Ted said with a shrug. "Doc Strange asked us similar questions when he was here."

Julian Strange was the family physician for half of Holden so it seemed. It didn't surprise Clare that he was already involved.

"We're just waitin' for the paramedics to show up and take Anne for a check-up. He told us to wait and that we have. It's been hours."

Clare was already working through the logic of the situation. This was all just too odd to not leave some clue. "What did he look like? It's been a dozen years since he left. I never knew him before but with all the rumors he might have information about Mom and Pop at least."

"Twelve years since Roger left her with a baby?" In a red dress with short dark hair, Annette showed very little resemblance to her daughter. Anne's facial features, immobile in her state of catatonia were those of her father, with slight softening. "You didn't miss much through not knowing him, girl. We barely saw the man when he was with Anne. He was a ghost, more of a drifter than a husband. He had a baseball cap on when I came downstairs this morning, black. And he wore a jacket with a logo on it. He kept his head down, but he was shaking, and he looked like he had been sweating a lot. It was dripping off of him."

"What logo?"

"You think you can catch up with him? You think he left clues to his whereabouts?"

Clare looked around the living room. "Ted if I'm being brutally honest, I wouldn't even know where to start looking for clues. I've got to start somewhere. The logo. Can you remember it? If it is distinct, it might be important."

Flashing lights became visible down the hallway as an ambulance pulled up on the driveway.

Annette's brow furrowed. "It was a sort of odd looking letter 'a' shape. I've seen it several places before."

There was a knock on the door. "Hello? We're here for Anne Bartow. Is anybody in there?"

Clare grabbed a scrap of paper and pencil from the floor where Grace had moved to watch the ambulance. Sketching a stylized 'A' as quickly as she could, she held it up. "Did it look like this?"

Annette took the proffered drawing, considering the sketch as she turned the paper around. Ted glanced at the paper then rose to answer the door. Anne just stared, vegetative.

Two burly paramedics entered the house, one earning a look of disapproval from Annette. The fact that he was black was not lost on Clare. Some people it seemed had bigger issues than keeping a tidy house and Annette's views were well known in the neighborhood.

"I'll help her up, thank you," she said when the paramedic moved to attend to Anne.

"Annette," Clare insisted.

"Yes, that's what he wore. That red logo was on the breast of his jacket." Annette didn't look her way, leaving Clare and Jeff standing amidst the Cameron family detritus, Dean silent behind them.

They followed the slowly-moving party out to the ambulance, giving them space as they ushered Anne ahead.

"What do you think?" Jeff asked.

"I have several thoughts. First, if Anne comes to, she might provide all the answers. One can only speculate what Roger must have told her to leave her in such a state. Second, the identity of our mysterious house guest might be revealed if we can find some prints."

"You think if it was Roger, he might have been that careless?"

"I think we at least need to act as if he was. There was a lot of suspicion that he had a hand in Mom and Dad's deaths. What if that's the fact he admitted? Would that be enough to cause Anne to lose her wits? I know that I have a place to visit in the morning."

"What do you mean?"

"That's not the first time I have heard Alden Labs mentioned today. I don't believe in coincidences."

Chapter Five

All Clare wanted out of life was a good night's sleep. Was that so hard to achieve? After the hassle at work and the feeling of all-round betrayal, Clare and Jeff remained up until the early hours dusting for prints. She found only one set that didn't belong. That they were in her parents' bedroom did nothing for her nerves. Clare had a restless night's sleep and woke as weary as she had been the night before.

It was Saturday morning; the working week finished. A quick liquid breakfast of icy water followed by juice that tasted of vinegar and was quickly spat out led to Clare leaving Jeff asleep in his room. She made the house as secure as possible, the windows locked and the front door barred from within. The back door was well-hidden under overhanging ivy. Jeff was right. It was much safer using just that entrance.

Under a light blue sky dotted with cotton balls of fluffy cumulus clouds, Clare made her way across town in the Impala, keeping the revs at a grumbling low for fear of disturbing the town's residents. The sun hit her car from the east at such an angle that it reflected off the hood, threatening to dazzle her senseless. At a set of lights, she pulled on her Wayfarers, earning a honk from the car behind. She ignored their waving protest.

Alden Research Laboratory lay across the other side of town from the mystery of her own wooded glade, sitting just North of the junction of Shrewsbury Street and Main. The lab had grown from a small satellite department of a nearby university to become a major employer in the town. There would be, in Clare's opinion, no Holden without Alden. Her father had worked in the labs for most of his adult life, fishing in nearby Chaffin Pond with colleagues during his free time. The pond was fed by a river that also provided water for lab research. It was no wonder she would find people at every turn who knew the family. Alden was a community within a community.

So it was that when Clare pulled the Impala to a stop in front of the lobby and climbed out to the parking lot, she felt on familiar ground. The pines surrounding the complex were a little more aged, but the main building, brown bricks and flat roof as was typical from the seventies, had not changed at all. Clare ran her fingers along the iconic Venturi Meter that had been one of the labs' first triumphs, used for testing water turbines. The pits in the cast iron shaft were deep and worn with time and exposure, the iron itself cold and lifeless. Clare turned to enter the lobby. A guard clad in brown moved to intercept her.

"Clare Rosser, is that you loiterin' round out there?" A friendly female voice called through an open door from within the building.

Clare turned. "Philly?"

A tall woman with curly black hair and striking brown eyes appeared in the doorway. "Well I'll be damned, it is you! What you waitin' out there for, girl? Come on in. Joe, let her in."

Accepting the invitation, and having no idea how she was going to get any concessions from a company who owed her nothing, Clare stepped past the guard across the threshold and into the embrace of her old friend.

"So how're you? It's been like forever." Phillipa Cookman flashed a smile. Clad in a figure-hugging black dress and smelling of expensive perfume, she resumed her seat behind the reception. "Still at the cop shop?"

Clare smiled. "Sure. Still trying to take over the music industry?"

"You bet. Char and I have a gig coming up at the Lucky Dog in Worcester Monday night. We have a band too. You gotta come check us out."

Not knowing where she might be by then, Clare said, "Sure. Char? You mean you and Charlotte Benson? You're still going strong?"

"Ten years now," Philly confirmed. "Our husbands play in the band. We are a modern day funky ABBA."

Clare couldn't help but smile. The memory of her two high school friends belting out songs with an acoustic guitar was one that would never fade.

"Glad to see you're living the dream."

Philly shrugged. "Not quite the dream I had intended for us, but you know. It pays the bills and allows me to perform. How about you? How's forensics? Everything you had hoped for?"

"It pays the bills," Clare said, repeating the phrase. "It's actually why I'm here."

Philly's eyes widened in interest, and she leaned forward. "Oh, are you on official police business or something like that? Do tell."

Clare took a breath. *Here goes nothing.*

"It's not actually *official* police business, since I'm just a forensic analyst."

"Bullshit. You work at Worcester PD. That's police enough for anybody round here. You do science. Alden does science. You're practically family. Besides, this Private Eye stuff is kinda fun."

"Well, funny you should say that..." Clare began, and stopped when a door opened on the other side of the lobby.

"Is everything all right here, Phillipa?" asked a man in his middle years, wearing a cream suit and sporting a white beard with flecks of black. The hair ran out before it reached the top of his head.

"Absolutely, Dr. Mayeux. Clare Rosser, this is Doctor Joe Mayeux, one of our senior engineers, responsible for the site. Dr. Mayeux: my old high school buddy Clare Rosser, now a cop."

"I didn't know the Sheriff had any detectives in Holden," Mayeux conceded.

"He doesn't," Clare confirmed, finding herself caught up in the lie and unsure how to extricate herself from it. "I'm Worcester P.D."

"Oh yes, what brings you all the way up here?"

Amused by the consideration that she had gone out of her way to find them, Clare brushed a loose lock of hair back over her ear and continued. "It's a bit of work and a bit of personal, sir. My pop used to work here a long time ago. I was reminded recently that you guys kept a box of his things in storage when he passed away."

Mayeux's face fell. "I'm very sorry for your loss."

"Thank you. It's nothing recent though. He passed twelve years or so back."

Mayeux nodded. "Before my time here; I was working at another facility then." He turned to Philly. "You have any idea where we might keep such effects?"

Philly clicked on a folder on her computer, scanning down the log. "They're probably in one of the sheds to the back of the complex. All our deliveries come into building W1, just behind the main office. There're a few scheduled to be torn down to make space for the new hydrodynamics lab. Probably the best place to start."

"You mentioned work also? We have among the best engineering and scientific staff in the country, all very highly educated. I doubt one of them has been thieving from the local K-Mart."

Clearly, Mayeux had a high opinion of the people at Alden. "No it's nothing that bad. We had reports of a break-in from a house in Holden. The burglar was reported to be wearing one of the jackets commissioned for the company's centennial." Clare pointed to the wall behind them where such an item had been framed and hung, the stylized 'A' in bright red on the black breast. "I was hoping, with your permission, to scan some security footage?"

This ruffled Mayeux's feathers by the way he frowned. Clare sensed potential defeat. How far could the lie take her?

"Just external footage?" Philly's intervention prevented whatever objection Mayeux was about to voice.

Ignoring him, Clare said, "That should be fine for now. I just want some idea if he's been hiding out here or not."

"Very well then," Mayeux had evidently come to a very quick decision. "I have a new project to supervise. I'll see if I can find someone to escort you about the facility should you find any information of use."

"Thanks for your time," Clare replied, already watching a security feed as Philly scanned her screen. Neither of them looked up as the old engineer left the lobby.

When the door clicked shut, Philly closed her eyes and shook her head, black curls bouncing from side to side. "Engineers. They're all the same, management or not. Paranoid about their secret projects, thinking they run the place. Sometimes looking after a bunch of super-intelligent scientists is like running a kindergarten. Their needs always outweigh the greater good."

"That being the advancement of science?"

Philly barked a laugh. "No, the creation of patents. Scientists are as greedy as anyone. They might preach about the good of mankind, but they are just after one thing: lining their pockets. Jim Mayeux is no different. He probably got jittery when you mentioned security feed because he doesn't want whatever he's working on to be out in the public domain."

"Why? What's he working on?"

"Damned if I know, Clare. I just man the desk and keep the paper moving." She squinted for a moment, looked down and prodded the ledger with her left forefinger. "There you go. We do keep a bunch of personal effects. It's an informal sort of lost-and-found at the end of the compound."

Clare's breath caught. Her friend had done it. "Can we go take a look?"

Philly rolled her eyes as if to say, 'What do you think?' "You can. I work here, at this desk. Remember?"

Clare stood back, the constant leaning over the desk making her back ache. A wave of dizziness threatened to send her to the floor. She staggered, grabbing the desk.

"Clare? What in tarnation...?"

"I'm all right," she insisted. "Just haven't slept well the past few nights."

"You might try eating once in a while too," Philly advised. "You're wasting away."

An uncomfortable feeling remained in Clare's bladder. "You have a restroom?"

Philly pointed to a doorway to their left. "I'm sure your guide'll be with us by the time you're freshened up."

As her friend had predicted, Philly was no longer alone by the time Clare returned to the lobby. A tall man with black hair in spikes wearing a pair of rimless spectacles perched on the edge of her desk, black shirt and jeans barely concealing his well-defined body. He laughed, his voice strong and confident, at something Philly said. She glowed in response.

Clare put on a serious face. "I hate to break up the party, but…"

Deep blue eyes directed at her. "That's quite all right. I've a feeling this day just improved immeasurably."

"Clare Rosser, this is Dom Holden."

He stood, several inches over six feet, towering above her. "Dominic, please." He extended his hand, which she took. Firm and warm, it comforted her. His scent was alluring, just a hint of cologne. It was understated but manly, nonetheless.

"So you are to be my guide?"

"It does seem that way," Dominic nodded toward the door through which Mayeux had left. "Shall we?"

"I'll get Joe out front to have a look at some CCTV while you are gone," Philly offered. "Last two nights, right?"

"If you would, please."

"No problem." Philly waved them off. "Have fun on site, you two." Philly's tone of voice implied to Clare that fun was paramount, and she expected full disclosure upon return. Some things never changed.

In the hallway beyond, Dominic was forced to curtail his loping stride in order to stay with Clare. "I hear your father left some belongings at

Alden." His voice was devoid of any obvious accent, but the even tone mixed with the sure way he spoke to betray a good education.

"Yes, thank you for sparing the time to chaperone me."

"That's quite all right. One of my projects is running, and it will take a few hours to compile data. It beats sitting around staring at machinery, and the company is infinitely better. Let's take a look. If we find anything I'm sure one of the guards will let you sign it out."

It was hard for Clare to avoid becoming engaged in the subtle flirting. But she resisted. This was not the time to lose focus. "Is this one of your projects?" She pointed at a set of wide blue pipes in an adjacent room, several instruments flashing up numbers on a panel beside them.

"No. That's just a series of water sampling points and component testing. It's been patented and approved. The board therefore feels it's safe to put the science on show. I'm working on a desalinization project down site. It's much more secret than some pipes. At least until we present our results in *Science*."

"Science?"

Dominic turned toward her. "Yeah, the periodical. Ever read it?"

Clare thought back to the stacks of old copies in Boston. The precinct never had anything like that in all the time she had been there. "I did a long time ago, but not since university."

Dominic flashed a pass over a sensor and opened a door, indicating she should pass through to the parking lot beyond.

With a grateful smile, Clare did so. She was certainly enjoying the easy nature of her guide. "I don't mean to pry. It seems you guard your secrets tenaciously here."

Dominic picked one of a fleet of Alden-branded vans, opening the door for her. As she climbed in, he said, "The board makes the decisions, and we follow their lead. They do oversee us after all. But science is for the good of all mankind. I like to think we may one day discover something that will change the world." He started the engine, and in short order, they were moving at a very modest pace through the Alden site, warehouse-sized laboratories crawling past either side, the faintest of breezes kissing her skin.

"So," Clare began after a moment's silence, "a Holden in Holden, eh?"

Dominic nodded. "It gets worse. I'm descended from Samuel Holden directly. I studied at Harvard for a time, within sight of Holden Chapel. It seems I am trapped by my family's legacy no matter what I do."

"I can relate to that," Clare murmured.

"How so?"

Clare started, forgetting that she hadn't just been thinking to herself. "These family heirlooms," she said by way of diversion.

They pulled up to one of the more dilapidated warehouses; a rusting affair that really looked ready to be torn down. The surrounding woods threatened to swarm in and overtake the building.

"Well, this is it," said Dominic as he opened his door. "Do you know what you're looking for?"

"Not really," Clare admitted. "I guess a box of some description."

Dominic got out and opened the door for her: A true gentleman. "I have plenty of time. Let's see what we can find."

Inside, the warehouse was in no better state. Trails of animal footprints in the dust, rat and something bigger, revealed the disuse. A strange smell hung in the air, mold and a stench of decay. It caught in Clare's throat. One large room, the warehouse must have stretched twenty meters in every direction to where foliage crowded up against windows stained green. Endless shelving was covered in plastic sheeting, protecting whatever was beneath from the environment. She wiped the dust from the surface of one, the plastic brittle and sharp as she touched it. The boxes beneath were warped with moisture, the surface of the reinforced cardboard sticking out like ribs on a malnourished child.

"They really didn't care about the contents of these boxes," Clare noted.

"Or the pursuit of scientific advancement blinded us to the simple fact that this lab had humble origins," Dominic added, brushing dust from his jeans. "Honestly, where do we even start looking?"

He pulled out a two-way radio, depressing a button with a click. "Phil, are you there?"

"Hey honey," came Philly's voice after a moment. "Had any success? I hope you're looking after the detective?"

"We're fine, aside from the dust coating the inside of our lungs. Listen, you have any idea where to look in this place? We could be here for weeks and find nothing of consequence."

"I can do better than that. It turns out that there was somebody snooping in the dark the past few nights, in your very building. The only camera that works shows someone rooting about in one of the far corners of the warehouse."

"Where's that security, Phil?"

The curiosity in Philly's voice changed to panic. "I'm sorry darlin', Joe's with me but we can't raise the other two on the radios. They could be anywhere on site. Watch out guys. You might not be the only ones in there."

Chapter Six

The radio fell silent. Dominic stared at the device. Clare was ill-prepared for any real confrontation, and she edged closer to her guide. Shadows stretched where once they had been unimposing. Every pathway through this maze of detritus was now fraught with danger. Sound magnified in Clare's ears, the settling of plastic sheeting, the creak of ancient shelving. And no backup.

For his part, Dominic did not appear fazed, though he now spoke quietly into the radio. "Phillipa, do you have a location for Clare's father's belongings?"

"Sure. There should be location labels on the end of each set of shelving. You want fourteen-s."

"Thanks. Call security over here. This place is a private facility and should be on lockdown."

Clare rubbed the grime from a plastic label attached to the end of the nearest unit. "If the sheriff shows up this all becomes a potential crime scene. I want to find my dad's stuff before it's confiscated. I'm not afraid; there's two of us. Okay, Two B."

Dominic scrubbed the nearest label to him. "Three C here."

She followed his gaze to a section where the lighting was intermittent, the faded luminescence of the strip-lights flickering and orange. "Well, of course it would be over there."

"Do you want to wait and get some more people?" Dominic suggested.

Clare brushed her hair back over her ear. "No. We're here now. Let's go have a look."

She allowed Dominic to take the lead, even though she was technically the authority here. Pulling on a pair of latex gloves, she followed her guide into the shadowed corner, producing a silver flashlight when the light became insufficient.

Their steps grew slower and more hesitant. The dust had been invaded with footprints, many recent. The banks of cardboard boxes muted sound, a pregnant silence threatening to burst with a wave of violence. Clare felt antagonism directed at her from somewhere close by, an itch on the back of her neck. She looked about the darkening warehouse and bumped into Dominic's back.

"What is it?"

"The shelf you want."

"There anything on it?"

Dominic moved to one side. "No, but it looks like whoever was here made a pretty thorough job of going through whatever once was."

Dust swept clear, the floor was covered with objects, empty boxes stored on the shelf beside it. On the far side of the open space, some blankets had been folded.

Clare knelt among the objects. They had been placed with care, equidistant from each other. She began to sift through them. Watches, photos and old stained coffee mugs had been lined up. "Why would someone treat all his rubbish with so much care?"

"Why do old homeless ladies push carts of aluminium cans around like babies?"

"For the scrap value, I always presumed."

Dominic shrugged. "Perhaps this is a similar situation."

Clare stood. "But look at the precision."

"Homeless doesn't mean unintelligent," countered Dominic.

A small china teapot caught Clare's eye, and she bent down to retrieve it. Wiping the dust clear, she examined the antique.

"Not gonna make much tea in that," Dominic observed.

Clare smiled. The pot was no more than two inches in diameter, white china painted in the black and pink of the Worcester 'Ruby Legs' baseball team. "My parents had a set of these. Many historical teams had them made. As long as I can remember the display always had an empty space. Dad had borrowed one."

Clare glanced back down. A sealed packet lay nearby. She retrieved this and opened it. Photos fell out, of her parents meeting some other man. Her father looked furious, his nose screwed up and his eyes wide with a glare; the other man wore a smile that could only be described as smug. Beyond that, the photos were too faded to be of any real use. Behind them, photos of her and Jeff.

Dominic had stopped poking around and was looking over her shoulder at the photos. His warmth was a reassurance.

"Cute kid," he said.

"Thanks."

"You know her?"

"I am her. This is most of Dad's stuff." Clare held up photos that had been folded and torn. What would anybody want with these photos?"

"Is there anything else?"

Clare picked up a wallet bearing her father's initials. "I think that's all of worth that's here." On impulse, she knelt and fingered the blankets. "These are sodden." She picked one up; the gray homespun fabric was heavy with fluid, which dripped onto the floor. It stank of something organic, vegetable perhaps. Replacing it, she pulled a tube and stopper from her bag, pushing the glass onto the fabric with care until fluid began to run into the tube. Once it was two-thirds full, she stoppered it.

Dominic wrinkled his nose. "That's awful."

"I've smelled worse. This warehouse should be sealed until a team can come in and give it a full examination."

"What about this guy you are looking for?"

Clare looked around the warehouse. The feeling had not lessened; someone was still watching them. "It may be nothing," she said in an attempt to allay her fear as much as quell the antagonism she felt from without.

Dominic locked the warehouse and they drove back to the main building in silence. Unsure of what exactly it was she was supposed to have learned in there, Clare gazed at photos of herself as a child. Who was this other man in the photo? Why did a drifter show interest in her family, and if it was Roger, why would he go to such lengths to conceal himself unless there was more to it? Was there a bigger connection?

"Philly, can you show me what you found on the tapes?" Clare asked immediately upon re-entering the lobby.

"I... yeah, sure," her old friend replied.

The black and white footage showed a figure crawling through a gap in the corrugated paneling, replacing it with care and then sorting through the various belongings. After placing them about the floor, the figure stripped and began vigorously rubbing himself down with the blankets. He appeared gross and distended, as if suffering from excessive water retention.

"He's soaked," Dominic observed, leaning forward so that his chest rested on Clare's shoulder.

"So he is," Clare agreed.

"But we haven't had any rain in weeks."

"Was he in the river? If he is homeless, maybe he was bathing." Clare waved the vial of collected water. "I'll get this analyzed. That should fill in the blanks as to whether this is our man. Look, I need to be off. I have a lot to think about. A good deal doesn't add up."

Dominic turned to her. "Maybe later we could...?"

"Maybe not," Clare interrupted the rest of his question. "I have to get these samples studied. Philly, thanks."

"Anytime, babe. You stay safe and get yourself looked at."

Clare left her friend with the perplexed scientist in the lobby. Climbing back into the Impala, she spared a glance for the road that bypassed the main building. There was movement in the distance. Someone still watched her. Uneasy, she pulled out of the lot and on to Main Street.

She needed to settle her nerves with a drink. Several diners flashed at her with garish advertisements for the world's best cup of coffee. Clare ignored them all until a large red sign came into view at the intersection of two roads, the stars and stripes hanging limp beside it. Friendly's Restaurant had been a favorite of both Clare and Jeff as they'd grown up, the frozen custard a local delicacy and sweet relief to the sour stress of their parents. But Clare was not after ice cream now, just a place to think.

Pulling her car into the parking lot, she let it idle for a moment before selecting a space out of public view behind the red-brick building. Satellite dishes poked out from the gray-slate roof. The owners wanted their customers to come in, stay for entertainment, and buy; it had always worked with her.

Clare pushed through the swinging door and waved at Gus, the bald, rotund owner. He beamed a grin and beckoned her to a booth near the kitchen, the wide blue and green plaid pattern on the back of the seating very retro. Clare accepted the invitation, sitting down with obvious relief. The morning barely over and already, she was exhausted. Pulling out the photos and information, Clare spread them over the table. In moments, with a minimum of fuss, one of the waitresses had filled a mug with steaming coffee. The bitter aroma of the coffee filled her nostrils as she inhaled, and eventually Clare smiled a thank you across the restaurant.

She opened the wallet, leafing through the contents. Chatter from around the restaurant began to lull Clare into a sense of relaxation that she embraced. There was a connection between the items the homeless man, possibly Roger Bartow, had gathered and her parents. She refused to believe that it was a coincidence.

Rolling the tube of liquid around between her forefinger and thumb, Clare considered the potential ramifications of what she had done. If Harley were ever to find out, it would mean her job. If Joe Mayeux were to call the department, she was done for. Well, it was what it was.

A shadow loomed over her, blocking out the light. The most recent entrant to the restaurant now stood above her.

Scruffy jeans full of tears gave way to a black Alden polo shirt, under which hulked a serious amount of muscle. Atop this bulk was the leering face of someone else she had not seen in years.

"Jonathon... Finely?" she guessed.

His lips edged into a slow smile, more that of a cat sure of catching prey than that of anybody pleased to be recognized. Not waiting to be asked, he took the seat opposite her. His eyes yellowed from what must have been a heavy night, he continued to observe her.

"Clare Rosser," he said at length. "I'll bet you never thought our paths would cross again."

Jonathon had bullied everybody he could lay his hands upon from kindergarten right through high school. Clare had been no exception, at least until Charlotte and Philly had come along. But now she was alone, with only her wits and reputation as a shield. He had truly become the man he'd threatened to be and was not better for it. With stubble going gray before its time and both ears pierced, he looked a mess. Clare's intrigue as to how this would play out began overriding her fear.

"Coffee?" Clare offered, looking back down at the photos and documents.

Jonathon leaned back and laughed. "I don't drink that swill, especially from a place like this."

"Steady now, John," Gus warned from the kitchen.

"Or what's the consequence, old man? You gonna do what you did last time? Cower back there and call the sheriff?"

"It's fine, Gus. I can handle a bit of trash," Clare called, bringing Jonathon's attention back to her.

He leaned forward. "I have a message for you. Stop prying into matters that are none of your concern. I followed you to tell you..."

"You followed me? You are aware of who I work for?"

That slow smile again. "I may not be one of those genius scientists, but I know what you aren't. A forensic analyst is not a detective. Stay out of it. Stay away from Alden."

"Or what's the consequence?"

Jonathon brought two meaty fists to rest on the table between them. "Or there might be an accident."

The barely suppressed rage in this man's body was enough to convince Clare she was outmatched. Was he using the warehouse as a refuge? Was Jonathon the person that had killed her parents? Not a chance. Clare thought for a second and burst out laughing.

This left Jonathon with a confused expression on his face. "What?" He frowned, looking around as if he were the butt of some unseen joke.

"Joe Mayeux put you up to this. He's so paranoid about his patents he would employ muscle to make sure his secrets remain secrets." Clare gathered up the photos from her side of the table, placing them in her bag. "You can tell your boss I couldn't care less about the clandestine world of hydrodynamics."

Clare rose to leave. Her legs trembled from lack of rest. This confrontation had not helped. There was a hunger in Jonathon that had not yet been sated. The need for violence was as strong as ever. Clare did not wish to be on the receiving end. She threw a twenty on the counter. "Get my friend some breakfast."

Gus nodded with a muted 'see you soon' wave. She had no idea if his worried face was for her predicament or the fact she was leaving Jonathon in Friendly's with him.

Outside, Clare made for the Impala, crossing as fast as she was able past trashcans and green, paneled fencing that kept them hidden from public view. Her heart sank when she heard the door crash open behind her.

"I'm not done with you yet," Jonathon shouted from the doorway. At least he wasn't terrorizing the restaurant any more.

Clare refused to stop moving, her steps desperate. She maintained an air of nonchalance. "I think this situation is all played out," she responded without turning. "Go back and have some breakfast."

There was a thud of boots behind her. A hand grabbed her shoulder and spun her about. Clare found it hard to stay on her feet.

"What the hell is your problem?"

"I don't think you quite got the message. I'm not convinced you understand the severity of your situation." Jonathon's eyes were fierce, poking out from beneath Neolithic brows.

"Still the bully? I swear there is a connection not quite right in your head."

"Truth is, I enjoy it," he purred, menace dripping from his voice. He reached back, his left hand balled in a fist. "This is so you remember our conversation."

There was a click, the hammer of a gun being cocked. "You let that go, son; there's a trip to the lockup for you, if you make it that far."

The voice came from behind Jonathon, who stopped and grinned. His eyes betrayed his repressed and unreleased fury; this could still go either way. "You gonna shoot an unarmed man, Sheriff Heckstall?"

"You look armed enough to me, son. Lower your fist and get outta here, or we'll see what you look like with a hole in your shoulder. Leave the lady alone."

Jonathon's gaze settled on Clare once more. The snarl on his face indicated he had made his decision. Clare tensed for the blow.

Chapter Seven

The fist never connected. Jonathon turned away, his arm dropping in Clare's direction with one warning finger pointed at her where the sheriff couldn't see. Not over, not by a long shot in her opinion. He began moving away.

The figure beyond was tall, standing with authority; one would have respected him even had he not been a cop. Sheriff Terrick Heckstall was a rarity. The beige uniform suited him, his black skin contrasting with the clothing. He held his six-shooter in both hands, the grip sure, the aim deadly. This was a man who had fought prejudice as he worked his way up through the system. Respected by the entire town for his uncompromising stance on any crime, he had been offered the post with endorsements from the entire town council. He took the Holden Sheriff's department and made it a force to be reckoned with.

"Keep on walkin', man," he said with a flick of his gun, his eyes piercing, rich voice strong and authoritative. "If I see you raise a hand against a lady in this town again, be prepared to lose it."

"You don't have the balls," Jonathon hissed. "You'd be out of a job before the wound closed."

"No, son. This is my town."

"Sounds like a threat."

The sheriff gave a slight shake of his head, his dead-eye stare unwavering. "Sounds like a promise. Go."

The Eyes Have No Soul

With a glance at Clare, Jonathon capitulated. Getting in an unmarked van she hadn't noticed on the way to her car, he revved the engine overmuch in one last act of defiance before making his tires squeal on the asphalt, rubber marks left in his wake.

The sheriff watched him leave, gun still raised. Only when the van had disappeared down Main Street did he holster his weapon. "You okay, kid? You look a bit pale and shaken."

"I'm fine. Thank you, Terrick. I had no idea what he was going to do. It was lucky you were around."

Terrick snorted. "Luck had nothin' to do with it. Gus had a panic button installed after the last time John tried his crap. An alert goes straight to the station. What set him off this time?"

"Alden. I was there picking up some of Pop's belongings. It looks like someone took exception to my being there. He said he had a message for me."

"That damned Lab. Full of paranoid geniuses." He pulled a small canister from his belt. "Take this. If you're gonna get involved with idiots like John, you'll need it sooner rather than later."

The side read 'Mace'. "Personal protection? Thank you."

"Of course, you would have better protection if you gave up that big city science dream and came to work for me. We both know you'd make one hell of a cop. You could work your way up in no time. If a black man can find his way to the top, why not a woman?"

"You would have me on my own with all those big burly men? I'd never get a thing done."

Terrick sighed. "A man can dream. I'm gonna escort you home in case Mr. Finely has any further designs. I'd stay off the streets for the afternoon. I'll send a patrol car your way a couple of times later to check in. There's somethin' about that one I can't quite put my finger on."

"Always has been," Clare agreed.

Terrick gave her a critical glance. "You been to see Julian Strange lately? You're lookin' a bit peaky."

"It seems everybody's looking out for me these days. I'm fine. Just a bit tired."

True to his word, Terrick saw Clare all the way home, not moving off until she was ensconced firmly in her house. For her part, Clare grabbed a bottle of water, a good book, and Steve the cat in that order, hiding in a chair from all and sundry until weariness overcame her. Of Jonathon Finely there was no sign. Yet his eyes never left her thoughts, those yellowed orbs haunting her to sleep.

Sunday morning found Clare still curled up in her favourite chair, high-backed, deep, and plush. The cushioned mahogany was patterned with lilies in faded shades of yellow. Steve the cat had moved elsewhere during the night, and she was alone, covered by a blanket. Good thing too, early mornings could be nippy with mist nestled in the hills behind her house.

Noise from the kitchen drew her attention. Still groggy, Clare attempted to tidy her hair and straighten her clothes before Jeff saw the mess she was in. Then she figured he must have covered her up so why bother?

"Screw it," she muttered before opening the door. The tang of bacon washed over her, the saltiness making her salivate. A crusty loaf had been sliced into inch-thick wedges. Eggs boiled in a pot, the steam causing the kitchen window to mist over.

"Morning, sunshine!" Jeff greeted her, his usual business attire replaced with jeans and a brown woollen sweater. "Slept in again?"

Hugging herself for warmth, Clare frowned. "I thought so, but I still feel like I could have another six hours. It never seems enough anymore."

"Clare Rosser, the waking dead," Jeff joked, and in that fatherly manner he had often assumed in the past, enfolded her in a hug. "My God Clare, there's nothing to you."

"I haven't been eating well. It's the job. Harley. It's very stressful."

The words were a poor excuse. Clare didn't believe them and Jeff was having none of it.

"Yeah, you have been saying that for a while. Ever since you had that virus a month or so back, you've been different. First things first, we get you fed, and then I'm calling Julian Strange."

Clare didn't have the energy to argue and let Jeff ply her with his cooking. She gulped her coffee, scolding her throat and having to cool it with another bottle of water.

"I'm not seeing Julian," Clare decided aloud when they had finished. She really did feel better, much more than she thought she had a right to. "What's the time?"

"Just before ten."

"I'm gonna sort myself out, walk up to Walgreens and get a blood-testing kit. I'll have the lab look at it first. I don't want anybody round here knowing my business."

"You still don't trust Julian after all these years?"

"No, I don't. Jeff, he knew about Mom and Dad. It's a small town, I know but he's never has offered any information about the night he called me."

After cleaning herself up and donning her favorite walking shoes, a gray pair of Abeo Rocs, Clare set off. The Doc's house was only a mile or so away. Even tired, she wouldn't take long.

A plaintive meow caused her to stop and turn as she crossed to the road. Steve padded after her, evidently disgruntled at her leaving without feeding him. She stopped, and he ran forward, pushing up onto his back legs to rub his head against her outstretched hand.

"Go on with you." She swatted his hind legs with a feather's touch, sending him scampering back toward the house, and began her walk before he had cause to follow again.

Crossing the track, Clare headed along Pleasant Street. It was warm out, a typical gorgeous Massachusetts September morning. Pretty soon, Clare had her sweater off and hanging from the strap of her backpack. With the sun not yet overhead, she stuck to the shadows, which were plentiful given the mix of pine, oak, and linden that vied for space above the road. Best of all, there was barely a sound but for the murmur in the distance of early risers on the highway into town.

"Good morning, Clare," called a voice from the porch of a green bungalow that lay beyond a garden littered with stumps, each mounted with a small wooden bucket full of vibrant red and yellow flowers.

"Hi Rachelle," she responded, not really wanting to spend any more time out than necessary; Jonathon Finely might still be lurking. Clare reached to check if she had the Mace at hand.

Rachelle Bishop, younger than her with dark hair tied back in a ponytail, crossed the garden to walk with her "It's nice to see you. You don't appear out as much as you used to." It was a loaded statement. In the year Clare had known Rachelle, she had proven perceptive and insightful. She also knew a lot, full of hidden facts and quotes.

"I've been busy."

"Doing what? Starving to death?" Before Clare could respond with what was becoming an automatic response about work, Rachelle went on. "The town committee has left it to me to round out the corners of the Holden Festival of Horticulture. I need volunteers to run stalls, raffle prizes, and sell drinks. Can I count on you?"

Caught on the spot, Clare stumbled for words. "When is the festival?"

"It's not until mid-October and it's only for three hours. There's gonna be farm animals, home-made jelly, pies, music, you can drive up and park at the lab." Rachelle paused. "What is it?"

"I... I'd rather not, if you don't mind."

"Why ever not?" Rachelle continued.

"I'm not very welcome at the lab," Clare admitted.

"Oh."

That's what she was after. "Come on, Rachelle, out with it."

Attempting to feign innocence and not doing a very good job of it, Rachelle said, "Well, I was up at the One Stop earlier and those three old women were there. You know, Sarah, Katherine, and Rebecca."

"I know them." The three old women in question hogged the small cafe inside the One Stop Food Shop, chatting about seemingly nothing for hours on end. They would gossip about anything and anybody, and if there was news of any sort, they had it.

"As it happens, Katherine wasn't at the One Stop yesterday. She was out on Main Street, having coffee..."

"...In Friendly's by any chance?"

"You've got it in one."

Clare let out a sigh. "Typical. So you had a near-perfect re-enactment of the whole episode?"

"Pretty much, yes. Clare, you need to be careful around types like that. If the sheriff hadn't shown up, you might have been in serious trouble. There's something wrong with Jonathon Finely. There's a darkness that you don't want to explore."

They neared the end of the road, stopping in the dappled shade of a grove that protected the bottom of the local graveyard, weathered headstones sprouting through the ground like a failed crop of corn, patchy and random. Clare steadied herself on the trunk of a nearby pine, the bark of the trunk rough on her hands. Her skin did feel dreadfully thin.

Rachelle held Clare by the shoulders. "Clare, you don't look well. Are you all right?"

"What is it with everybody? I'm fine. But if it will give you any peace, it is the reason I'm out this morning."

This seemed enough for Rachelle. "Good. You may not see it but it's clear as daylight."

"Thanks for your concern. I'll be sure to let the gossips know if the doctors find anything."

Rachelle meant well, Clare understood this. It appeared she had taken no umbrage from her gruff dismissal, scrutinizing her before throwing up a brief wave and starting back to her house. Yet Clare now felt on edge. Was there really something wrong? She felt weary, sometimes dog-tired. She needed to pee a fair bit. She had been described as a girl who liked to drink a lot by Dr. Strange, the family physician, when once referred by her parents. And losing weight? She held her hands out. "Well that's always a good thing," she said aloud and started up the path between the graveyard and Reservoir Street.

In only a few minutes, she had crossed the road away from the graves, caught in the glare of the sunshine as it began to beat down from on high. She stopped to swallow down the contents of a bottle of Evian. Only a couple of streets ahead, the One Stop faced Walgreens across Main Street, two titans of the town intent upon retaining the customers of the other and yet wholly dependent on their co-existence. The One Stop was compact in comparison to the majestic structure of its neighbor. It was the way of things. Even in sleepy Holden, the super-corporations of the world had gained a foothold. Eventually, she had no doubt the One Stop would become a Wal-Mart. The Big Y was already on the boundary of the town, the monstrosity that it was. Clare considered for a moment crossing to the food store to give the elderly trio a confrontation to gossip about. Then she changed her mind and turned to Walgreens. Her health might be a topic of discussion to many, but to Jeff she had an obligation to be sensible.

"There's nothing wrong with me a few good meals wouldn't sort out," she said to nobody in particular. An elderly couple stopped and stared at her for a moment before shuffling into the parking lot behind Walgreens. She would prove to all that knew her that Clare Rosser was as healthy as a horse. For that reason only, she opened the door.

Chapter Eight

The cavernous interior of Walgreens yawned out in front of her, sterile and clean as if she were standing in the Worcester Precinct morgue. White flooring, aisles where shelving resembled dominos primed to fall, staff in blue for the registers and white for the pharmacy. It suited Clare's needs since she was able to remain relatively anonymous in such enormity.

She looked about, worried, until she found the target of her search. Jena Baxter had been the manager of Walgreen's since it had opened the year before. She also happened to be the victim of a robbery Clare had helped solve with forensic analysis of the perpetrator's DNA. A gang of jewel thieves had been apprehended as a direct result and Jena's engagement ring, in time, returned. Clare had become friends with Jena and she needed a friend now.

"Clare, so good to see you," Jena said as they embraced. The dark blue trouser suit she wore barely shifted as opposed to Clare's sweater, already twisted and rumpled on the strap of her backpack. Jena was the epitome of good management, her blonde hair short and business-like, her smile and manner formal yet welcoming. "What can I do for you today?"

"Jena, I need a favor."

Clare looked about them. The few customers in on a Sunday morning were preoccupied with their own business, teenage girls trying on free samples of eyeliner and a middle-aged man trying to look inconspicuous but failing in spectacular style as he poked through goods on a knee-high shelf.

"Don't worry about Rob," Jena reassured her. "He has his own problems. In here every Sunday buying… whatever he buys. He's got a thing with chatty Sarah."

"You mean Sarah from across the road?"

Jena nodded. "Between the two of us, a sledgehammer probably ain't enough. Not that he really has to worry. She's in the One Stop all day with her cohorts. She's probably with them all night too."

"No wonder he looks sheepish," Clare replied, and the two of them burst into laughter. "Can we borrow your office?"

Jena's face became instantly serious. "Of course we can. This way."

They passed through two sets of double doors at the back of the store and into an austere but functional room.

"I'm not one for decoration. I'm barely ever in here to be honest. I prefer the action on the floor. So what's up?"

"I need to get hold of a blood testing kit but I need to be discreet about it. Can you get me one?"

Jena pursed her lips for a moment and then sat down at her desk to log into her computer. A few minutes of quiet tapping passed. Clare sat and waited.

Jena smiled. "Well, would you look at that? We had a delivery last night containing several of the kits you want, and one of them was damaged and had to be disposed of due to sharp parts. What a crying shame. You wait right here."

Clare sat in the office, the silence enclosing her like a shroud of cotton wool. She began drumming her fingers on the desk, unsure if an anonymous test would even work. There were always chinks in the system, loopholes from which confidential information could be gleaned. If emails from presidential candidates could be made public, surely blood test results were small fry.

Clare was on the verge of panicking and walking out altogether when Jena returned, a blue box labeled 'Home blood test kit' in her hand. "This all you need?"

"I want to mail it as soon as possible when I'm done. Can I use the basin in your washroom to scrub up?"

"Feel free. I'll be on the shop floor. When you're done, just leave the kit sealed and addressed. I'll see it mailed within the hour." Clare must have looked dubious for, as Jena was about to close the door, she added, "You got my wedding ring back. It's been in the family two hundred years. You can trust me, Clare. You're safe in here."

Clare smiled in response. "I know." For just a moment after the door closed, she believed her own words. Then thoughts of the warehouse intruded into her thoughts, and Clare got to work.

A single prick on the side of her finger with a sterilized lancet and, with a few squeezes, blood freely flowed. She filled an inch long plastic container with a bit of effort. Her blood was thick and sticky. From all the fluids she had taken, Clare expected the opposite. A quick click and the container was sealed. Writing a name, address, and a few personal details, she sealed the vial in polystyrene housing, marking the name of Worcester Medical on the mailing slip. By this time, her finger had ceased bleeding, and she left the office as if she had never even been there.

Outside, there was a strange kind of quiet, even for a store as sparsely populated as Walgreens. Jena stood by the entrance talking to one of her staff, a middle-aged woman who, by the look of her streaked mascara, had been crying. Other staff stood around in two's and three's by the cash registers, quiet, their faces pale, eyes wide.

Seeing Clare, Jena laid a reassuring hand on the shoulder of the woman she had been talking to and came over. "All done?"

"Yes. Jena, what's going on? I feel like I've come out to the end of the world."

Jena swallowed, taking a few breaths to steady her nerves. "We just received word from the family of Luke Morris, one of our cashiers. He was found dead in his bedroom this morning. The woman you saw me with, Pauline, had been calling. He was late for his shift."

"Jena, I'm so sorry. Is there anything I can do?"

Tears began to brim in her friend's eyes. "No, there's not really. I'm gonna sort out the mail and send everybody home out of respect. Clare, he was only sixteen."

"Do they have any idea what happened?"

Jena pointed at the front window. "Why don't you ask them? One of the guys popped over there for a coffee during their break, and they were gossiping about it. Clare, they knew before we did."

"That does it," Clare decided. "Those three seem to know more than is good for them. It seems at almost every turn, they have the jump on the rest of the town. Jena, thanks for your help. If I find anything of use, I'll be sure and tell you."

Leaving Walgreens, Clare paused on the sidewalk, staring at the One Stop. Her heart had been thumping harder of late, as if inside her, there was a battle going on, but between her and what? After thirty seconds, her pulse was still racing, so she crossed without waiting for her heart to calm, pausing for a yellow Sunday School bus to pass first, the frenzied waving of children greeting her as it went by. She raised her hand in acknowledgement, but no smile touched her face.

If Walgreens was grand and orderly, the One Stop was anything but. The store lived up to its name, selling anything and everything, aisles crammed, rotating displays at the end of every walkway. Clare ignored the shelves of Twinkies and Zingers, so often her first port of call, seeking out the small cafeteria at the back. The scent of coffee was earthy and pungent in the air, the ground beans making her mouth water. A few brown tables with laminated cream surfaces sat beneath a sign proclaiming in bright red letters the home of the best cup of coffee in Massachusetts. As she closed on the counter, she heard what she was after. Three elderly voices cackled. A group of fair-haired old women hunched over a table, staring at a screen. Beyond the counter, a bored looking teenager in a blue and white striped apron and white paper hat waited for the order that never came.

"Would you look at that?" exclaimed one of the elderly women as she stood. Rebecca was wearing a red sweater, the sleeves pushed up above her elbows. Her short hair still held hints of the red from her youth. "I knew no good would come of that one. He was always staring at me whenever we walked past."

"It's because you cut such a fine figure, dear," white-haired Sarah replied, her multicolor knitted cardigan too tight in places, the stitches ignored and pulling apart.

Both women cackled. Katherine, the third of them, remained quiet for a moment. "Listen," she said, holding her hand up.

"Dispatch, we have another," said a deep, officious-sounding voice. "What the hell is going on here?"

"Just secure the area, Troy," a voice advised. "Federal agents are en route. They have jurisdiction and will deal with the incident. Just stop anybody getting too close. Okay?"

The voice set off alarm bells in Clare's head. Where had she heard it before?

"Gotcha," the other voice replied.

"Right, what else is there?" Sarah asked, elbowing her way closer to the screen. "Have a look at his record. Is he a delinquent?"

Intent upon the screen, the three women had no idea they were in turn the subject of scrutiny. From the corner of her eye, Clare saw the long-suffering barista shift behind the counter, as if he were building up the courage to say something. Whether to her, or the three women, Clare had no idea. She fixed him with a glare, and he resumed his impassive stance. Cupping her hand and waggling it to indicate she wanted drinks, she raised four fingers and mouthed the word 'cappuccino' at him. The barista nodded and got to work, tapping coffee grounds into their fixings and setting the milk to frothing. The three elderly women never even noticed.

"There. Would you look at that?" Katherine's announcement was nothing less than triumphant. "I told you. He's got a record as long as his arm. The kid is practically a vagrant, a bad seed growing under the branches of a rotten tree. That one came to a suitable end."

"How did he compare to last night's vic?" The way Rebecca used the shortened term of the word 'victim' grated on Clare's nerves, and she clamped her hands on the edge of the table behind which she stood. Nobody on the force said 'vic'. Some people watched too much *CSI*.

"Well, the guy last night was hardly the biggest of sinners, but he wasn't exactly a saint. They were both from disruptive environments in one sense or another. This one's parents divorced, last night's had his own juvie record and barely stayed out of jail. Somebody's targeting the products of broken homes."

"See what else the scanner brings up," Sarah advised. "There might be more nearby in West Boylston."

"So that's how you do it," Clare said aloud, causing all three women to jump.

"How dare you sneak up like that?" accused Rebecca, the fiery temperament associated with her hair very much in evidence.

"How dare I? What right have you to go round prying into people's lives like this? What is that? An internet police scanner?"

Katherine slammed the lid of the laptop shut, the Apple logo glinting off the silver cover in the glare of the fluorescent counter lighting. "It is nothing. You saw nothing."

Clare's simmering rage began to boil over. "You know damned well who I am. What I am. All of you do. You," Clare pointed at Katherine, "were at Friendly's yesterday when I was being threatened. All three of you sit here casting aspersions until the whole town gossips. I heard about myself from a neighbor not half hour ago about everything I got up to yesterday with the Sheriff. And now you are sitting around once more, talking trash about people, judging them before their bodies have even gone cold."

"How dare you presume to judge us?"

"Judge not, lest ye be judged." Clare was not one for scripture, but these three brought out the worst in her. "You three are modern day Graeae. Katherine, Rebecca, and Sarah of Holden, who with their all-seeing laptop and nasty barbs perform their own cruel sorcery on a town."

"You see fit to judge us? You are hardly from what one could call a model family." Katherine's retort stopped Clare in her tracks. "Yes we know what you are. Your parents were far from the top of the social pile, girl. Given that your family is surely cursed, the fact that you came out on top is a miracle. And look at you now: Stick-thin and white as a sheet. You may as well be your mother."

"You didn't know my mother," Clare shot back.

"Girl, practically the whole town knew Jane Rosser at one time or another. She had more boyfriends than it was possible to count, always in and out of trouble or some fella's bed. 'Harlot' didn't begin to describe her. It came as no surprise to us when she got knocked up as she did, by a man other than Ched, *while* she was still with Ched. The oddest thing was that he stayed with her to let her have somebody else's child."

Clare's stomach tightened. The photo in her possession began to make sense. Her legs threatened to wobble, and her throat went dry, beyond the normal constant thirst.

The photo from the day before was still in her bag. She reached for it, passing it over the table to the three old women. "Was this the man?"

All three squinted at the photo before Katherine looked up at her, suspicion written all over her face. "Why should we help you, girl? All you've been to us is rude and demanding."

Clare pulled out her Worcester P.D. accreditation and showed them.

"You aren't police," Rebecca countered. "You can't do a thing. We know our rights."

"Do your rights include hacking, appropriation of personal and private information, and illegal misuse of Federal property? One phone call and cop or not, I can have that laptop seized and your houses searched. I might not be police, per se, but I know plenty that are. Now tell me about the photo. Is that the man?"

The threat had clearly registered with the three old ladies, mollifying them. "That is the man. Probably your father," Katherine confirmed. "He wasn't around long enough to make much of an impression. He stayed in town maybe only a couple of weeks. His name was Bert or Judd or something like that. He came and went, so to speak.

You were here nine months later. Your pop never forgave your mom, but he stuck with her."

He never forgave me either, not really.

"Is that it?" Rebecca interrupted Clare's introspection, obviously eager to get back to her snooping.

"Not quite. What's going on in this town?"

"We don't know. Bad kids getting comeuppances happen everywhere. There was one last night, another this morning. We only just heard about the second. Then the Feds took all coverage off the airwaves."

If that were the case, there would be no point going to the latest scene. "Where was the boy found last night?"

"Laurelwood Road, right down at the bottom in the woods. Your police Captain Harley took a personal interest. He went in earlier with a team." Katherine said this without referencing any information. She was cleverer than the little innocent old lady she purported to be. Clare turned and left the three of them in a state of confusion, the argument not concluded. Harley was at another crime scene in her town? One they wanted to keep quiet? Clare felt a profound sense of déjà vu. She had a house to visit.

Chapter Nine

"If you go down to the woods today, you're in for a big surprise..." Clare part hummed, part sang the tune as she walked through the woodland of southernmost Holden, only a mile along the BB&G from the crossing by her house. Yet as close as it was, this part of town was a whole world away from the rural peace of her home.

She had taken the time for refreshment and a pit stop before calling a cab. The walk wasn't that far, but the weariness was taking its toll so much that after only a few minutes into a very brief cab ride to Laurelwood Road, Clare found herself dozing.

"You all right, miss?" The cabbie, a graying man nicknamed 'Chin' for past boxing glory, had asked. Clare opened her eyes; he looked worried and unsure of what to do.

"Chin, I'm fine. It was just a bit of a late night."

"We're on Laurelwood. Where is it you wanted to go?"

"This will do for me, thanks."

Clare paid and got out. He would only be a call away. So she entered the deepest and darkest part of town, home to the real reclusive, humming a tune that seemed ironic given the mystery surrounding the death of Luke Morris.

Just for a second, the trees opened out and she could see the hills beyond, that out of town monstrosity 'The Big Y' dominating the ridge amidst the beautiful Massachusetts skyline. It was only across the train track, not really all that far away. Yet the development of that grocery giant was a whole different world.

The gargantuan shells of houses began to emerge from the woodland as she neared the end of Laurelwood Road. There was no movement from within but the houses were so huge that to see anybody would be unlikely. Even wildlife was avoiding this dark place today.

The road curved back on itself in a loop. Clare had reached the end of Laurelwood. A disused basketball hoop on a pole of rusted black metal stood in the middle of the road, the plastic base into which it was planted cracked and leaking sand. Someone didn't want visitors. She was undeterred; the overhanging trees and resulting gloom led to memories of the night her parents were found. Could that have been Harley on the radio?

The Morris house was right at the end of the switchback, shrouded by the trees. "You really did appreciate your privacy," Clare muttered in an attempt to break the silence. It resumed just as quick, and she concluded that since she was about to break and enter, which could get her thrown on the wrong side of the prison bars, maybe she should remain silent.

"Help you?" called an elderly voice from within the trees. A gray-haired woman in a blue blouse embroidered with daisies and a brown skirt had come onto the road from one of the other houses.

Getting used to the lie, Clare flashed her credentials, hoping the woman didn't get too close. "Police. I'm just here to do a little follow-up. Do you know what happened here? Did you see or hear anything suspicious in the last twenty-four hours?"

Squinting in the gloom under the trees, the woman pushed back loose strands of gray-streaked brown hair in an unconscious way. "Not anythin' that would point to who did this, that's for sure. Your people though, they were very unusual. Turned up in black cars they did. No flashing lights, nothin'. If paramedics hadn't shown up to remove poor Luke's body, you could have been mistaken for thinkin' someone was bein' arrested."

"What did they look like?"

"Suits mostly, black. It was gloomy when they showed up, no fuss, no ceremony. The parents were taken away in one car, body in an ambulance. Then the trucks arrived."

"Trucks? Down here?"

The woman pointed at the branches above and for the first time Clare saw damage. Branches snapped off, twigs hanging loose. "Two of them. Came through like ghosts. It damn near looked like an eviction with what they were emptying out. Then one of those Feds starts knocking on all the doors, yelling that we oughta leave for a few days. He spooked Mary over there with all the fuss, and the family are all probably away hunting deer."

"What about you?"

She smiled. "Me? I've lived here all my life. No Fed in a suit's making me get up and out of mine. Laurelwood was named for my great granpappy. Laurie Oaken."

The name was familiar. The Oaken Clan had been in these parts since the founding of the town. This must be... "Alice?"

The woman smiled, revealing a mouth of decaying teeth, totally at odds with her smart sense of dress. "You know me?"

"I think you knew my pop, Ched Rosser?"

"Ahh, know him I did. You're young Clare then. Dreadful shame what happened to him and your mom."

This time it was Clare's turn to self-consciously brush her hair over her ear. The run in with Jonathon Finely came to mind. Who could she trust? "Well, if truth be told, I think this might be same thing. I've no basis in fact. Not yet. Just a hunch."

Alice's smile fell, fear replacing the welcome in her eyes. "Tell me you aren't serious."

Clare leaned back against the trunk of a pine. "I am. I just have a feeling."

Alice stepped back. "Be very careful, young Clare Rosser. The Mandigon is dangerous. It's best left alone, if that's what it is."

"The what? Mandigon?" It was too late; Alice Oaken disappeared back into the woodland. No closer to any answers, Clare turned back to the Morris house.

Pushing through the crowded branches, Clare found she barely had space to move about outside the house. Branches tapped on the windows in the gentle woodland breeze. In some cases, they were bent across and many were snapped with the force of the removal from the night before. Evidence would be contaminated. Someone had been in a hurry.

She made her way to the front door, noting that already the yellow crime scene tape hung loose at the side of the entrance. Clare pushed on the door. It creaked open.

That's great. Way to let everybody know I'm here.

She slipped inside. The scene gave her a bad case of déjà vu. There was no hallway, so the main door opened directly into an extended living room, utterly devoid of any furnishings. The walls, painted a pale shade of lilac, had darker patches where once there must have been paintings. Dusty chandeliers hung from the ceiling. Several piles of boxes were piled without care on cement flooring edged with spike-studded gripping. By the way they were partially ripped up, they had recently held carpet. Only the hearth showed any evidence of recent use, a residual heat in the ash.

"Not much to go on," said Terrick from a doorway to the left, making Clare jump. "Don't ask the obvious question, girl. I knew you'd find your way here as soon as you heard about young Luke."

"I might have gone to the other house."

The sheriff grinned. "No, you wouldn't. Take a look round here while they're preoccupied elsewhere. That's what I'd do, so I assumed it's what you'd do too."

"It's logical," Clare agreed, fingering the small button depicting logic she still wore from her days at university. "But why do you need to look around?"

"Because this happened in my town, and the Feds came in without so much as a word. That irks me. They haven't finished though. Look around. Talk me through what you see."

Clare looked about the room. "It's messy. They were disturbed. If this were the only crime scene, it would be spotless. My parent's room was sterile. Not like this. I can only assume that if I'd not gotten to the house when I did, the same would have happened. Every trace presumably removed."

"And that takes us to the scene of the crime," Terrick concluded. "Come with me."

Upstairs, the bedroom that must have belonged to Luke was the only door that was shut, more crime scene tape plastered across it. Terrick reached through the tape and pushed the door open.

Being careful to avoid the web of tape, Clare ducked low and entered the room. Inside, all that remained of the boy's possessions was the metal bed frame. The walls were grimy with mold, the windows clouded. "It's funny," she observed. "This looks a lot like the warehouse I visited yesterday."

Terrick peered through the window, sniffed, and stood back. "What's that scent?" The sheriff kneeled so that his head was level with the window ledge. "There's a residue here. How is it that they missed it?"

"I don't know. Maybe it's an embarrassment of riches. The Feds went elsewhere because a fresher kill places them closer to the killer."

"In this case, let's expect the fox to return." Terrick scratched at the residue. "Smells like polish remover."

"Maybe that's why I can't smell it," Clare decided. "I'm too used to the scent."

Terrick pulled on the window, causing it to protest for just a moment as the residue held it down. After coming free, the window shot up in its runners, the old style cord holding it aloft. "That ain't no polish remover. Not if it can do that. There's more out here," he said as he leaned out, "Look."

Clare peered over his shoulder. There was a gap in the woodland, where branches had been pruned back and the dirt trodden into a path. "So there's a path leading into the woods. Maybe that's how the Morris family get in and out. That must go down toward the railway. Want to climb down?"

Terrick pulled back in. "After you, girl. There's a door downstairs. I'll be using that."

What was I thinking? Her cheeks flushed with embarrassment over this sudden departure from her usual logical approach to her analysis of a situation, Clare followed Terrick down through the empty house. The door in question had no fingerprint dustings on it, as if it hadn't been touched. Clare pulled a latex glove from her pocket, a leftover from the Walgreens testing kit, and tried the handle. It gave easily. Terrick took the lead, crouching down where the gravel of a semi-finished concrete pathway became woodland dirt. "No footprints, at least nothing under a day old. There are scuffs leadin' into the woods and look." He stood and pointed at a series of gashes on the bark of a pine that had all of its lower branches cut right back to the trunk. Residue had formed in the cuts, pine sap off-colored by a foreign agent. Clare pulled her mini forensics kit from her backpack, scraping some of the residue from the tree into a small jar. "There's an organic smell to that, not just pine sap."

It was on the tip of her tongue.

Terrick wet his forefinger and started to rub at the pine.

It hit her. "No, Sheriff, stop." Clare's hand shot out, grabbing at Terrick's wrist and pulling hard. "That's Mescaline. I'd stake my life on it."

Terrick pulled his hand away. "How can you tell?"

"There's a scent about the fluid, organic, natural. Yet it's markedly different to the pine. It's from the Peyote cactus, that's where the scent comes from."

"You can tell all that from a scent?"

Clare smiled, eyeing the scratches. "It's a guess, but I bet if you touched that, pretty soon you'd be seeing pixies. We had a case once,

The Eyes Have No Soul

not too long ago, where a mescaline addict killed a family by setting their house on fire. It was the drug that led us to him."

"Thought they don't make mescaline any more. It's not economical."

"True. He was chewing Peyote buttons, dried out cuts of the cactus. His hideout stank of them. When the detectives caught him, he was staring at a garbage can. I doubt he ever realized that he had killed that poor family."

Terrick sniffed at the gash. "It doesn't smell like the residue in the house."

"The scent isn't exactly right, like it's mixed with something else. It would make sense that the scent should be in the house too, unless it's from a different source." Clare took one more sniff of the pine-scented residue and sealed the jar. "What else is there?"

Terrick pulled his gun from its holster, holding it low in front of him. "Nail polish remover and mind bending drugs being found in trees. This is too damned weird for me."

Clare took a long swig from her water bottle. "Don't you love a good mystery?"

"I like crime the way it should be. There's a crime and a criminal. I catch the criminal and they go to jail. I'm old school, girl."

"No, those alpha males in Worcester are archaic in a bad way. You're more of a John Wayne type of old school. Right is right and all that."

Clare took the lead along the path through the woods. The narrow leaf-covered track opened wider as they walked away from the house. There was a crisp scent in the air, more fresh than musty and over-bearing as it had been at the Morris house. Clare almost felt as though this were just another pleasant walk in the woods, were it not for the nagging sense of something wrong in the back of her mind and her companion wielding a handgun.

Occasionally, Terrick would stop and comment on footprints. There were no more scratches, probably because of the wider path, she supposed, and then the path ended.

Clare stepped out onto the tracks of the BB&G railway. Silence. The bright sun shining down on her gave no warmth.

Terrick scuffed around in the nettles at the side of the track. "That's it then. End of the line. Our killer could have gone anywhere from here. Worcester for instance. Or your house."

"Gee, thanks."

"Goes past your place, this track," Terrick added. "Just an observation. So what do you want to do now?"

"Get these samples to the lab and do a little digging around of my own. It's time to find out where the fox stores its kills."

Chapter Ten

Another restless night and Clare was back in the precinct. The events of the weekend had conspired to make her forget that she had a fixed and ultimately futile interview only three days before. While she expected the lewd references and chauvinistic putdowns just out of earshot, this time she was on a mission.

The labyrinthine hallways of Worcester Police Department were uncharacteristically clogged with refuse, fallen bulletins lying like leaf litter on yesterday's forest floor. Discarded plastic coffee cups and stirrers in nooks instead of bins, the stale liquid within full of congealed creamer. She gulped her water instead. It was not that people couldn't move about, but having been used to a certain level of disarray in her place of work, Clare was surprised the standard had fallen yet further.

Getting into the lab before anybody else, Clare was afforded first crack at the equipment in some measure of privacy. The samples were prepared and in the mass spectrometer before Alison showed up with Helen and Sunny close behind.

Helen nodded toward her office, the offer of privacy unspoken.

"No thanks, I'm fine. I just needed a little time away from this place."

"Are you sure? I can't have my team working at any less than a hundred and ten percent."

Clare indicated her desk, information spread about in haphazard fashion. "I'm already on it. Maybe I should just forget about detective work. I was always best at this job, anyway."

Helen smiled. "Good. Well, work hard, team. Drinks are on me tonight. Daniel's playing the Lucky Dog."

"Acosador? The medical examiner?"

Quietly, Helen added, "He's got a soft spot for you, Clare. He phoned up earlier asking for you."

Clare controlled her breathing, feeling perspiration sprout on her brow. Helen had already been in? Did she know what Clare was doing? In silence, she hoped the flush would be mistaken for embarrassment over male interest.

"Always the matchmaker, aren't you? I have to go down and see him, actually. Thanks for the information, boss. That'll make everything comfortable down there."

'Down there' was not all that far away. One flight of stairs and about a hundred meters led Clare to the morgue, home to Daniel Acosador, the resident Medical Examiner. There had been others over the years, but Daniel had risen to prominence following his transfer in.

Other than his medical prowess, Daniel was an acclaimed musician. The multiple facets of his personality were a mystery to women. Many had hoped to unlock them, only for him to show disinterest. So how Helen knew he held an interest for her was beyond Clare. She pressed the buzzer, feeling the vibration as she held the button a little too long.

The door opened inward, Daniel Acosador motioning her through. Not one to waste time on words, he turned away. Clare couldn't help but notice the way the muscles of his shoulders bunched through his greens beneath that long brown ponytail; what was most alluring about the man was he appeared to have no conscious understanding of how wild he drove women. Even Clare was not unaffected.

"I'm glad you came," he said in that rich baritone that melted hearts. Daniel never turned, only halting at the wall of drawers in which rested the unfortunate deceased. His jaw clenched and unclenched beneath the beard that threatened to sprout in all directions, yet accentuated his allure. The twelve stainless steel doors were spotless, much as the rest of the room. They reminded Clare of one of those gameshows. *Pick a box and win a prize,* she thought as she looked the room over.

Daniel turned and Clare realized she was staring again. She pushed the ever-loose strand of hair back over her ear. "What was it you needed? I don't normally get summoned to the 'cradle of death'."

Daniel smiled at the honorific. Everybody used it. "I wish you were down here on purely social reasons, Miss Rosser. However, we have a quandary. One you might well be interested in." He pulled open the second drawer from the right, middle row. The steel slab rolled out in near-silence, respectful of its passenger. Clare was thankful for the sterile and frigid nature of the room. This should have reeked, she thought, but nothing overlaid the scent of industrial cleaner.

"That's awfully small," Clare said of the sheet-covered lump on the slab.

Daniel poked at the body with dispassionate hands. "True. Wait 'til you see it. There's not a lot left. Our unfortunate friend here would have suffered at the end." Daniel turned back to the sheet. "Have a look but be warned, this is not your usual victim."

Daniel stared at her for a moment. There was such passion in his face, cheeks aglow, lips parted as if he wanted to warn her about something else. Maybe let her into a secret. Yet he said nothing more.

Pulling back the sheet, Daniel revealed a monstrosity, a twisted gargoyle of human remains with skin as dry and faded as ancient cracked wallpaper. The face was not much more than a suggestion of features on a skull, the hair still attached. Worse, this was the body of a child. This could have been Luke Morris but it was impossible to tell.

"What the hell did this?"

"Pathological reports are still being compiled. You'll have them in a day or so."

"What about bloods?"

Daniel shrugged. "That's the thing. There wasn't any."

"This... child?" Daniel nodded at her assertion. "Was exsanguinated?"

"Not only that. The corpse is devoid of any moisture whatsoever. This is complete dehydration."

"And you brought this to my attention why?"

"Because I heard you might have a vested interest in this case. Besides," Daniel pulled open three more drawers, revealing bodies similar to the first victim, "this is no longer a coincidence. There's a serial-killer on the loose."

Clare swallowed, holding her breath as she looked over the cadavers. One was a small girl. The two remaining bodies were larger, but still somewhat shrunken.

"This is hideous," she said, leaning over the nearest body. There was no rictus of pain or contorted sign of a struggle. The body appeared to have just laid there while it dehydrated. "What has this to do with me?"

"Two of the bodies were brought in from Holden just recently. I thought you would like more of a look at what had transpired. Word has it you were already at the crime scene."

Terrick? He wouldn't have done that to me? Clare was afraid to speak the words aloud.

"You okay?"

Clare looked up to find Daniel staring at her, his eyes bright, expecting her answer. "Yes, I was there. I live in Holden, as you well know."

"I'm not the only one who knows," he replied. "Word gets around."

That meant Harley. Daniel drew close. "Did Helen mention we're playing tonight? You busy? Gonna be lit." He smiled out of the corner of his mouth with a self-assured lift of his head.

Something about his accent pulled at her in a magnetic way. He was a lodestone, and Clare could not avert her eyes. The grisly nature of the situation disappeared. What was it? Was there a hint of Spanish? Portuguese? Russian? Acosador: where did that come from? Clare wanted to ask so many questions but all she could manage was a weak "Yes."

"Excellent." Daniel turned, and the contact was broken. "The Lucky Dog, eight o'clock. I look forward to seeing you in the crowd. That is if you can avoid Captain Harley and make it out of the building in one piece." He flashed a well-manicured hand, the nails filed to points. "It'll be quite the show. I will be honoured to have you attend."

Clare brushed her hair back over her ear and then held her hands in front of her. "Yes. Eight o'clock. Lucky Dog. Fine. I'll see you then. I look forward to it too." She turned to leave, Daniel evidently engaged in another examination. On her way out, she glanced in the glass of the door and caught him staring after her. The look on his face was indecipherable, yet her stomach tightened at this man watching her.

Emboldened by the previous encounter, Clare decided it was time to find the janitor and lay that particular beast to rest. In her current mood, work could wait. He had watched her ever since she had joined the department. Never intrusive yet always there. Worming her way through the hallways, Clare descended into the bowels of the precinct where offices and jail cells made way for cluttered piping and dim lighting. The pipes clanked and groaned as water pushed through them. It was the only accompaniment to the hum of machinery. Clare noticed a musty smell that made her think of graveyards. Given the look on the janitor's face when she saw him last, he might well be a grave keeper, or at least a taker of souls.

Pipework opened out into huge generators, the beasts of burden that, unseen, powered the entire precinct. It struck Clare as illogical that such a source of power was in proximity to pipes full of scalding water, but her pondering was cut short by her arrival at a simple white door that read 'janitor'. She leaned on a cabinet for a moment, pulling her hand back suddenly as she touched something soft. Dust came back on her palm. There was a perfect print left in the dust where she had leaned.

Clare tried the door. With reluctance and a squeal as metal scraped the floor tiles, the door gave. For a moment, there was the sound of banging. Clare assumed this was just the equalizing of air pressure on both sides of the doorway. She pushed into the room.

"Hello? Is anybody here?"

Clare's call was met with silence, no echo, the walls muffled with equipment and cleaning uniforms. On a table, an electric kettle had steam drifting out of its spout. An empty mug stained brown enough that whatever amusing quote had been on the outside was barely legible, contained a dry teabag. Small sachets of creamer lay in a blue plastic tub nearby.

"Tea in a place everybody drinks coffee," Clare observed, amused at the notion. She felt her mouth going dry at the mere prospect of a drink and moistened her lips with her tongue. Somebody had until very recently been in this room. Nobody had passed her on her way down so it was logical to assume that the kettle had been set to boil and the janitor had been called away.

Feeling reinforced by her returning logic, Clare closed the door and continued to pry. A chest of drawers yielded little bounty, just more bottles of bleach and industrial-strength cleaner, the chlorine of one such bottle causing Clare to withdraw rather quickly when the scent went right up her nose. A piece of plastic at the back of the bottom drawer caught her attention. She checked the doorway once again. There was nothing. She was alone. Moving two of the bottles, she reached in and withdrew a faded identity card reading 'Crime Scene Cleaner'. The name read 'Juan Menzes' but the photo was too faded to recognize. Clare pocketed the card, intending to run a search later. Time was passing, and Helen would begin to ask questions if she didn't put in an appearance.

Clare was about to give up the hunt when she spied a fold of black material with a zipper hanging from the corner, sticking out beneath one of the cushions on the couch. She approached the couch. The nagging feeling that she was no longer alone threatened to overpower her senses. Taking deep breaths, Clare willed herself onward.

She lifted the seat of the couch, ancient, crumbling foam from within spilling onto her hands and the floor. There would be no doubt she had been here. Beneath the seat laid a black jacket. She pulled it out with her free hand, the other still holding the cushion. When she saw the stylized red logo on the breast, Clare let the cushion fall free in a shower of foam.

"Alden Labs. It's the same jacket." It reeked of body odor. There might have been an organic hint to the smell as well. Finding some plastic sheeting, Clare wrapped the jacket into a bundle and planned her escape. Surely, the janitor would be back any second. There was no way he would leave his lair unguarded for so long. He had been in the warehouse sorting through her father's pictures. He had been watching while they discovered his work. He had no doubt been somewhere nearby while she entered his lair. But why would he do that? To mock her? To show his power? That he could do all this under the nose of the Force? Had he intended to draw her here?

In a panic now, Clare began to sweep the foam detritus under the couch. Would it make a difference? Probably not. It was clear someone had been here. The jacket would be missing at the very least. It had been hidden, or was it bait?

Her vision blurred as she began to panic. This was not like her. Clare closed her eyes and took several deep breaths to try to regulate her thumping heart. Picking up the wrapped jacket, she looked over the room. It was as tidy as it was going to get. If this had been left for her, she couldn't change anything now, regardless.

Clare backed out of the janitor's room, closing the door with as much stealth as a mildly panicking woman under a lot of stress could manage. It slammed shut. She looked around. Nobody was about, just the humming machinery and the water pipes. Clare gathered her wits, starting back toward the promise of humanity. She had chosen to come down here alone. Now, she felt like prey.

Picking up her pace, Clare began to feel decidedly light-headed. When was the last time she had eaten? Or had a drink? The thirst came quick and fast but she had no water. A bang somewhere behind Clare caused her to jump.

In desperation, Clare began to run, her pumps thankfully quiet on the tiled floor. She reached the stairs and took them two at a time, glancing behind her more than looking where she was going. Was there movement in the shadows? He was gaining on her, coming for her. Still looking back, Clare rushed out into the hallway and screamed as hands held her tight.

Chapter Eleven

"Whoa there," Tina Svinsky cautioned as Clare tried to fight her way free of the tangle.

For a moment, Clare struggled with an imaginary foe, doe eyes looking out at her from a man's face completely devoid of emotion, hands locked like clamps around her wrists. The bundled sheeting dropped to the floor, mercifully remaining wrapped. Clare followed it, wrenching her opponent toward the jacket until she came to her senses and realized who she was fighting against. "Tina?"

"And you're back in the room. Clare, what's up? You're white as a sheet."

Clare glanced back down the corridor. No movement. Had she imagined it? "There was definitely someone following me. I swear it."

Tina followed her gaze. "Down there, hun? That's just the janitor, the furnace, and a bunch of mechanical gizmos."

Clare grabbed Tina close by the shoulder. "I know. I've had the weirdest weekend. I think he might have something to do with my parents' death." She retrieved the bundled jacket and pulled Tina into a walk, eager to put distance between them and the janitor's lair. "You know about the murders?"

"I don't think it's common knowledge in the precinct yet Clare, but yes, I'm aware. I was just coming to find you. Helen said you came down to see the M.E. He had no idea where you went after. I was just starting to head back, and I heard you running. Clare, I'm so sorry this happened to people in your hometown. But there's such a thing as coincidence."

"This is not coincidental, Tina. The way the crime scene was cleaned was a repeat of what happened to my parents. Those kids, I saw them. There can't have been a drop of moisture left in those bodies."

"Yeah, but two…"

"Four. Daniel has four bodies in there. The two boys from Holden were in there with two others. Someone's been very busy. And there's more. I learned that Pop had his belongings in storage at Alden Labs. I went over there to look for them and someone had beaten me to it."

"How could you tell?"

"They had taken Pop's stuff and laid it out on the floor of the warehouse in order, like they were cataloging it. Tina, I wasn't the only one there. Once I got all of his stuff out of there, I was followed and threatened."

"You think this is linked?"

Clare wiped her brow. It felt as though it should be slick with sweat, but there was no moisture, just a pulsing heat that radiated from her temple. "Maybe these events are. It gets more complicated. When my parents were killed, several things really stuck in my mind. First, the way the crime scene had been cleaned. Back when I was studying forensics, it was drummed into us how thorough you need to be. Their rooms were stripped bare by the time I arrived, which could only have been a matter of an hour or so after they discovered my parents. I saw this same practice yesterday at Luke Morris' house. I challenged Harley on this back when I was a student."

"I remember the story well. It's a miracle you ever made it into this precinct. I'm really clueless as to how you did it."

Clare shrugged. "I've no idea. Maybe I have a guardian angel. Or maybe I don't give them cause to doubt my work. But that wasn't the only coincidence from the weekend, or from the night ten years ago. When it happened, a lot of suspicion fell on Roger Bartow, who had been in a relationship with Anne Cameron in the next house over from ours. He disappeared right after it happened, and nobody has seen him since. Until he made an appearance last Friday. He showed up unannounced, in their house, bundled up to the eyeballs, wearing a jacket bearing a very distinct logo. It's the same logo that's on this jacket." Clare brandished the jacket wrapped in plastic. "This jacket that Alden Labs issued on a very special occasion. I need to get this to the lab and test it."

"For what?"

"For everything. Tina, believe me when I say we found some very funky residues at the house. I think they were rushed because of the two murders. Somebody's attempting to cover up what's going on here. I suspect the same was true twelve years ago."

"And there were bodies in the morgue?"

"I don't think they will be there long. Daniel wanted to warn me. That is he wanted to warn me and invite me to his open mike night."

Tina's face lit up. "All-comers at The Lucky Dog? I wouldn't miss it. Do you think he's inviting you along because there's more to say? More perhaps than he could tell you here?"

Clare stopped walking. "I don't know. Maybe."

Tina's enigmatic smile lit up her face. "Darlin', I'm sure there's a whole bunch you don't know about him. If you got out more instead of hiding away in your country museum, you might see a different side. So are you coming?"

"I promised Daniel I would. I want you to do me a favor though. Hang onto this for me until later."

"You're serious about this connection."

"Yes, I am. For years, they have blocked my every turn trying to find out what happened to my parents. Now, I think I have a chance of tying at least some of the pieces together."

As they talked, Tina's route took them away from the forensic labs and up past the interview rooms toward her own office. However, when they reached the hallway, Clare found her path blocked by two burly middle-aged detectives.

"Fitzpatrick. Aulenbacher. What do you want?"

"Miss Rosser, come with us please. The Captain has a few questions for you in regard to an ongoing investigation."

Tina looked ready to jump in front and defend her. Clare forestalled her friend with a warning glance. "Whatever the Captain needs. Lead the way, guys."

The detectives escorted her down the hallway, one on either side of her. Clare mouthed the word 'later' before turning toward the inevitable confrontation.

"It must be very important for Captain Harley to send two of his biggest and best to escort a mere analyst into his majestic presence."

Not a word in reply. Clare's taunts fell on deaf ears. This lot were obeying instructions to the letter. They arrived outside Harley's office to find Terrick Heckstall on his way out. Clare's face turned to stone. Could he really have reported her? Surely not.

Terrick opened his mouth to speak, and one of the detectives moved to block them. "Not now, Sherriff. You can worm your way out of this one some other time. Go on, now. Get."

The dismissive way the detective dealt with him caused Terrick's jaw to clench. He drew himself up, ready for a confrontation.

"Just try it," the second detective sneered, spoiling for a fight.

The first detective smiled in satisfaction; the taunt had hit its mark. He wanted Terrick to lash out.

The sheriff was too experienced to succumb. "Clare, I'll see you soon," Terrick's voice was tight with the strain of repressed fury.

"Only if you keep your job and don't end up on the other side of the prison bars," Harley bellowed out his open doorway. "Rosser, get in here!"

Here we go. Clare took a deep breath, straightened her clothes, and entered the lion's den once more.

Inside, Andrew Harley waited behind his desk, his face red with fury, reeking of sour onions. He was stressed. Mike Caruso sat in one of the chairs opposite him. Clare would be forced to take the remaining chair, lumpy and worn as it was, designed to intimidate, to make her uncomfortable. She decided against it, remaining on her feet.

"Sit down, please." It was an order not a request.

"I think I'll sta..."

"Sit. Down." This hadn't begun well. Harley's tone brooked no argument. With the two older men studying her, it was old-school intimidation. Clare held her head high, as if she were the one in control here. *Always own the room, seek to dominate your surroundings.* She had been taught that at school in Boston. Even the shyest person could employ a mask. Clare wore her mask now, slowly taking the seat as if it were her right.

"You reconsidered the position then? Excellent, I accept." This wasn't going to go well so she might as well fire the opening salvo.

"Cute. I'd consider my words with far more care were I in your position."

"And what position exactly would that be, Captain Harley, aside from being sandwiched between two old men?"

Mike Caruso bristled. Surrounded by the folds of a pale blue jacket and trousers that were badly tailored and meant to fit a larger man, he looked swamped by material. He held aloft a report, a scrawled signature at the bottom.

"You were witnessed entering a crime scene yesterday in the town of Holden. This scene had been sealed and was off limits."

"All I saw was some police tape, already broken, in a house out of your jurisdiction."

Evidently not expecting a comeback, Caruso waved the report at her, his face reddening. "This is a Federal investigation and, as such, the jurisdiction is not given to you to..."

Clare ignored him and looked at Harley. "If this is a Federal investigation, where were the agents? Where was the notice keeping people off the premises? Why are you in possession of Federal documentation? Correct me if I'm wrong Captain Harley, but you are Worcester P.D., not FBI. If you've dragged me in here to discipline me, where's Helen? Where's *my* Captain?"

A slow smile crept across Harley's face. "I am your captain," he purred. "As of this morning, Captain Latchford is on indefinite leave of a medical nature. He might not last the day. I've been given the forensics department as part of an overall reshuffle."

"The Chief would never allow it."

Harley chuckled. "The Chief spends his time at City Hall or on the golf course. By all means try to go through me to him and see how quickly you end up suspended. This isn't the first time you and I have clashed over this subject, Miss Rosser. This particular investigation is far above your pay grade. You have been told before. Keep your nose out. You and your pokey little town Sheriff will leave well enough alone. Despite your aspirations, you are an analyst, not a cop. Rest assured that the only reason you aren't being marched out of here right now is the fact you were not the person responsible for breaking the tape."

Mike Caruso had remained silent during this exchange, watching her. Clare refused to acknowledge the man, though she could feel the avarice in his glance. Whether it was her personally, or the proximity to the authority wielded by his superior, she could not tell. "Where are you going with this, Captain? No rules have been broken. There was nothing to convince me that I wasn't allowed in. I broke no tape. I followed correct protocol to the letter and was accompanied by an armed member of the local department. Surely the fault must lie not with me but with those you are seeking to protect behind this façade. Perhaps, if they had done their jobs properly, instead of rushing off to the next crime scene, this might have been avoided. Why don't you tell me what's got you so paranoid?"

Clare felt a warm glow from within. She was focused. Alert. She realized that for the first time in years, probably since joining the department, the fire had returned.

Harley held out his hand for Caruso's report. When Caruso handed it over he placed it with a couple more of the federally sealed files in the evidence box and pushed it in Caruso's direction. "Take this down to records."

"Yes, boss." Deprived of his sport, Caruso directed a sour look at Clare as he retrieved the box. This was not over from his point of view.

Clare couldn't care less. They had ample opportunity to get a shot in at her and had not done so. This intrigued her, put her in a position of power. Harley waited until the scowling Caruso had exited the room before closing the door and turning to her. He perched on the desk in front of her, looking at her for a moment. "You're lying to me."

"Prove it."

Harley lurched forward, his hands on the arms of her chair causing it to shove back several centimetres with the force of the contact. The squeal of metal on the tiles beneath made her wince. His face was only a fraction away from hers. She could smell the coffee and cigarettes, feel the heat as he exhaled. "There's a distinct difference between what you know and what you think you know, Miss Rosser. You should be careful."

Clare stood, forcing Harley to back up. Her legs threatened to wobble but she refused to show Harley any weakness. The threat was real. "If you want to get rid of me, get on with it. Otherwise I have a job to do."

"Watch yourself," Harley warned. Clare ignored him as she opened the door and slammed it behind her. As she walked down the hallway, oblivious to the stares of people passing her by, Clare came to one conclusion. *He doesn't know I've seen the bodies.*

Chapter Twelve

What else had Daniel been trying to tell her in the morgue? Clare mulled over this at her desk in the gloom of the dimly lit lab. She certainly didn't want to advertise that she was here. It was after eleven, the evening having passed in a whirlwind of jacket analysis overlain by Daniel's rugged face watching her across the floor of the Lucky Dog. Potential stains had been swabbed, stray hairs analyzed. Clare liked working in the dark. It was refreshingly cool, a comfort quite unlike the invasive heat of the Lucky Dog. It also meant that she had less chance of catching her own reflection in the glass. She didn't have to look in the mirror to see she was losing weight. Could it be cancer? Clare dismissed the notion as paranoia. Finding her parents' killer was too important to succumb to either the thought or the illness.

She turned back to the results of the mass spectrometer. The formula '$C_{11}H_{17}NO_3$' flashed up in the results column. The chemical composition of mescaline.

"Weird," she muttered to the empty lab.

"This whole damned quest of yours is weird."

Clare looked up from the report as the door to the lab closed, oiled hinges silent as the grave. Tina Svinsky poked her head above the dull-gray filing cabinet protecting Clare from immediate prying eyes.

"Did you get anything?" Clare tried without much success to hide the anticipation in her voice.

The diminutive blonde glanced back out the doorway then approached on soft feet. "I could lose my badge for this."

"I promise, just five minutes."

Tina gave one more fearful look to the doorway. "This means that much to you?"

"Yes, it does. Tina, it's my parents." Clare stood up from her leather-cushioned high stool. "Look, if it will make you feel any better, I'll lock the door. Okay?"

"Who's gonna notice? It's the middle of the night."

Clare snapped the lock shut, watching the hallway for a moment. A janitor was polishing the floor off down the hallway but other than that they were alone. Certainly, no Captain. "Harley can go spin for all I care. That guy has been a pain in my ass ever since I joined the department."

Tina grinned. "And you in his for far longer, showing him up like that."

"He's a sloppy cop, a wannabe politician, more of a cowboy. He doesn't deserve to be in command, nor do any of his drinking buddies." Clare felt that Tina was stalling. Holding out her hand, she said, "Come on. You went to all this trouble appropriating the information. Let's have a look at it."

"Don't you want to know how I got it?"

"No." With the desperate look of a cornered rat, Tina produced a brown paper folder. "Once you go down this road, you had better produce something pretty goddamned spectacular to keep our asses out of jail. You understand what it means to break Federal Law?"

Clare took the proffered document, holding it between forefingers and thumbs as if to merely touch it would seal her fate. "I will suffer contempt of court and gain the reputation of low-level traitor, a probable jail sentence. Oh, and I would lose my job."

"That would be the start of it." Tina's voice lowered to a whisper. "Word has it that on more than one occasion, Harley has been crossed. Those who fell afoul of him were transferred out of the department to sheriff's offices in the middle of nowhere. They're never heard from again."

An amused smile touched the edges of Clare's lips. "Ostracized because the offices are so remote?"

Tina's face grew deadly serious. "No. The offices are perfectly contactable. The officers were transferred but never reached their destination. They never made it."

"You can see how I feel it's a grand conspiracy," Clare urged.

"Well, what are you holding there if not a grand conspiracy? The original file was sealed by powers much higher than you or I. They did not want the world to know what happened to your parents. This information gets found in your possession, they will bury you so deep it will be like you never existed. You'll be their first suspect."

Clare flexed the file and Tina placed one hand over her own. "Just think about this. No turning back."

Clare frowned at the document. Temptation had been left far behind. This was compulsion. She had to know what had happened or more could perish. "No turning back," she said with determination and ripped the seal.

The file was Clare's Pandora's Box. Now the information was loose. Her heart began to race as the enormity of what she had just done settled about her shoulders.

Tina walked round behind her, leaning against the wall.

The wallet contained a thorough report on her parents' life history. "Everything is here. This isn't just about my parents' death. Tina, they have Jeff and me in here too, information about our family from before we were born. They've been watching us."

"Odd. That's far more than needed for a crime scene report. What does it say about the deaths?"

Clare flicked through the pages, turning them over and placing them in a neat pile as she read. The front page of the copy was dated only a couple of weeks after her parents' death. Harley had been playing with her mind. Did he want her to go after the report? It was too late now. She had taken the bait.

"Here we go. The pathology report states that judging by the condition of blood vessels and especially the greater vessels and heart, Ched and Patricia Rosser died from hypervolemia." Clare looked up. "That's fluid overload in the body causing heart failure. Yet, there is all this information about the bodies being dry, nearly desiccated." The pages slid apart, revealing two photos. Clare's entire body tightened, her face flushing as her heart went into overdrive. "Oh dear God. Look."

Clare pushed the report to Tina, photographs containing two dried and twisted bodies spilling out."

"Jesus, Clare, I'm sorry. I just scanned the file. If I'd known those were in there I'd have warned you."

Her eyes welled up. "I saw the bodies in the morgue earlier and I thought it would all look the same. But it doesn't. It can't be when the faces are those of your own parents. Look at their faces. I mean really look at them. Twisted, mouths wide. They suffered before the end." She wiped a tear away from her cheek. "They're on the brink of mummification. Yet the report suggests they were filled up with liquid to the point their hearts gave out. The traces of salt in the bodies confirmed this. It's crazy. Even drinking litres upon litres of water would still cause the body to flush most of what isn't needed away."

"So, you are thinking that either the pathology report is incorrect, or that what... something drained them?"

Clare nodded. "That's exactly what I am thinking. What if they were filled up until their hearts burst and then drained? Why Harley felt the need to sit on this is beyond me. Whatever sociopath dreams up such a complicated method of murder is some sort of genius or not human."

"Not human, indeed," Tina snorted a laugh. "This isn't an alien conspiracy, Clare. There has to be a rational explanation for all this."

"I didn't see anything rational about a collection of bodies in the morgue that looked exactly like this. But I'll bet if we test those victims, they have the same trace in their blood as this." Clare pushed a piece of the report that had come loose toward Tina. The same combination of elements flashed on her computer screen.

"Mescaline..." Tina's voice was full of wonder, and not a little confusion.

"Exactly. I think someone drugged my parents and did this to them. Look at this. There's a series of small scars punctuating the upper arms. I'll bet if we go downstairs and take a look, we will find the same scarring. There's a serial killer out there, and he's been around this area before. He killed my parents, and now he's back. And this gets even stranger."

Tina looked perplexed. "How can this get any stranger?"

"This sample is one I took from near the crime scene yesterday." Clare indicted the computer screen.

"So that makes you think it's the same perp?"

"Yes and no. This is a comparison microscope. Take a look at the two samples. The left sample is what I took from the scene. The right is a sample of my own blood."

Tina leaned forward, looking into the binocular apparatus. "Okay, I see your blood cells on the right, but the left is clear."

"What you don't see is blood plasma, but with next to nothing in it. No cells, leukocytes, platelets. Also blood plasma alone is usually a straw yellow color but as you can see this is completely clear."

"Like something has removed all the good from it," Tina surmised.

"That's right. Normally, it would have dissolved nutrients, glucose, amino acids, enzymes, and hormones. I ran an arterial blood gas test on this sample. You know what I found? Waste products like high carbon dioxide and lactic acid. This looks like a plasma expander except it's tainted by natural cell detritus. I found a similar sample at Alden labs, on the jacket. Tina. I think the janitor is involved, possibly directly responsible." Clare went to take a swig from her water bottle, the liquid within barely seeming to moisten her parched tongue. "You understand the dilemma here, of course."

"Damned right I do. Clare, I made a copy of that file for you. Let me destroy the pages now you've read them. Anything you're intending to use the information for won't stick. If you take this public we go to jail. If you have any grand plan, you're gonna have to go so left field they don't see it coming. Nobody has blood with no blood cells in it."

Clare frowned. "Don't forget to add in the fact that we have a stolen police document in our possession and the author of the report would probably prefer to kill me than talk to me. Harley has something to hide, and he's baiting me with it. He's always telling me to keep my nose out, to stick to what I'm good at. I don't think he has the faintest idea what I'm good at." Clare realized she sounded scared. She was. This job was becoming a hazard. At least if she'd made detective she'd have had a gun. "You know, it was a bit too personal today. I swear if Mike Caruso hadn't been in the room, Harley would've punched me."

"He's not the author of the report."

Clare stopped gathering up the loose paper and photos. "He's not?"

"Not if this signature is to be believed. The crime scene report is signed Detective Jarret Logan, a Worcester detective working with the Feds. Harley is only mentioned as one of the investigating officers."

The name wasn't familiar. One of the men in her kitchen all those years ago? "I've never heard of him."

"Me neither. Can I borrow your computer?"

Clare closed her analysis and stepped aside. Tina took the helm and logged into the system. "Logan…Logan…Lovell, Lorimer. Here we go. Jarret Logan. He transferred to Bernardston from Worcester, early October…Jesus. He transferred within weeks of your parents' murder."

Clare leaned in, frowning. "How convenient is that? What's he listed as doing since then?"

"Well, that's the oddity. There's no record of him at all beyond the transfer. No 401k, nothing. Even if he'd taken a desk job and sat enjoying coffee and donuts for the last decade there would be some sort of entry. Instead there's a whole load of big fat zip. We've been automated for twenty years. Records are too good now for that."

"Now maybe, but the network wasn't the same all over the state. It might be paper only out in the farthest reaches."

Tina turned in the seat. "What are you thinking, Clare? I know that tone of voice."

Clare sipped on a new bottle of water. "Harley doesn't want me poking my nose into this business here. The person named on this report isn't here. He's upstate."

"Clare, there's been no contact with Bernardston for years according to the system. I couldn't even tell you whose jurisdiction they're under or if there's even a department."

"Exactly. So whose to stop me taking a few days personal leave and going traveling?"

Tina stood. "I hate to break it to you, but you aren't exactly in the best of health. The constant weariness you suffer, this obsessive drinking. Clare, I don't think…"

"I don't want to hear it." Inside, Clare knew Tina was right. The sooner she knew what was up, the sooner she could put it to bed.

"I'm just saying I don't think you should go driving into the wilderness alone, hun. Who knows where you'll end up and in what state?"

Clare took a deep breath. "I can manage. I need to go. I need to find this out for myself. You need to get this file back, broken seal or not."

Tina looked down to the file, the cracked seal very obvious. "I'll see what I can do with this. But remember, we broke the seal on a Federal document, one you didn't have access to. Somebody will notice, and when that happens… well you had better be in another state, better on a different planet for the trouble that will come."

"I'll be discreet. I promise. I want to know why Federal Seal protected those men in my house. Someone down here is killing people. This Logan could be the only person able to point the finger."

"There are enough crazies in this world, Clare. You don't know why he's there. If you're determined to do this, for God's sake get a gun. At least have the capability to protect yourself. This Logan might be able to finger Harley, but he might also be out of the picture for a very valid reason. What if he was the one doing the killing?"

"Then I'll find a way to make sure he doesn't do it ever again. I've seen enough twisted bodies in the last day to understand this killer is out there, active again, and has to be stopped. The photos of my parents only give me more resolve."

Tina handed her a small phone. "It's a burner and is untraceable. Keep this on you. I want to have some way of contacting you."

Clare regarded the phone in her hand. "I wonder how soon you'll need to."

"Hopefully never, hun. Keep your eyes peeled. It's a wild world out there."

Chapter Thirteen

An all-nighter, that's my excuse. Trying to catch up on what I missed Friday. Make it look good, convincing. Clare fretted, knowing that she needed to be in early and present her best possible face. Yet she was fighting her ongoing fatigue and had to let Helen know she was taking leave. She was a planner. Rational. Logical. Yet here she was, about to drive off into the middle of the state, through woodlands and backwoods, armed with only a name on a sheet. A hunch. Life was becoming unexpected in the most bizarre of ways.

Too tired to drive home, Clare had curled up under her desk using her backpack as a pillow. So now she was not only dirty from the rock bar, yesterday's clothes, and a diesel-infused joyride with Tina, but she lacked deodorant and smelled strangely fruity for it. Her back ached and her side was numb from the unforgiving floor Clare at least was able to clean herself up to a degree in the restrooms.

The morning crawled by, the air in the lab oppressive and cloying. Clare kept her head down. Her colleagues filtered in over time, offering brief, reticent greetings. Clare wished they were friends, she really did. Yet colleagues they remained. With what was to come, that was probably for the best. The less they were associated with her, the better it would be for them when everything came crashing down. Inside, she was terrified. She kept an almost constant watch on the door, her stomach contracting every time somebody walked past. It was inevitable. Harley would find her again. He would walk through that doorway soon.

"Can I have a word?" Clare jumped. Helen had approached in the middle of Clare's internal deliberation.

"Of course, boss." Clare followed Helen into her office, closing the door behind her. *Here we go again then.*

Instead of the seat and the frank appraisal, Helen turned and reached up to her face, holding her chin with one hand. She turned her head one way and then the other. "You aren't well."

Without aggression, Clare removed Helen's hands and turned away. "I'm fine."

"Clare, I've been a forensic analyst for the last two decades. I can spot things, you know. You might be kidding yourself into believing you're fine, but you aren't. Drinking all this water, the constant weariness, and the way you are just wasting away to nothing. Have you considered submitting a blood test, specifically one for sugar levels?"

"No," Clare lied. "And I'm fine. I've just been working myself too hard."

Helen looked sceptical. "I've approved your leave. Goodness knows you need it. May I suggest that whatever you think you're going to do during your time off is done with discretion? The constant clashes with the captain are beginning to have a negative effect on the department. I'll back you Clare, but only so far. You need to find that spark. You need to remember who you are."

Helen was only looking out for the department. Clare understood this. Everybody in authority in the precinct was some type of political animal. It still smarted to be scolded by a woman she respected.

"Who am I?"

"You're a fantastic scientist. Logical, driven, intelligent. This you..." Helen pointed at her. "This is not you. This is not the postgrad so full of passion and verve I brought into the team despite obvious objections to my decision." Helen stressed the word 'obvious' with raised eyebrows. "You go find yourself, Clare. Your erratic behavior doesn't just reflect on you. Remember that. It reflects on the department and on my ability to make sound decisions. Come back to us as you once were, not this shell with a devil on her shoulder."

"I'll clear my head. I'll find the answers."

"See that you do. Good luck."

The tone of dismissal was clear. Clare left the office without another word, finding Sunny and Alison outside.

"You didn't just quit," Sunny accused her.

Clare smiled, the expression not reaching her eyes. "No. I'm taking some leave. I think if I didn't, Helen would force it on me."

"Is there anything we can do?" Alison's face was a mask of concern.

"Yes. Watch out for any abnormal test results involving synthetic drugs. I'll be back in a few days." Clare reached under her desk for her bag and left the lab to the sound of Alison asking in a confused voice, "Abnormal? We deal in abnormal."

Keep walking, Clare. Calm. Poised. Show no weakness. Clare made it out of the precinct step by faltering step, looking at nobody and in turn hoping that her demeanor rendered her invisible amid the Tuesday bustle. It was fortuitous that she saw neither Harley nor Tina. She just wanted to disappear. No fuss.

She made it to the Impala, standing like a bastion from the sixties in the parking lot. The creaking door and the ancient leather were welcome reminders of her life outside of this building. For the moment, nothing else mattered. Once safely inside, she sighed, and placing her hands on the steering wheel, Clare leaned forward until her head touched her forearms.

"First step: get out of here alive," she said to the car. "Next step: see where you can take me."

The engine roared into life at the second attempt, and with as much care as she had taken in the precinct, Clare edged the Impala out onto the road. Her plan was simple. Get a gun and some clothes from home then drive off into the wilderness. Exactly how Tina had put it. She checked the burner. No calls. No immediate repercussions from last night's adventure.

She headed north up Main Street under a crystal blue sky with the window down. It was one of those days full of subtle, pleasant warmth, the sun not as high as it had been a few months back. The gorgeous day was at odds with Clare's mood, yet she softened as she warmed.

As she drove north out of the city, she mulled over Helen's words. "Go find myself? Erratic behaviour? It's just not me." Yet her mind worked the words every way it could, seeking out the logic behind them. Helen believed in her. No. She had faith. That wasn't just belief. That was acceptance in a greater good that provided no proof of its existence. A good that meant Clare needed answers without the confines of a lab. Is that not what she was striving for? Mentally she was fine and yet Clare worried for her health. Her arms were thinner. She'd never had fat in abundance, yet it seemed her clothes were slipping more and more on her increasingly skeletal frame. Her eyes were sunken in the rear view mirror. Pretty soon she stopped looking at the traffic behind altogether.

When a police siren began to wail behind her, Clare jumped. The streets had become very familiar. Worcester had become Holden. The One Stop faced off against Walgreens a couple of hundred metres ahead of the space she pulled into.

Shaken, Clare took a deep breath as a patrolman stalked the driver's side of the Impala. She had an illegal gun and no registration. If he asked to look in her bag she was screwed. She wound down her window like any good law-abiding citizen.

"Good afternoon miss. May I have your license and registration, please."

The officer stayed upright. As Clare flipped down the sun visor to grab her documentation, she realized that she recognized the voice. "Well thanks, Terrick," she muttered as she handed over her license. "They bust you down to patrolman now?"

Terrick went through the motions of examining her license, giving it a cursory glance. "You could have chosen a better place to go haywire,

Clare. Everybody that knows you will be watchin'. I have to at least make it look like I'm upholdin' the law."

"What do you mean, 'go haywire'? I was just driving home."

"Drivin' is not how I would describe your recent actions. You drifted into the opposite lane, failin' to signal. Seemed to me you were on autopilot."

Clare did feel weary, the euphoria from her impending journey having disappeared entirely. Is that why she found herself suddenly so close to home? "Well this is just fine. Ruin my life twice in two days why don't you?"

"I think you'd better come with me, Clare," Terrick suggested. "Bring your things."

In a moment of desperation, Clare wished she had her gun. She was not sure on what side of the fence Terrick lay. It was probably a bad idea given how he had dealt with Jon Finely. Clare reminded herself the sheriff wasn't the enemy and she didn't know everything that had happened in that office. In the end she did as bidden. A few people had gathered in the distance, onlookers desperate for a bit of action. Among them Clare saw the three elderly women smirking. She kept her head high and her face dignified as she locked her Chevvy and at Terrick's direction climbed into the back of his patrol car. He then took the driver's seat and pulled back out into the traffic.

"Shouldn't you have frisked and cuffed me?" Clare said after they left the crowds behind, acid dripping from her voice.

"Why? I never placed you under arrest. You never caused a scene."

"Then what are we doing here, Terrick?"

"I wanted to clear the air. I suspect you are under the misapprehension that I somehow informed on you yesterday."

"You saying you didn't?"

Terrick nodded. "That's exactly what I'm sayin', girl. The Chief of Worcester P.D. called me up himself Sunday night and asked if I could spare some time to come on down and talk to a Captain Harley."

"You sure it was the chief?" Clare was intrigued enough to give Terrick the benefit of the doubt.

"Man, I have no idea. Could have been the god-damned janitor for all I know. But I take on faith because if it wasn't and I refused to cooperate, then I get the Holden electorate hollerin' at me for obstructing a Federal murder investigation."

"What did Harley say?"

Terrick chuckled. "He doesn't like you much; him and that subordinate of his, a greasy guy with ill-fittin' clothes. Looks like a clown dressed him."

"Mike Caruso," Clare provided.

"Yeah well they spent an hour grillin' me about what we were doing there. How we were messin' with a Federal investigation and all the usual bull. Caruso was desperate to implicate you on somethin', anythin'. I reckon I got a good fifteen to twenty years on you, girl. I've been round the yard a few times. I know how this game's played. I gave them nothin'. Truth is all I spoke. Fact of the matter is we touched pretty much nothin' inside the Morris house. They just concentrated on the house so I had no reason to lie. Everythin' you found was outside, more or less. I think they'd have charged you with trespass had you been there first but they knew damned well they set up a crime scene in my town without even tellin' me. In truth, I think they were embarrassed at being caught out."

"And what did he say about the rooms?"

Terrick paused while he turned left onto Holden Road, the graveyard on their right. He motored on down past Clare's turning away from the town, the police station and all inhabited parts of the area.

"Where are we going?" Clare said, suspicious.

"Relax. No need for you to panic just yet. I have somethin' I want to show you. Now the one thing I did take from that so-called interview is the fact that your Captain Harley was under pressure from above."

"The chief?"

"I don't think so. I've met the old man. He's in it for the fun nowadays. No, this is comin' from a different direction; A separate agency perhaps."

"Like those in my kitchen? The spooks I never saw."

"It could be the case."

The time had come for admission. "I have a name, Terrick. Logan. He filed the report on my parents. Harley was a foil, there to distract me when I showed up at the crime scene. Detective Logan did the work, and was transferred soon after."

"Where?"

"Bernardston."

Terrick considered this for a moment, keeping his eyes on the road. "That don't add up."

"Exactly. I suspect he may have not been entirely enamoured of what was going on. These murders; the response is too fast, as if somebody is waiting for them to happen. As if…"

"… they already knew about it," Terrick finished. "I get the impression that someone is either helpless to act, or they are consciously allowin' these murders to take place and hidin' the evidence."

"Not hiding it well enough this time. Logan is the key. I track him down, and maybe find all the answers. Like why he was carted off so soon with no obvious reason or word from him since."

"You a girl on a mission," Terrick declared. "But you can't go drivin' round the state in your condition. Look at you: You'll be the death of someone if not yourself."

"Well I have to try. The next time I go back to the precinct I'll most likely be arrested. See, I…"

"Don't tell me, Clare. The less I know, the better it will go for you. If I know nothin', then they can't force it outta me."

"But if I don't make it through this, someone needs to know the truth."

Terrick remained silent for a moment. "You'll make it through this. You won't be drivin'. I'll take care of that."

By now Terrick had taken them far out from Holden. While the route through Paxton was a viable way to get to Worcester, Clare had seldom taken this road out of town. The woodland was dense and lush, the well-protected oak and birch that made up this part of Massachusetts not yet succumbing to the onset of less clement weather.

Terrick pulled to a stop on the verge of a side road that wound up a gradual incline and disappeared to the left. "Okay. Out you get."

Clare climbed out when Terrick opened the door. It was still pleasant, mild and somewhat muggy. The air was strong with tree sap and the earthy funk of moldy, decaying leaves. The utter lack of a breeze meant that there was no sound other than their footsteps.

"Well, this is nice," Clare noted. "We came out here to hunt chipmunks?"

Terrick looked about, seeking something. "What do you see here, Clare?"

Unsure if this was a trick question, Clare answered, "Trees, dirt. I see a road with a sign bearing the words 'Entering Paxton' on them in the distance. Down there to the right is a lake. I think it's called Asnebumskit Pond. I guess whoever named it must have been drunk at the time. The next town along, Paxton; If I get complete silence I bet I can hear the traffic."

"But what does it mean?"

"I don't know, Terrick." Clare's temper was frayed and she was becoming tired of riddles. "That I have a long walk home?"

"To you this is the next town along, or the pond, wilderness. To me it's much more profound."

Suddenly it all made sense to Clare. "We're standing on the line of demarcation. Your jurisdiction ends here."

"Exactly. My powers extend out of Holden, north just past Trout Brook, just southeast of here, east to Greendale and west into… well pretty much into the middle of nowhere. My jurisdiction as Chief of Police in Holden has its limits. Within these boundaries, I hold sway. Here I can fend them off for a while, protect you. But beyond this invisible border I have no power. The same cannot be said for Worcester P.D. and Harley. Nor can it be said for the State police and certainly not the Feds. One thing I learned yesterday, one immutable God-honest fact. You crap in their pond, mess with their business and you certainly feel the blowback. You start rippin' up crime scenes, no matter what's been done, and those political borders disappear, my protection ends."

"Where does that leave us? The answers are out there. The killer is still at large, I think under the roof of the very institution that has sworn to deal with such monsters. Terrick, I saw the bodies. I saw what had been done to those kids."

Terrick's face was incredulous. "You sure you saw it right? You've been erratic of late."

Clare nodded. "There were four bodies. All kids, or teenagers at most. There's more. I've seen the report on my parents."

Terrick raised his hands in a defensive gesture. "Girl, I said I don't need to know."

"You just offered to drive me to Bernardston. It's best you know fully what you're getting into. I might be labelled a Federal fugitive at any moment. Do you, in your position, want to be caught up in this?"

"The way I see it, you kidnapped me off duty and forced me to drive you around at gunpoint, seeing as you might be labelled a Federal fugitive at any moment." There was a twinkle in his eye. "But I think you might be safe. There's lots of odd things goin' on in the state. Strange people keep appearin' as if from nowhere. It's got the cops jittery. You're one of us. You know how we all hate mysterious circumstance. I get the impression they're gonna be real busy for a few days."

"I don't follow."

"There's all manner of oddities occurrin', in this state and further afield. Just watch a bit of news when you get home, girl. You may find out that a body-sucking demon is the least of your troubles. I'll be takin' you back now. Get some rest and pack some things. For God's sake, have a meal. I've got to tell the station I'm takin' a bit of leave and settle things with my wife."

Clare grinned. "I'm sure she'll take to you running off into the middle of nowhere with a younger woman ever so well."

"She will," Terrick affirmed as they climbed back into the car, the front passenger seat far less criminal for Clare. "There're bigger issues here. You can't solve 'em on your own, not in your state. Candace appreciates chivalry."

"Even if the act makes you an outlaw from your own force?"

"You let me worry about that. Let's get you home."

It took no time for Terrick to drive her home. Clare realized that Terrick hadn't overestimated the boundaries of his domain. The borders of Holden really weren't that great. Letting herself in through the kitchen door, Clare considered the woodland that bordered her property. Was this person out there? Did they know the terrain just as well as she was beginning to suspect they did? The Morris house wasn't all that far away.

The tunnel loomed in the distance, giving Clare chills. How times had changed. She wished it were not so close, not there at all. She needed a means of defense.

Her father, in one of his more lucid moments, had shown her his skills with a handgun. As a child she had been banned from a closet in the one spare room upstairs. Most of the time he kept the room locked. Out of habit she had rarely gone in since their deaths but now was not the time for caution. Clare needed protection.

Unlocking the spare room she headed straight for the closet. Under a pile of old coats was a cardboard box. She lifted it out, placing it atop a chest of drawers and removed the lid. Inside lay her father's old Smith and Wesson revolver alongside a box of bullets. She lifted the gun out, cold steel with a wooden handle. The box was only missing a couple of bullets. Maybe Pop hadn't used the gun much. She opened the gun and filled the chambers, placing the box of bullets alongside the gun in her bag.

Underneath the gun lay a packet of documents, folded and placed in an unsealed envelope. Clare pulled the packet from the box and sat on the bed across the room, flicking a sidelight on. The envelope contained photos, a signed contract, land deeds and a letter. She picked up the letter.

"Ched, I realize this won't mean much to you, not now, but I'm sorry. When I was first introduced to you and Trish, I never expected that I would end up with feelings for her. It was unexpected, and unfortunate that our meeting led to such circumstances as happened. I don't expect your forgiveness but try to see it in your heart to not blame your wife. The affair was all my doing. I got to know you both too well. I sought it out and she ended it. That you're left with a reminder of my time in Holden is an inescapable fact. I regret our agreement cannot come to fruition. You'd have been a good family. I must make amends as much as I can. I have enclosed the land deeds to a plot in a quiet street, up against the hills.

It's the best I can do. I have found an alternate host for our original arrangement. I shall not be returning to Massachusetts. With Regrets, Bud Maygan."

Clare folded the letter back up and replaced it. So the man who had given her life now had a name. And through his guilt he was responsible for her house. Yet the answers she now sought would not lie in this museum. They lay out in the wilderness with a detective she had never heard of.

Feeling safer armed, Clare returned to the kitchen. On the table rested several letters, the foremost postmarked 'Worcester Medical' with Jeff's name on it. Ripping the envelope with no care for the letter inside, she pulled out one piece of folded paper, crisp and thick. It was not a detailed note, just a couple of sentences. The note was signed 'Dr Burren', whoever that was, and countersigned by Julian Strange. Clare's legs went weak as she fixated repeatedly on the words 'contact us urgently', reading them again and again. The name at the top was Jeff's but it was her blood that had been tested. Her heart thumped and her stomach tightened. It couldn't be. Not now.

Chapter Fourteen

Early morning found Clare staring at the wall across the living room, not seeing it as she considered her future. "Contact us urgently," she said for the umpteenth time. Steve stirred on her lap. She had others to consider in this, even if they were tiny. The killer had struck four times in quick succession and then nothing. Three days since the last murder and there was no obvious motive, no clue as to how he was even going about the grisly task. Just the evidence in a document she could never use showing her parents died the same way. The only way to beat whoever did this was to find the information in a place nobody suspected. She had to find the missing agent. Harley wasn't gonna help her. It was a necessary decision, Clare wanted to put the letter to the back of her mind but found it hard to do so. Shoving it in her bag along with the rest of yesterday's mail, she hoped she had time.

Her constant weariness combined with the lack of sleep left her in a bemused state. Nothing seemed real. She made coffee, downing two or three cups before she realized what she was doing. Still thirsty despite the liquid sloshing inside her stomach, Clare forced herself out of the kitchen.

"What's up with you?" Jeff asked as he stumbled down the stairs, fighting his way into a brown woollen sweater. "What was that letter from the hospital?"

Clare paused. He had never read the name on the front. Her secret was still somehow safe. "I... Yeah. They want me to come in for some tests. That's gonna have to wait though. I'm going upstate for a day, maybe two."

"You don't look in any position to drive," Jeff pointed out.

"I know. I'm hitching a ride. If you need me, I'll have my cell. Are you staying much longer?"

"Long enough to keep ol' Steve fed. I can work from here and in truth I'm enjoying the silence. I might have a visitor from Boston as well if that's allowed under house rules."

"Fine with me, Jeff. Anyone of note?"

"It's just a friend from work, a colleague. You don't know her."

"Her?" Clare smirked. Jeff had never brought anyone out from Boston before. "Should I hang about and meet Miss 'Friend from work a colleague'?"

"You'll meet her soon enough sis, if all goes well." Clare realized she'd been so obsessed with seeking closure for the dead, she'd ignored the living. She promised herself that would be remedied when she returned.

"That's great. I'll be in touch. Just don't make too much of a mess. Try to leave some food in the fridge."

A car pulled up on the drive, and the horn honked.

"My ride," Clare said. With a farewell scratch behind the ears for Steve, who whined his displeasure at their parting once more, she grabbed her bag and went outside.

Terrick waited in a brown Lincoln of a similar age to her Impala, a good thirty years old. The door creaked in the same arthritic manner when she opened it.

"I swear this must be some ex-pat community of Cuba, the way we all drive around in relics," Terrick said as she buckled up. He was dressed in civvies, brown leather jacket and jeans, no sign of a badge or a gun.

"Either that or we just have really refined taste," Clare beamed a smile. "This isn't your usual flavour."

The Eyes Have No Soul

"The car belongs to Candace. I had to promise not only would I take care of you but if she gets so much as a scratch, I have to drive her for a year and she gets a new car."

Jeff waved from the doorway as they set off, keeping a firm hold on Steve. The tortoiseshell cat tried in desperation to extract himself from Jeff's grip, presumably to run after her.

"Everythin' all right there?"

Clare stared at the dash, her eyes losing focus. "Goodbyes can be hard. For everyone."

Terrick glanced across at her. "You're holdin' onto that bag real tight. You luggin' the family jewellery about?"

The letter she had opened the day before weighed heavily on her mind, like a lead weight in the bag. To avoid the conversation, she pulled out the gun, her hand glancing off the frigid metal before she got hold of it. With deliberate movements she held it up for Terrick to see.

"A Smith and Wesson. Nice. Old too. You don't see 'em much anymore with everyone packin' glocks."

"It was in the family. I have no license."

Clare's admission surprised her more than the sheriff. He just shrugged. "Let's hope you never have to use it."

Clare watched her brother recede into the distance as they drove along Sunnyside Avenue, turning left onto Main Street. The fire station and St Mary's church passed them on the right and, in no time at all, they were out of Holden and halfway to the next town, Rutland. She sipped at a bottle of water, the compulsion to drain it threatening to overwhelm her. "Yeah, they'll be fine. What about you? How does Candace feel about her husband aiding a potential fugitive?"

"She feels her husband is too damned old to be drivin' young ladies out into the middle of nowhere lookin' for trouble. But she knows it's the right thing to do." Terrick looked askance at her. "That gun's not the reason you're claspin' that bag so tight, girl. Come on, what's really up?"

Clare closed her eyes and took a deep breath. It was difficult to admit to herself, let alone tell anybody else. "I submitted some blood samples to Worcester Medical and I got this." Clare pulled the letter out and waved it.

"What's it say?"

"They want me in as soon as possible."

Terrick slowed the car. "Jesus, girl, we should take you there now. It could be serious."

"No. Terrick, we need to find answers. We need them now. This can wait. If it had been that bad they'd have called me direct. As it is, I think it might just be diabetes."

"Don't know much about that," Terrick admitted. "Insulin and needles; is that the one?"

"Yeah. You get thirsty a lot, and tired. They can control it once they diagnose it. It's a gradual illness."

"But you should still go. I can take you."

Clare turned to regard her driver. "Let's try to get some answers first, then hospital. If I go back to Worcester, I'm probably getting arrested, and the killer is free to suck the life out of whomever he wants. We need to go back armed with information beyond the control of Harley."

"I sure hope you're right." Terrick's voice was full of doubt. Clare had no more to say on the subject. If diabetes was what she had, she didn't have much time left before she became seriously ill.

Clare came to alone in the car. The metallic creaks of the engine told her she hadn't been left alone for long. A solid-looking building rose up to the left of the parking lot, the shadow of which kept her out of the direct glare of the sun. It was early afternoon already. She licked her dry, cracked lips, and finished off her bottle of water.

"There you are," Terrick said, poking his head into the car. "Thought you were gonna sleep all day the way you dropped off."

"It's been hours. Did we stop? How far did we get? Petersham? Orange?" They were the next two towns along the highway. Clare hadn't learned all the places.

"Bernardston."

"What, already?"

"Girl, you went out like a snuffed candle. I wasn't gonna wake you to point out hills and waterfalls. This here's Crystal Watson." Terrick stood back to reveal a rotund young woman with short brown hair and a smile who raised a hand in greeting. "She'll take you in and see to your needs. Then we got a meeting with the chief."

Impressed, Clare climbed out of the Lincoln. "You don't hang about."

Following her host, Clare used the restroom and in short order was back in the reception of what appeared a recently-refurbished police station. Three cells, all clean with their bars slid back, sat opposite two small offices. Several potted plants were on the sill of the internal window.

"It's quite cosy for a station," Clare observed. "Would be great to have my precinct this tidy. But for the cells you'd just think it was an office in any small town."

Crystal smiled. "You can't escape the fact we are what we are, honey. The town's so quiet we've not had to use the cells at all in a year or more. Doesn't mean we can't have a few home comforts."

Terrick approached with another man, muscular and well-fitting in his police uniform. "Better?"

"Much. I haven't slept like that in days. I could use a drink though."

"Clare, this is Jim Deane, chief around here."

The police chief extended his hand. "It's a pleasure, ma'am. Terrick here says you're on a bit of a fact finding mission. Come into my office and let's discuss it."

Clare shook the proffered hand, her own being engulfed in his grip. With Terrick at her side, she followed the chief into his office where they sat down in functional, basic wooden seats opposite him. Clare went immediately for the jug of water that had been placed between them, not failing to notice the glances of misplaced amusement from both men.

"So what can I help you with?" Chief Deane leaned back in his chair, very much at ease in his surroundings.

"Jarret Logan, a detective out of Worcester was reassigned here a decade or so back. We believe he has information crucial to a case I'm looking into."

"And what would that be?"

It was more information than Clare wanted to give but clearly, it was the only way to deal. "It's multiple homicide of a very strange nature. The bodies appeared drained of all liquid."

Deane's eyebrows rose at this. "Jarret Logan, you say." He pulled out a report that had seen better days, old proper typeface with worn staple binding. Flicking through it with a doubtful look on his face, the chief eventually dropped the report onto the desk. "I can't help you there."

This stunned Clare. It was not the answer she assumed she would get.

Terrick noticed the look on her face and asked, "You mean you have no record of him?"

"No record of him, never heard of him."

"That can't be," Clare said, crestfallen. The wooden seat felt much harder. What was she to do now?

"Can. Is. I've been Chief for eight years, since this building was built. Before that I was a patrolman in the department. Look about you here. We aren't exactly an army. Your man here says that Worcester has no record of this office. Either someone has sabotaged your records or just never bothered to keep in touch. We used to be policed by the Shelburne Falls department of the State Police. Some joke we are so far removed from anywhere of note in Massachusetts that we may as well be Vermonters. Maybe someone in the big city had problem with us. As it is, we keep ourselves to ourselves. As long as Bernardston is free of crime and Pioneer Valley is safe, I'm a happy guy."

Clare walked out of the Bernardston Police Department dejected and confused. "I just thought it would be so easy. What a fool."

Terrick waved thanks to Crystal Watson, who watched them leave as they headed north through the town.

"He had no idea," Terrick concluded. "He wasn't interested, just very provincial. I get the feelin' he didn't want any trouble comin' his way."

"Maybe there was more to this little set-up than we saw," Clare supposed.

Terrick laughed. "Hey girl, now don't be seein' ghosts where there ain't no shadows. You've already caused enough of a ruckus back in Worcester."

The phone Tina had given Clare began to ring. Clare put it on speaker. "Tina?"

"Hey there sweets. How're you hanging?"

"I'm thirsty," Clare admitted. "I'm with Terrick. You?"

"Anxious. Clare, I think Harley suspects. There are rumours around the department that someone broke into the records rooms and messed with Federal documents. They aren't confirming who or what yet."

Clare thanked Tina in silence for getting her to copy rather than retain the documents.

"The place is on lockdown, Clare. They are calling everybody in to account for themselves. Everybody, do you understand? When they can't find you..." the unspoken consequence was thick in the air.

"What do you think I should do?"

"Stay close to the sheriff, and keep your head down."

"You should keep yours down too."

There was a sigh from the other end of the line. "That's not hard, sweets. There's all manner of weird going on down here at the moment. I'm on a rape case with Caruso where the perp is damned-near impossible to detect. There was footage from the hotel, yet every time we look at the tapes he's a ghost. Nobody can remember him."

The name 'Caruso' caused Clare to shudder, pushing herself back into the worn fabric of the Lincoln's passenger seat.

"Listen, I have to go. Stay safe Clare. Are you alone?"

"No, I have Terrick with me."

"The sheriff? Good call."

"Thanks for the approval," came Terrick's dry response.

There was a pause. Tina clearly had not expected a conference. "Look after her, Sheriff. And stay away from police stations. If they decide to hunt you, better be in the wildest backwater imaginable. Harley's tenacious." The line clicked off. Clare sat in silence.

"So we can't go home, and we have no leads," Terrick surmised. "It's time for food. You look starved. Pie?"

"Sure," Clare sighed. "If we're gonna go all *Deliverance*, I guess we'd better stock up first. Did you see anywhere on the way in?"

"I noticed a couple of good-lookin' places. There's an Italian called Antonio's up by the highway and somewhere a little less conspicuous up here on the left."

Clare waited in anticipation as Terrick drove at a painfully normal speed through Bernardston. As the buildings began to increase in frequency, she noticed a large lake off to the right in the distance.

"Fall River Reservoir," Terrick said, noticing her stare.

"It looks peaceful."

"Hah. In this part of the state, look in any direction and all you get is a whole lot of peaceful. Here's the restaurant."

On their left, a light brown building, wide and squat with a dark brown roof caught like a bug beneath a spider web of powerlines, emerged from the treeline. The sign out front read 'Four Leaf Clover'. Clare wished a bit of their luck would rub off on her.

Terrick pulled into the parking lot, the Lincoln bumping over the gaping cracks in the asphalt. They parked under the shade of a giant Linden tree, next to a quaint white house with a blue roof, well away from the road. The parking lot was busy, and they merged with the traffic.

Clare attempted to give Terrick a stare that implied they could have parked closer.

He picked up on it. "It's best to remain unobtrusive. You may not have noticed but we've been tailed since about a mile out from the station back there. No, don't try and look. Just act normal. There's a red Chevy just pullin' into the lot. Get out, act normal. Go into the restaurant. I'll be watchin'."

Clare did as bidden. Her heart was thudding in her chest. Blood pounded in her ears and she felt faint. The day was cloying and hot, the sun paining her eyes as it shone off the cars around her. Near the exit, a cherry-red Chevy Malibu was pulling in. It moved past. Clare wanted to turn and stare at the driver yet she kept her head straight.

"Okay marked him," Terrick confirmed. "Old dude, grey hair stickin' out seven ways from Sunday, bearded."

"What do we do?"

"We go eat; try not to make a fuss."

Clare pushed through the door, wishing nothing more than to get inside and away from the view of their pursuer. She was met by the bustle of a restaurant in full flow of the lunch shift. People crowded round the bar making it difficult to hide. Clare squeezed round them and leaned against a counter covered in vases. Cocktail glasses hung upside down behind the counter.

"Help you, darlin'?" called a redhead in a red-patterned blouse. Her name tag bore the name 'Julie'.

"Got a table for two? Somewhere quiet?" Clare asked, wondering how the hell there was any space left for anybody.

"Sure thing, foller me," she said with a smile, swishing her way between two rotund men, one who swatted at her behind.

"Nuff o' that, Clyde," she admonished him. Clare gave him a look. If he did the same thing to her she wouldn't be as forgiving.

Terrick chuckled. "Way to keep a low profile."

Julie led them to a booth obscured on the far side of the restaurant by the bar. It offered concealment from the entrance. The sides and back of the wooden booth reached past her head and Clare settled as far in as she could get.

"Coffee in a sec, kay?" Julie offered.

"That'll be great, thanks." Terrick replied, flashing the waitress a smile.

Julie waltzed off to retrieve the steaming jug of filter coffee, leaving Terrick watching Clare.

"Well, you got any plan B?"

They had nowhere to go, no clue to follow. They had come up short at the very first attempt.

"No I don't. I think however the best plan will be to survive the next few minutes." Clare tilted her head in the direction of the route they had taken round the restaurant. An elderly gentleman with tufts of hair sticking out all over the place peered around. He made eye contact with Clare, frowned and approached the table.

Chapter Fifteen

As the old man approached, Terrick whispered, "Don't make a move."

Clare realized that not for the first time in her life, she was totally out of her depth. The night her parents had died, it was all bluster and phony confidence that had gotten her back into her house. Now her confidence was hanging by a thread. Physically she was a wreck and Terrick knew this. If he couldn't diffuse this situation and something bad happened, she was done for.

Before she could take another breath, the old man had entered their booth and sat next to her, looking back and forth between the two of them.

"Steady, neighbour," Terrick said in a low voice. "This booth is taken." A click under the table reinforced the steely gaze as Terrick cocked the hammer of his until-now concealed pistol.

"Calm it down there, Sheriff Bart," the old man shot back in a fierce whisper. "Give a feller a chance, why dontcha?"

This earned a glare of such fury from Terrick that it could have melted steel. Despite the tension between the two men, the sheriff maintained his composure. "Why don't you tell us why you are here?"

Julie returned with coffee, noticing the newcomer. "Why, hi there Wilf. Thought you were gonna miss the special today an all. You stayin' here with these good folks? Not your spot on the counter?"

"Yeah I'll be sittin' here with my friends. I'll have coffee, me darlin'. And then the special."

"How 'bout you folks?" A man across the restaurant waved a coffee mug at Julie and yelled her name. She shook her head and turned back.

"Pot roast for me, please, and the sausage and gravy biscuit for my friend," said Clare.

"Give the check to me, Julie," Wilf said. "It's my treat."

"Sure thing." Julie smiled and moved off.

"You don't have to," Clare said, once they were alone.

"We're fine, thanks," Terrick added, his tone still cold.

"Nonsense," Wilf replied. "In addition to a free meal, let me give you this as an appetiser. Jarret Logan."

This sent Clare's warning bells into overdrive. "Where did you hear that name?"

Wilf smiled. "Jim Deane wasn't always chief of police in this little paradise. He may hold the position but he has no instinct and wasn't there the day Logan came to town."

"Wilf O'Reilly," Terrick wondered aloud.

"In the flesh," replied their companion. "You might lose the badge when you retire, Sheriff Heckstall, but it's in you. Police work's all you know and it's a difficult habit to break. Let's say I keep tabs on the department, from afar." Wild hair bristled with anger as Wilf leaned forward. "The department's not what it once was. The chief's more concerned about politics now than policing. They wouldn't know a mystery if it jumped up and bit them in the ass."

"But you do?"

They paused as Julie swept in with a round of coffee before hurrying off.

"So there was a day, a decade or so back, when this guy shows up at the station, such that it was. He was a tall drink of water, short dark hair. The perfect lookin' city cop. He presents me with transfer papers from Worcester, signed by some lieutenant or other. Now I can tell you here and now he wasn't lookin' very happy. When I sent him on his way, he didn't get mad. Looked sort of resigned to his fate, as if there weren't nowhere in the world for him to fit no more."

Clare's heart had clenched at the words 'on his way'.

"What do you mean you sent him on his way?" Her question was asked with caution. The last thing she wanted to do was frighten this old man off.

"Well I saw it like this. We didn't need anybody else, and we certainly weren't gonna have some punk-assed lieutenant from Worcester ordering us around. They had always treated us like poorer cousins as it was."

"Was there anythin' else of note?" Terrick asked. She gulped down her coffee; it was only just below scalding temperature and she felt the hot flush as the liquid hit her stomach.

"Yeah there was. He looked like he knew something was up; Kept glancing out the door behind him. I think he wanted a safe refuge, from what I initially had no idea. It was like he never expected to get that far. When I sent him on his way he refused to go. He asked about a case that had happened back then. A couple of strange deaths had been reported. These people looked like they had been sucked dry."

Clare's blood turned to ice. The twisted faces of the victims in the morgue returned to her. The report of her parents, the copy safe in her travel bag, suddenly felt like a lead weight.

"Sucked dry, you say?" Terrick watched her while he repeated this; maybe he was looking for signs of a possible reaction.

"Yup," Wilf continued at a whisper. "Sucked dry, but somehow still chewy, if that's the right word. It looked like someone had hooked in a tube and just drawn the life out of 'em. I swear, it looked like somethin' supernat'ral. They were well-preserved, but an animal must have gotten to 'em. They had strange marks up their arms. Looked like lovebites. Claw marks too, like they'd been gripped."

"Did you take any photos?"

Wilf fixed her with a steely gaze. "Girl, this is the wilderness up here. Nobody knew the deceased and they had no identification. In all honesty the guys wanted rid of the bodies and the case. How Logan knew about it was anyone's guess. He reacted like you when we told him everything was gone. I gave him the case notes and sent him on his way. We don't like strange things transpirin' round here. We certainly didn't want a media circus in Bernardston. The less people as knew about it, the better. Your Chief Deane was a rookie and out on patrol when this went down. He wasn't part of the investigation, and we kept it that way."

"You keep saying 'we'," Terrick observed. "Who else was involved?"

"Sergeant Pete Carter, one of my oldest friends. He died soon after. I saw no reason to tell anyone about this. With Pete dyin' of old age, and Logan takin' all the evidence, it just went away."

"It hasn't gone away," Clare said. "The same thing is happening right now. We had hoped Logan would be able to help us."

"You don't say?"

Clare nodded, the futility of the situation frustrating her.

"Well girl, your answers don't lie around here. That's one thing Deane and I agree on. You need to try up round Ashby. That's what I told the other guy."

"What other guy?"

"He was a little guy, this other. The polar opposite to Logan, twitchy and staring. I didn't trust him. Said he was on a taskforce to transition officers who excel in the hope of training a new generation of statewide law enforcement. I sent him on too, said he could catch the first guy if he hurried. He was only hours behind."

"Was there anything else remarkable about him?" Clare suspected it was the janitor. Small and staring; that was him all over.

"Not that I care to remember. He was ordinary, unremarkable until he stared at me. Then the eyes were so bright, at least they seemed that way. He also had a fruity scent about him. Come to think about it, so did Logan."

"What makes you think of that?" Terrick asked.

"She had the same scent on her breath when I first sat down. In fact, he had a look like you as well, the first guy, Logan. Gaunt, as if the very flesh was being eaten from within. He really looked like he needed to be somewhere in a hurry, just didn't seem to know where." Wilf pointed at Clare with his fork. "Strange how you remember these things after such a long time."

The Eyes Have No Soul

"Strange indeed," Terrick agreed.

"Listen. You want a tip? If you're gonna go poking up around Ashby, be very cautious. If I were you, I'd approach it out of state."

"How so?"

"Because Harley's got everybody looking for you two, that's why."

Clare let go of her coffee cup surprised, causing a clatter and a few of their closer fellow diners to turn their heads. "How do you know that?"

Wilf smiled and pulled out a portable scanner. "This is one of many. There's a lot of weird crap goin' on these days. It don't hurt to stay clued in. Follered you as soon as I heard Chief Deane chasin' your name with Worcester. Do me a favor. If you're dead set on this, remember the word 'Viruñas'."

"Who's that?" Clare asked.

"Beats me. The second guy had it tattooed on his forearm. Hid it up pretty quick too when I spotted it. Stay away from the sheriffs too. Nasty bunch round there."

Lunch came and went quickly after Wilf's strange warning. Given direction, Clare once again felt that familiar surge of purpose. It was good to be back on the trail. Without worrying about the check, Clare used the bathroom before joining Terrick in his car. The engine already idling, he shifted into gear as soon as her behind touched the seat.

"Fortuitous," was the only word he uttered for ten minutes during which time they passed the small Italian restaurant, Antonio's, crossed the I-91 and headed at a leisurely pace toward the Vermont town of Winchester through craggy hills and dense pine forest. They passed a sign hammered to a couple of rough pine logs, faded yellow text on a cerulean background bearing the words 'Welcome to New Hampshire'.

Upon passing the sign, Terrick let out a sigh. "A night's respite. If anybody's been followin' us, they'll stop at the border. Cops up here're much more provincial."

"How's that gonna help us? We have to go back into Massachusetts to reach Ashby."

"It's as old Wilf said. They won't be looking for us in this direction. If Jim Deane made contact with Worcester, the last place they knew we were was Bernardston. Nobody but the old cop and his dead partner know where Logan went, so unless you go announcin' us, we have a moment to breathe."

"Unless feds are on the case," Clare pointed out.

"Don't go creatin' problems for us, girl. Let's deal with what we have in front of us."

Terrick was right. Clare felt the sting of her insides fighting against whatever was ruining her. Why worry about a hypothetical situation when they had actual concerns. Pushing her hair back behind her ear, Clare said, "So what's the plan? Do you know this area?"

"Some. You see that great hill up in the distance?"

Clare watched for a gap in the trees. When they opened out, the horizon was dominated by a squat but very broad peak, the forest ending in pale gray granite.

"That's Mount Monadnock," Terrick said. "Around it is the town of Jaffrey. I know a few places to stay that are out of the way, and only twenty miles or so from Ashby. We camp out here tonight, and hit Ashby in the morning, ask around about anything that might have happened a decade back. They must have stores and restaurants. How's that sound?"

Not liking the sound of 'camp out', Clare shrugged. "We have a place. That's a start."

Camping out turned out to be two rooms in a lakeside hotel called the Woodbound Inn, next to Contoocook Lake, which sprawled south of Jaffrey. Clare especially enjoyed the wood-panelled rooms and the open fire, which she set to a blazing roar just as quickly as she was able. After a brief meal with Terrick, Clare returned to her room. It was not late but despite the morning's sleep weariness was ever-present. Clare closed the curtains and lay down atop the plush maroon comforter, stitched into diamonds, and watched the flames flicker in the hearth. She had no idea how long she lay there listening to the crackle of burning wood. One moment the fire was alight, bright yellow flames reaching heavenward and the next moment she was looking at glowing coals, far more sedate but still very alive with heat.

Clare shook her head, reaching for a drink. How long had she lain there? The room was very warm, and she felt rested but hadn't registered sleep. Was this insomnia? Was she now in a semi-catatonic state where she could not tell the difference between the two? Unable to settle, Clare could no longer just lie there. She reached into her jacket, hanging on the chair, and grabbed both her cell and Tina's.

The clock read 3:42 am; she must have slept at least some of the time yet she still felt exhausted, her stomach in knots and her bladder full again. Instead of seeing to herself, Clare settled back onto the bed, too weary to move any further. She considered Tina's phone for a long while. There was one number stored in the quick-dial, presumably to another phone that Tina held. Clare's thumb hovered over the send button for what seemed an age before she placed the burner out of temptation's way on the table by the bed. If Wilf O'Reilly could detect a conversation, surely more advanced technology could do so too. That would be her quest for answers over in an instant.

Clare looked at the other phone. The Wi-Fi bars indicated good signal. Clare grinned and opened a search engine. *What was that word? Vironas? Verunos?* She tried several combinations before a complete lack of sensible results led her to the answer.

"Viruñas," she said to the empty room.

The logs crackled back at her. Clare entered the word into the phone. When a grinning face appeared on the screen, she yelped, throwing the phone across the room. It landed screen up, staring at her. Shaking, she drew her knees up and buried her face in her legs.

Chapter Sixteen

Daylight crept in under the heavy velvet curtains. The room was warm and scented with pine from the still-smouldering logs. Clare lay on the rumpled comforter, still wide awake.

A polite tapping at her door made her jump.

"Terrick?"

"You decent?"

"Come in, it's unlocked," she called.

The door opened and Terrick entered, closing the door behind him. "You look like crap," he observed. "Did you sleep?"

"Maybe; What day is it?"

"Thursday."

Interview day plus six.

"What's wrong? You look like you've seen a ghost."

"Terrick, I know what Viruñas is."

The sheriff pulled one of the straw-colored cushioned seats from the window to the side of her bed. "Go on."

Clare brought an image to the screen of her cell. In it, a pale-skinned humanoid creature with glowing red eyes and several missing teeth crawled toward the front of the picture. A straw hat obscured much of the body but it had trousers on. Clare flicked to another screen. In the dark, an emaciated creature bound with a minimum of muscle stared at the screen, mouth agape. Its skin was a pale gray but again, it was the eyes that were the focus of the picture. They shone pure white.

"There are more pictures like this, Terrick. Every depiction of this creature has glowing eyes, as if there is nothing behind them but a lust, a hunger that knows no satisfaction. It's as if the eyes have no soul in them whatsoever."

"Or they don't realize what's going on, like a substitute character for an everyday man, like a werewolf."

Clare laughed. "Now you're talking like a loon. Such things don't exist."

"Okay, so that is a Viruñas. What has it to do with these murders?"

"Well first it's pronounced 'beeruhnyas', and it's a legend based in Colombian folklore. The creature itself is also called a Mandigas and is believed to be a depiction of the evil one, I guess meaning Satan. It's often depicted as a handsome man who steals the souls of the people. There are other stories that tell of Viruñas being a werewolf-type creature, presumably with the same goal. It's really all very sketchy. What they do have in common is what he does to people. He scratches them with talons. His victims then just lay down and allow him to take their souls."

"Just lie down and take them…" Terrick repeated in a mystified voice. "How the hell would one do that, if it existed? Which it doesn't."

"That's not all," Clare continued. "The stories speak of the bodies of his victims. Twisted and thin, like agonised shells of the people they once used to be. Sound familiar?"

"So you're sayin' that what, this janitor of yours with the word Viruñas on his arm is some sort of legendary copycat?"

"The tales go on. Though they originated in Colombia, centuries ago, these stories tracked the path of Viruñas northward through Central America. Each country tells its own tale, sometimes about Viruñas, or the other name he took, Mandigas. The trail leads up through Mexico, into the South-Western United States, the last report of such tales being that of a native tribe in the early twentieth century. Always sporadic attacks, grouped presumably to not betray a pattern."

"Or because your legendary monster only needs to feed every so often."

Clare felt a weight pressing in, as if the creature was there, menacing them. "Always six attacks. There's only two more to go."

"Yeah. If this was a creature out of legend, Clare. I think you're over-reactin'. What you've got here is a guy whose probably seen the same website you've read. He's a copycat."

"If that's the case, where's the mescaline coming from?"

"This cactus still grows, Clare, the guy could be using it because he's deluded, or a very clever psychopath. Maybe he's just tryin' to resurrect a legend."

"Whoever this is, we need to get to Ashby and find out what happened to Logan. Someone will have a name, a witness. If he ended up there we need to find something. My parents can't rest in peace until we nail that scumbag."

The eyes haunted Clare in silence as both she and Terrick prepared for Ashby. She came to the realization that not only was her body rebelling against her but her mind, her very essence, was altering. Never in the past would she have entertained the concept of a flight of fancy directing the search for her parents' killer. She was beginning to believe in instinct, in something other than what she could analyse. As they neared the crossroads where route 124 would take them from New Hampshire back into the metaphorical maelstrom that was Massachusetts, she imagined a road full of cops waiting for her. Weapons would be raised, the lights of the cars flashing red and blue in the shape of a huge pair of glowing eyes. Everywhere she looked Clare saw them. A chipmunk on a branch watching her: Eyes. Another driver coming past, waving a rare greeting between travellers: Eyes. Shadows in the trees: Eyes.

"What's wrong?" Terrick's voice was full of concern. He turned to look at her: Eyes. Clare's breath caught. She threw her hands out toward them. The creature. It was beside her.

Clare blinked. It was just the sheriff, who was now struggling to control the car. Terrick braked, causing the car to spin ninety degrees to a halt. A truck coming from the opposite direction flashed them a couple of times and Terrick waved them on.

"What the hell, Clare?"

"I... I'm sorry Terrick. I don't know what's going on. The creature, the Viruñas. I started seeing it everywhere. In the woods, walking beside the roads, even you. I have the strangest feeling I've seen it somewhere before. It feels somehow... familiar."

"Yeah well whatever, keep your hands down girl, or sit in the back. We're little more than a mile away from the State border and we're tryin' to remain nondescript. The sooner we get you to a hospital..."

The reminder caused a knot in her stomach, on top of the pain she already felt. *The sooner I have to admit there's something really, really wrong with me.*

"We can't do that. Not until I have enough evidence to keep us out of cuffs."

"What if it kills you? Clare, you're looking worse and worse."

"I don't care."

Terrick said no more, just shook his head and resumed driving.

Not far down the road, they passed the Massachusetts State sign, the chickadee sat on mayflowers in front of a blue background. The woodland never changed, still the same dense mix of elms, ash, linden and pine, all grown to dizzying heights where the forest had lain undisturbed. At least they never came face to face with a wall of police and for that Clare was thankful.

"Feelin' a little on edge?" Terrick asked, noticing her increased unease.

"I just don't know how this is gonna go down," Clare replied. "We assume that Logan came into Ashby by the most direct route."

"Therein lies your problem, Clare. There's no direct route into Ashby. The roads are a spider web of routes around here. Logan could have taken any one of a dozen combinations and been captured, lost at any one of them. Or he may have just given up entirely. Look, I'm just tryin' to set a bit of perspective here."

He was trying to make her feel better in his own gruff way. Terrick took no prisoners when it came to tolerance. He would never mollycoddle her but he was honest to a fault. The heavy scents of the forest took a back seat as the woodland withdrew from the sides of the road. A green sign at the side of the road read 'Willard Brook Conservation' and Terrick nodded.

"Almost there. Now be careful here, girl. I've heard things."

The whoop of dual sirens caught him by surprise as two black and white cars marked 'Ashby Police Dept' sprung out behind them. The noise was so loud Clare had to initially cover her stinging ears.

"Crap." Terrick punched the wheel. "Any ideas?"

Clare turned to look behind. "There's four of them, two in each car. Can we outrun them?"

"Yeah sure. Let me just press the hidden button that turns the Lincoln into a Ferrari. We were tryin' to remain unremarkable."

"And yet here we are, caught all the same."

As if to reinforce their situation, one of the cars behind nudged them with deliberate force, causing Terrick to lose control for a moment.

Clare grabbed the edges of her seat with clawed fingers, finding her strength was now barely sufficient to even hold on. "Terrick, just stop the car. We aren't getting out of this one without a fight."

"I warned you, girl. These are a different sort. That's a bad idea."

Clare grabbed her bag, rummaging for the gun.

"That's a worse one. Leave it. This lot'll shoot first, ask... no they won't even ask questions."

"Why? Who are they?"

The answer came quickly. Terrick slowed to a stop, pulling the Lincoln off the road onto a triangle of bare brown dirt that formed as two roads intersected. Power cables crisscrossed the air overhead, leaping from one picket-fenced house to the next. Small sycamore trees shone red, their leaves about ready to drop for the winter. One half of their escort pulled in front to block any escape. The other parked at an angle behind them. The only noise came from idling engines.

"Whatever you do," advised Terrick, "don't give them cause to anger."

"Why not? We haven't done anything wrong as far as they are concerned."

"And yet they stopped a car drivin' within the limits, trappin' them as if they expect flight."

Four men got out of the vehicles, blocking the two doors. They obstructed the light, their black uniforms throwing the interior of the car into shadow. Clare marvelled at how similar they looked. They all wore moustaches, were all barrel-chested with guts barely contained by their belts. None were younger than perhaps forty.

"They develop clones up here?"

Clare's quip had no time for a response. The doors were opened.

"Out," a heavyset man wearing a broad-brimmed black Stetson, demanded. Most of the muscle had turned to fat but Clare suspected he wouldn't shirk from enforcing his stunted demand.

Terrick indicated that they should do as asked.

Clare climbed out of the car, an effort in itself given how her nervous legs wanted to collapse under her. She eyed up their captors. Every one of them seemed predisposed to violence. The day was quiet; even nature was sitting this one out.

"Can I help you officers? What appears to be the problem?"

"The problem woman is you opening your mouth without being asked," broad-brimmed hat shot back in a tone of voice that suggested she not do it again. "Spread 'em."

Clare was manhandled round until she had her hands spread on the roof of the car. On the other side, Terrick had been placed in a similar position. Hands frisked her far more intimately than was necessary, lingering between her legs and on her chest. Clare endured it, hoping that her scrawny state gave them little satisfaction.

"Hey now," Terrick shouted. "I'm a cop. That's not what you…"

His voice was cut off as one of the patrolmen on his side of the car slammed him into the Lincoln, winding him and leaving him to collapse on the dirt.

"Boss said silence, meat." The patrolman kicked Terrick in the stomach twice for good measure.

"You want the same?" Broad-brimmed hat growled in her ear. "Just make a sound. You're in my pond now, bitch. You might wish you'd stayed in New Hampshire."

Clare refused to move or make a sound. She could hear Terrick's groans but she couldn't see him. She would not give them the satisfaction of a beating.

This fact dawned on the leader. He leaned into her, making it very obvious he was enjoying this situation. His breath reeked of coffee and onions. After a moment he stepped away.

"Chief, this is Montgomery. We've got 'em, coming in from the east on Main."

"Good job, sergeant," approved a voice through the radio. "Bring them in quietly. No fuss. Worcester will want them intact... mostly intact. Harley's orders were specific."

Grins spread across the faces of all four officers.

Clare's heart nearly stopped when she heard the name. *He knew. All along, he knew where we would be. How?*

"You two, go on ahead. See that our route back is undisturbed." The patrolmen grunted an affirmation. Clare's hands were cuffed behind her back before she was bundled in the rear of the cop car. Terrick had to be dragged up as they cuffed him. He was dumped beside her, barely conscious, blood dripping down his face from a cut above one eye.

By the time this happened the first car had left the scene and was a distant speck far down the road. Congratulating each other, Montgomery and his heavyset clone took their seats and prepared to set off. They had only gone ten yards or so when a shuddering impact threw them all sideways. A black van had appeared from the other road on the intersection, slamming into the front of their car with violent force. Clare felt her head collide with Terrick's chest as the spinning car forced them all to one side. He groaned in response, still only semi-conscious. Clare tasted the warm iron tang of blood in her mouth. The car skidded to a halt. Moving her head from side to side, everything felt in place. Just a cut lip. The same couldn't be said for their two escorts. The driver was unconscious, Montgomery screamed in pain where the impact had crushed the front right wing of the car into his legs, shattering the bones.

Within moments, three figures clad in black and wearing balaclavas appeared from the van, wrenching Clare's door from its hinges. Hands reached in and, despite her struggles, removed her with surprising care. Two men set her on the wooden flooring inside the back of the van and then disappeared to help the third retrieve Terrick. A fourth figure dressed the same watched her from behind the wheel of the van.

"Who are you?" Clare's demand came dry and raspy from a stressed and parched throat.

"If you want to live, stay quiet."

Chapter Seventeen

Clare twisted, attempting to get around Terrick and out of the van. If the report was taken she was screwed, Harley off the hook and the janitor free to kill again.

One of the masked men grabbed at her leg, causing her to bash her shoulder as she crashed to the floor. Pain blossomed and she cried out.

"What in the hell are you doing, lady?" The voice was surprisingly youthful. "We're trying to save your life here."

"My bag," she gasped. "We need to get it. All is lost otherwise."

This caused a moment's contention among their captors, or rescuers. Clare had a hard time working out which. She took a gamble. "Logan. We're here about Logan." As an afterthought she threw out, "and Viruñas."

That did it. Three of the masked men turned to look at her in alarm. One had familiar eyes and a certain set of the jaw that reminded her of… someone.

"Get the bag," said a voice Clare couldn't fail to recognize. Those blue eyes shone at her from behind the mask, concerned.

The van stopped and one of the figures jumped out. In quick order, the bag was retrieved and they moved off.

The men in masks sat in silence as the driver navigated a twisting track through dense woodland. Clare watched Terrick, too scared to look up at her captors. He groaned several times but otherwise showed no sign of returning to consciousness.

One of the masked men, the one Clare was convinced was familiar, leaned down and checked on Terrick, peeling one eyelid back. "Stunned; He'll make it."

"Make it to what? Should I be thanking you or trying to dive out the back of this van?"

"Where would that take you?" Laughed the driver, a woman. "Even those cops have no idea we exist. How're you gonna find your way back to civilization?"

The woodland eventually opened out to moorland for a while, before they plunged back into darkness down a track just wide enough for the van. Behind them, Clare saw people moving a barricade into place as they barreled through the dense forest.

"What's going on out there?"

"Protection," said blue eyes and turned to face forward. In moments the track opened wide enough to permit Clare a view of a two-storied wooden house built entirely of logs. The trees reached over the roof leaving the building entombed in leafy shadow.

"Get him out," said blue eyes. "Take him upstairs and check him over." To Clare he asked, "What did they do to him?"

"I couldn't see exactly. It looked like several kicks to the midriff. He fell down beside the car. Then there was whatever happened when you hit us." The tone of her voice left no uncertainty as to who she blamed for that particular incident. Clare watched helpless as Terrick was manhandled, albeit with some modicum of respect, out of the van and into the log house.

"It's a necessary evil. We can't have them tracking us. You're too important."

Clare barked a laugh. "Important? You could have killed us in there."

"Yet here you are. You should know all about taking calculated risks. Why are you in Ashby in the first place?" The question was rhetorical.

"I think you know more about my business than I do. Why don't you get these cuffs off and we can talk?"

Blue eyes nodded. "Do it."

The smallest of the four brought a set of picks out and jimmied the cuffs off. The instant her hands were free, Clare dipped into her bag and pulled out the gun, pointing it at blue eyes.

"Back! Get Back! I want answers. Now."

"Steady," warned blue eyes, raising his hands slowly aloft. He waved his team away. "Clare, don't do anything rash now. You aren't among enemies here."

"Prove it. What are you doing with us?"

"We're giving you a safe haven. Wilf O'Reilly said you would likely be coming to see us."

The name caused Clare to waver. "This… this was a set up?"

"Not as such. You've wandered into something here, Clare."

"You say my name like you know me."

"I do." He pulled his balaclava off, revealing the dark hair and chiselled jaw that had so recently made Clare forget her woes.

"Dominic? What the hell?" The gun became a dead weight, tugging on her arm until she lowered it, dropping the weapon to the floor.

Dominic jumped back in alarm. "Whoa!"

Clare smirked at him. "It wasn't even loaded. Serves you right though. Why didn't you say anything?"

"We couldn't afford to be recognized. When I say you've wandered into something here, I mean exactly that."

"I'm only looking for whatever killed my parents."

"And that led you here?"

"A lot has happened," she conceded. "To both of us, it seems."

"I have no doubt. Suffice it to say I don't just work at Alden. But look at you. Last week you appeared a bit thin. Now you're positively skeletal. Clare, why aren't you in hospital?"

"Because that guy is out there, killing people to appear like a monster."

Dominic nodded. "Viruñas. What if I told you he's not out there mocking a monster but in fact killing to feed."

Clare leaned back against the interior of the van. "I'd say you're insane, but for what I've seen. The husks of children were twisted and empty. My parents the same. There's just nothing on earth that can do that to a person so quickly."

"There's more," Dominic pushed both doors open as wide as they would go. "Come inside. Let's at least get you warm."

Clare brushed a loose lock of hair back over her ear. As she ran her fingers through her hair, several strands came loose and remained entwined in her fingers. She looked at them, confused. "When the body is under heavy stress, hair is often the first thing to go…"

"Inside," Dominic ordered. "Now."

The interior of the lodge was like a normal house, albeit somewhat larger in scale, more like a mansion. The logs were facia designed to blend in with the outside. Clare conceded they did a great job. Warm, spacious and welcoming, she collapsed into the deep plushness of a forest-green chair, exhausted. The home was spacious and airy, their few captors also discarding their disguises now they were away from the wider world.

"Here," Dominic offered a glass of water.

Clare took the drink and attempted a demure sip but ended up draining the glass in one go.

Dominic's face darkened. "Wait and don't move."

In a matter of moments, he was back with a small black pouch. He produced a pen-like device and a small meter into which he stuck a narrow white strip. "Hold out your hand."

Clare did as bidden, allowing Dominic to swab her pinkie. He placed the pen next to it and depressed a button.

"Ow," Clare said, attempting to pull her hand away.

Dominic's iron grip prevented this and after dabbing an initial drop of blood away, he dipped the small strip on the end of the meter into the second drop that had swelled as if eager to leave her body. The device bleeped a few times before the screen lit up.

Dominic sighed. He turned the meter around to show her.

"It reads two hundred slash eleven point one. What does that mean?"

"The numbers are the two international standards for measuring blood glucose levels. By either one of those, your blood sugar is abnormally high. That means either your pancreas is failing to produce enough insulin because of overuse, which I highly doubt, or because the cells that produce insulin are being attacked by your immune system. With the weight loss and the way you gulp down water, it looks like you are well on the way to developing diabetes."

It was the letter from the hospital all over again. Putting the issue aside had been a mistake. All came crashing home now. "How long have I got?"

"Before you become incapacitated? You have a week, maybe two. It depends on the ketoacidosis."

"The whosyacidwhatsit?"

Dominic sat down opposite her. "Ketoacidosis is what happens when your body can't get the energy it needs to function from sugars. If glucose is absent, the body looks for the next best source. That's fat. Once all the fat reserves are used up, protein. Your body will literally eat itself alive to survive. The by-product of this is called ketones, a toxic sludge that builds up in your system over time and does all manner of damage. If not treated, you will eventually fall into a coma and die."

"How is it you know so much about this?"

"Come with me." Dominic held out a hand, which Clare gratefully accepted and refused to let go of once he had pulled her upright. He led her from the lobby of the house up a broad staircase of deep-stained oak that split in two directions just before reaching the second floor. The climb was a strain on her legs, Clare breathing heavily by the time they reached the top. They took a left on the landing, their steps muffled by a series of Paisley-patterned rugs until they stood at a large door. Dominic took a deep breath then led her in.

What appeared to be an old man lay in a hospital bed in the middle of the room. Heavy velvet curtains were drawn across the windows, only a slither of daylight coming in. The old man was wired up to a series of machines, all of which showed steady signals. Other tubes went into his throat. His face was sunken, shallow, and pale from a lack of outdoor exposure. His chest fluttered with each shallow breath.

Clare moved to the side of the bed. In a hushed voice she asked, "Who is he?"

Dominic came to stand beside her. "Clare Rosser, may I present Jarret Logan, or at least what's left of him."

It took only a moment. "Jarret... Logan? Detective Logan?"

"The very same."

"How long's he been like this? What's wrong with him?"

"Massive internal trauma just about sums it up. He's been this way the best part of a decade. I've only been on the team for the past five."

"Team? What team?"

Dominic beckoned her away from the bed, to an adjacent room in what turned out to be a suite. The nurse, who had remained silent and unobtrusive when they entered, joined them.

"Clare, let me present my sister, Ellie."

Ellie smiled and for the first time Clare noticed the same blue eyes and dark hair.

"Strong resemblance," Clare observed.

"Good genes," Ellie replied and shook Clare's outstretched hand. "Dom's not kidding about the trauma. Jarret's been in a coma for the entire time we've known him. He survives on nutrients passed into his stomach through that tube, fluids by drip and oxygen into his lungs. He's basically a tomato plant in a bed."

"Has he ever given any sign of coming round?"

"We don't expect him to. What you see here was built to protect him after he was attacked."

"You mean he was found in this state?"

Dominic and Ellie exchanged glances. Dominic finally turned to her and took her hand in a gesture of reassurance. "He was tracked to the outskirts of Ashby, where he was found unconscious in the woods. Something was attached to him, draining the fluids from him."

"Something?"

The records are sketchy but yes. It was described as humanoid in nature but bloated and pale, with bright, glowing eyes. It held onto him like this." Dominic grabbed Clare by the upper arms, clenching tight. "The records show that upon discovery the creature fled at inhuman speed. It's nearly impossible to detect anything other than fluid excretions."

"I have some."

"You do?" Ellie became animated. "If we could get those samples and cross check them. You don't happen to have seen the results?"

"Sure. They were damned weird. The fluid we found was bereft of almost everything except blood plasma and waste products. It was like as if everything useful…"

"…had been stripped out of the blood," Dominic finished.

"Exactly."

"There's more," Ellie added. "Take a look at his arms."

The three of them crossed the room to the unconscious Logan, whose arms rested atop the bed. Ellie folded back the sleeve of his pyjamas up to reveal a series of horrific scars. Clare counted five of them, in an arc below a raised circular scar that looked to have never healed.

"Any theories?" Ellie asked.

"I have a couple. First that there's a guy, a janitor, in Worcester P.D. that's attempting copycat killings based on ancient folklore."

"Do you believe that?" Dominic asked. "I mean do you really believe it, right down in the depths of your soul?"

Clare looked down upon the living corpse beneath them. The eyes were partly open. Underneath the pupils were dilated enough to show there was never any hope for poor Jarret Logan. No soul rested in those eyes. Elvis had well and truly left the building. "No. The evidence, as much as I wish it, points to another conclusion. I found this website only this morning called grail dot com that describes ancient myths and legends. I saw the bodies of the children, so twisted and empty. No man, no copycat could do that. I found mescaline traces in fluid at one of the crime scenes but it was natural, not manufactured. I'll bet that's what killed my parents. I'll bet..."

"Go on," Dominic urged. "You're ready to take that step. Science is not enough. Belief is a powerful tool in the right hands."

"I think those marks are where the murderer injected mescaline into the body of the victims and the circular scar above is where it sucked the life out of them. Cut a hole or something." Clare pulled the FBI file from her bag and flicked through. "But the reports state that my parents died of hypervolemia."

"When they found Jarret, the creature was still on him, feeding. No more contact than hands on his arms, in the exact place of the scars. Jarret had eluded the man chasing him, the man that spoke to Wilf in Bernardston. Yet he couldn't elude the creature. Viruñas hunted him down and caught him out in the open. The creature incapacitated him, filled him with its own fluid which would normally cause heart failure, and drained him."

"But he didn't die."

Dominic smiled. "Jarret has a strong heart. We estimate the creature knew it was being hunted and didn't have time to complete the feeding. It was right. It only executed a partial procedure but that was enough to render Jarret the way you see him."

"Why show me all this?" Clare moved her hand around the room, indicating the horrific scene about them. "I'm hunting this thing too, but if it is what you say it is, how do I stand a chance?"

Ellie looked to her brother for evident approval. Getting the nod, she said four words that bound Clare's next choice in unbreakable chains. "Logan was becoming diabetic."

Chapter Eighteen

"It wasn't a surprise. Jarret was chosen because he was displaying the right signs. An initial blood test confirmed the early stages of type one or juvenile diabetes. From there Jarret knew he only had so long before he would become incapacitated."

"But what has this to do with diabetes?"

Dominic took her hand. "Viruñas hunts diabetics. Specifically it appears to hunt those who have not yet been diagnosed or in rare cases, those who are having trouble coping with the illness. Anybody already on an artificial insulin regime is ignored. They tried luring the creature with diabetics off their regular dose. It didn't work. Come look at what we know."

Clare followed Dominic out of Logan's room into another lined from floor to ceiling with shelved books. "Nice reading material," she observed.

"Sometimes there's not a lot to do. I've read most of these. Look at the desk."

By a grand window exposing the autumn forest outside, a desk was burdened with stacks of documentation in paper files.

Clare pulled out the copied Federal document and placed it on top of the rest. "I think this belongs here."

"Keep it. We already have a copy."

Caution overcame intrigue. "Who are you? Who do you work for? Why are you here and not Alden?"

"Who I work for is not for me to say. Trust me that they want the same thing you do though: an end to the killings. Why I'm not at Alden? They believe I'm at another location. I have a cover, of sorts." Dominic picked up various files and showed them to her. "We have infants, teenagers, and adults. All have been taken and drained. Every decade without fail this happens, going back centuries. The creature emerges, takes half a dozen and then disappears. It must have gotten easier lately. The rise of diabetes is alarming."

Clare looked through the proffered files. "These people are quite old."

"True. Juvenile, or type one diabetes hits kids a lot but it's not limited to the young. Sometimes you are genetically predisposed to get the disease. Your body might catch a virus and react for example. Many who were perfectly normal and did nothing wrong in their lives become afflicted by the disease. It was only when the creature made a mistake and let a victim escape that it came to our attention. It sucks the goodness out of its victims, absorbing the nutrients and most importantly, the concentrated blood glucose. We suspect that it cannot absorb nutrients by the usual method of ingestion and developed vampiric tendencies. Diabetics make perfect victims. They are already weak, disoriented, poisoned by the by-products of their own body by the time the creature takes them. They don't put up much of a fight. It's those specific by-products the creature needs, foremost of all, the concentrated levels of blood glucose. Undiagnosed diabetics give off an aroma in their breath akin to pear drops or nail polish remover. We believe the creature tracks them using this with advanced scent receptors. That's how it stayed ahead of the game with poor Logan in there. The plan was to put Logan in the creature's path, and trap it. But the creature fed on him. By the time we caught up it was almost too late."

"Have you tried faking the aroma? Surely that's safer than placing an already-ill person in harms' way?"

"It was tried back in the seventies. Strategically-placed 'victims' were left in the area of the creature. It avoided them completely. Viruñas isn't feeding mindlessly. It is conscious, self-aware, and very,

very dangerous. The plan was to find someone who knew the risks and was willing to go the extra mile. It took thirty years for the hunting cycle to coincide with someone willing and able."

"That's why he was at my house. Logan was tracking the Viruñas."

"From what we understand, he was hoping to get in the way of the creature. He was, however, delayed."

Clare barked a laugh. She knew exactly where this was going. "Harley."

"He's involved all over the state. The guy is a pain in the ass. He has people everywhere, including Ashby. It's a good ole boys network round here."

"Can't you do anything about that?"

"Not directly. He has a role in this that has yet to be determined and there aren't enough of us involved to be able to ferret out his secrets."

"Oh he has secrets all right. At the moment, he's working his way to becoming the chief of police in Worcester. Harley has ambitions above his station. You put that man in politics and he's gonna do all sorts of damage to the city."

"He's doing worse than that. He's linked somehow with the creature."

The temptation was too great. Clare realized she was being led into this but the faces stared up at her from all the folders. Lives extinguished before their time, ill or becoming so; all had deserved a chance at life. Diabetes should never have been the end of them, not if they were careful.

"Can I sleep on it?"

Dominic leaned over the files, looking up at her. "Of course you can. Terrick needs time to recover. Tomorrow we'll take you out to where Logan was found. It might put things into perspective."

Saturday morning came far too quickly. Although the bed was soft and the room dark and comforting, Clare felt ill at ease in a house set up as a hospice for just one man. Jarret Logan had no quality of life here. His body was a shell, being kept alive by people guilty of losing him. Clare found sunlight greeting her through the dense foliage that pushed at her window as she considered her next move. Risk becoming another soulless almost-corpse, or seek the medication she now knew she had to have.

Wandering the house, Clare eventually found the kitchen by way of the scent of cooked food and fresh bread. Breakfast was laid out and Terrick sat at the grand mahogany table. It was far too splendid a room for something as mundane as breakfast. Framed artwork decorated the maroon wallpaper and yet more bookshelves filled one end of what appeared more like a drawing room in an Edwardian mansion than a kitchen in a secluded log house. Terrick looked every inch the beaten man, slumped over his meal.

"How do you feel?" Clare asked as she sat down and helped herself to coffee and toast. She downed a glass of orange juice, barely noticing the taste as the liquid filled her stomach.

"Like I've been kicked in the gut several times and someone barrelled into me."

Terrick's deadpan humor wasn't lost on Clare and she smiled in response. "Could've been worse."

"True. They tell me nothin's broken, though I'm bound to ache for a few days and pass blood every which way but how. Truth be told, those deputies were so overweight they got in the way of each other tryin' to get in a good kick. I've had worse, given better."

Clare didn't doubt this for a second. Terrick was a tough old nag and had probably taken a beating or two in his life.

"What about you?" He pointed at her. "They wouldn't tell me anythin'."

Clare raised her hands in a gesture of defeat. "Diabetic; According to the blood sugar readings I'm headed to the morgue if I don't sort myself out. My body's eating itself alive but the situation is much more complicated than that now."

"What's more complicated than getting yourself to hospital? Sort it out, girl. If you aren't here this goes away and everybody forgets."

"Come with me." Clare stood.

Terrick groaned and stood to join her. She led the way to Logan's room, opening the door. The body was alone.

"Who's he?" Terrick asked, staring past her but not entering.

"He's Detective Jarret Logan. He was diabetic and the creature got to him. It's real, Terrick. He was a lure intended to draw it out and he perished in all the ways that matter. That's a breathing corpse in there, nothing more; A meat sack."

Terrick gave her a suspicious look. Clare didn't need to ask what he was thinking. "I haven't made my mind up yet."

"But you're thinking about it."

"I am. Nobody has asked me outright to commit to this but there have been four deaths which means there are two more to come. Always six kills and last time Logan was the sixth. After that this thing disappears for a decade. What you see here is guilt over the failure to protect a human life already in the balance. If I can do something about it, why should more people suffer and die?"

"Noble, Clare, but what if the same thing happens to you?"

"Let's make sure it doesn't."

It's not like I really have a choice.

The pair resumed their breakfast, Clare consuming far more than was good for her. She figured at least hunger wouldn't affect her as much as thirst, though both were becoming more of an issue as each day passed. Dominic joined them in the lobby of the house when they had finished.

"Ready to go?"

Terrick looked to Clare, his face questioning.

"Sightseeing," she replied. "It might help put things into perspective."

"Whatever. This quest of yours for answers is at an end. Get to the hospital already. Let others deal with the monsters in this world."

"Will you at least take a look?"

Terrick nodded. "Looks like I ain't got a choice. Those dumbass Ashby cops probably have my car, if they didn't already smash it to bits."

Dominic laughed. "They're nothing if not petty and vindictive," he agreed. "Don't worry. The next journey is not far for you, and we have you a new ride. One even the sheriff's wife might like."

The reference to his title caught Terrick off-guard. "How do…"

"Don't bother," Clare said by way of cutting off the obvious and unnecessary question. "They know everything. We've been playing catch up the entire time. If I had to guess, I'd say they knew about my illness before I did and engineered our route."

Dominic gave her a mysterious wink and opened the front door. Outside, a brand new silver Chrysler sedan waited for them, engine already running. The windows were tinted, preventing anybody seeing inside. "For you sir; A replacement for the car you lost, and your inconvenience."

Terrick was struck dumb. He pointed at the car, his face alive, mouth attempting to form words.

"Yes it's yours. You drive, Sheriff, we'll sit in the back."

"Is it safe?" Clare asked as they got in the car. The leather seats were unblemished. Clare had never owned a new car. Everything felt unusual, sterile. "Won't they be on the lookout for us?"

"They'll be watching for a damaged black van, one that no longer exists. They won't see a couple of new sedans cruising through town. These things are a dime a dozen round here. Drive on, Sheriff."

Terrick encouraged the car forward with a little gas. "Where are we?"

"North of Ashby, where nobody ever looks."

Clare glanced behind. A four by four in a shade of deepest metallic green stayed close. "Our guardians?"

"In a manner of speaking. They will be useful in discouraging anybody from following us. It's a shame the local police found you before we did or they might not be necessary."

The gates opened and Terrick took them down the track they had entered the day before, pulling back onto the highway after checking it was clear.

"Just drive through town," Dominic instructed. "Don't do anything crazy. There's an incident brewing at Worcester County jail and they've sent several officers down there to help quell the unrest. But they've still got a presence here."

Terrick's beaming grin emerged for the first time since they had arrived in Ashby. "Don't tempt me, lad. I might do so just to see what your boys are capable of."

Dominic's face showed concern and Clare took his hand. "He's joking. Really."

Her back-seat companion nodded but remained holding her hand. Clare really felt skeletal in his presence. She looked inside herself. There were the usual aches, the constant need to pee and a hunger that just never appeared to be satisfied. Overall she felt a weariness; a fog that would not lift. Now it was all linked, all pushing her toward her destiny. Her pain now had a name: Diabetes.

Buildings passed by as they came to the main street of Ashby. The police station was a strange converted trailer, cars lined up outside including the car crumpled by the van.

"The whole front right wing's crumpled," Clare observed. "How did anybody survive?" The words came out a lot more accusing than wondering.

"I'm sorry about that. We aimed specifically for the front."

"We're still here," Terrick said by way of acceptance. "They can trace the plates and what will that tell them? Only that I'm not from around here. I ain't without resources myself."

More houses passed, all owned by the affluent judging by their size. Dominic wasn't kidding. There were high-end sedans everywhere. The street opened up for a moment to show a quaint parish church with a small spire in the distance. Then the scenery returned to dense foliage revealing nothing except a large restaurant marked 'The 873 Café' that had seemingly been carved into the forest.

"People like their space up here then," Clare said. Nobody replied.

Ashby disappeared into the background, claimed by the forest. They were alone on the highway but for trees, powerlines and the green support vehicle. Dominic had been right. Nobody had noticed them. How would anybody notice a guy being tracked down and killed in this wilderness? They needed an advantage. They needed someone to draw the creature out, make it desperate.

Out of nowhere an open section of land appeared, the trees only dead trunks now, the branches bare of leaves.

"Those aren't trees ready for winter." Clare opened the window to get a better look. Cold air cut her face, stinging her eyes. "Those trees are dead. What happened here?"

"Time to pull over, Sheriff," Dominic let go of Clare's hand to point off to the left.

Terrick did as bidden, stopping the car. Everybody got out and they stood as a group looking over the dead terrain.

"It's so alien," Clare said.

"Been like that ever since the Viruñas got to Logan. Chased him down in a car, ran him off the road right into the middle of the forest and started feeding right there. They reckon he was getting desperate both for food and time. But for the wreckage they would never have found him. It's so uniform around here. The trees died within a year, the death spreading out a few hundred metres in every direction."

Clare turned back to the car. On the other side of the road the trees were dead too, but not as far back into the forest.

"It's like someone dropped a biological bomb on the landscape."

"That's exactly what it looks like. We found this in the past. There are records of forests dying out where the creature had passed. Something it releases poisons the ground. Imagine the damage it would cause if it were to get into a hospital in the middle of a city rather than picking on vulnerable individuals in the wilderness?"

Clare stared at Dominic for a moment, and then smiled. "I've got an idea."

Chapter Nineteen

Dominic's demeanor changed in an instant, assumed an air of if not business, at the very least authority. "You will do this for us?"

"I feel you always assumed that I would. Just tell me one thing. How far gone was Jarret Logan?"

"The last blood test he submitted showed his blood sugar nearing the maximum reading a testing meter can cope with. He was pretty sick. Yet for all of that he wanted nothing more than to catch Viruñas. He was approached just before your parents became the creature's victims. The night of their death, he argued with Harley about hunting this thing down. They came to blows. Harley already had influence by then and skipped the chain of command to have Logan transferred. He has a history of transferring those he fears."

"So I understand. Why's he involved in all this anyway? Whoever your paymasters are, surely they don't have to deal with the likes of him."

"Sometimes in order to remain anonymous, one has to play in another's backyard. They often have a different set of rules. Harley is the big fish in the Worcester pond. He has been for over a decade. You should know, Clare. You've been dancing to his tune your entire career. The time to trade up is coming soon. Ask yourself this: Why has Andrew Harley been so persistent in keeping you from trying to become a detective? Is it because of a misogynistic desire to suppress the advancement of women? Or is there something more…"

"He had Jarret transferred out of Worcester shortly after we recruited him. There's a possibility Harley knew the detective was unwell. Maybe he knew with what. Despite my organization's best-laid plans, Logan still ended up dead or as near as was possible before we could close the trap. Viruñas had an advantage."

The chill breeze was beginning to numb Clare's hands. She moved back to the car. "I'm getting out of this wind. This place reeks of death."

Getting in, she pulled the door to with a loud 'clunk'. Terrick and Dominic continued to talk outside, the conversation appearing to become animated as the sheriff waved his hands about. Clare watched from under drooping eyelids, not even trying to listen.

"Hey," Dominic's gentle voice said.

Clare started. "What?"

"You dropped off there."

Clare looked around. She was inside the car. Terrick was still outside, stood a few metres toward the skeletal treeline, looking away from them. "What'd I miss?"

"Just the conclusion of our heated debate about what's best for you. From my point of view I'll be honest; I want to see this thing captured or dead. I won't beat about the bush here, Clare. You are the best chance, perhaps the only chance to see that come to pass. It's not about the person for me, even though it's you. It's about some unholy creature killing innocents. It's about seeing an end to the murder."

"And Terrick? His view is somewhat more protective."

"The sheriff would see you in hospital right now, on an intravenous drip of insulin and fluids. He's right to want that for you. He's a good guy, going out of his way to protect one of his own. But he understands duty. He knows both the gravity of the situation and the next step you need to take should your resolve be adamant."

"It is. This man... this *creature* killed my parents. I need to find it, look it in the eye, and ask what they did to deserve death. Was it personal or was he just hungry? Perhaps you both need to consider that I know what's best for me."

Clare emerged from the Chrysler, aching. She moved with next to no sound, the hushed whisper of the wind through dead trees the only noise. The cold made the backs of her fingers prickle as the blood rushed to withdraw from her extremities. She shivered, wrapping her arms about her body.

Terrick made no movement to indicate he knew she was there. "If this is about vengeance, we part ways right here. I'll not get involved in a blood feud between you and some skulking nastiness."

"Yet if you could do something to make a difference? If you could stand up and say 'I count. I'm that person who is going to stand between you and them. They will live on because I'm gonna do my darndest to make sure you don't succeed and they die, even if it costs my life.' Would you be that person?"

Terrick didn't reply. Clare understood why. "I know you already are. What I've come to realize is I can be that person too. There are people depending on me. Strangers I will probably never meet. Two more people have a chance at life in this moment. Who knows how many more would be saved in the future if we stop this now? Six more? Sixty? Six hundred?"

Terrick turned to her. "And what are you doing about Harley?"

"He's tied up in this, for sure. If these people refuse to finger him after everything, I'm not gonna go after him directly. If we find any evidence that implicates him, so be it. This is not about personal vengeance."

"No?"

"Not any more. It was once but there are bigger issues."

"Well if you ain't gonna go all Inigo Montoya on him, I guess I can help you a little further."

Clare stuck her left thumb up behind her back so that Dominic could see. "Now's not the time for spur of the moment heroics, girl. You need a plan. It has to be well-conceived, thoroughly considered with every possible weakness eradicated. This is your life we are talkin' about and if I'm on board, you'll not be losing it on my watch."

"I have a plan," Clare admitted. "Don't know about flawless but it's not gonna put me out here in the wilderness to die on my own. Let's get in the warm and we can discuss it on the way to wherever we're going."

Clare turned with Terrick to find Dominic stood by the open passenger door. "This is where we part ways," she said with a smile.

"Why?"

"This is my journey, Dominic. I'd love it if we meet again, but we can't catch this creature out in the wilderness. Look what happened to Logan. If anything that's proof you just gave Viruñas too much space to vanish. We need to trap it in an environment it has a much harder chance of avoiding detection. Plus, you have your hands full with Logan and Alden. Allow me to do this. My way."

Dominic nodded. "Okay, so you're gonna try and pull it back into the city? We tried trapping it before. You think you stand a better chance?"

"Exactly. With surveillance technology as advanced as it now is, we can track it. I know exactly where to focus our efforts."

"Will you do me a favour before you go back? There are some people I'd like you to meet who can help you with your plan. It is on the way to Worcester. With the increased police presence due to the prison situation, they might be able to help you get back in undetected."

"Where are these people?"

Dominic nodded toward Terrick. "He knows. He'll see you there safely. In the meantime, I've stocked you with as much relevant reading material as possible. You don't want to get caught in possession of that, by the way. It's somewhat incriminating."

A leather briefcase sat on the backseat, alongside a holstered gun. "What's that for?"

Dominic smiled. "In case you ever need use of a gun that can actually fire. I don't know where you got that hand-cannon you waved at me but had you loaded it and squeezed the trigger, you'd have more likely blown your own hand off. It was in dreadful condition. That's a

Walther P99 right there. It has minimal recoil and is already loaded. If you point and squeeze, you might actually hit something."

"See her safe," Dominic instructed Terrick, who nodded. To Clare he said, "I'll be watching. If you're sure you're up to the task, good luck."

Terrick turned the car and began to head back toward Ashby once Clare was secured in the passenger seat. She still felt weary but that was never going to leave her. It was the kind of weariness that one didn't mind, like a child waking up too early on Christmas Day. Clare had direction and purpose. More than that, she had a deadline. In her case, it was literal. If she didn't draw Viruñas out soon she'd be too incapacitated to do anything about the remaining killings. She might fail and become another Logan.

"Are you havin' doubts?" Terrick asked.

"No. Not at all. Any conflict in my mind was cleared up the moment I saw Jarret Logan. I won't become a victim like him. Or my parents. Now's not the time for that. Let's find these people and see what they have to offer."

Clare looked out the window for a moment. The white 'Welcome to Ashby' sign flashed past. "You sure we're going the right way?"

"Yeah. The place Dominic told me about is off a road to the south. Keep yer head down and we'll be through here in no time."

"Let's hope so." She reached over to the backseat of the Chrysler, the pale-gray leather of the passenger seat creaking as she hauled the case through to the front. Flicking the clasps open, she cross-checked mental notes she had made at Logan's lodge. Dates, names and as many previous victims as she could recall. Inside lay several laminated folders marked 'Special Investigation File.' She gathered the top two and closed the case, placing it in the foot well.

Clare stared at the dates on the recovered police files, noting the expected similarities. They were onto it in a big way.

Terrick took a right. The sudden change in direction caught at her stomach, reminding her she had overeaten. Closing her eyes, she took a series of deep, slow breaths.

"You ok?"

"Can we stop somewhere along here? I want to get through these files before we lose the opportunity."

Terrick nodded, muttering under his breath, "Barely started and already we stop."

Clare smiled inside. Terrick would know this was important.

A couple of minutes later a huge lake came into view on their right, stretching off to a distant treeline, the surface calm and undisturbed by the breeze that had made the skeletal forest so unappealing. Terrick pulled off the highway onto a dirt track, a couple of scrawny pines the only thing between them and the water. Clare looked out the window; they were so close to the lake's edge it gave the impression of disappearing under the car.

Across the road, what seemed the entire population of Ashby had gathered at a street-fair; the scent of spiced chicken wafted toward her, mixed with the sweet smell of cinnamon on waffles. Clare's stomach flipped and she gulped down what was left of her bottle of water, draining it in one go. Trying to ignore the travel sickness, she continued.

The two kids who died here ten years ago were killed just before the transfer of Jarret Logan. "These records all tie in with the last round of deaths, including my parents. Yet nobody at Worcester has ever mentioned Logan…"

"You think Harley's people'd let on if there was a grand conspiracy?"

"The file Tina copied: It's here. The author of the report is a John Hope on this version, not Jarret Logan."

"Who? You think it's the same man?"

"I believe so."

"That means someone on high has been messin' with these reports."

Terrick was right. Anybody party to this would be deep in cahoots with Harley.

"This report seems to say that somebody responsible for the mishandling of the investigation had been relocated. There's more at play here than just covering tracks."

"Harley," Clare said aloud, banging her fist on the plastic dash. The captain's influence amongst his peers reached for many miles, far out of Worcester. Clare knew her prejudice against the man was likely to colour her views, yet what other answer was there? *Four kids this time, you evil son of a bitch. Twelve on record, who knows how many more before that?* He might not be directly responsible for the killing but he was damned-well responsible for keeping the facts from the public, leaving nothing more than whispers and rumours. Indirectly or not he was hiding the killer, this abhorrent monster that drained kids dry, from detection and ultimately justice.

But why keep her close? Then it hit her.

"Because when the time is right, I will conveniently disappear, another unsolved mystery," she said aloud, causing an old lady who was passing by to stop and stare at her before scuffing on up the sidewalk. "Don't you see? Harley is hiding somebody and doing his darndest to make sure there's no paper trail. I think I know why the Ashby cops were waiting for us. I'll bet somebody was coming up here to make sure I suffered a similar fate to Detective Logan. Somebody, or something."

Chapter Twenty

"We'd better get goin'", said Terrick. "The longer we wait here the more chance they'll see us. You feelin' better?"

"I'll live."

Terrick waited for her to put the files away before starting the car once more and moving off. The street fair continued unaffected by the loitering of strangers and the last suggestion of Ashby was soon out of sight behind them.

Clare settled back to wait as Terrick drove them down the road. The car bumped across repeated cracks in the asphalt, the yellow markings barely visible. The dense forest was interspersed with areas of stagnant pooled water, more dead trees clawing through, as if once again desperate for life. The sun shone down on these areas, attempting to give them beauty through light. Clare was dazzled by the reflection. She imagined a creature with glowing eyes, grinning as it slathered over an immobilized victim. Clare imagined how the children must have felt before they were drugged into insensibility and it twisted her insides.

"Are we far away?"

"I ain't tellin'," Terrick replied with a smile. "Sometimes, you just gotta trust that the right decisions been made, and go along with it. Destiny forms part of belief, girl. Have faith in a bigger plan and acceptance of both the plan as well as your place within it. Just trust that I'll get us there. It's not far."

"I can't wait. I've had enough of driving through forests."

Terrick's face gave nothing away, a slight smile tugging at the corners of his mouth. What wasn't he telling her? He remained silent.

In time, the tedious forest road became interspersed with signs declaring their impending arrival in the town of Fitchburg. Clare knew little about the place, except that the residents were heavily devout. And so it proved to be. Even on the outskirts of the town, placards had been placed in neatly-trimmed flower borders proclaiming obedience to God, adherence to His Word and the damnation of those who would not. Other than the abundance of religion, the town was much like any other. Stars and Stripes hung from every available flagpole, three-story buildings loomed about the centre of town, worn at the edges but cared for. Newly-painted window frames gleamed in the bright sunlight, standing in stark contrast to crumbling red brickwork. Weeds sprouted from cracks in a worn path within stepping distance of a glorious fountain erected in His honor. People traversed sidewalks, cars filled the roads. It was nothing out of the ordinary, except for the sign on the church.

Terrick had reached the middle of the town and was waiting to cross what passed for the main junction in the town, where three highways met when she first spied it. The hall was red brick walls filled with huge arched windows and set off with a grand white spire. The parishioners of this particular church clearly knew they were the centre of town. A majestic and yet pride-filled building that seemed to say, 'There are other churches, but this is *the* church.' They passed around the front, revealing both the name, The First Unitarian, and a sign.

"Failure to choose may become the choice we have to live with," she wondered aloud.

"Never were truer words spoken," Terrick agreed. "Not all these churches spend every waking moment denouncing each other."

Clare reassessed her opinion of the First Unitarian. She was slowly failing, her body crumbling from within, yet she had chosen to act with positivity. She would live with that.

"I've made the right choice," she declared.

"So you have, girl. You're believin' that now, for real. They said only tell you where we're goin' if you came to some kind of decision. You're not capable of drivin' across the state in your condition and they wanted me to help."

"Religion helps put it all into perspective. This is certainly no kingdom of heaven, not with monsters like this left to roam free and kill at will."

"Be that as it may, there's still no guarantee you'll catch it. We're headed into the Leominster State forest."

"Oh joy," Clare groaned, "back into the woods again. What's there?"

"It's a commune where we'll find you help."

Clare thought for a second. "The Rainbow Warrior Writing Retreat?"

Terrick shrugged. "Maybe, I was just given directions. It looks like we aren't the only ones headed that way either."

Clare watched the wing mirror as Terrick edged the car over to the side of the road. In the distance she saw a silver car. "How can you tell?"

"They've been changin' speed as I've done so. Up and down both. They stay the same distance. They caught us up just before Fitchburg. Got close then edged back. Happy to sit there unless we do somethin' drastic, I'll bet."

"Who are they?"

Terrick laughed. "Damn, girl. What am I, psychic? Why don't we just stop and ask 'em?"

"Might not be the best idea. They must be from Ashby. What plate was on the car?"

"It's unmarked. When they caught us up, I spotted four heavies in there. You know, like the size of the deputies that used me for field goal practice. Maybe they worked us out and are lookin' for a nice quiet spot of revenge. Harley left more of 'em up here than we thought if they're free to chase us down. If I were you, I'd loosen that toy gun o' yours in its holster. You might yet get some practice. Just do it real subtle, like."

Clare reached down to the foot well. "I've already got it." She placed the Walther in her lap. It felt reassuring to have the compact weight resting on her thighs. While she wasn't likely to sign up as a member of the NRA, in this situation she felt better for having a means of self-defence. With her deteriorating state of health affecting her insecurity, it was doubly welcome. "Now prove it to me. I wanna see them react."

Shaking his head, Terrick eased the car to a halt. "It's a bad idea. Just don't stare at them." At first the unmarked car began to follow suite, maintaining distance. As it became obvious they weren't going to sustain the facade, the silver car sped up and overtook as Terrick signalled off the road. Clare tried to get a good look as it shot past; several large men filled the car. One watched them from the front passenger seat. Their eyes made contact and in that instant Clare came to a realization. *We're being hunted.* Their pursuers turned off at the next available junction.

"Too crowded," Terrick observed. "Too near population. They'll catch us again in the forest."

"Then make sure they don't."

Terrick pulled back onto the road, accelerating past the road where the silver car was mid-turn. There was a distinct squeal of tires as the driver sought to join the chase.

"East Princeton," Terrick muttered as a sign flashed past. "We have to go left."

"Where does this lead us?"

"We go through the forest which means windy roads and less visibility. There's a very distinct white house down this road a few miles on the left. We turn right there. Then a mile down that road there's a crossroads just after some open land with a hill to the right. If I don't make it, you have to go up that road onto the hill. You *need* to get up that road. You got all that?"

"White house, turn right. Open land on a hill then crossroads. Go up the hill. Got it? Don't do anything suicidal and let's hope it won't come to that. You got it?"

Before Terrick could answer, his wing mirror exploded.

"They're shootin' at us, girl."

Clare turned. Behind, the silver car was closing on them. She could now see the four men silhouetted inside, though she could not be sure they were the same deputies. One of them was attempting to get a bead on them, his gun waving around as he coped with the wind. He fired again, the bullet ricocheting off the trunk and out of danger.

"Ashby's finest on their day off," she observed. "Our secret is definitely out."

They were already doing seventy along roads that twisted with frequent irregularity.

"Feel free to dissuade them," Terrick suggested. "I'll try to hold her steady."

Clare wound down her window and turned, kneeling on her seat, the Walther in her left hand. "I'm right handed."

"They don't know that. Just squeeze off a few."

Clare waited until a bend in the road gave her a decent view of the car behind, and squeezed the trigger. The right headlight exploded in a shower of plastic and glass, causing the driver to swerve. Unfortunately their pursuers refused to back off, closing the gap until the two cars touched. Clare attempted a shot at the front wheel just as they hit a bump. Her shot went high, hitting the gunman in the arm and causing him to drop his weapon in a spray of blood. Another bump from behind caused Clare to hang on for dear life as she was shunted off-balance.

"They don't want us gettin' away. Buckle up, girl. We need to make some sort of populated area or they'll run us off the road."

Clare secured herself as Terrick upped the speed. The car behind matched them. For the next few minutes it was a dogfight. Both cars swerved across the lanes of the road.

Please, stay empty, Clare prayed as they hurtled down the wrong side of the road. Another nudge found Terrick compensating the direction, curses streaming from his mouth.

Clare tasted blood and began to panic until she realized it was just a bitten lip.

Then out of nowhere buildings materialised.

"Is this enough?" Clare asked.

Another bump, this one forceful, caused her head to whip back into the headrest. "Guess not."

A fork in the road appeared out of the woodland. Across the road to the right, adults shepherded children in uniform.

"They're about to cross," Clare warned.

Terrick began to honk the horn. "We slow down, we're dead."

The children moved toward the crossing, shepherded by their guardians. The scene was on them in moments. The driver behind had no such morality about collateral damage, attempting to pull alongside them.

Terrick swerved left, still beeping at the schoolchildren. The other car followed but the foremost adult, a man maybe in his twenties, jumped forward as one of the kids attempted to run across the road. With a thump that made Clare wince, the other car hit the man, slowing back as the driver wobbled and lost control in a spin.

"Did they get him?" Terrick's voice was thick with concern.

Clare strained to see. "He looks down, but moving. Maybe they just took out his leg. Keep going. They'll be on us in seconds."

It didn't take long. "White house," Clare pointed to their left. Off to the right a narrow road disappeared into the woodland at the bottom of a low, wide hill that emerged above the treeline.

Slowing only enough to take the sharp right at speed, Terrick allowed their car to drift until the tires gained purchase once more, sending them shooting off into the shady twilight of a road barely used.

"Too much dust," Clare said as she looked behind them. "They'll know exactly where to look."

"We need to ditch this car and get on foot. We'll have the advantage if we can outpace them. You wounded one of them. The rest don't look up to a mountain hike."

Clare stared down at her own withered hands. "I hate to be the one to break it to you Terrick but I'm not exactly in shape for a trek either."

"Yeah but we know where we're going. They don't have that luxury."

Clare took a series of slow, deep breaths, trying to calm her thudding heart, fuelled by adrenaline. "I wish I had your confidence."

"We're gonna have to dump the car, or at least hide it. Maybe they'll miss it."

The hill rose to the right of them, its lower flanks steep and packed with trees straining toward the light. In what seemed like moments, the forest withdrew, the fields of a farm stretching off to their right. The open space before the crossroad appeared, cattle-trimmed grass and a gradual gradient providing no cover at all. They were running out of road.

"Nothing there," Clare concluded after a brief examination. "A couple of barns up the hill. That's about it. We're gonna have to try for the treeline." As the road swept around the hill to the right, Clare watched for signs of pursuit. No movement. "Maybe they did crash."

"Hitting a person won't stop people like that, girl. They looked far too determined. They're out there, believe me."

The open space ended as they passed the tree-line and just as quickly the junction appeared.

"Go left," Clare suggested. "We can stash the car and double back."

"Could end up walkin' right into them," Terrick cautioned.

"We're gonna have to risk it. You don't want to take the right track and lead them right to the commune. We don't have time to argue."

Terrick took her suggestion, easing the car down the slope until a gap in the trees presented itself. Clare grabbed the case of documents and exited the car, being careful to close the door quietly. The leaf litter was deep underfoot, the forest floor twisted and tangled with roots as she squelched and slipped her way through the undergrowth. "Now the hard bit," she said in hushed tones. Her legs were already like jelly, her head fuzzy with ongoing weariness. How was she supposed to make it up the hill?

Chapter Twenty-One

They had only gone a matter of meters when Clare's legs began to give way. The irregular surface would have been fine for a fit and healthy Clare Rosser, used to outdoor terrain and a regular hiker since childhood. It was not the case anymore.

Terrick caught her as she began to crumple.

"I... I can't," she gasped, sweat running down her forehead. "It's too much." A chill ran down her back and she began to shiver.

"You have to, girl. You stay put and we're done. Your mind is stronger than your body. Remind yourself of that fact and get the hell up."

In the distance Clare heard the whine of an engine labouring at speed. Was it the Ashby deputies? Terrick pulled her forward despite her body protesting with shocks of pain. They made it through the trees to within sight of the road they had come. Terrick hissed, "Get down!"

Clare dropped as much as fell to the ground, laying prone amongst a bed of mountain laurel.

Terrick cautioned her to silence with one hand and they ducked low behind a clump of ferns. The silver car, dented and scratched down its left side, sped along until it reached the junction. One of the men, the same guy who had kicked Terrick and then driven off in the first squad car the day before, climbed out of the damaged passenger side, his movements laboured. With a groan he knelt down and examined the road.

"That way," he called back to the car, pointing in the direction they had taken. The silver car edged forward, allowing him time to get back in, before heading off down the track.

Terrick watched the car until it was just behind them and pulled Clare to her feet. "We got minutes at most. We gotta get you up that hill, girl."

"What if they see us?"

"Try stayin' on your feet for more than two minutes and leave the what-ifs to me."

They emerged onto the road and for a moment Clare was blinded by the glare of the sun as she stared unthinking right at the golden ball of light.

"Idiot," Terrick cursed, and dragged her forward.

With no will to resist, Clare stumbled on, her only conscious contact with the outside world the hand that yanked with dogged determination at her right arm.

"There's a trail off to the left, where the hill is steepest. Let's hope they think we went to the farm for help."

Clare blinked as the dazzle began to lift from her eyesight. She was left with a thumping headache pulsing across her temple. Each 'thump' threatened to collapse her once again but she fought with a primal urge: a survival instinct. One footstep became ten. Ten became twenty. Twenty became fifty. Were they winning?

"This will do for a moment." Terrick took them off the track into a part of the woodland where the trees were denser. Pines had bunched together in a near-impenetrable wall. Clare stopped in the lee of one tree that stood out from the rest, wider and taller than its fellows. Leaning against it until her forehead touched the rough bark, she stood there gasping for breath.

A single gunshot rang out from the slope behind them. Clare's sight had only returned enough that she felt rather than saw a bullet shatter a branch only feet from her head. She lifted the Walther around the side of the trunk with her right hand and squeezed, emptying the clip just as Terrick had instructed her. When she lowered the empty gun and looked to the sheriff, his face was a mask of disbelief.

"When you can see them..."

Clare looked to the gun and back to Terrick, not quite comprehending, then around their barricade.

Down the hill behind them there was movement. Some, if not all of the Ashby deputies stalked them. Clare had trouble focusing on the distant woodland with the way her head was throbbing.

"Move up the hill, real slow like," Terrick whispered. "I'm gonna see if I can get round and hamstring them. They won't see you from here, as long as you stay low and stay quiet."

"Terrick that's insane. There's four of them and one of you, and they have guns."

Terrick pulled his own gun from his belt. "I fancy my chances, girl. Just make your way back there."

Not giving her a chance to respond, Terrick silently disappeared into the woods. Clare remained where she stood, trying to decide if moving was a good choice. Surely staying still just presented her as an easy target so she decided to try it.

"Sheriff," boomed the deep voice of a man down slope. The word echoed through the woods. "We've no quarrel with you. Just give us the girl and you can go."

"Ain't gonna happen," Terrick's voice bounced back from Clare's right. A barrage of gunfire erupted from down the slope a hundred metres or so from where Clare hid, tearing into trees in the direction from which the sheriff's voice had been heard. Even from this distance the noise was deafening. Clare put her hands over her ears.

The gunfire ceased; the silence was deafening. "Sheriff, give it up. You guys got nowhere to go. If we don't get you, the wilderness will."

A single shot rang out from higher up the hill. There was a yell and the crash of a sizeable body dropping to the undergrowth. The gunfire erupted once more from downslope. This time it was sustained.

The Eyes Have No Soul

Clare took this as her cue to drop back from her hiding place. *Damn, Terrick can move fast,* Clare moved toward where she guessed the shot had originated.

Some of the shots from below strayed in her direction and Clare froze for a moment. Down the slope the three remaining Ashby deputies climbed the hill, unloading clip after clip from their assorted arsenal of handguns. What sort of manhunt involved such firepower? Was she really worth all that noise and destruction?

The woodland opened out into a glade, at one end of which rested a large granite slab. Trees grew to either side, the branches giving her hand holds to pull herself up. Clare feared she didn't have strength sufficient to the task. She pulled out the phone Tina had given her, looked at it for a moment then depressed the speed dial. Before the number had even completed she cancelled it. What good could her friend do for her out here? Clare was alone.

Behind her there was a rustle of foliage. Clare turned to find a fourth man stalking her, cradling his right arm with his left. A large patch of red stained his plaid shirt. Despite this he grinned through a heavy brown beard at her.

Clare backed up to the granite face, not taking her eyes off the man, reaching about with her hand in a futile effort to find a loose piece of granite for a weapon.

"This is the end of the line, girl," he taunted. "You got nowhere to run. You look about ready for the creature. Nice and scrawny. That's how he likes 'em. Still, ain't nobody as said we had to deliver you whole and unsullied. He just wants what's inside you. I figure fluid's fluid. What matter if some of it's mine?" The grin became menacing. "Those three are off huntin' your friend. It's just you an' me, girl."

He moved forward, spreading his arms with a grunt. The pain from his wound was obviously an issue but the lust in his eyes was stronger. Clare had seen that same look far too often in her job, contained on the faces of the old-man cops in Worcester. She prepared to mentally isolate herself. He was right; it was just fluid. Survival was what mattered.

A single shot rang out and her barrel-chested antagonist stared down at the hole in his chest in momentary confusion. His mouth gone slack, he looked toward her, his face questioning. Blood spittle dribbled from one corner of his mouth and his good hand came free, touching the red plaid of a shirt now darkened with blood. He pitched forward, landing face-first on the trampled tracks of countless small footprints that made up the glade's floor with a lifeless thump.

Another shot and another scream. Clare turned to run but as she did so, a gloved hand clamped round her mouth, leaving her unable to call out. Worn leather assaulted her nostrils.

"Don't make a sound," whispered a female voice directly into her ear. A woman with such strength would easily subdue her in her current state. "There're more of them out there, many more than were just chasing you. Your friend's in peril. Stay quiet, don't move and you might both get out of this alive."

Clare nodded that she understood and the hand released her mouth. She massaged her jaw, remaining otherwise stationary. Two more shots rang out followed by the crash of heavy bodies into the foliage, then a minute later another shot. Two more followed. All the while Clare remained motionless, trying with increasing desperation not to pee herself.

Terrick appeared at the edge of the glade.

"Thank God," Clare called out, taking a step forward.

Two things happened. Her unseen saviour grabbed her by the shoulder, dragging her back, and someone she had never seen before stepped into the glade behind Terrick, a gun pointed at the sheriff's back. Well-muscled, he wore combat fatigues in shades of greens, browns and black. While Terrick's face was calm, composed, his captor looked anything but relaxed. Eyes surrounded by more camouflage paint darted around the glade and sweat dripped from his forehead. Spasmodic movement made it very clear he was trying to remain an elusive target, but from what?

"Call off your hound," the gunman ordered, looking past Clare. "If I hear even a rustle in the leaves this one…"

A single shot rang out from directly above them. The gunman's head rocked back, ruptured by a bullet before he had a chance to finish his sentence. He dropped to the ground, bereft of life, the word 'dies' still partially formed on his lips. Clare tried as best she could to not look at the gore sprayed beyond him, brains, blood and skull.

Terrick dived forward, out of the aim of the gunman's dying reflexes. When it became apparent that no further violence would be done upon him, he climbed back to his feet, dusting his clothes down.

Clare turned to the woman behind her. Masked in a balaclava, she had piercing blue eyes, intelligent and knowing, that seemed to read every thought in Clare's head.

"Come with me," the masked figure instructed.

Only once Terrick passed her did Clare begin to follow.

The track, while not steep, was still arduous for Clare. Several times she had to stop to catch her breath for fear of collapsing. In time they crested the hill, to find a shallow valley beyond in which several buildings had been built around a series of fields. The forest provided a protective ring around the outer edges of the commune.

Their mysterious guide stopped to allow Clare to breathe in the majesty of the scene and then said, "Call your friend. Tell her you are okay."

"What?" Clare realized that she still held the burner in her hand and nodded, letting the speed dial complete this time.

"Clare?" Tina's voice was concerned. "What is it? What's wrong?"

"Tina, I'm okay. I have leads on the case, major leads. Believe me when I say this is a game changer."

There was a pause. "Whose making you call me?" Tina's voice was suspicious.

"Nobody's *making* me call you. I just needed..."

The masked woman took the phone from Clare's hand, putting it on speaker. "Detective, you have one chance to capture this creature."

"Clare? What creature?"

"Tina," Clare pleaded, "you're gonna have to take a lot on faith here. Believe me, this is all a hell of a lot more twisted than any of us ever guessed a week ago."

"Detective, carry on about your business. There's far more at stake here than just one person's history and well-being."

"Who is this? What are you doing with Clare? What creature are you talking about?"

"What I am doing with Clare is much the same as what I'm doing to Clare. She's very sick, detective. I'm saving her life. Who I am is not important. That we have your friend and will ensure her safe delivery to you is. You have a decision to make in the next day, that being to take a stand against the unholy creature that walks the streets of your city and to put an end to it."

"There's nothing worse here than corruption."

"Exactly; but ask yourself this: what is really behind the corruption? Gather anybody you trust, detective. Time is against you now. You'll be contacted tomorrow. Be ready."

"Wa…"

The phone was switched off. Their masked host dropped the phone onto the rocky path beneath their feet and smashed it with her heel.

"Well that's great," Terrick said. "How're we supposed to call anybody now?"

"We have all your information. We shall provide you with a new phone, one that's actually untraceable. Your detective friend has some tricks, but she doesn't have our resource."

"You make this sound like some sort of set-up," Clare accused. "Like this was all intended to happen."

"Moves, and counter-moves." The gentle descent into the valley did nothing to put Clare at ease. "You were meant to be hunted in this forest. Did you not hear the words of the guy that almost had you? 'You look about ready for the creature. Nice and scrawny. That's how he likes 'em.' This is a hunt. You're the prize. Now we have time to turn the hunt on the hunter and prepare a trap."

The Eyes Have No Soul

It all clicked into place. She knew what she had to do. "You're right," Clare agreed. "Except last time your hunt failed, didn't it. Last time you didn't know about those who follow where this... thing dares to tread."

"We don't know it all," the woman admitted. "I have a feeling your plan is different to Logan's."

"Let's get inside and I'll talk you through it. But I'm not going another step until you tell me who you work for." Clare planted her feet and folded her arms.

The masked woman tipped her head to one side as if listening to something, and then nodded. "Very well; the organization I represent is called ARC."

Chapter Twenty-Two

It dented her pride to admit, but Clare needed help to make it into the mansion at the centre of the complex. At first just Terrick helped her. When she became too much of a burden for the sheriff, their guide stepped in. Nobody in the fields seemingly paid any attention to this strange trio moving through their midst. Maybe they were used to it.

Clare didn't remember much more than impressions once they entered the mansion. The place was big and airy, in complete contrast to the cosy feeling of Logan's private sanctum. The flight from Ashby had taken so much out of her she was focusing purely on her own pain. It meant she was still alive.

"Lie her down there," the woman said.

Clare felt a firm surface beneath and smelled wool. She was on a bed.

"What's that?" she heard Terrick ask.

"Same thing we gave Logan. It'll allow her body to function the way it should for a while longer."

"Insulin?"

"Of a sort. An initial jolt of fast-acting insulin to get her body back on track with a greater dose of slow acting insulin to abate some of the symptoms."

Clare felt a sharp prick in her shoulder. She didn't have the energy to jump or cry out, but managed to turn her head toward the woman. She had removed her balaclava, and had a pretty face with small lips pursed in concentration, framed with well-styled white hair.

Their guide had noticed the movement. "You will have answers later, Clare Rosser. You've had one hell of a day. This next shot will help you sleep."

Clare felt another prick in her arm and her sight blurred. She heard a discussion but what was said was lost as she lapsed out of consciousness.

Where am I?

Clare blinked awake. By the light streaming in through the window it appeared to be morning, the sun barely above the trees. Without moving, she assessed her surroundings. She was in a converted attic, vertical beams of polished wood supporting the roof. The window was to her right, bordered by bookshelves built into the eaves.

She stretched, expecting to groan in pain but finding instead that while she ached, it really wasn't all that bad. Wiggling her fingers for a moment, Clare sat up, almost bumping her head on the ceiling. Confused, she looked herself over. *Still dressed, well that's something.* Her hands were skeletal, veins pushing the skin up. A needle connected to a drip had been inserted into the back of her hand. She sighed. Somebody else had finally taken the step she refused to.

"Why do you feel so much better?" The familiar voice of the white-haired woman asked from the other side of the room. "Insulin is carrying glucose around your bloodstream once again. You're worse than I think anybody told you, almost as bad as Logan was. Would you like some water?" The woman offered Clare a glass.

Grateful, Clare took the drink, taking only a couple of small sips. She studied the liquid; she was no longer thirsty, a feeling she had never expected to feel again. "They... the guys at his house said I had maybe a week."

The woman sat down on the bed beside her. She was older, yet still radiated a luminous beauty from skin that appeared younger, smooth with barely a wrinkle. The eyes spoke volumes though. Wisdom, intelligence, and a certain amount of pain had been experienced during her lifetime.

"A week till you drop dead, certainly. But not a week before you're incapacitated beyond the ability to function. You were pretty close to reaching that point yesterday. What were you thinking? Exhausted, depleting your energy reserves; barely slept in days I'll bet. Your lack of thirst shows you aren't beyond redemption but only an idiot refuses to listen to their body."

"It's not like I had a choice," Clare said, hurt by the accusation that after what everybody had said, still a stranger was taking her to task.

"You have spirit, I'll give you that," the woman conceded. "And a will of surprising strength; I have no doubt that comes from the day you found your parents dead, if not earlier."

Clare decided she had had enough of these cryptic observations. "Who are you, and why are you here?"

The woman smiled. "Direct, too. That's admirable. My name is Ellen Covlioni. You've made it this far, you deserve to know that much."

"Ellen. What is ARC?"

"That's one question too far," said a second voice from the doorway. A man stood there, lean and scraggly with a small but unkempt beard, glasses and an oversized set of retro eighties-style headphones around his neck. He stepped into the room. He wore a red t-shirt with a picture of Devils Tower, the mountain used in Close Encounters as a place to meet the extra-terrestrials. Clare certainly felt in an alien situation now.

"Clare, this is Scope."

"What, did your parents hate you at birth?"

Scope chuckled, more of an amused exhalation of air than any actual laugh. "I'm a sniper among other things. The nickname suits me."

"So that was you up on the ridge? I thought it was Terrick." Then the realization hit her. "Where is he? Is he okay?"

"He's fine," Ellen assured her. "He went to go pick up your vehicle earlier this morning, once he saw you were safe and recovering. He will be along soon but he doesn't need to hear this conversation."

"Why, am I in trouble?"

Ellen smiled. "Not from us. However, it's safe to say there are those out there baying for your blood."

"Harley," Clare spat.

"Indeed. What do you know of the man?"

Clare reached into her bag, producing the transfer letter. "That he's connected to all of this somehow. He had the same thing done to Logan. Look what happened there. I never knew we would end up in Ashby looking for answers, yet we were expected it seems. Those guys hunting us said I was food for the creature and by that I presume we're talking about Viruñas. That ties Harley into the creature somehow. For a long time I was convinced I knew who the creature was. There's a janitor who works in the precinct who seems to have an unnatural interest in my life. I found a bunch of Pop's things at Alden Labs, where he used to work. Samples I took from the scene showed a liquid that had many of the properties of blood, but nothing that makes blood useful, like all the goodness had been stripped out."

Scope nodded in thought and looked to Ellen. "She's got most of it worked out."

"That's not too far from the truth," Scope agreed. "The problem you have with a creature that hides its identity for a decade at a time is that your opportunities to tag it are limited." Scope pulled a chair across the room, the feet scraping along the wooden floor causing Clare to wince. He placed it opposite her, sitting down. "I think we've reached the point that you know this thing isn't entirely normal, yes?"

"Not entirely normal? It isn't natural."

"Actually it couldn't be any more natural if it tried. Viruñas is a primal force, a very ancient creature. It could be that Viruñas the man isn't even aware of his, shall we put it, other side. It may be that in order to suppress that side of him, he has to sate the appetite."

"Like some sort of vampire?"

"In a sense it is, yes. Viruñas draws the fluid out of its victims, taking what it needs and expelling the excess liquid. Always six kills, always once every decade. You've seen the evidence."

Clare thought for a moment. "The Grail Website is your doing?"

"Indeed. It's a location for urban legends with a basis in fact."

"What are you saying? That it's immortal?"

Scope lowered his voice. "There's a reason urban legends exist. What if demons were real? Heaven, Hell, the whole shebang? What if those who were destined to take a trip South never really left, bereft of morals, lacking anything but the primal urges: Hunt. Feed. Maybe even reproduce."

There it was. "You don't think this is the first Viruñas, do you? You're not just hunting one."

"Told you she was smart," Ellen said, approval warming her voice. "What we kept from public record were the exact dates of the past killings. They're always individual kills on six specific dates, every decade. Ten years back there was a double killing. This year…"

"There was another double kill," Clare finished. "Luke Morris and the other kid died close together. There's another Viruñas."

"Only a few times in history has it been recorded," Scope provided. "Can you see what importance we attach to this?"

"Destroy the creature and you destroy the legacy," Clare answered. "Or at least this part of it. How do you know these are the only Viruñas?"

"These deaths only occur every decade, and in a specific geographical pattern. If there were more, the pattern would be random. Do you see now how your willing participation is so important and at the same time so perilous?"

"You're not hoping to use me as bait for just one," Clare concluded. Suddenly she felt a lot less positive.

"That is indeed true," Ellen agreed. "These double kills may be a way of hiding numbers, or a method of weaning if we are correct about offspring."

"So were Viruñas to have a child, it might be a way of introducing it to its heritage." Clare pondered this, stroking the back of the drip in her hand, feeling the needle in her vein as she disturbed it. How alien it was to have something reside within you that was not meant to be there. Is that how the creature felt? "Or there is something the child can't get through normal nourishment. Either way undiagnosed diabetics suffer."

Scope smiled. "There you have it. The crux of the matter is that diabetes is on the increase, especially in America. If we don't take this chance, we might lose the opportunity to end the creature and if possible, its line. Now what's your plan?"

"Whoever planned this last time intended to isolate the creature, yes? You gave it the scent and intended to lead it into the middle of nowhere so you could be sure that nobody would get hurt. What you didn't expect was what happened, because someone was onto you. All your secrets and your mysterious organization, still you were beaten to the punch."

"That's harsh, but fair," Scope admitted.

"What's harsh is that Jarret Logan was sacrificed without need. I don't intend to be isolated in a forest when I lead this creature into a trap. I'm going to be surrounded by a buffet."

"Go on," Ellen said, evidently hooked.

"I want to put out an alert to the entire region, Worcester and surrounding, detailing the symptoms to look out for, gather everybody at a hospital and wait there to see what happens. If you are dead set on trapping this thing, you need bait on a scale that makes it impossible to resist. Drive this thing wild with longing until it just comes drooling in to feed. If it can track the scent of an undiagnosed diabetic like you seem to be implying, the scent of many will be irresistible."

"That's crazy," Scope burst out. "The sheer numbers are insane. Plus you're gonna get every lunatic hypochondriac who thinks they can get attention walking in off the street."

"True, but someone will have to sort the wheat from the chaff and as they do so, we build up a ward of diabetics. The Viruñas isn't interested in anybody else. They don't have the right condition to nourish it. It will have to come for the honey pot. It won't be able to help itself."

"Have you thought of a hospital?"

Clare nodded. "I have, but this is where it gets really crazy. I want misdirection. I'm gonna get on television, radio and wherever I can to tell everyone to go to a public place, free buses or something, that will take them to St Vincent's. There's a new wing scheduled to be opened. It's currently empty and should provide good hunting ground for the creature."

"How about using the Union Station bus depot?" Scope suggested. "It's got plenty of capacity for people to park up. It's in a public place and is within easy transport distance of St Vincent's."

"That it is," nodded Clare. "However, you will transport everyone that comes looking to UMASS. I don't care what it takes just keep them away from the new wing at St Vincent's. That's where I'll be. I hope that the failure to find a smorgasbord of diabetics leaves it hungry with only one choice: To attack me."

"You want security?"

"At UMASS, yes definitely. You're gonna have a lot of scared and confused people there. At St Vincent's, no more than we need to take in there. I want it to be able to track me without fear of capture. I'll take Terrick and Tina. They should be enough to watch my back. Plus, they're the only people I trust. No offense."

"None taken. It's your party." Scope shared a glance with Ellen. "How long do you need to set this up?"

Ellen shrugged. "A few hours should do it. There's already chaos with the breakout from Worcester County Jail."

"What breakout?" Clare asked.

"It happened last night. Someone blew a hole in the wall and most of the inmates escaped. Staffing's always been an issue there and half the guards were out on strike. Is it a coincidence? I think not. This was intentional, and the escapees aren't too worried about resuming their unlawful activities. Worcester's become a very dangerous place."

"It was already a very dangerous place. We'd better get started hadn't we? How long am I gonna feel this way?"

"You have maybe half a day before you start feeling ill again," Ellen replied. "It's really just abating the symptoms. It's not a cure. If we fill you with normal insulin the creature will notice and disappear. We could give you more…"

"Forget it." Clare tugged at the line in her hand. The pain was sharp but pain meant life. "If I run into this creature sooner than expected, I want to be a tasty meal, not an under-ripe banana."

There was a polite knock at the door.

"They said it was okay for me to come up now," Terrick said from the doorway. He smiled at her, an expression of delight on his face showing his relief.

Ellen stood. "Indeed it is, Sheriff. Time is, as always, of the essence. You will have to move, and move quickly once we set things in motion. Do you have somewhere you can lay low for a few hours?"

Terrick looked confused. "Why not stay here?"

"Because people will come looking once word gets out. You need to be in place and ready to act, to stay ahead of the local authorities. You see there's a problem. Your Captain Andrew Harley has raised the stakes. He's had Clare listed as missing and a fugitive by Worcester P.D., in connection with the deaths of the very children whose murders you've been trying to solve."

Chapter Twenty-Three

"I'm on the F.B.I. wanted list..." Clare's heart began to thud. The sound of her blood rushing in her ears threatened to drown out the conversation. "Harley knows about Ashby."

"That would make sense," Terrick agreed. "The way I understand it, they're like his own brute squad. Linkin' you to the deaths of children puts you on the radar of every enforcement agency in the country."

"Time to prove how quickly you can move," Ellen advised. "Give us three hours to put your plan into play. How long do you need to get where you're going?"

"Two at most."

Ellen considered this. "Fine. In an hour Scope will remove the drip, then you've got twelve hours before you start to fail. In the mean time I want you to take this."

Ellen unzipped a small black pouch, producing a black pen and a pot of small strips. She gave them to Clare.

"What is this?" Clare asked.

"It's a blood glucose testing kit. From this point on it's the most important thing in your life."

An hour later, with the drip removed, Clare led Terrick back out into a well-kept parking lot, the asphalt fresh, spaces painted white. Her bag seemed to weigh heavy with the new kit and supplies. She turned the new phone over in her hand. Tina's number was already on the speed dial. As they passed members of the community, nobody spoke to them. It was as if they didn't exist.

"What if somebody here is a mole?" she wondered aloud.

"Girl, that's crazy talk. Everyone here's totally preoccupied with themselves. I had to reassess my opinion of the place too," Terrick said. "I casually mentioned the shots fired and nobody had heard 'em. They aren't just self-absorbed hippies. In fact the majority of them are artists of one form or another. This is more in the nature of a spiritual retreat, a place for them to come and find themselves. They sure don't know why you're here and I'll bet most don't care either."

Clare opened the Chrysler's door, the metallic silver paint heavily scratched through the recent contact with the pines. The door made a creak not unlike her Impala. Suddenly Clare missed her car with its ancient leather and bony steering wheel. "Does the commune work?"

"I dunno. Saw some beautiful paintings and some stunning sculptures last night. They really do pick em." Terrick brought the car to life and moved it out of the parking lot.

He paused for a minute as they reached the crossroads. The day before they had gone down the pine-shadowed track opposite, pursued by Ashby's finest. He looked both ways, watching for movement.

"You don't think we got them all?"

"After yesterday I'm thinkin' a little caution might be beneficial." Terrick leaned forward over the wheel, his arms crossed.

"True, but they aren't going to show themselves, not if they have any clue what happened."

"They'll know we're comin'. We've been to Ashby. Now we've taken care of their brute squad. It's clear where we're headed."

"We're going to my house."

Terrick snorted. "Don't be a fool, kid. That'll be the first place they check."

"Then make sure you got your gun ready, Sheriff. I'm checking on Jeff and I'm checking on Steve. Once I've done that we can go wherever you like."

The closer they got to Holden, the more nervous she became. This wasn't coming home from work. This was, metre by metre, closing in on a series of choices that could leave her a hero, in jail, or dead. As they passed up the hill to the crossroads at the centre of Princeton, Clare saw the first road sign for Holden and Paxton.

"Route thirty-one," she breathed.

"How you holdin' up, Clare?"

"I feel like I wanna wet myself. That sign was poignant. There's no escaping your future. Just look at this place."

The road ahead was cut with turnings, left, right, all leading to destinations unfamiliar. She didn't know this place anymore. The pale peaks of whitewashed churches jutted out of the skyline, offering salvation, but was there any deliverance here? Would any building on the road ahead truly offer her sanctuary from the threat she sought to evade? "I'm making blind choices with no idea if I'm doing the right thing. Is it all a game?"

"Maybe it is, girl. For someone it's just moves and countermoves. We were meant to be out here, bein' led around by the nose until we were attacked, saved, knocked unconscious. Choose one. Was it the good guys, testin' your mettle? Or was it those of a darker nature, seekin' to prevent you makin' contact with them. When all's said and done, you got powerful friends, and lethal enemies. Who's on what side? Damned if I know."

They drove out of Princeton, Clare counting the churches as they passed. She spotted thirteen in all, though doubtless there were more. The streets were empty, as if everybody knew of the danger abroad and cowered at their altars. Clare didn't have that option. She switched the radio on, only to hear reports about Worcester and the growing crime spree. No wonder people hid.

Out into the forest once more and Clare was able to suspend her sense of disbelief. For moments at a time it wasn't real. Trees crawled by, choked with vines, swarmed with fern fronds and all that existed was her visual connection, to each of them, in the instant they shared. In that microsecond, she could forget.

It became harder the closer to Holden they got. Each bend in the road, each isolated house was more and more familiar, drawing Clare back to the reality of the situation. She wanted Terrick to go slower and slower. They crossed the small bridge over the River Quinapoxet and Clare sighed.

"Feelin' ill again?"

"No not yet. It just feels like I'm coming home for the last time."

"Girl, if you think you're gonna lose, you'll probably find a way to make it happen. Your detective friend and I won't let you down."

"But there's still so much information that's not straight. The trap might work, yet we can't guarantee the creature will show up. Harley's out there looking to put my neck on the block. This could spiral out of control quickly."

"Look at how far you've come," Terrick countered. "You're a tougher kid than most city cops, Clare. Jarret Logan would be proud to see you continuin' his work. We just got to last these few hours before the plan gets set in motion. Then you won't have time to worry."

They passed the Gale library, the modern building made in a pseudo-Gothic style with a tower and long, haunting windows. She really was home.

"Someone's gonna see me at some point," Clare pointed out.

"If you wanna put in an appearance, leave it till the absolute last moment. The more as see you, the quicker Harley finds out."

The library disappeared into the trees behind them. Once more they were at the crossroad on Main and Highland. The graveyard stretched out in front, Walgreens down the road to the left. "I'm home. If ARC watches over me like they promised, Harley'd be mad to come after me with witnesses."

"It only takes one bullet, Clare," Terrick cautioned her. "He doesn't need to even show up. You ask your new friend Scope how far away one can be to take out a mark. I've got a nice safe place for you where they won't expect you to show up."

The blue house came into view as they drove down the hill. The entrance to Pleasant Street appeared beyond it. "Home."

"Think rationally, girl," Terrick urged. "This is tantamount to suicide. Don't give it all up on a whim."

"I can't call Jeff. I need to see he's all right."

Terrick took a deep breath, then looked forward to the road and resumed driving, instead taking a left into a spur of Reservoir Street that looped back toward the centre of town. "No. Make what threats you want. I've gotta protect you, even if it's against yourself. Argue with me on this, I'll arrest you. I still have that power, believe it or not."

Clare was about to spit out a vile response when Terrick's cell began to ring. He glared at her to remain silent as he pressed the speaker button.

"Heckstall here."

"Sheriff, its Deputy Marcus White. I know you're on leave right now but we got a situation. You got a moment?"

Terrick motioned Clare to keep her head down. Gone from his face was any trace of argument. Now he expected to be obeyed. "I'm on my way to the lake, Deputy White. What's goin' on that can't be handled by you guys?"

There was a pause. Terrick's question had been loaded and carried the promise of reprisals. "Well sir, we have a couple of Federal agents waiting in your office to speak with you. They are after your help concerning the whereabouts of one Clare Rosser. Sheriff isn't that..."

"...The girl from Friendlies and the One Stop. Indeed it is."

"They want to discuss her with you."

Terrick cut off the call. "They're trying to track me."

"What do you mean?"

Terrick grinned. "Marcus used two key words: Moment. Concerning. Seriously, who uses language like that round these parts?" He pressed the call-back button. "Sorry Deputy, bad signal. You were saying?"

"She's a wanted fugitive."

"And also a person of such immediate threat that these agents need to interrupt my fishin' trip right now? Convince them to come back tomorrow mornin'. I'll be back by then."

Terrick turned his phone off. "Lucky I didn't take a squad car. They're all lowjacked. Do you see now why you can't go home? They're watchin' you."

"Where else is there? They'd likely be watching your place as well."

"I can think of one place. Laurelwood Road."

Clare picked at the yellow crime scene tape. The trees were as pungent and invasive as ever, leaving not much more than breathing space. It was hard to not feel claustrophobic with the police net closing in around her. Here she was at the centre of the spider's web, the deadly Harley all fangs and poison.

"Let's get in," encouraged Terrick, watching the road from the gap in the trees. There was nowhere to leave the Chrysler that wouldn't mark the house out as occupied, so they had parked it a hundred yards away, before the loop at the end of the road.

Clare picked at the tape one more time, freeing it from the door. The lock had been bashed through with a hammer and the door swung ajar. This time the hallway was utterly spotless. "They came back."

Terrick pushed past her, gun drawn. "Does that surprise you?"

Clare followed him in. The house reeked of lemon-scented cleaner, as if scoured of any memory of the family who had once lived here. "What do they get from keeping the family away?"

"Nothin'. Could be they just don't wanna come back. Somethin' real grisly happened here, remember; Bad memories."

Clare walked through to the kitchen. Even the sink had been scrubbed to a shine. There was hardly a clear view from any of the windows. Perfect as long as nobody knew she was here. "Maybe they just couldn't come back to the scene of such tragedy. I wouldn't blame them."

"Maybe. I'd say make yourself comfortable 'cept there ain't anythin' t stairs to sit on. At least you're safe."

`lare pulled out the phone Ellen Covlioni had given her. "I might as \ make decent use of my time here."

rrick appeared dubious. "You think that's clean?"

"There's only one way to find out." Clare dialed the forensics lab. After a couple of rings, the phone was picked up.

"Hello?"

"Alison?"

"Clare? Dear God, where have you gone? This place has gone nuts looking for you. Have you… did you do what they say you did?"

"What did they say I did?"

"There's an all-points out for your arrest. They say… the kids in the mortuary. They say you had a hand in that."

"And you believe them? Have you spoken to Daniel?"

There was a short pause. "Well I… no…"

Clare snorted. "Gee, thanks for the vote of confidence."

Alison's voice was stressed, weary. She began to whisper, the line crackling with interference. "You have to understand it's crazy here. It looks to me like they were lying in wait for you. The moment you didn't return the place was turned upside down. Harley marched in here with a whole squad of his men and demanded to know your whereabouts. He was furious like everything was taking too long. The prison break has everybody on edge. All vacations have been cancelled and everybody's working double shifts. The entire precinct is in chaos and Harley's taking every advantage. Protocol's been thrown right out the window. Helen was nearly dismissed on the spot when she refused Harley's goons access to your desk. They produced a warrant and just went about rifling through your stuff. Laptop, drawers, everything. You realize what sort of power they have if they're producing warrants in advance."

"Are the bodies still in the morgue? The kids?"

"That's the funny thing. They were incinerated. Daniel never said who the order came from."

Clare's stomach sank. That would have been primary evidence against the janitor and Harley. "Did you get any photos?"

"Yes, but it'll take me a moment to find them. Can you hang on?"

"I'll hang up. Look for large elliptical markings on the upper arms. They might look like big hickies. Call you back in a couple." Clare switched the phone off.

"Well?" Terrick leaned against a doorframe, tapping his gun on the wall.

"They're tearing the precinct apart trying to frame me. Looks like you were right. It only stands to reason they would be staking out my house if they're going after you too."

Terrick nodded.

Clare redialed, putting the phone on speaker.

"Got them," Alison said. "Wide, flat hickies on both arms of each of the vics. It looks like someone had a big ol' suck on the kids. What are they?"

"Our method of death," Clare confirmed.

"How does something kill by love bite?" Alison asked, confused.

"You wouldn't believe me if I told you. Let Tina Svinsky know."

"What..." Alison's voice trailed off as from outside the house came a woman's piercing shriek. "Help! Somebody help me!"

Before Terrick could stop her, Clare yanked the kitchen door open. The woman's frantic cries echoed through the woodland. Clare craned her neck, seeking the origin of the scream. There was a shroud of silence in the trees. Something was wrong.

The outline of a house loomed out of the gloom to their right, obscured by the crowded trees. "I'm going," she decided.

"Clare, no!" Terrick hissed.

A shot rang out. The doorframe by her head exploded.

Chapter Twenty-Four

Time slowed. Clare felt the residual warmth of the bullet where it had passed her face. Splinters shattered outward from the door. A startled bluebird spread its wings. Clare discerned every detail of its miniscule feathers as they angled to propel it to freedom.

An impact brought her back to her senses. Terrick had dived to her aid. Clare found herself sprawled in the doorway, the sheriff on top of her.

"You all right?" He mouthed the words. There was no sound in her daze.

What just happened? Clare feared to speak aloud, taking several deep breaths.

"Clare!" Terrick shook her with one hand, his voice sounding miles away.

She focused on her saviour. "I'm fine," she said, unaware of the volume, only registering that she was speaking at all by the vibration in her throat. "Ears ringing."

"You some sort of lunatic? You're more important than some screams." Terrick hauled her back into the house, pushing the door as shut as it would go on the mangled frame. They waited a few minutes for the ringing to subside to a dull ache.

Another shot rang out, the kitchen window erupting in a shower of glass. Clare screwed her eyes shut, protecting her face with her hands. Pine scent wafted in through the shattered window.

The Eyes Have No Soul

"He can't see us," Terrick decided. "He's tryin' to pin us down. Clare, what in Hell's name did you think you were doin'?"

Another scream, followed by the sound of a struggle and one more shot rang out. Clare ducked on reflex. Footsteps scuffed on gravel. A door slammed on the house, creaking as it swung back open. A car pulled out, the tires skidding as they fought to gain purchase on the road.

Terrick rose from a crouch, peering over the edge of the scoured aluminium sink now full of glass and debris. "You're gonna go out there, aren't you?"

"We can't hide here and do nothing," Clare argued. "Right is right."

"Damn if they didn't put some sorta superhero juice in you along with insulin."

Clare chuckled, the sound far richer than any she had made in over a week. "Maybe they did. I'll have to get me some more. Come on."

Clare leaned in the direction of the ruined door and found Terrick's arm blocking her.

"Not that way. Go out the front. If the shooter's got a bead on us, let's make him work for his prize."

Clare turned without comment. At the front door, Terrick took the lead, his gun held by confident hands low in front of him. Clare had no doubt about his reflexes.

They edged out of the house, back down the track between the pines, taking a route to the left of the kitchen. Clare kept watch to their right, looking for any sign of movement and praying there was none. They reached the threshold of the road. Terrick paused, watching.

"What is it?" Clare whispered, unable to see past the sheriff's much larger frame.

"There's a set of tyre tracks comin' from that big white house next door. Go."

Terrick dashed to the cover of the foliage in the middle of the looped road. Clare followed on his heels, squeezing in behind him, wedged between a tree trunk and the rusting post of the basketball net she had seen when last on the road.

"He was in those woods, between the two houses," Terrick said in a low voice. "That's the only place he could have kept watch on both sides. Look, up there." He pointed.

In the midst of the pines a space had been cleared and a rudimentary attempt made at nailing wood to one of larger trunks. "Was he in that treehouse?"

"Looks like it. Those tyre tracks come from near there." Terrick stood up.

"What are you doing?"

"He ain't there no more. It was him that drove off. The question is why?"

"It's a very random place for a shooter to wait," Clare agreed.

"Or a very specific one if he knew there might be company. Come on."

This was madness. Walking out in view of someone intent on shooting them was not how Clare had planned on spending her time waiting for the green light. She concluded Terrick was right. As they passed through the dappled shade of the driveway, moisture dripped from above, hitting her head. She wiped the wetness away, not compelled to absorb it. Clare felt somehow invincible, as if nothing could faze her. It was why she'd opened the door in the first place. Even the total silence that had resulted failed to discourage her. The wildlife had been frightened off by gunshots. Curiosity was also a factor. This place held answers.

Terrick kept his gun ready as he stalked the driveway. There was no hiding place. Clare followed close to him, expectations high. This house was in total contrast to its neighbor. White, clean and majestic with a tall chimney rising above several wooden gables, it was well maintained. A garage stood open with space for several vehicles inside.

"The front door's open," Terrick noted.

Clare made for the house. Terrick hurried to get in front and only managed to reach her heels as she pushed the door wider. He grabbed her shoulder, spinning her around to face him. "You want to take the gun? No? If not then let me..."

His voice trailed off as he regarded the scene behind her.

Clare turned back. "What the Hell?"

Above polished mahogany floorboards, separated by low-hanging globes of light, were mounted row upon row of antlers, stretching hungrily toward the center of the hallway as if their owners were ready to clash in rut. Among the antlers were interspersed sometimes the heads and sometimes the entire bodies of smaller animals, warped into hideous positions by whoever had stuffed them.

"It's a taxidermist's dream," Clare said, unnerved by the horrors staring down at her. "Foxes, wolves, owls, bats. Dear God, what is that?"

"Some kind of stoat or weasel," Terrick supplied.

They both stood staring at the creature for a moment. Jammed into the skull of the grinning animal were what looked like doll's eyes. The effect was frightening.

Floorboards creaked above. Somebody was still here; the woman that screamed? Clare stepped back, feeling a prod in her back. Turning, she found a skull, empty eye sockets glaring at her from waist height, twisted horns spread wide. Directly below, a duck was mounted with horns, its head twisted and beak appearing to scream. Next to it a rabbit had been mounted in a similar pose but looked even more wrong. Clare couldn't figure out why until she took a step down the hall.

"That... that thing has two heads. Right, that's it. I don't care who these people are, they can damned-well fend for themselves; Freaks."

She backed toward the door, and was ready to turn and escape the house of slaughter when a whimpering sounded from the stairs down at the other end of the hallway. Her words sounded suddenly hollow. Victims were victims.

"Go," she ordered when Terrick glanced in her direction, the sound of another being in distress overcoming the urge to flee. As the sheriff navigated the trophy room Clare followed close behind.

"I hope there's another way out of this nightmare," she muttered as they passed through a doorway and began to climb in the direction of the weeping. But the nightmare had only begun.

They reached the first floor. Clare stopped. She held Terrick back with one hand. A trail of fluid led between two rooms across the hallway. Hinges groaned. Someone was opening a window. She heard a whimper. A door slammed below. Clare's ragged breathing filled the silence. Her eyes darted around the hallway, searching desperately for the threat.

Clare panted, her hand tight on the bannister. She was weakening.

"Careful now," Terrick cautioned and pressed past. He peered through the gap where the door to the right hinged, grunted and pushed his way in.

Clare followed, gagging on reflex when the stench in the room hit her. Something very bad had happened here. The curtains were drawn and Clare could only see outlines as her eyes adjusted.

Terrick crossed the room, throwing the scene into stark contrast as, with a violent jerk of the drapes, he let light in.

"No," screamed a voice full of fear and panic. In the corner between the bed and the wall a woman held her hands up, shielding her face from the light. She had her knees drawn close to her chest, blood dripping down one side of her body.

"Clare," Terrick turned her attention from the woman to the bed.

"Terrick, it's got another." She wanted to step closer but the stench was strongest on the bed. The body of a boy lay, arms straight as if they had been pinned. His torso was warped in a grotesque parody of humanity. Legs twisted and bruised, one of them bent backward where something had wrenched at it. The belly was shrivelled ,the skin so taut around the ribs they had burst through in places. The bedsheets were covered in waste where he had soiled himself at some point during the assault.

"He's like the others. He looks like he's had the life sucked out of him. But he's not dried out. He's still fresh."

The woman whimpered and Clare turned back to her. Shaking, she cowered from them, holding one hand over her face, the other on her bleeding side. Clare reached out to soothe her and the woman jumped.

"Get back! Leave me alone!"

Clare knelt beside her, attempting to be as unthreatening as possible. "It's okay. You're safe. Was that you screaming outside? Were you the one we heard?"

The woman nodded in a series of staccato movements. "Look what it did to my Cliff; My poor Clifford Lee." She stared at the floor, purposefully avoiding the scene, her hand on her forehead. Every few seconds she lifted her face toward the bed and turned away, quaking.

"We need to get her out of here," Terrick said. "This ain't good for nobody."

The woman resisted initially but with gentle coaxing allowed them to get her to her feet and out of the room.

Clare made a decision to avoid the room with the trail of fluid, choosing a different door at random. As it happened, she chose what must have been the master bedroom. Sitting the woman down on the white bedcovers she pointed in the direction of an adjoining door. "See if that's a bathroom. Let's try and get her cleaned up some."

In moments Terrick returned, cloths and a bowl of water in his hands.

Clare soaked one cloth and wrung it of any excess. "What's your name, love?"

She appeared totally lost. "What's... my name? I... Dana. Dana Burke." With lucidity came a fresh bout of tears. She put her hands to her face and began to weep.

"Careful," Clare warned. "You've a wound on your side." She dabbed the blood away, earning several winces for her efforts.

Terrick dug through a sideboard, bringing a medical kit back with him. "Gauze, tape. Whadda you need?"

Clare daubed away more blood, reaching up under Dana's blouse. Puckered skin met her fingertips. "Not a lot. If that last shot hit her, it only grazed the skin. It's a surface wound."

In quick order Clare had Dana bandaged, and with a fresh bowl of water cleaned up her face. "Dana, can you tell me what happened?"

Dana stared into space, her voice haunted. "I… there was someone in here." For a moment she stared, and with juddering movements at first, began to rock.

Clare reached up with a gentle hand to touch Dana's face. "Dana, has Cliff been ill?"

Eyes wide open, unshod tears glistening, Dana turned back to her. "He was getting better. Both he and his cousin caught a virus that hit the high school. It laid them low for a week but that was a couple months back."

This revelation sounded alarm bells in Clare's head. "Dana, who was his cousin?"

Dana closed her eyes, holding them shut with one hand as tears ran down her face. "Luke. Luke Morris."

Clare shared a look with Terrick. "From the house across the street. Dana, what happened to Luke?"

Dana's head shook slightly from side to side. "We don't know. He took ill a week back, acting all strange, drinking loads, walking around at night. Then one morning Luke's dead and there are Feds everywhere."

"And Clifford? Was he ill like that too?"

"He'd been off hunting with his pa and some friends. First time he'd felt up for it since the virus, but they brought him back early. He said he felt unwell. He was hungry, and thirsty. Tired, but wouldn't sleep. Just like Luke."

With the description of every symptom, Clare's stomach knotted more and more. "…and there was no end to the drinking. He just didn't seem to fill up."

"What about the man in here?"

A haunted look came over Dana's face. "Is that what it was? A man?"

"Was it not?" Terrick asked.

For the first time Dana seemed to recognize the sheriff. "I was out... shopping. Cliff was tired so I just let him be. I got back from the Big Y with a crate of water bottles and the kitchen door was open. I came upstairs to check on my boy and there was this... thing on him, pinning him down. All I could see were his feet sticking out."

"What did it look like?" Clare urged. "This thing you saw?"

Dana closed her eyes, squeezing tears out as if trying to expel memories. "It was pale and fat. No not fat; bloated. And hairless. I came into the room and it turned, staring at me. It was gloomy in here and I swear... those eyes, they glowed white. Then it spoke." Dana drew a shuddering breath. "It was no more than a whisper: 'I have his soul', it said and climbed off the bed, making for me. I ran, slamming the door behind me. I never looked back. That's when I came downstairs and shouted for help at the kitchen door. Then someone started shooting at me." The realization came to Dana as she said the words, and she looked to her side, seeing the blood. "Oh God..."

"You're fine," Clare said. "They only grazed you. I've patched you up. Nothing some rest won't cure."

"Dana," Terrick said, kneeling down to get in her line of sight.

"Yes, Sheriff?"

"I want you to give us ten minutes then dial 911. You get me?"

"But you're here now."

"That's true. But with everybody that's going to show up, we can't investigate this properly. I need you to act as if we were never here, okay?"

Evidently confused, Dana nodded. Terrick rose and took Clare's arm, escorting her from the room.

"Get what you can, we don't have long. You do realize what this means, don't you?"

Clare nodded. "Viruñas isn't acting alone. Somebody's helping it feed."

Chapter Twenty-Five

She took a couple of long, slow breaths to steady herself before entering the room. The corpse lay there, twisted and empty.

Clare stared for a moment. "Not that empty," she observed, speaking to poor Clifford. Fluid wept from the patches on his upper arms. "He didn't finish his meal."

Taking the blood glucose meter Ellen Covlioni had pressed upon her, Clare inserted a testing strip from a small pot in the pack and dipped it into the fluid that oozed from the wound. There was a strong smell of acetone in the room, particularly around the corpse. Clare tried to avoid looking at the face while she worked on the wound but she could feel sunken eyes staring at her as they would have been staring at the creature as it drained the poor boy's life away.

The meter bleeped, a red warning light coming on. The machine read 'High'.

"You poor thing; you were very ill." Clare had done all she could and left the room. This would not be her fate.

Outside, Terrick waited. "Confirmed?"

"Yeah, this kid's readings were off the charts." Clare held the meter up for Terrick to see. "Ellen said if the meter reads 'high' it's run beyond the range of numbers programmed in. Your blood sugar's at a level you need immediate medical aid. Poor boy. Sometimes the body just rebels and you've got little to no hope. Even without a monster hunting you down. That's five now. One more and we lose the chance. The creature's gonna move fast. Clifford wasn't drained. There was still fluid seeping from the wounds. It was disturbed by the mother before it had completed its feed. Terrick, we need to move faster. We can't afford to wait for them to set an evacuation in motion. By the time that happens, it may have struck for the final time." Clare leaned toward the bedroom. Dana was repeating the same words over and over.

"No soul in those eyes. No soul in those eyes. No soul… No soul…"

"I think her cork has popped," Terrick said. There was no attempt at humor in his voice; Terrick meant every word and the world was a poorer place for it.

"We can't leave her like that, alone."

Terrick folded his arms, leaning back and balancing his shoulders on the flowered wallpaper of the hallway. "I'm open to ideas."

"You aren't gonna like it. We may well be broadcasting our whereabouts."

"This is, as they say, your party. Remember we may be on borrowed time. We've escaped Harley's men in Ashby, but that's bound to have been reported. We've left prints everywhere here. The agents who cleared the first house appeared from nowhere and rapidly so. They may already be on their way if they haven't been redirected into Worcester. We got lucky here, Clare."

This gave Clare a moment to pause for thought. "What car did the shooter use to escape? He was keeping watch on the road, yet the sound of a vehicle originated back by the house. Why did he need to escape so quickly? Why not leave the way he arrived?"

"You said the creature hadn't finished feedin'. Perhaps it was being led to its next meal."

"Perhaps. We've got an idea of what Viruñas may look like when exposed if it looks like the legends. But what about when it's not feeding? The lore said it walks among us, a normal man. Don't for a second assume that this thing crawls off into a hole for a decade. It could be hiding in plain sight. What if it needs to complete feeding in order to return to normal? This could be a way of prolonging its life."

Terrick appeared doubtful. "Could it hide that for so long?"

Clare grinned. "There's a few days every month where I'm somewhat different, you know. The point is the same. It may be just a biological condition."

"Stop it feeding and it doesn't return to its human state. Then you just look for whose missin'. It's a needle in a haystack situation, girl."

Clare led the way outside. The sun was well past its peak now. What was taking them so long? A dull ache had returned to her midriff and she was beginning to feel thirsty again. She didn't have long left before she was back to square one.

She stopped at the open garage door. Made of heavy oaken planks, the garage was more like a giant musty-smelling wooden cave, housing a collection of imposing four by fours. One was missing. Dana's car sat beside the gap, engine idling. Clare reached in and turned it off, removing a couple of bottles of water from the passenger seat. The unfortunate boy wouldn't be needing them.

"You want to get the ball rolling?" Clare tipped her head in the direction of the missing vehicle.

"We won't have long," Terrick's voice was a clear warning. He dialed a number and waited. "Deputy White. I want you to run some names for me. All vehicles registered to Dale and Dana Burke, Laurelwood Road. Yes, I'll hang on." He covered the mouthpiece. "Somethin's up. I can hear a lot of action in the background." He removed his hand.

"Okay. Got it; A one-eight-seven." He put the cell in his pocket. "Let's get out of here. Once Marcus started referencin' this address those Feds were out of there like a shot."

"What did they say?"

"I'll tell you in good time, girl. Car first, then escape, then we talk."

Clare began to flag even as they hurried to the waiting Chrysler. She had pushed herself too hard.

Terrick's face was a mask of concern as he helped her in. "They'll be here any second. Hold on." Terrick turned right up the private drive of one of the large houses. When they reached the house he veered to the left.

"What the hell are you doing?" Clare shrieked in alarm.

Terrick remained silent, manoeuvring the car through the trees until he hit a wooden fence head-on. He grimaced as he did so.

Clare threw her arms around her head, expecting a collision but not finding one. The car turned left and slowed.

"That'll do it," Terrick decided.

Clare opened her eyes. They were on a road but not the same one.

"Holt Road," Terrick provided. "This should buy us enough time to get out of here."

"You don't think the Feds will notice a gaping hole in a fence?"

"That was back from the road. They'll not see a thing before it's too late. Now onto the missin' vehicle; we're lookin' for a 2004 Chevy Colorado truck, painted in brown and green camouflage."

"Well that shouldn't be too hard in a state full of hunters."

Clare's sarcasm didn't go unnoticed, Terrick grinning in response. "State police're monitorin' all major roads. There's an APB out on the truck but they're mostly focussin' on lookin inward to keep the escapees contained. No connection at this point to what's happened behind us. We'll be lucky if they spot it before the Feds cotton on, but at least we'll have a lead."

Terrick's phone rang after a couple of minutes. They had made it to the corner of Holt and Main. He pulled into the parking outside the Black Cat Quilt company. "You're on speaker," Terrick said after activating the phone.

"Why?"

"I have another agent with me," was Terrick's evasive reply. "Please go on."

"The Chevy was spotted running a red light as it got on the I-90. Camera snapped it."

"Heading what direction?"

"South."

"That's it," Clare said. "They're going into Worcester for the last one."

"We don't know that."

In the background at the other end of the line there was a commotion. Sounds of a scuffle erupted, followed by glass shattering.

Clare stared at Terrick without comment, waiting for Deputy White to say something. After about a minute the creak and taps of a phone being retrieved from a place of concealment showed someone had it.

"Sheriff, are you still there?"

"Yes, deputy; what was that?"

"It was the Feds, sir. They were still here. They had us at gunpoint. Is that her with you, sir? Is that Clare Rosser?"

"Yes it is," Clare said before Terrick could answer.

"Ma'am, they're really hurtin' to get hold of you. They didn't say what but seems you know some stuff they aren't happy with you knowin'. They made a grab for the phone but we stopped 'em. Think they wanted to trace you and race you at the same time."

"Did they flash any badges when they came in?" Terrick's voice was suddenly suspicious.

"No, but they were dressed like Feds, all suited. They had a black Fed car, asked Fed questions."

Terrick moaned. "Marcus since when did you ever speak to the FBI before? Kid this ain't no episode of Supernatural. They could be Goddamned mercenaries for all we know."

"Well they sure knew how to find you, boss. You'd better be far away on your fishin' trip as they're headed right for you. They said it was your badge for this."

"Boy if I live to see you again, you're on traffic duty forever." Terrick's growl would have been funny but for the imminent threat. He cut off the apologising deputy, throwing his phone to the foot well of the car. "So we've got a diabetic-munchin' vampire on the loose, possibly fake cops huntin' for us and we are going where exactly?"

"You need to head to the Charter TV3 studio in Worcester. We have to try, Terrick. We've got to do this for the kids who've died already. It's all for nothing if we fail to act."

They passed Alden labs, the reception building flashing by in a blur of red brick and trees. Clare wondered if she would ever see her brother again. She would get healthy for his sake. She smiled as she considered those words. *As healthy as somebody with a life-threatening condition could be.*

The grand entrance to Mountview Middle School appeared to their left, the building set back from the road and connected by a half-mile linden-lined avenue. Clare had always imagined her kids would one day attend the establishment, back when she was young and the harsh realities of life hadn't set in. Alcoholic parents and a lifelong quest to get answers had seen to that dream. Clare had no idea how she would cope if the chance came along.

She was still imagining what could have been and what might yet be when from below them, on the interstate, a cacophony of sirens began to blare. Terrick slowed to a stop.

"That's no coincidence," he said as five black-and-whites in convoy charged south toward Worcester.

Clare was perplexed. "Why are we watching them?"

"They can't reach us. The nearest exit is a couple of miles down and they can't jump concrete K-rails."

"What about those guys back in Holden? If those uniforms are after our car, doesn't it stand to reason that the fake Feds have access to the same information?"

Terrick moved off without a word. After a couple of minutes of silence he said, "If it was us they spotted. Girl, I don't know whose chasin' who right now. Are they Tina Svinsky's cops? Harley's cops? Are they huntin' us? Protectin' us? That lot were already en route to somewhere. Stop seein' ghosts in every shadow."

"Best not take the chance. Let's just get where we're going and worry about whose behind us…" Clare's voice trailed off as she realized Jeff knew nothing about what was going on.

She dialed and as the phone rang, she whispered, "Pick up... pick up."

"Yeah?"

"Jeff?"

There was a pause. "It depends whose asking."

"It's your sister."

There was a loud sigh of relief. "Clare. Where the hell are you?"

She put the phone on speaker. "I'm around. Is everything ok? How's Steve."

"If cats could pout, your tom-cat would be sulking like a hero. He misses you. When're you coming back?"

There was an element of desperation in his voice that indicated everything was not as it should be. "Jeff what is it?"

"I've been in and out of this place as work allowed. You know your Wi-Fi is really shoddy."

"Bad wiring; Jeff get to the point."

"I came back yesterday and these guys in an unmarked black sedan were peering round the house, in the windows, checking the doors. I challenged them and they said they were Feds. No IDs though. They started asking questions about you: Where you'd gone, who with, conversations you and I might have had."

"You tell them anything?"

"Not a word. They threatened to arrest me but never followed through. Clare they're outside now."

While it was her brother, it didn't sound like him. The confidence, the brash and cynical approach to life didn't resonate through like it always had. Something had happened since they had last been together. "What else, Jeff?"

There was a silent pause.

"Jeff? What's happened?"

"I tried to go out a few hours back. They started shooting. Or rather they allowed some guy with a sniper rifle to take pot shots at me. He damn near took my head off!"

The Eyes Have No Soul

"Sniper rifle eh? Sounds familiar," Terrick said as he concentrated on the road. "Looks like they got their marks selected carefully. And so close by."

"What's that mean?" Jeff asked.

"We just had a run in of our own with the shooter, only a couple of streets away from my house." Clare said, her voice sounding weary in her own ears. She grabbed a bottle of water and took a swig. "There's someone... something on the loose out here, killing kids who are ill with a certain condition."

"What's that got to do with you, Clare? Why go running off like you did? You work in a lab."

"You know the hospital was trying to contact me?"

"Yeah."

"I have that same condition. It's diabetes, Jeff. Like Mom and Pop had. The thing that killed them, it's killing again. I'm trying to stop it."

"Why you?"

Clare stared out the window. A black-fronted store with the words 'Joey's Limousine Service' plastered on a sign passed by. "Because there isn't time for anybody else to do what must be done. Look, I..."

The wing mirror outside her window exploded in a cloud of plastic and glass, shattered by a bullet. Down the road in front of them, about two hundred metres off, a squad car blazed into life. Clare turned. A black sedan trailed them, closing on them fast. A guy in the passenger seat leaned out and took aim. It was Ashby all over again. They were trapped.

Chapter Twenty-Six

"Down there! Turn!"

Terrick wrenched the wheel to the right. Where Clare's Impala would have resisted with stubborn tenacity, the Chrysler's power steering took the abuse with good grace. The back of the car began to slide out and Clare held on to the inside of her door, trusting the seatbelt to do its job.

Behind them the police were the first to make it to the junction. Unless they were lucky this chase would be very brief. Then the squad car did something unexpected. It skidded to a halt, blocking the road with its length. The two officers opened their doors, using them as cover while they began to shoot at the car that had been following. Sparks came off the vehicle as shots were fired from up the road; the battle had been joined.

"Looks like those two guys are movin' quicker than you expected," said Terrick, his eyes on the road, the pursuit forgotten for the moment. Nevertheless he looked like a man expecting to be arrested at any second.

"The ARC people?" Clare looked at her phone. There was nothing on the screen. No missed calls.

"They don't strike me as the type of people that'll call you an' tell you every little detail; need to know and all that. Just take advantage of that incident back there. No cops, no Feds. Believe me, they'll be swarmin' all over us when you tell them exactly where you wanna be sendin' everybody."

"Let's just get there as quickly as we can," Clare said, feeling strained. The sensations of discomfort were coming back at an accelerating rate. A dull headache had spread through the back of her skull. Already one of the spare bottles of water had been emptied; Clare didn't even remember drinking it and yet she still thirsted. It would all be for nothing if Viruñas already had a target marked.

After a couple of turns in the road took them from the edge of woodland to the sculpted landscape of a large business-park, a sign appeared on their right bearing the name 'Charter Communications'. Rows of cars were parked around what looked to be a large gray warehouse.

"This is it," Clare decided.

"How you wanna play it?"

"Straight. We go in, say exactly who we are and hope they listen to reason."

"And if they don't?"

"Well you always have your gun," Clare said with a wry tang in her voice.

Terrick didn't appear amused.

"We could threaten them a bit… if necessary. This is important. It's not like its ABC World News. We are trying to save people here."

"Let's leave that as a last resort, eh?"

Terrick pulled into a visitor's spot near the front door and waited for Clare to get out before switching the engine off.

She found relief in the fact that they were so close to the entrance. It would make for a great getaway, though where they went from here depended on their next meeting.

Terrick opened the door to a reception glowing from every angle with bright neon lights. A series of free-standing boards proclaimed the various shows. Jordan Levy, Mayor's Forum, Worcester News Network; all were unfamiliar to Clare. Large plasma screens broadcast news from other channels all round an extensive lobby and proceeded to heat the room to a near-uncomfortable level. Clare felt somewhat oppressed, sweat beading on her brow. A circle of squat red leather seats had been placed in the centre of the room so that no matter where one sat, several of the screens intruded upon the senses. Above them, running around the wall like a giant electronic border was a red lettered feed with yet more news and what Clare presumed to be stock prices. A reception desk stood empty in front of them. Clare checked the monitors on the desktop. "Switched off, not locked. I guess it's because it's Saturday. Maybe they don't all work on the weekend."

"Thought you said this was a local station?" Terrick commented as he stood staring at the screens, not having taken more than a couple of steps into the lobby. "Looks more like Times Square."

"Can't criticise them for having a little ambition, I suppose. Hey!" Clare began to protest as Terrick hauled her across the lobby to stand in front of one of the screens. The ABC World News logo, gold and spherical, rotated in one corner. Jeanette Wingrove, the famous anchor of the program with her business-like attitude and striking bleached-blonde hair, was talking about a prison break.

"…and linked to the prison break there appears to be more information regarding the fugitive." Clare's stomach clenched upon hearing that word and seeing a picture that looked strikingly familiar. "Dr Eva Ross is wanted by police in connection with ongoing events across the State of Massachusetts."

"That's not me," Clare accused Terrick. "That's not funny."

"Watch," the sheriff said.

"Chimney Crest Manor, a mock-Tudor hotel in Bristol, Connecticut which dates back to the nineteenth century has been ablaze for the past two hours. Despite the damp conditions, and the presence of seven fire crews, the fire is still raging out of control. Police have not yet ascertained the cause, though several victims have been pulled from the fire. Be advised that some of these pictures may not be suitable for younger children."

The camera switched to a handheld, shaking as the cameraman jostled through paramedics. Peeking through a screen, the cameraman revealed several men in bandages.

"It's funny, your comment about the civil war," Terrick said. "Look at what they are wearing. That's army uniform."

"Looks like Civil War period costume," observed Clare. "What's going on there? Something is happening to one of them."

The view was partially blocked, but crystals were forming on the screen around another of the patients. Through the opaque material, something writhed before becoming still. At that moment, the cameraman was bundled out of the medical area, but not before a paramedic pulled back the screen to reveal an empty bed.

"As you can see, this hotel has been host to some very unusual events," the reporter continued. "Police arrived very quickly, and efforts are being made even at this early stage to ascertain the identity of those responsible."

The camera panned round to reveal several police, and amongst them, Mike Caruso stood with Andrew Harley, a lean-looking guy and an aging musclebound character who looked like a doorman gone flabby. The camera flicked to an impromptu press conference Caruso was leading.

"We believe this event to be linked to a number of such occurrences across the northeast, through Connecticut and up into Massachusetts. It is important that you contact us should you or anybody you know suffer episodes of sudden amnesia. We believe the couple responsible for these events are using drugs to render people uncontrollable while they commit these atrocities."

"Those two look very smug about something," Clare noted as she pointed to a couple of strangers on the screen behind Caruso. "I swear I know that doctor they're after. She looks very familiar."

"Try looking in the mirror sometime," Terrick said. "You two could be sisters."

Clare snorted. "Jeff's my only family. So Harley and Caruso are out of town. Good. That means two less of them directing the search for me and maybe a bit more confusion in the city. It could work to our advantage."

"They're gone but not forgotten," Terrick cautioned her. "Once this stunt of yours gets out they could be back in a matter of hours. There's nothing to say the report being shown there is live. The footage could've been filmed hours ago and they could already be on their way. I'm hopin' this gives us a fightin' chance is all. What do you need?"

"Let's find a studio that's operating," Clare said. "We need to tell people what to look for and where to go. With any luck Viruñas might get wind, or at least catch a scent. Let's get on air."

"Hi," said a voice from a doorway to their right. A petite blonde in a black blouse and jeans stood in the light of what must have been a restroom or kitchen holding a mug of coffee. "Can I help you?"

"You work here?" Terrick asked.

The blonde gave an exasperated look. "No, I come here for the free coffee, especially on weekends."

Clare laughed in response, bringing a smile from the blonde and a scowl from Terrick. "Hi, we're cops," she said, flashing her badge and encouraging Terrick to do the same.

"Oh. Is someone in trouble?"

"Maybe; I was wondering if you could point us in the direction of the broadcasting studio."

The blonde gasped. "Dwight?" She bit her bottom lip as if imagining indiscretions. "Well it's about damned time. He's been cheating on his poor wife with any woman that'd open her legs to him. He tried it on with me once or twice. I wouldn't give it up for that creepy old dude if he was the last guy on earth."

"Well let's see what we can do to put a dent in Dwight's perfect day then," Clare said, warming to the woman. "What's your name?"

"I'm Hollie. Hollie Turner. Come with me but stay quiet. If the production team sees me it'll probably mean my ass, not that one could call a dead-end reception job desirable."

Hollie put her coffee down with a bang on the reception desk, the strong smell and splash of liquid causing Clare to lean involuntarily toward the source of hydration. She yearned for it.

"We don't have long," she warned Terrick. "It's really wearing off."

Hollie looked at the pair of them in confusion before turning to lead them away from the lobby and down a hallway that was just as much an assault on the senses as the entrance had been.

Clare caught Hollie wincing at one particularly garish neon pink sign bearing a picture of an aging man with a brown toupee. The receptionist explained, "Imagine the ego if we were a national network. Here we are: studio two; the grisly lair of Dwight Perlman. Whatever you want to do, you do it in there."

Above the door, a red light glowed with the words 'on air'. Through the window, the inspiration for the neon sign sat atop the man's head.

Hollie unlocked the door with her pass and ushered them in. She remained outside.

The studio was a simple set up, the smart, functional nature of the cameras and desk before a light-blue background at odds with the garish hallways beyond. Clare was relieved for a moment until a balding man with shirt-sleeves rolled up to the elbows crossed the studio to hiss at her.

"What the hell are you doing in here? We're live. Nobody comes in. That's the rule." He waved his clipboard as if to emphasise the point.

Clare flashed her badge. "We need a little air time. It's an emergency."

"That's totally out of the question."

Terrick loomed behind Clare. "Listen pal, we ain't askin'."

"I don't care who you are or where you're from, there's protocol to be followed and you don't..." His words were drowned out as the music announcing the resumption of the live broadcast began to play. The desk lit up to reveal in all his self-important pomp, Dwight Perlman.

"Welcome back to Worcester tonight... Hey!" Perlman protested as Clare shoved him, chair and all, from in front of the camera. Brown wig tilted to one side, the middle-aged man attempted to retaliate, moving his ferret-like frame back into the picture.

"Wait there," Clare ordered.

"Somebody get security!" Perlman's voice grew high in tone with desperation. He was no bigger than her.

"That won't be necessary," Tina Svinsky interjected, flashing her badge as she entered the room with three uniformed officers hulking behind her. "I'm Worcester P.D. We need a broadcast to go out, so stay on her."

Where had Tina come from? She had all but disappeared in recent days. Clare decided to worry about her friend's recent whereabouts later; it was all she could do to stand up. She swept her hair back over her ear, and said, "My name is Clare Rosser. I am an analyst for the Worcester Police Department. If you have been following the national news recently, you will have seen that this great city of ours has been subject to many strange incidents. I am here to tell you that they are not isolated. Please listen carefully. If you or any of your family, especially children, have any of the following symptoms please report to Union Station where there is ample parking. You will be bussed to the new wing at Saint Vincent's where there is sufficient capacity for all."

"If you or your family have suffered excessive thirst, combined with hunger and or fatigue, or recent and extreme weight loss and have cracked dry lips, please come in. If your child's breath gives off a fruity aroma, bring them in."

Tina leaned in from behind the camera, handing Clare a scrap of paper marked 'read this'.

"All medical bills will be paid for in the event of the symptoms being proven diagnostic of type 1 diabetes…" Clare looked up at Tina in disbelief. This would get the crowds flooding in. She looked back to the camera. "Union Station to be driven in by bus to St Vincent's. If you go straight to the hospital you will not be admitted. Thank you for your time."

"That went well," Tina observed, watching the glaring face of the usurped Perlman as he huffed at the intrusion. "Will it do any good?"

"It's our only hope," Clare replied.

"Your new friends called me about an hour ago with instructions. They asked if I would follow your lead. Seems they consider you very valuable, Clare. They told me about your condition. I'm so sorry, sweetie."

"You've already helped here, Tina. What else have you planned?"

"I've a few friends in the precinct, those not exactly enamoured with what's going on in Worcester. Some of my boys were on the lookout for your car. When they saw you headed this way they radioed in."

"Then that was them by the interstate?"

Tina indicated two of the officers behind her. "These two stepped in for you."

Both nodded in her direction.

"You have my thanks," Clare said with genuine appreciation. "What about the car behind us?"

"They never made it."

Clare found the answer satisfying. "Here's what we learned in a nutshell. This is organized. The last death, there was a lookout. Each time there are six killings. I'm being framed by Harley and there have been only five deaths. We nearly had the creature earlier, right near my house. It's out there; caught mid-feed it will be desperate to hunt again. If it sees that broadcast, it knows where to come for a feast and we have a chance to trap it and end this."

"Creature? What've they been telling you?"

Clare shook her head, scarcely able to believe she was convinced of this, yet there it was; belief, firm and strong. "I'll tell you everything soon, I promise. You've known me for years. I'm asking you to trust me."

"What if we are too late?"

Clare looked down at her hands, the flesh beneath the skin withered, eaten from within. "Then there will be at least one more death on our conscience."

Chapter Twenty-Seven

They exited the studio the same way they had come in. Two squad cars were parked next to Terrick's Chrysler. In the distance, the evening traffic was punctuated with sirens as emergency services dashed all over Worcester. It had only been a matter of minutes yet the sky had darkened considerably.

"It's a lot to ask to expect people to go straight in to the terminal. We need to give them an hour. If Viruñas or whoever's in cahoots saw that broadcast, they'll need to get there too. They won't attempt the terminal. It's too busy. They might lay in wait at the hospital. We won't know until we get there."

The sirens sounded closer and Clare began to shiver despite the warm September air.

"I think Harley and his goons got wind of your broadcast," Terrick said.

"They won't be able to stop a tide of humanity, not once they all start moving to Union Station. I'm hoping Andrew Harley underestimates the average Joe's desire for free medication."

"I'm hoping he's too distracted to notice all sorts," Tina added, waving a piece of paper in Clare's direction.

"What's that?"

Tina grinned. "It's just his remote network login. He's not the only one with friends in low places. Let's get to a computer and find out

The Eyes Have No Soul

what else he's been doing. The prison break's turned this city upside down. There are some mad, twisted people out there."

Clare frowned. "When did the world become so warped?"

Tina shrugged. "Depends how you look at it. When was it ever not the way it is now?"

Clare looked at the skyline, what passed for skyscrapers in the centre of Worcester piercing the gloom of the evening sky. It was still beautiful, always worth fighting for. "It'll be dark soon. It's harder for them to spot us in the darkness. Let's go hunting."

The closer they got, the more nervous Clare became. Every set of lights held a potential ambush. Every car that passed them could be agents under cover, looking for two women and a black man. Terrick's car had been marked when they were followed, so yet again they were forced to swap. With no other choice, Clare sat next to Tina in the back of one of the squad cars, trapped behind the reinforced grill that kept the criminals in and the drivers safe. Terrick sat alert in the front, looking every inch the seasoned officer. Safety in numbers was Tina's mantra. They were four. Harley's men were looking for two.

They had gone a mile east and turned down Burncoat Street in the hope that any who discovered Terrick's car and the intended destination would simply not be looking for them there.

"Tell me again why this plan's gonna work?" Tina asked. "There's no logic."

"Breadcrumbs," Clare replied. "The creature…"

"Stop calling it that," interrupted Tina. "It's just a man."

"It is not," Clare countered. "If you'd seen what it did to Jarret Logan you'd know it's no man. You saw the photos. You saw the reports. What man sucks the life, the very soul out of another? This is gonna work because the police will have to follow the trail of people. We need to see everybody safe. I believe there's a connection here, a link between Harley and this thing. I'm going to make myself the only viable target, appearing exactly where I said I would be, it will have no choice to strike."

A siren began to wail as a car on the other side of the road shot off to the north. Clare's heart thumped with the unwelcome surge of adrenaline to an already-overtaxed body.

"Hey, it's okay," Tina said. "There's a heavy police presence tonight. Not all of them are hunting you, sweetie. Those escapees are all over the city."

With traffic at a standstill, Clare took the decision to park away from the hospital. Her broadcast had been taken to heart and people had begun to pour into the city center. Once they parked up, the walk to Saint Vincent's was no more than a mile. With every step Clare's sense of impending doom increased. Had Terrick not been by her side, she feared she would have stopped and turned away.

The enormity of the nearby DCU exhibition centre slid slowly past as Clare kept watch for squad cars. It was a busy Saturday night; people swarmed outside the entrance to the convention hall, the name of what Clare presumed to be the latest boyband sensation glowing from an electronic billboard. She hoped the four of them would get ignored in the excitement.

Across the road from the DCU stood Saint Vincent's Hospital, the modern brick fascia elegant and simple. If a hospital could look inviting then this was a good start.

Clare stopped to stare.

"Keep walking," Tina advised. "Let's not stand out."

They crossed the road against the general flow of pedestrian traffic. Even if someone was watching for them it would be unlikely they would spot individuals in this much humanity. The flow of people didn't stop once they entered the hospital either. The makeup of the population changed. Instead of animated teenagers, now along the yellow marbled floor walked medical staff decked out in uniform, patients in wheelchairs or moving at a delicate pace with the aid of loved ones or crutches. With cafes and a small shopping mall along the central atrium the general hubbub was loud.

"You've never been here before?" Tina asked.

"I never had any cause to," Clare replied. "I always went to Julian Strange in Holden if I ever felt unwell. The nearest I have been to a building this size was the precinct."

"Talk about a sheltered life," Tina said before chortling. "They want you to forget that you're in a hospital with all this. It's distraction; the ultra-modern face of medicine, fitting in with the commercial lifestyle. It's not all like this."

Tina wasn't kidding. The press of humanity lessened as they passed further into the bowels of the hospital. By the time they rounded a glass-clad bend to the new wing, they were but four, the last person a few minutes away.

"Why so empty?" Terrick asked. "It's brand new."

"It opens on their timeline, so not for another week." Clare replied. "The wing is fully functional though, which will be to our advantage."

A thick blue ribbon hung on the doorway, ready to be cut in a ceremony. Tina lifted it aside and pushed through one of the glass doors. Clare followed, the two men close behind. The rooms were dark, the only light coming in from the hallway behind them. The random collection of fluorescence left the wing looking like an alien landscape. Everyday objects such as chairs and desks were thrown into bizarre stark relief by the various hues of yellows, blues, and pinks. Clare stared around the empty wing. The hygienic scent of a hospital ward untainted by neither ailing humanity nor the constant application of cleaning fluids left her unsettled.

"Clare, come here," said Tina.

Obedient in her detached state of mind, Clare crossed to the computer terminal where Tina had logged into the Worcester P.D. database.

"I think you're gonna want to see this." Tina's voice was mysterious, holding the promise of long-sought answers.

Clare sat down, looking over the screen. She couldn't see the wood for the trees in her current state, until she noticed the date. "That date's last week. Those are the chem-analysis on the samples taken from the Morris house back in Holden."

Tina was still speaking but Clare was lost in the statistics on the screen. The samples must have been of the fluids excreted by Viruñas. Trace elements of human blood, elevated toxicity and… "Mescaline…"

"The drug?"

Clare leaned back, massaging one withering hand with the other. "Yeah, that's how it subdues its victims. It injects them and they don't even realize what's happening until their heart stops."

"What's that?" Tina pointed at a fourth sample.

"Some blood we found. I've already looked at that." Clare clicked on the test results. "I don't see anything out of the ordinary. Wait. There's a DNA match."

Intrigued and excited, Clare moved the pointer to the flashing red icon and clicked. What showed on the screen was both a revelation and a bafflement at the same time.

"Andrew Harley; twelve and a half percent."

Chapter Twenty-Eight

"So it's him but not him?" Tina had one eyebrow raised in confusion.

"It's a relative," Clare answered. "Autosomal DNA is shared between family members. The more distant you are the less you share. Kids share fifty percent with their parents for example. A match of this type puts it at either a great grandparent or a cousin. Harley is on the database because we all are. This test could have picked up any member of his family, or shown that we were related if that had been the case."

Tina scanned the information again. "Just Harley, which is damning in his case. Your name's nowhere to be seen, sweets. Doesn't matter what Harley claims now. If they check your samples against these, they'll find nothing in common. You're clear."

"That's a relief," agreed Clare. "But the fact of the matter is that whatever's going on, Harley is not just concealing a random person while they go about killing. He's protecting a member of his own family and he's been doing so for well over a decade."

Recent memories of Harley and the doomed Jarret Logan struck Clare. She pulled an ID from her pocket, showing it to Tina. "What if they aren't on the police payroll but work for a third party?"

"Juan Menzes?" Tina asked. "Whose that?"

"It's the janitor. It has to be. I found this in his room."

Terrick tilted the pass, squinting. "You still think it's him?"

"Too much adds up, Terrick. Harley is protecting a member of his family while they're given carte blanche to slaughter innocents. Where else to hide the man than in plain sight?" A thought made Clare pause. "Are these results public record, Tina?"

"Not quite. Any hacker with a modicum of computer skill could probably find them. Why? Do you think this might be how your man has been identifying targets?"

Clare shrugged. "Perhaps. Let's say samples get submitted and are recorded on the hospital system. Harley gets alerted by somebody when a particular blood glucose reading is recorded, and sends the menu to his cousin who picks up the takeout before the victim is alerted to their medical condition."

"That's grasping at straws," Tina countered.

"And yet look what's happened lately. How else are Harley and his squad getting to these places so fast? Come to think of it, he looked pretty close with that tall guy in the footage on TV. Who was he?"

"The guy he stood with at the fire? That was Gideon Homes, the chief administrator over at Worcester State. Eva Ross, the woman Mike and I interviewed, she worked for him before she fled the state."

"Would he have access to such records?"

"Sweets, he runs a prison hospital for psychos. I guess he'd have connections to whatever or whoever he likes."

"Then they might have spotted my results. They might go after Jeff…"

The door rattled from the darker recesses of the wing. They all went silent.

"That wasn't from the direction we entered," Tina whispered. "Someone's already here."

"Move," Terrick ordered.

Without thinking, Clare followed the command, hurrying from the open-plan central wing into one of the hallways to their left. Dim emergency lighting helped conceal her. There was no way anybody in the bright light of the entrance could see one woman hidden down a side passage. Or so she hoped. Tina stood guard in front, gun held low as she watched for movement. From their hiding place Clare watched Terrick direct the officer into a position behind a large column across the lobby. Between them the two men should hit anything that walked into that particular killing ground.

Another door rattled, this time closer and insistent. Someone was getting frustrated. Then a movement in the corner the room caught Clare's attention. A man shuffled into view, the features of his face obscured by the shadows of a post so only the paunch of an older gut was exposed. He had on a grey jumpsuit with the letters W.S. in large black letters on his chest.

"Worcester State," Clare whispered directly into Tina's ear.

"We couldn't find them all," Tina whispered under her breath, her lips not even moving. "Now we know why."

More bodies shuffled into view behind him; one became two, then three, then five. All stood still, staring around the wing.

Clare held her breath. Spots began to appear in front of her eyes. When she finally exhaled, the lead convict smiled. "Welcome Clare."

How did he know that was me?

Tina turned her head toward Clare, shaking it. *Do not engage with them.*

Clare checked behind her. Down the hallway was a door. More so, it was a means of escape or a place to hide. She felt safer with options even as nervous sweat began to trickle down her brow.

The convict took a deep breath. "Nectar; I can smell your fear. I can taste your illness. I see why HE wants you. What a meal." The convict paused, cocking his head to the right. The others began to do the same.

"Yes, Lord Iuvart," the group intoned as one.

Clare glanced toward Tina, the group behaviour confusing her. The convicts moved forward, spreading out.

"Stop right there," Terrick ordered.

For a moment the level of command in his voice held the five fast. The foremost of them sneered in the direction of the column where Terrick was hidden. "You need cover and a gun, little sheriff?" He began to laugh. "You think that will be enough for you?"

"I'll take my chances." Terrick rounded the column, firing a warning shot at his opponent. The bullet ricocheted off the tiling inches from where the man was about to step.

The convict paused but only to laugh more. The sound of his voice echoed through the hallway. "You think we're the only ones here? That we came alone? Two of you won't be enough to hide her. We have her scent. We only need to keep her for him. He comes."

A wicked grin lit up the face of the rotund convict, his eyes catching what light there was, appearing to glow. Clare stood immobile as his face began to change. Maybe it was a trick of the light but he seemed to be swelling and distending, his face losing its natural shape to some weird elongation.

"Go," Tina hissed.

The rest of the men spread out, two on each of Joe and Terrick's hiding places. The foremost began to stalk Clare's refuge.

"Clare, go!" Tina shoved her, breaking her stasis. Tina leapt toward the man, his face a combination now of pain and triumph.

Clare stumbled toward the door. She could move no faster than a rapid shuffle. It was all the aching would allow, her muscles screaming in protest at the violation of their disparate state. The door resisted her initial attempts to pass through, stiff hinges unused to motion coupled with her returning state of weakness. She had to push forward, get safe.

"Get out of here," Tina yelled, moving from the shelter of the hallway into the fight. She fired her gun at one of the Worcester State convicts. The noise that resulted was a double-pitched roar so alien in nature it left a ringing in Clare's ears. *How did that come from a man?*

It was enough to spur Clare into action. She shut the door and flicked the lock. Turning, she found herself in another hallway, the only lights being those from the DCU across the road. A door opened down the end of the hallway, another escapee spotted her and gave chase.

From where the energy came Clare had no idea but she ran. There was no way these guys were going to catch her. Sounds of fighting punctuated with inhuman screams echoed down the hallways of the deserted hospital wing. She wanted to get as far away from them as possible.

Darkness in the hallway merged with a deeper black of open rooms, sealed from the outside. It was the only way Clare could tell she was making ground. Behind her the footfalls, faster and heavier, made headway over her own. She rounded a corner and found herself faced with two doors: more hallway and stairs. She had no time to think. She shoved the door to the hallway wide open, then ducked through to the stairs, locking the door behind her.

She crouched behind the door, her eyes closed. The footsteps reached the doorway and paused. A slow, laboured breathing came from the hallway. The fetid stink of bad breath reaching through a gap. A gap? The door had caught on the bolt of the lock. She'd been too quick, not checking it was actually shut. Clare opened her eyes a crack. After a moment the prisoner moved off down the hallway.

She rested for a few seconds, catching her breath. Thirst pulled at her. Was it all to be lost in the labyrinthine vaults of this unused hospital wing?

She crept down the stairs, afraid that at any moment the pursuer upstairs would realize his mistake and double back. Two flights down and she was on another level, still disused and empty of equipment. It was poorly-lit and lacking in anywhere resembling a hiding place. Clare pushed through a doorway on her left and let it shut behind her. She closed her eyes, listening for any sign of movement. Was that an echo of more fighting from above? It might have been her imagination. Opening her eyes again helped little as they adjusted to the dark. The floor was deserted. Reaching out to one side, Clare followed the hallway by touch, her fingers trailing along ceramic tiles, smooth and cold. Her footsteps echoed down the hallway. Compared to the wing above, this floor was a shell of a building. Clearly the big opening was only reserved for one level.

An idea struck Clare, and pulling out her phone she activated it. The light on the screen was just enough to give the hallway eerie green definition, to show her the way. Many of the doors lacked handles. Quite often doorways lacked doors altogether. Clare hid behind a door with a steel lock, closing and bolting it as slowly as possible to avoid any noise. There was the faintest of clicks as the latch engaged. Her sanctuary was sealed for the moment. She shifted a metal instrument trolley across under the handle. It didn't quite reach but the handle wouldn't turn fully. She prayed it was enough. Her friends would find her. They would reach her first. They had to.

Taking a deep breath, she leaned against the far wall, her legs wobbling. The wall was solid, real. Not a monster in the dark. She turned to switch the light on, and paused. "Night vision," she growled, fearing her sight would be ruined by the dazzle; she was no good blind in this world of darkness. She had to keep it together.

After a few minutes, she realized this was a bathroom of sorts. She would only be able to keep this up for so long.

The use of her phone's light revealed windows behind panelling. Clare pulled one panel back on its folding hinges, wincing as it squeaked. Her elation at a potential escape route turned to rapid dismay as she realized that she was still several stories up. Below her, cars filled the street outside Saint Vincent's, the drivers oblivious to one woman's waving from an insignificant portal above them.

There was a click from behind her. The handle was being tested. It moved down and up, tapping several times against the metal surface of the trolley. Scraping metal on metal. Clare backed into the corner. *Move on, you bastard.*

The handle stopped. Clare remained still. She counted silently. One. Two. Three. Four. Five.

The door shuddered. Someone battered it from the other side. Clare screamed. She looked for some kind of weapon to defend herself with. The room was devoid of anything useful.

Again and again the door shuddered. Under colossal impacts the lock held. But for how long? Another barrage and the whole door began to come out of the frame.

She ran to the window, desperately trying to pull one of the panels loose but her strength gave out. She tried to dial Tina but the signal was so faint the phone barely registered.

With a devastating blow that splintered the doorframe, the door toppled in. Clare shrunk back, dropping her phone.

"Such a doomed family," said a voice from the doorway.

An average size, he wore a dark overcoat with a hoodie underneath. His face was concealed by the hood and the shadows of the dark room. The voice was familiar. She had heard it at the precinct.

"I know who you are. I know what you are: Viruñas."

A dark chuckle emanated from the shadow. "A name I haven't heard in a very long time. A man left to his own devices in a room deep below a nest of self-serving vipers often goes unnoticed. I have watched you for years, known you for even longer. This day would always come. It was inevitable. Overlooked by you, by everybody, I have been free to feed, free to live. Exactly how I've wanted it."

"Do you think you are here by choice? That I did not know of your attempts at misdirection? I never sought to hunt those that were not destined to satiate me. There's a bigger endgame at play here, Clare Rosser. We are just the beginning, you and I."

Viruñas stepped fully into the room. One more step closer to Clare and a hallucinogen-filled end to her life. He was enjoying this, savouring what was to come.

"You won't get another child. They are all safe."

"I don't need one. I have you. There are answers you do not have, daughter of Bud Maygan. There are victims of your own life that you cannot hide, those you do not, will not ever know. You do not know what you are, what you could have been."

Viruñas tilted its head to the right, observing her. From within the deeper shadow of the hood, two points of white began to glow. His eyes filmed over as he prepared to feed.

Clare's legs began to buckle. She grabbed at the window ledge. Fear coursing through her body, the adrenaline threatening to overwhelm her. The thud of her heart sounded in her ears and still Viruñas watched as if waiting for something.

"Let go, Clare. Your fate is at hand. I can taste the disease filling your veins." He sniffed, and the shudder that resulted reviled Clare. Had she the energy she would have fought back, but she could barely stand.

Viruñas breathed in, sucking back drool. "It is ambrosia to me. I knew this day would come the moment I fed on your mother and her husband. I could taste your future in their blood. I've watched you for years, you and your delicious brother."

The shadow flickered. In an instant the creature appeared in front of her. Still she couldn't see past the glowing eyes. This wasn't a pleasant end to life. This was a dark and deliberate death, the realising of one's worst fears. With delicate care, Viruñas traced his fingers down the sleeves of Clare's shirt. The material fell away. He placed a hand on her right arm, just below the shoulder, thumb laid on the inside, fingers clasping one by one in an iron grip.

"No," Clare moaned as he lowered her to the floor, seemingly beyond her control.

"Yes." As he raised his left hand above her a strange oval puckered mark began to force out of his palm, the skin rising, forcing itself into a ridge. The skin contracted underneath until the centre of his hand split open to reveal a large fleshy sucker, joined to his palm by an umbilical. The nails, already with pointed tips, secreted a clear fluid that glistened in the faint green light of her phone's screen. Clare began to draw in rapid shallow gasps, transfixed by the glistening appendage. Her body rebelled, remaining tense and taut even as she willed it to action. The sucker twisted back and forth, fluid dripping onto her arm. This was it. Caught by her own plan she held onto her last breath, her stomach tensing.

"You're apples, ripe on the tree and ready to be plucked," he hissed and jabbed his nails into her arms. Pain exploded as mescaline surged into her body. Clare twisted, trying to get free.

Viruñas held her tight, pinning her arms to the floor. The mescaline overpowered her body, keeping her placid. The monster held her easily and leaned down, its face next to her ear. "Time to feed." Something warm touched her arms where his hands held her. The suckers latched on and Viruñas shuddered again.

Clare felt the suckers clamp tight, spreading wide. Pain exploded as something was forced into her arms. Clare tried to scream but her voice had gone. Then suddenly she was free. Viruñas hissed as somebody moved behind.

A flash in the dark and the creature fell away.

"Pluck this," Tina Svinsky said, unloading her gun at the monster.

Chapter Twenty-Nine

A howl of pain filled Clare's mind, a warbling roar that distorted into deep bass mixed with piercing treble. She put her hands over her ears, collapsing to the floor and curling into a ball. Her upper arms throbbed, five small wounds on each like needlepoints of fire lancing into her body. She didn't have long.

"Clare, are you okay?" Tina asked, her voice slowed as if someone had lowered the pitch.

Clare shook her head, trying to clear it. "What happened? Where did he go?"

Tina switched on the lights and Clare's head began to swim. The walls flattened and appeared to merge, lengthening into one flat boundary, the room disappearing off into infinity. This was happening far too fast.

"Clare!" Tina appeared in the middle of the endless white, the angles of her face shifting as if something lay beneath it. "Stay with me girl. That thing's still out there. I wounded it; shot it in the shoulder but it moved like lightning to escape. It bounded all over the room before it fled."

Clare sat up, leaning over to examine the blood on the floor. The droplets were of the purest ruby-red, shining up at her, rippling, swirling.

"Tina. It knew we were here. The ruse failed. It chose to come here. It was after me." Clare's own voice sounded deep and slow. Time was beginning to stretch out.

Then everything snapped back into focus. Clare saw the room with painful clarity. "There you are, sweetie. Welcome back. We need to get you outta here."

"Wait. Tina, I have to explain. He got me." Clare pointed with her right hand to the marks on her left. "He filled me with mescaline. It's working faster than it should. Normally it takes an hour or so from ingestion. I'm gonna act very strange very soon. It's all a hallucination. Whatever I do, keep me close. With the diabetes I just don't know if my body can last."

"But this creature…"

"It needs to feed. You wounded it. The pleasure of choosing and hunting its victim won't matter anymore. This'll be in my system for a good twelve hours. Look after me."

"You won't be the strangest thing I've seen in here," Tina replied, her face shifting as her nose seemed to Clare to want to make its way across to the right of her now-angular face.

Clare reached out to track it with her finger, finding nothing but air. Something deep inside held on, reminding her that this was the creature that had done this. Her head started to throb as strong arms grabbed her waist and lifted her aloft.

"I'm flying," she said, her own voice rising as high as the air on which she floated. She began to laugh, spreading her arms wide as the endless portal opened up above her, welcoming her into its midst. The white light disappeared, being replaced with a latticework of red lines that began to swirl and distort. In Clare's distance, fireworks began to explode, bright and filled with sparks of red and green.

"Who are they?" said a voice so slow and languorous it took an eternity for the words to filter through.

"Harley's. They're from the precinct." The words all mingled into a cacophony for Clare as all words merged into one. Clare felt herself lurch backward and down at an impossible angle. The sensation refused to dissipate. Green lines surged under her feet, shooting up into the midnight sky as she dropped like a stone into the abyss. "Help me," she cried.

"She's fading."

In the midst of the lines, two points of light stared at her, unmoving. Were they stars? No, they were eyes she could never again escape. Only the blackness of unconsciousness would spare her from the gaze. Clare began to let go.

"Can you hear me?"

She must have still been hallucinating; it all sounded so real.

Yes? I can hear you. What do you want? Who are you?

"Come on, girl. Come back to us," the voice said, insistent.

I'm here. Can't you hear me..? Am I alone in here? Where is here?

"You're going to have to wait for the patient to come round in her own good time, Sheriff," said a deep male voice. "If she even makes it there may yet be organ failure. She's on the critical list for a very good reason. She should have been given medical treatment a long time ago."

The debate raged on the other side of a wall keeping her from consciousness. She pushed against it and the wall remained firm.

"...without good cause," said the first voice, familiar. "She chose this."

Tina. TINA. Clare rallied, forcing herself against the invisible wall until it shattered. As it did Clare wished for a second she had remained in the dark recesses of her mind. Light came flooding in, enough to sting her eyes so hard she groaned. The scent; she was still in the hospital. No, it was different. The cleaner was missing from Saint Vincent's. She was somewhere else.

"There she is," Tina said through a grin.

"You had us worried there for a while, kid," Terrick added. "Runnin' off the way you did. Crazy fool thing to be doin'."

"You try standing there with a convicted murderer chasing you down and no means of defence," Clare croaked, still very drowsy. Her eyelids weighed tons. It was difficult to keep them open. This fog-filled world was similar to that of the mescaline-fuelled hallucination, just with none of the whimsy. She raised her hand to her head and groaned; not only for the world-class hangover she was suffering with but also that her hand was once more bandaged to a drip.

"Where am I?"

"A private recovery room on the wing in UMASS where your misdirection seemingly sent half the population of Massachusetts, and every hypochondriac and freeloader contained therein."

"Julian?"

A stern man with a military bearing and short-cropped iron-grey hair watched her from behind Terrick, leaning against the wall by the door, stethoscope wrapped around his neck. He had a straightforward, no nonsense kind of look about him. Dr Julian Strange had been a source of mistrust for Clare during her childhood and ultimately was responsible for her decision to choose forensics as a career. They hadn't spoken in quite a while. Not since the night her parents had died.

"You almost didn't make it," he observed. "You're in the latter stages of advanced hyperglycemia as well as suffering poisoning by mescaline. Mescaline? What were you thinking?"

"It wasn't exactly my plan to go out and get high," Clare said. She managed to focus her eyes. The room was as severely white as Saint Vincent's. Vertical blinds hanging across glass windows allowed a view of the wing. Outside the main room was crowded with people waiting for assessment.

Tina adjusted the bed, tilting it higher so Clare could make herself more comfortable.

"So what happened?" she asked when she was settled.

"You sure you want to hear this, Doctor?" Terrick asked of Julian Strange.

"No, probably not. If it's tied in to what you've done here though I think I had better."

Terrick nodded.

"In a word," Tina said in hushed tones, "Harley. Well not him directly, but beat patrols who report to him and are well known for handing shall we say, his work. What's the last thing you remember?"

"I don't know. It's impressions mostly. Like the whole world had turned to angles and you were all distorted. There were fireworks."

"Do you remember gunfire perhaps? There was a lot of that," said Terrick. "They were neither as accurate nor as insistent as us. You had a few crazy moments there, kid. You were on another planet with whatever that guy put in you. I thought we were gonna lose you, girl."

Clare shuddered. Those eyes still watched her from inside her mind. "Trust me Terrick, you wouldn't want to be in my head. That's not an experience I would ever care to repeat."

"Does that mean you're done?" Tina seemed very intent on the question.

"No. We didn't start all this and risk everything to give up at the last hurdle. We almost got that thing."

"And we almost lost you, sweetie."

"It's worth it. I'm gonna have to do it again if Viruñas…" Clare looked out into the ward again. "Wait, how long have I been here?" Fully awake now, she realized that she felt none of the symptoms. There weren't as many people in the ward as she had first assumed while drowsy. Clare began to panic.

"Clare it's Sunday evening. You've been unconscious for just over eighteen hours."

"What?" Clare jerked upright, the drip catching on the rails along her bed and pulling tight against the skin of her hand. "Ow! Tina, you know what's at stake. Terrick, how could you let this happen?"

The question was unfair, and Clare regretted it the second the words left her lips. "I'm sorry," she added. "That was uncalled for."

"It was." Terrick gave her a stern look, "but it's understandable, kid. Just don't make a habit of it. We've all gone through Hell for you and the story ain't over yet. There's worse to come. You nearly didn't make it."

"Well I'm here now. What's been done to me?"

"Half a day of drips and gradual insulin administration," Julian provided. "We almost have you stable."

Clare gave the doctor a flat stare. "Take it out."

Julian just looked at her for a moment, blinking. "I'm sorry?"

"Julian, I'm asking you to take out the drip, before I rip it from the back of my hand. It can't end this way."

"Told you," said Tina.

Julian's eyes narrowed. "You know the insurance is covered by..."

Clare began to tear at the bandage on the back of her hand, wincing in pain as the needle embedded in the vein was disturbed.

Julian stepped in and immobilised her arm. "Clare, I've never known you to be crazy like this. You were always so sensible. What happened to you?"

"I found belief in the strangest of places."

"You found religion?"

Clare's gaze softened. "Julian, not all belief is religious. Let's say a new world has been revealed to me, one you might not be prepared to accept. I have one more task to do before I can get treatment for good and all. In order to do that I need to be untreated." Clare looked to her arm, blood weeping around the edge of the pristine white bandage. "With your good intentions, it might already be too late but I have to try. Please Julian, remove the needle. Let me make my own decision here."

Clare's impassioned plea had the right effect. Julian nodded. "I'll need a moment and a smaller bandage from that cabinet over there." He nodded in the direction of a set of narrow metal drawers by the door which Terrick began to explore, the shriek of metal on metal grating on Clare's ears.

She took a deep breath. "It feels like I'm asking this question far too often but how long do I have before I end up back in here?"

Julian loosened the bandage and withdrew the needle, causing Clare to wince in pain and squeamish discomfort as the blood that had welled underneath poured out. A quick dab with a sterile wipe and gauze and medical tape sealed the wound in. Julian held a gentle but firm finger over the back of her hand. "Hours? Clare, I clearly do not need to tell you that you aren't well but I cannot compel you to remain here. You are not rehydrated. You have insulin in your system, both administered here and what is remaining from your pancreas as your own body destroys the beta cells that provide it. Yet that will not be enough to sustain you for long. Take a look at yourself in a mirror. You're an old woman in a young woman's body, frail, weak. I implore you to see reason."

"Not until I see this monster captured, or dead." Clare swung her legs out of the bed, preparing to stand.

"What monster?" Julian asked, looking at Tina and Terrick rather than at her.

Clare stood; her legs were weak and the floor was ice-cold, but standing was manageable. All she had left to lose was her life. Terrick knew the truth, and the look of horror in Tina's eyes showed she had at least some faith. "It's a creature out of legend." Clare pointed at the barely-healed scars on her own arms. "This is how it gets you. We found marks on every victim. If we don't stop it, we lose it. I will die to catch it if necessary. That is the extent of my faith."

Clare had hoped to baffle or shock Julian into some sort of understanding but instead he stared at her, as if she had just confirmed already-known facts for him.

"You've seen it," she accused. "Julian, what's going on? What do you know?"

"I told you we weren't lyin'," Terrick said to the doctor. "You wanted to hear from the girl confirmin' what we were sayin' and now you have it right there."

"It can't be true," Julian said, baffled.

"And yet she's livin' proof of the thing," the sheriff argued. "This was supposed to be the sanctuary, and instead it's a honeypot."

"Sanctuary? Honeypot?" Clare was equally worried and baffled. "What's happened?"

Julian rubbed his right hand over his forehead. "There was an incident. Clare, I have to show you something you might not be in a state to witness. We have no choice. Come with…"

"No," Clare gasped, "not now."

The three other occupants of her room turned to follow her stare. Outside Andrew Harley stood in the main ward.

Chapter Thirty

Clare felt her legs give way.

Terrick caught her before she collapsed, sitting her on the bed. He turned his back to the scene behind him, blocking her from view of the window.

"Let me see," she hissed, grabbing his top for balance and leaning to one side.

"Steady, girl," Terrick cautioned. "Not too far. It's one way glass but you make a lot of noise and he'll get suspicious."

The scene outside unfolded very publicly. Three of Harley's men waited behind him, all intent upon the man blocking their way.

Tina grabbed Clare's arm, pulling her back.

"What do you think will happen if they spot you?"

"I don't care. He's the one that did all this to me. Arrest him. Test him. Blood tells all."

"Can you positively identify him from the other night, sweetie?"

"No but..."

"Did you witness him kill any one of the children you believe him to have murdered?"

"I can't. But I..."

"Then we have no grounds for an arrest."

Clare stopped struggling and fixed her friend with a stare. "If you weren't a federal fugitive it would be a lot less complicated. Clare, he knows you're in here. Listen to him."

"I'll deal with this," Julian decided, slipping out the door behind Harley's goons.

Outside Harley's voice had raised as he shouted at the other medic. "Doctor, where is she? This is a federal matter and as such my jurisdiction takes precedence."

"What appears to be the problem here, Captain?" Julian said, assuming an authoritative manner. He was taller than Harley and stared him down.

"Julian Strange," Harley turned at the voice, his subordinates forming a loose circle around him. "Always popping up where you're least wanted. You're harbouring a fugitive. Hand her over."

Julian feigned innocence. "I've seen a lot of sick people in here, Captain. Whether one of them is a fugitive isn't my concern. Treating them is."

"You're holding Clare Rosser and she's coming with me," Harley growled.

Julian flipped open a folder he carried, scanning down the names. "You must be mistaken, Andrew, to believe you have any rights in this place."

Harley attempted to push past him, reaching for the door. Julian held up a hand to the captain's chest, preventing him from taking a step. "In this hospital, in *my* ward, my duty of care to the patients is the ultimate priority. You can attempt to intimidate anybody you like but you have no say on the fate of one of my patients until they are in a state to leave this ward. *When* she is in a fit state of health, *if* she even recovers, then you can interrogate to your heart's content. Until that moment you will desist attempting to bully the staff of this department. Do I make myself clear?"

In a moment of great personal satisfaction for Clare, Harley was lost for words. He stared up at the taller man; Julian stared back, unafraid. Two men used to getting their way. This was nothing other than a home win.

"I'll be returning with a warrant," Harley threatened.

Julian leaned over. "I don't threaten easily. Get your court order. The most that can happen is the release of information. Patients. Come. First." He continued to face down the bulk of the captain, who backed away seconds later through his men. Clare jumped when Harley punched the window behind which she was shielded on his way out. After a few moments, Julian came back in.

"Thank you," she said, for the first time in her life feeling genuinely grateful towards him.

"I meant every word I said," Julian admitted. "You're sick. That being said, I only came because the hospital called requesting cover. I have a feeling we won't be seeing the last of Andrew Harley today. There's people in here far worse than you."

Clare noted the glances passing amongst her companions. "Okay spill, you guys. What else have I missed?"

The private room across the hallway was dim, lights turned down. The young lady within was unconscious, which was a mercy. Dripping with sweat that soaked into the sheets of the bed, her bloated body fought to stay alive with a dogged tenacity that belied natural order. Her stomach was swollen to the size of a heavily pregnant woman, veins sticking out all over the surface as they tried to cope with containing an invasive force. Her hands and feet were also swollen through excessive fluid retention. It was no wonder the bodies were so twisted and agonised when the creature had finished with them. She should have been dead.

"When did you find her?" Clare watched with the rest of them from an adjoining observation room. They all spoke in hushed tones for the girl's survival was balanced on a knife-edge. Any upsetting of the equilibrium might kill her.

"She was among the first brought in," Terrick said in low tones, "wastin' away and sponge-dry. They diagnosed her with a simple finger prick test but anybody could've seen what was happenin' to her. She was put on a drip and left in this room. Shortly after the floodgates opened and people started turnin' up left right and centre. She

The Eyes Have No Soul

must've gone wanderin'. As it was a nurse was checkin' for free space and found her like this on the floor, a man leanin' over her in a room, hands on her arms. She disturbed him and he fled."

Those eyes; Clare shuddered at the memory. "What... what did he look like?"

Terrick pulled out a notebook and flicked through some pages. "The nurse's words were 'emaciated, almost skeletal with glowing, white eyes'. Everyone laughed it off but she was insistent. Sound like your guy?"

"It does." Despite the warmth of the room, a chill passed over Clare. "Where'd he go?"

"Straight out that window, once the alarm was raised."

"That's got to be a two-story drop. Who found the body?"

Tina laid a hand on Clare's shoulder. "I'm sorry, Clare. No body was found."

Clare grinned, taking Tina aback.

"Not the reaction I'd have expected."

"Don't you see? He can't be far away. Viruñas feeds by killing his victim through fluid injection, overloading the heart, and then sucking the goodness out. You ever tried sucking on a piece of fresh sugar cane? Try filling it with so much fluid it bursts. It's much the same. This poor girl's heart should have given out but it hasn't."

Julian appeared animated at this. "The application of such a natural process in medicine could be incredible. Imagine a fluid injected directly into a body that..."

"You ain't thinkin' about exploitin' this I hope, doc," Terrick growled. "Look at her. Poor girl did nothin' but get ill and now she's a human water balloon. Maybe ask her about that once... *if* she recovers."

"The creature can't be far away," Clare surmised. "He needs to feed. Think about it. He was feeding and it's his Achilles' heel. He forces the fluid from his body into another. They die from hypervolemia. He has no fluid left to give. It's all in her. He's gonna need a quick score or he dies."

"You think?" Tina appeared sceptical. "You've been hell-bent on blaming that janitor for all of the world's ills and he looked fine to me."

"There's more," said Julian. "I took samples of her blood after we found her. The plasma's flooded with mescaline. I administered diluted insulin to the sample to see if there would be any adverse effects to the girl. The sample disintegrated."

"You mean the insulin did its work?" Clare asked.

"No. Everything in the blood was destroyed. Platelets, blood cells. They all just collapsed. We can't treat her until her body stabilizes and is clear of the creature's fluid. There's an unknown element that reacts to the insulin."

"I need to get out there," Clare said. "You all supported me this far. I need a little bit more from all of you. We need to set a trap. It was my plan to be the bait for the creature in St Vincent's and we almost had him. We have a trough overfilling with goodness in here but he's not getting back in to feed without exposing his true nature."

"What do you need?" Tina asked. By the look of exasperation on her face, the detective's patience was wearing thin.

"When a school of fish are threatened, they form up into a ball to try and confuse ocean predators. That's what we have here. A bait ball; we need to separate individuals from that ball in order for the predators to hunt. I need to be that lone fish. I need to get out of here. He has my scent now. If I can place myself in his way we can draw him out. If I'm right, and Juan Menzes is Viruñas, I need to find him and confront him. If I'm lucky, all you need to do is bear witness. You have to let me after him."

"Where do you need to go to now?"

Clare smiled. "Take me to the precinct. There's something weird going on. I need your help to work out what."

"Girl," said Terrick, "if you die and go to heaven, on your tombstone I'm carvin' the words 'There's somethin' weird goin' on'. There's been somethin' damned weird goin' on since I met you a week back."

"I must protest Clare," said Julian. "If the complete course of medicine isn't administered, the hyperglycaemia and ketoacidosis will become life threatening in hours."

"Then that's how long we have to find it. Terrick, I need you to remain here and stay vigilant. You might argue but I need somebody I trust to watch over these people. They've done nothing beyond get ill. That's the real kicker here. Type-one diabetes is an attack by your own body. There's no warning, no cure." Clare thought for a moment. It all became so clear. "No cure… Julian, can you get me insulin?"

The doctor's face lit up with approval. "That was a quick change of heart."

"It's not for me. If I can get close enough to the creature I'm gonna stab it. This being hunts diabetics. Why? It can't ingest sugar through normal means so it needs to feed on the sugar in their blood. Manufactured insulin will affect it severely. That's why it only goes after the undiagnosed. Those on the road to recovery will poison it."

Terrick didn't appear convinced. "Why don't you just take a gun and fill it with holes?"

Clare brushed the loose hair back over her right ear. Several strands came loose, sticking to her fingers. Her body was in mild shock; the hair was always the first thing to go. She ran her right hand over the wound on her left arm, wincing as she did so. "This is payback. I'm gonna kill it."

Back in her room, Clare found a brown envelope waiting on her bed. "What's this?" She picked it up, turning it over in her hands. On the back were written the words 'keep digging'.

"Okay who did this?"

Terrick shrugged. "We were all with you, girl. If you got a guardian angel, it's comin' from a different place than us. Open it up."

Clare did so, emptying the contents onto her bed. A series of colour photographs fell out, spreading out on the sheets. Each showed the janitor washing blood off of his hands."

"Where's he doing that?" Tina picked up one of the photos, taking it into the light to examine.

Clare didn't need to look. The dim lighting, the brick walls, the cleaning equipment behind him all led to one conclusion. "It's his lair under the precinct. I've been there once before."

"That's a lot of blood," Terrick observed. "Looks like he's been visitin' a slaughterhouse."

"Keep digging," Clare mused. "I wonder what they mean. There was nothing else there when I went looking before."

"Look at that wall, it doesn't line up with the window." Terrick pointed at one side of the photo. He was right. The brickwork disappeared behind the wall.

"I never noticed," Clare admitted.

"It's easy to miss. It's been done very well. I daresay that a janitor didn't do that without help. He does appear to have connections."

"Then I'm definitely going there next," Clare decided.

"Harley'll be waitin' for you," Terrick warned.

"I'm not without resource," Tina said, "and he's not the only captain in the precinct. I'll get you down that rabbit hole and back out again, sweets. What we find there had better be worth it."

"Something tells me we will find more than we bargained for," Clare said, lost in the photo. Her contemplation was disturbed by Julian returning to the room. In silence he handed her a clear plastic case containing a syringe, two loops for fingers on the base for a better grip with the thumb plunger. The needle, which looked impossibly thick, was covered in a second plastic sheath.

"Just remember to remove that cover before you use it. That's rapid-acting insulin. Near instantaneous."

Clare held up the syringe, staring at the clear liquid inside. "Is that a lot?"

"If you let me treat you that would keep you going for a couple of months. The amount your body produces is miniscule. You get all that in you, your blood sugar will plummet and you're hypoglycaemic in minutes, a coma soon after and dead not long past that. Be very careful."

"Won't they notice so much going missing?"

Julian nodded. "Eventually, but you let me worry about that. Good luck."

Clare nodded. "Thanks, doc. Terrick, stop fidgeting. I know you want to come with me but I need you to do something else while you're here. Look over the security footage. I'm not saying Viruñas isn't who I think it is but he had to get in here somehow."

"I reckon he must have needed no more than a few minutes to paralyze and fill that young lady. I'll look for anybody comin' in that much before she was found. If I find anythin' I'll let you know. Keep yer phone on."

"Are you sure this is the only way?" Julian urged.

"It has to be. There's too much muscle around here now, too much attention. By putting myself out there I have a chance to draw Viruñas to me, as desperate as it is."

"You sure you're seeing things the right way?"

Clare took a deep breath to steady her nerves. He was only looking out for her. "Explain what happened in that room. Rationalize those symptoms. Did you see the bodies in the Worcester morgue? Did they look like my parents?"

"I never saw your parents," Julian admitted. "I just knew they were ill and that you had to be there."

"And who told you and why weren't you there? Julian after all of these years, with the way I am, I think I deserve that much truth."

Julian looked nothing more than a man who wanted to bolt. Terrick must have noticed this too. He moved to the door, blocking it with his bulk. He his arms and frowned. "Answer her, doc. Girl's been through far too much pain already for you to leave this wound festerin'."

Julian sighed and perched on the edge of the bed. "Truth is I was there, in your kitchen with Harley and Jarret Logan. I called you before I was driven to the crime scene. Nobody was supposed to know we were even there. Harley went apoplectic when you showed up. Accused us all of informing you but had no proof. Tracing calls was more basic back then. Logan bore the brunt of it and took the long walk."

"You know what happened to Logan?"

"I do. I presume from that tone you've seen him. That would lead me to infer that his foolhardy sacrifice somehow inspired you. He was already ill and the plan was coming to fruition. We kept his condition secret from Harley and the others. Or so we thought."

"We? Julian, I know who 'We' is. Terrick and I met them yesterday. Tina's been in contact too. This is a choice I've made and I have to see it through."

Julian's face grew wide-eyed and desperate. "Clare, don't go down that path, I implore you."

"I have to, Julian. If you know what happened to Logan you know I've volunteered to do the same job. My way. There's time yet and I have a creature to catch."

Julian remained silent as he considered a response. As a conclusion was evidently reached he nodded and raised his hand to his mouth. Speaking into his cuff he said, "Bring them in."

Chapter Thirty-One

Two large men appeared at the door. Terrick moved aside and the pair, both with hair clipped close to the skull and the bearing of military officers trying their best to remain inconspicuous, filed into the room.

"What's this?" Clare asked Tina. "Where did the other guys go?"

"After I found you the situation deteriorated rather rapidly. They remained behind to see to the rest of the escapees. I was advised we would get replacements."

The foremost of the two, with green eyes in a face that was worn with experience, allowed his mouth to edge up into the slightest of smiles. "We're protection detail, miss. We'll see you safe to the precinct and back."

"I have no doubt."

The second of the pair threw a zipped duffel bag onto the bed. "Put that on. It'll keep you inconspicuous."

Clare opened the bag, pulling out the garments within. "A boiler suit, a baseball cap and a hoodie? This will keep me safe? Where's the specs and the false beard?"

"Just waiting for you to dress, miss. The beard comes later." The second agent spoke in a tone that said he wasn't joking.

"Clear the room then, guys," Tina said, grabbing anybody male and shoving them to the door. You can all protect us once we are ready."

Once the door had closed behind the retreating form of Terrick, Tina turned back to her. "I'm not gonna ask you what you think you're doing. Nor am I gonna lecture you on the futility of going right into the one place where at least fifty percent of the entire inhabitants want you in chains. What do you expect to get out of this?"

Clare stepped out of the hospital gown someone had seen fit to robe her in. Catching her reflection in a mirror, she winced. Bones stuck out everywhere. It was hard to spot any muscle on her gaunt frame. She was reduced to a fraction of the woman she had been. "I'm going to find a conclusion. There's something evil, something morally rotten at the core of that precinct. Even if it isn't Viruñas then we do what we were meant to do and put an end to someone else's foul practice by doing our job."

Tina helped her pull the boiler suit on over her underwear. It was small, yet it still felt painfully loose, the material coarse and scratchy at the seams. Clare suffered worse than the distraction of clothing. "We don't have long," she sighed.

Fitting the hoodie atop the boiler suit bulked Clare out somewhat. She pulled the baseball cap on, tipping it down low. The syringe case went in a pocket on her chest. "Okay?"

"You'll do," Tina said and signalled to the agents.

A few minutes later, a man nobody had laid eyes on before walked out of the emergency diabetic treatment ward flanked by what looked like three cops. Clare kept her head down and her hands in her pockets. The makeup applied to her face to fake stubble was still sticky and it was all Clare could do to leave it be. Her companions moved at a steady pace beside her. She was running out of time and yet was still willing to push herself to the edge to accomplish a common goal. The creature was out there, watching, waiting for a chance to jump in and finish what it started but it would never make the hospital and the poor girl it had assaulted. Not with the crowds filling the ward.

The hallways were so crammed with people they had to walk single file; all seats were taken and many had to stand and wait. She felt a sense of satisfaction that at least part of her plan had worked. People who might have ended up victims were safe. But the gratification was overlain with the unconscious girl's face, swollen to bursting. It was an image that would haunt Clare. "Who are they?"

"Your hypochondriacs mostly, or those that think a good dose of sugar will make them appear diabetic." Tina stopped as an elderly couple shuffled past to search for a seat. "Many are just lonely and want the attention. Most of the severe cases, the ones that matter, have been treated already. You've helped a lot of people." Tina's tone spoke of pride, all directed at Clare.

She couldn't bring herself to defend her choices, or take credit. Not as long as it was out there. There were no words left. She touched the case to reassure herself. This was her final gambit.

They made their way down to the parking lot, taking the elevator, inching through the human traffic. Outside two buses were unloading more people who headed straight back past them. They climbed into a squad car, the two agents stripping and pulling patrol uniforms atop slabs of muscle while Tina drove. Clare kept her eyes fixed firmly at her feet, a picture of subservience while inside her mind she pondered over what she had missed when she had been in the precinct before.

"Take these," green-eyes offered, handing her a bottle of water and some pills.

"What are they for?"

"Pain relief. Your symptoms will return much more quickly now you've been taken off the medication a second time." He knew about the retreat?

Clare took the pills and swallowed them down, emptying the water bottle without pause. Her stomach clenched at the sudden influx and her body cried out for more; an ocean could not satisfy her now.

"What happens if I'm recognized and they try to arrest me?" she asked as they pulled off Belmont Street and into the precinct's parking lot.

"We stop them. By whatever means necessary. We can be persuasive."

"You're going to come into the main precinct of the city police and lay the smack down? I'm impressed."

"They were the ones that carried you out," said Tina. "They took down most of the escapees while I was searching for you."

"Our orders are to only step in if we have to, Miss. When the situation became untenable in the hospital we took action. Think of us as your shadows. This here's your party."

"There are a lot of good people inside. Not everybody is on the take. I don't want innocent bystanders getting cut down in a firefight. Let me take the lead and figure out what's going on. If the situation becomes untenable, do what you have to. I assume all phones are tapped?"

"Number listed 'support' is on your speed dial. We were told you might issue such orders. A mutual friend said to say that the best you're getting is constant communication. There's still a mission to complete. Turn your phone on and dial. We'll listen in from this end."

"This mutual friend is one who likes watching from a distance?"

"Perhaps, miss."

There was no use trying to strike up a conversation with them. Clare did as bidden, placing her phone in the same pocket as the needle. It was into the lion's den or nothing.

The car moved with purpose into the underground parking of the Worcester city precinct. Clare kept her head down, sneaking an occasional glance outside. For a Sunday night the place was buzzing, barely a space free.

"This isn't gonna work," Clare said, worried. "There's too many in."

"They're all in by the look of it," Tina agreed as she parked the car. "Might not be a bad thing though; many bodies and all that. You're only a janitor after all."

With a warning glance at their escort, Clare climbed out of the car, almost choking on the fumes in the garage. Normally bustling, the area was frenetic with cars coming in and out.

Several officers recognized Tina and waved. One or two others made to intercept her and were headed off by the first group.

"I don't like this," Clare said.

"Like it or not, we're here now," her friend replied. "Just stay behind me, look like you know where you're going and hope there's no human roadblock set up for us under the building."

Trying her best not to breathe, Clare followed at a pace that was no more than sedate. Only one hallway led into the precinct from the underground parking and it was full with people going both ways. The atmosphere was oppressive. The acrid tang of sweat hung in the dead air of the sub-level, the body heat of so many raising the temperature to a cloying discomfort. As luck would have it, most of the bodies moved in a particular direction, along corridors taking them to the building's central stairwell.

Only once were they stopped, and then by an officer called Chris who recognized Tina.

"They call you in too, detective?" he said, his voice dripping with anticipation. "They've got everybody coming in it seems."

"Why all the fuss?" Tina looked up at the giant of a man. Standing easily over six feet tall, the young officer's muscly bulk kept them protected from general view. The hallway that took them down to the janitor's lair was only a couple of metres away. Clare wanted to dash for it but felt already like her legs were going to give way. She had to conserve her energy.

"They've got everyone who holds a badge out calming the streets. You've got the Worcester State breakout, strange and unexplained deaths, rioting. Reports of people showing up with strange, distended features. Take your pick. The incident room's full of it upstairs. Also we're on the lookout for a member of the forensics team whose supposed to be behind it all, though that last bit I don't tend to believe. Harley issued an order to find her. Name's Clare. Clare Rosser."

"I'm just giving this guy the tour, or by the looks of it personal protection. I'll be up and out shortly after." Tina indicated with a nod of her head toward the parking lot.

Chris nodded, and moved off.

Clare stood staring into space, ignoring those that passed. Weirdly distended features? Bright, luminous eyes in the dark? She swore she'd never sleep again.

A noise intruded upon her thoughts. "Hey, guy. Move, will ya?"

Clare shook her head, her eyes focusing on a heavyset man frowning at her. "I wanna use the can and you're blocking the door."

Clare turned. Sure enough the men's bathroom was behind her. "Uhh, sorry," she grumbled in a scratchy voice that was as deep as she could muster, and moved out of the way.

The man looked at her, a strange expression on his face. "They'll employ any special case nowadays," he muttered and pushed past, causing her to stumble against the wall.

Clare recovered from the push and caught sight of Tina up the hallway. She hurried to make the ground up between them. "Sorry, I got caught up."

"There's too much thinking going on in that head of yours, sweetie. At least the disguise works. He's one of Harley's."

Clare pushed past her friend, her heart thumping at how close she had come to discovery. "Let's get this done. I can't take much more."

They moved away from the bustle, echoes of the hectic rush following them like the harassment of an overly excited spirit. The building was a mass of anxiety. Officers in body armor barging past as each new incident was announced. All around them cops called out for reinforcements, or tried to drag others to the garage. The air reeked of nervous sweat, warm and sickly. Clare felt hemmed in by it all, as if the walls would crumble on top of her. She shrank down a little more, stooping as she stumbled along. Only once they had passed through fire doors did they feel truly isolated.

Tina took the lead, her gun out and held low as she crept on silent feet through the boiler room. They moved past the pipes clad in silver-coated insulation and colossal boxed machinery that Clare remembered with a familiarity she wished she didn't have.

"This is all a bit too much like Freddy Krueger for my liking," Tina said in a low voice as they reached the janitor's room.

"I thought the same thing myself when I came down here before," Clare agreed.

"And you came down here alone?" Tina tried the door. The handle didn't move. "Locked."

"Kick it in," Clare suggested. "If we find something, it's not like they can say we didn't get a search warrant. This is our own building and it's just a janitor's closet."

Tina considered this for a moment and kicked the door right beneath the handle. With a splintering crunch the door gave, swinging inward on protesting hinges and hanging half-open.

"It's all right guys," Tina said over Clare's shoulder. "We won the fight with the wooden door. No casualties."

Clare chuckled in spite of the situation. "Let's get to work."

Tina pushed in with Clare closing the door behind them. There was no way of disguising the fact they had broken in. This was all or nothing. "Stay by the door, guys," Clare said, "we don't want any surprises."

The room appeared exactly as it had during Clare's previous visit. Buffers stood in order by their cans of polish. The sofa had been left the same despite Clare's discovery. It was almost as if it hadn't been touched at all. This made Clare pause.

"What?"

Clare pointed to the side of the room where a small cupboard hung above the table with the kettle. "If that's a false wall, I think this is all just for show. That seat is how I left it last time I was here. There are no prints in the dust. Nothing's moved in a week. I really think the janitor's playing us false. There was never anything here to discover, unless he planted the jacket to keep us off of something worse."

Clare moved to the wall, following the brickwork past the orange glow coming in from the skylight. Running her hand over the surface, she traced the mortar, old and crumbling until a point about two feet from the back wall. "It changes here. The mortar's newer. The bricks are near-identical but not exactly the same."

"It is however, enough to pass a cursory glance." Tina joined Clare in examining the wall. "Here's where it cuts off. This…" She poked at the join where plasterboard had been sealed with more plaster. "This wasn't meant to be here."

"Who'd notice a place so deep and hidden in this fetid labyrinth?" Clare began to feel woozy, tired. She stepped back, leaning on the back of the sofa.

"Y'all right?" Tina looked concerned.

The ache across Clare's middle had returned.

"No," she admitted. "But let's get in there and maybe I'll get one step closer to feeling better."

Tina searched the surface of the wall. "If this is detached and there's a room behind it stands to reason there's a door." She reached a coat hook embedded in the wall and stood on tiptoe, taking a sniff. "That's fresh oil."

Clare stood up, the anticipation overcoming her ailment for a second. "Who oils a mounted coat hook?"

Tina grinned. "Let's find out." She pulled down on the hook. There was a click and a six-foot high part of the wall receded. Tina pushed at the segment and it rotated, revealing a narrow corridor.

"Ingenious," Tina remarked, sticking her head into the gap beyond. "This ain't deep. There's another door. Metal."

Clare followed Tina into the corridor. Between walls, the path was clean to the point of fussiness. Unlike the room behind, this had been kept spotless.

Tina edged sideways along to the other door. "It's just a bolt at this end, nothing special."

"Can you see anything in the room?"

"No, it's covered." Tina gave the bolt a yank and it moved freely. She tried the handle and it opened without fuss. The detective peered into the room and on reflex, gagged. An instant later, a waft of carrion swept over Clare.

Chapter Thirty-Two

Clare doubled over, vomiting what water was left in her stomach between her feet. The stench of death, decaying flesh and embalming fluid fought to equalise between the two rooms. It was a struggle to breathe. Clare held her nose, steeling herself against whatever was to come.

"You don't have to come in here," Tina cautioned her. "In fact, I wish you wouldn't."

"I've come too far," Clare insisted. "There are answers in that room."

"Perhaps sweetie, but maybe not any you may like." Tina pushed the door wider, the noxious breeze subsiding as the airway increased.

Following her friend, Clare was glad she had already puked. "Tell me this isn't real."

Tina turned on the light, an ancient chandelier with broken crystal appendages and three upturned light bulbs, one of which flickered. Opposite a series of paintings had been affixed to the genuine external wall. Each painting depicted grotesque scenes: humans feeding on humans, supernatural beings lording over rituals, sacrifice, sex, every sordid practice the mind could imagine and many it could not. On the walls to either side hung a collection of decayed human body parts. Entire legs, the skin torn and irregular, the flesh shrivelled and black, lay in a pile, a yellow fluid. Clare remained frozen to the spot, her eyes fixed on the human remains.

"Clare," Tina said. "Snap out of it."

The pungent smell was so strong she had to force herself to breathe. She turned away only to face a series of hands severed at the wrist, clawing at the cloudy glass jars in which they were preserved.

Clare backed away. Something brushed her shoulder. She turned. A string of eyeballs hung from the shelf above, the eyes tied by the optic nerves. Many were desiccated, the flesh withered and tough. Others were fresher, the whites yellowed and cracked, the irises a mix of brown and blue. Blood stained the walls and coagulated in puddles on the floor. Scarlet stains mingled with older black. Worst of all, atop shelves near the ceiling, two human heads stared across the room at her, the eyes lidless. The skin was taut over one of the skulls, but the other, still fresh, caused her to cease moving altogether. Clare stared into the dead eyes, all other thoughts banished.

Tina moved forward, picking up a small photo that rested on the mantelpiece of an unused fireplace. "Recognize anybody? Clare! Come back to me."

Clare turned to her, trying to exclude the horrors around. "I'm sorry, Tina. That head on the right. It's Clifford Lee Burke. Terrick and I found him dead just before the broadcast, drained like the others. The fifth victim. Whoever dismembered him did so in the last day."

Clare noticed a picture on the wall. The photo was faded, but the likeness was clear. Harley and the janitor both grinned at her out of younger faces. "Confirms what we knew. They're related. They could have been brothers in days gone by."

Clare opened a small closet sheltered in a relatively unscarred corner of the room. Inside she found three boiler suits, all without a mark on them. Hung next to the clothing, wrapped in a plastic sheet she found a butcher's leather apron. Pulling it out, she examined the garment through its plastic protection.

"Blood?" Tina asked.

"It appears to be soaked right in to the leather. He spends a lot of time practicing his craft." Clare replaced the garment. "So where do we start? Prints? Blood?"

Tina looked around the room and echoed her comment. "Where do we start indeed?"

"I know. Gather your forces, Detective. We're putting an end to Harley."

Tina pressed a button on her phone. "It's me. Get down to the basement with everybody you can find."

Clare took the phone from her pocket. "Hold tight, boys." Before there was any chance of a protest, Clare dialed.

"Hello, Alison Gunn."

Here goes nothing. "Alison; it's Clare. You busy?"

"Clare, are you crazy phoning here?"

"I'm crazy. I'm desperate. I'm a dozen other words. Listen, I'm onto something and it's huge. Is the team all in?"

"Are you kidding me? With all that's going on? I don't think any of us can remember the last time we slept."

"Grab the team, get all the kit you can and meet me in the janitor's closet in the basement."

"But…"

"Alison, just do it. You know I'd not be calling if it wasn't important. This one's a career-maker." She put the phone away. "You boys still out there?"

"We're good," said one of their escorts.

"We're gonna need your skills soon. We might have to fight our way out of here."

Clare replaced the phone in her boiler-suit pocket. "Well what do we do about all this?"

"Don't touch anything else," Tina said. She was right. Clare began to go through a mental list of what they had disturbed while in the room. It wasn't much.

She closed her eyes; trying to avoid so much gore and twisted hideousness was impossible. Yet when vision was removed, those eyes still watched from the darkness, following her everywhere, waiting to taste her.

"The guy's got to be around here somewhere."

"A guy?" Tina's response was loaded with sarcasm. "More like a ghoul."

"We got a code for being a ghoul?" Clare quipped.

"We could always get him on code five-nine-four: Malicious mischief."

Clare shook her head. "Sounds too much like a badge of honor to me. This guy's going down for whatever we can pin on him."

Out of the corner of her eye Clare saw the door to the room move. She tensed.

"Clare?" It was Helen.

"In here."

Helen pushed the door open and stepped in. Her face went pale, nearly as white as her hair. Sunny and Alison followed bumping into her as she stopped in her tracks.

"Oh dear God," Alison gasped.

Sunny stuttered, trying to get words out. "Why…Who?"

"Right under our feet," Clare said, her voice flat, emotionless.

Helen crossed to her, still visibly shaken. "Is this what you meant? Is this why you left?"

"Not directly. Look, I need to get out of here. The stench, all this… It's too much. I need to sit." Not meaning to, Clare barged past her friends and into the narrow corridor. Her legs were like jelly, her stomach in knots. She gripped the wooden cladding on the back of the false wall, pain lancing into her hand as splinters pierced her skin when she pulled away.

Not caring about evidence she slumped onto the couch, staring unseeing at the entrance to what everybody had perceived to be the janitor's refuge. The plastic case dug into her chest. Four people entered; their two escorts led two suited men into the room. She didn't look up.

"What is it, Tina?" asked one of the strangers.

"Go look, Hank," Tina answered and knelt down in front of Clare until her face filled the limit of her vision. "Don't come apart on me now, girl. Not this close. Not after everything you've done."

That one sentence may have saved her. *After everything I've done...* She shook her head. "Got any water?"

Tina handed her a bottle, which Clare opened and gulped down. The two other cops quickly reappeared, both ashen-faced.

"You all right, Rosser?"

Clare looked up, recognising the cop as a rookie detective Tina had been training, Dwayne Codd. "Hey fish," she said, using the nickname he had very quickly picked up, "only a small case of type-one diabetes. There's nothing for you to worry about."

"Jesus, you should be in the hospital."

"She was," Tina said. "Some things are more important. Now you've seen what's in there, your thoughts?"

"They've been trying to pin this on her for the last week. I don't believe it."

"Harley's machinations. This isn't the end of the search, detective. We need to find the janitor. He's Caucasian, about five feet ten tall, brown hair fairly short, long sideburns, slim build. Wears a blue boiler suit like that one."

Tina pointed at her and Clare realized she was still dressed like a member of the cleaning staff. She reached up to take the cap off and Tina prevented her. "Don't, not yet."

"But Fish recognized me. If he does, surely everybody else will."

"And if you're normal Clare Rosser, walking shoes, prim and proper with the habitual hair-flicking, can you hide?"

Her friend was right.

Helen came back into the room, still visibly shocked. "I've got the guys cataloguing everything and taking photos. Clare, I don't suppose an apology would suffice? This is huge. There's enough in there for several teams to pore over. I've got to call some more in. I'll be back."

"Where did all those body-parts come from?" She asked Tina. "Our morgue is secure."

"Is it?" Tina replied, thinking. "That's a bold statement. Nothing's ever that secure. You still think this is your guy?"

The question flummoxed Clare. She stood, despite the effort. "Honestly, I thought so. This creature sucks people dry. It doesn't chop up its victims and store their bodies. It's feeding and moving on. What we have here isn't survival. This is much more macabre. I expected to see the janitor looking withdrawn but he was completely normal."

Tina barked a laugh. "Forgive me for saying so, but Clare, have you looked in a mirror lately? You don't exactly look normal."

"But I'm accounted for," Clare vouched. "I've been with you the past two days. Terrick's keeping an eye on things in UMASS and I've not left his side for several days before that."

Clare shrugged, even that movement making her muscles ache. "You're right to ask. I would. The fact of the matter is that the janitor might not be what I'm after but he's a means to an end. He's Harley's cousin."

The room fell silent as those not in the know processed this information.

"How do you want to play this?" Tina eventually said.

"We have to find this guy, no matter what. It has to be on the quiet though. I don't want Harley knowing I'm here. With the chaos in the precinct he will find out eventually but let's try and reach a conclusion first."

"Several of those body parts are still oozing fluid," Tina offered. "Not to mention the head up there. Somebody's been gathering carrion this very day."

"The morgue," Clare blurted out. "But Daniel would never allow access."

"Then you have to conclude either that Daniel doesn't know, or that he does. It's simple."

Clare lurched to her feet. "We need to get to the morgue. It's not far away."

"And if you're spotted?"

"That's what these two are for. One way or another, this ends tonight."

Clare, Tina and their two bodyguards made their way through the underbelly of the precinct. The morgue was so close, yet when she had been here before, Clare was merely unwell. Now she was desperately ill and every fibre of her being screamed out for help, quashed only by the dogged determination she possessed to see this task through. *If this ends tonight, I'm taking six months off.*

Clare smiled at her own comment.

Tina noticed. "What?"

"I was just thinking I needed a vacation."

"No joke," was Tina's sarcastic answer.

Clare's phone began to ring. She motioned her companions into a dark room, leaving the door cracked open for light. It was Terrick.

"You got him?"

"No, sorry girl, he's a no show. I just wanted to let you know that girl succumbed to the assault. She passed away not five minutes back. If Viruñas were to return, he'd have to start all over again."

"Crap. That could put him anywhere and in the condition he's in, he might be getting desperate. Have you got anything on the security footage?"

"Again, nothin'. Its complete chaos but I'll keep lookin' for you."

Clare switched the phone off and replaced it. "UMASS is a bust. He's long gone. The girl died too."

Tina looked to the floor. "That's a bad way to go. I just hope she was so out of it she never knew."

There was silence in the room. Perhaps out of respect for another lost innocent, perhaps because of the futility of this madcap hunt.

"We need to move," Clare said. "The morgue's down that hallway then left. There's a stairwell to the right. If we meet anyone coming it will be from that side."

As quietly as she was able, Clare led her companions out into the hallway. Her heart began to thump in her ears. Flashes appeared in her eyes as the stress on her body threatened to overwhelm her. Her breath came in rapid, shallow pants; sweat began to trickle down her forehead, dripping into her eyes and gathering like tears in the hollows where flesh had filled her face beneath them.

They reached the final corner before the morgue. There was a clicking out of sight to the left. Clare held her hand up bidding the rest of them to wait. Leaning forward, she gripped the wall for support and edged toward the corner. A man stood, back facing them, locking the door with one hand while he gripped something in the other. He wore the same boiler suit as her and stank of offal. It was him. Clare withdrew the case from her pocket and opened it, her fleshless fingers slipping easily into the loops at the base of the syringe.

Clare glanced back over her right shoulder and nodded. In an instant Tina and the two agents were round the corner, guns drawn, pointed at the janitor.

"Freeze!" Green-eyes raised his gun. "Put your hands where we can see 'em! Now!"

The janitor turned his head, dropping the key to the morgue from his right hand. He raised his hand over his head, his eyes wide, mouth hung agape in disbelief. He clearly hadn't expected company. That was as far as he moved.

"I said hands where we can see 'em," insisted the agent. "Don't make me put a hole in you, sir. Turn around."

The janitor complied but slowly. He turned to face them, revealing the front of his boiler suit bulging with concealed objects.

Clare stepped out from behind the protection of the wall and the janitor's face changed from disbelief to a snarl, his jaw jutting forward.

"Open your suit," Tina ordered. "Do it now. Slow and deliberate. Don't give my man here a reason to shoot."

The eyes emptied of anything resembling humanity as all reason fled the man. The janitor reached to the zipper of his suit with his free hand, still supporting the load with his left forearm and jerked with twitching movements. Nothing happened.

Smiling, staring right at Clare, he grabbed the material to either side of the caught zip and tugged.

Chapter Thirty-Three

For the second time in under an hour, Clare retched. This time there was nothing left to come up. The torn boiler suit spilled more body parts to the floor. Two hands, one still attached to an arm, ears, a small foot, broken bones and sinew tied in a knot. Clare couldn't look away. She had no energy to move.

The ARC agents didn't suffer from the same affliction, leaping forward to take hold of the janitor's arms, wrenching them behind his back as they shoved him up against the door to the morgue. He didn't appear to care. The whole time they manhandled him his eyes fixed on her. It was the steely gaze of a predator, not the defeated visage of a doomed man. Another hand had caught in his zip and hung there until gravity claimed it and the hunk of flesh dropped atop the rest.

"He has a key," said Tina, who had remained beside Clare, her gun trained on the man. "Take it." She turned to Clare. "What do you want to do with him?"

"We can't throw him in a cell, not yet. If we do that, this place is so corrupt he'll be released within the hour."

The janitor chuckled; a soft sound but a triumphant one nonetheless.

"That's right, you keep on laughing, smiler. You're going down forever." From the way she gripped her gun, the wide eyes and the grimace, the situation threatened to get to Tina. She was terrified and trying hard not to show it.

"I don't think so," the janitor countered, indicating the grotesque scene on the floor. "I am Legion. I am many. You cannot stop the moon. You cannot stop darkness. It is inevitable." He stared straight at Clare, taking a deep breath and tipping his head back in pleasure. "Ahhh, pear drops: My favourite. Some things you cannot stop. Some people are destined to be free, some to die."

"Which are you?"

"I'm free, do you not see this? Incarcerate me. He will release me. He always does. There's a war coming and I've chosen my side."

The janitor watched her now. Not cocky, just certain. As twisted as the man obviously was, he had accepted his fate if not embraced it wholly.

Clare tightened hold on the plastic sheath, ready to remove it and end the creature for good. As she did, Helen approached from the direction of the janitor's basement refuge. It had become a full-on crime scene by the looks of the people coming and going. She couldn't do this now, not among all these people. She slipped the syringe back into its case, clicking the plastic shut and tucking it into a pocket. A few people followed Helen. Clare recognized Mike Caruso among the number, oversized suit flapping about him like the blue robes of some distant eastern nomad. It didn't matter if they saw her now. This was out in the open.

"What the hell?" The detective stared at the mess on the floor, not having recognized Clare in her disguise. She kept her head down.

"We'll need his clothes as evidence," Helen advised.

The ARC agents donned latex gloves, peeling the outer garment from the janitor. Underneath his vest and boxer shorts were bloodstained. Clare turned away as they stripped the man of all decency as well as clothing, only turning back once she was sure he had donned the two-piece orange prison uniform provided. He looked undaunted by the treatment. In fact to Clare he appeared expectant, holding his cuffed hands out toward Caruso.

"No. Not this time," Caruso said, not making a move toward the man.

Not the expected acquiescence. The janitor's eyes hardened. "The Captain... my cousin..."

"Will be informed in due course," Clare said aloud, causing Caruso to turn and stare at her as if seeing her there for the first time. "We already have you linked to him by DNA results. It's only a matter of time until crime scene evidence is re-examined to link him further. Tell me, where have you been the last few days? Holden, perhaps?"

"You..." Caruso pulled his gun on her. "You're under arrest..."

"Oh Mike, don't be an idiot." Tina reached out and pushed his gun down. "You know as well as anybody what's going on here. The fact that you addressed him the way you did speaks volumes about whether you're implicated."

Caruso frowned, holstering his weapon. "You think it ends with this? He's done this before though not for about ten years. Last time I was there to conceal him. Looks like this time he's not so lucky."

The hardened eyes of the janitor filled with rage and he leapt at Caruso, hands clawed.

Caruso stepped to one side, knocking the man down on his face where several officers pounced on him. The tide was turning.

"Wait," Clare cried, "stop it. Show me his arm."

One of her colleagues stepped back, revealing the elaborate tattoo on his right forearm. Inked blue and white, it appeared to be letters in a foreign language.

"I can't read it," Tina said, stooping to stare at the pinioned arm.

"I doubt anybody here could. It's South American, derived from the Incan language. It means 'Viruñas'."

"How do you know this?" Caruso asked.

"Research, detective. There's a monster out there draining people dry, and this guy's hacking up the corpses for his own sick pleasure."

Caruso looked at her like she was mad. "These are murders, plain and simple. There's a killer out there. A man."

"Mike, stop kidding yourself," Tina urged. "You've worked for Harley long enough. What Clare says is true." Tina spoke loud enough so the growing crowd could hear. "The samples are a matter of public record, certified by our own forensics team. You're all welcome to examine them."

"So it comes back to you," Clare said to the janitor. "What are you: Some kind of freakish ghoul? A Viruñas wannabe? His personal wet-nurse, cleaning up his leavings?"

"All of the above," he responded, his eyes still passionate. Whatever this man's problems were, a fierce belief shone from his face. "He's promised me eternal glory if I but serve him." He cackled. "My cousin too; we serve at his behest."

"I think you can put him in a cell now," Tina decided. "We need to pay the captain a visit."

At the back of the crowd, a detective, one of Harley's from what Clare could recall, began to back away toward the stairwell. "Stop that man!" she shouted.

Several of those nearest turned to pursue him, only to find that as soon as he reached the stairwell, he was forced back in; two more ARC agents, automatic rifles raised and aimed at his head, followed him through.

"This situation is contained, Dr. Rosser. You'd best go give the captain the good news before the word spreads."

Mute, Clare nodded. Had she won?

Her heart still pounding, nerves shattered, Clare stumbled away from the scene, pulling herself up the stairs, her failing body resisting with pain. Her legs were burning by the time she had climbed to the office level. Her heart felt ready to give out. *Please, not yet.*

Feigning a strength she lacked, Clare strode down the hallway. Those that recognized her despite the boiler suit stood back; her two ARC agents were close behind and they were not to be messed with. Not this night.

Throwing the door to his office open, Clare stormed inside, the anger she felt at such a desecration overriding her natural cautious nature. The door crashed against the wall, the noise hurting her ears, and closed on the rebound.

"What the hell do you think you're doing, man?" Harley asked, the shock in his voice betraying his ire at the intrusion. He placed the phone back in its cradle.

He hadn't recognized her. She removed the baseball cap and threw it onto his desk. "I might ask you the same question," Clare retorted. "Did you think that you could carry on covering your tracks for all this time and nobody would notice? Or did you seriously believe that the people in this station, this city, even this county would remain blind to the facts?" Clare wanted to throw it all in his face before he had a chance to gather his wits. *You sly sonofabitch; How dare you. How DARE you abuse the trust of those that rely on you as a leader?*

Harley leaned back, dispassionate, his face hiding any surprise. "Well, well, well... I think the only fact here, Miss Rosser, is that you have overstepped the mark for the last time. I know about the FBI file."

Clare stared at him and just for a moment the captain began to sneer. This inflamed her more. She balled a fist. The best defense was a good offense. "Congratulations. I know about Detective Logan. I've been to Ashby, and despite your puppet captain's best efforts, I got to the truth. I know about the connection to the janitor, your cousin. The detestable individual who dismembered those kids, accounted for my parents, and just spilled somebody else's guts on the floor downstairs. Logan knew this too, but he's not in a position to tell the tale. I have proof that will attest to all of this."

Clare gauged the captain's response as she delivered this blow. She was in her element now and he was getting angrier by the second. *You come at me and you have nothing. Logic is cold. Merciless. Absolute.* She licked her lips, feeling the dry skin cracking under her tongue; she was so thirsty, so tired. Some things were more important than health. A resolution required resolve. The cold lucidity of facts fought inside her with the tight knot of anger she maintained. The best combination was a balance of both.

The captain stood, stepping round his desk with the confidence of a predator stalking trapped prey. He was a good six inches taller than her, an imposing man to stand off against despite his age and burgeoning weight. Harley leaned over her, his mouth by her ear. She could smell the stale reek of sweat, the soured cologne. His muscles were taut, straining to reach for her. He was afraid.

"You listen to me, you insignificant little bitch. You will hand over the folder regarding your parents, now. You will give me any evidence you believe pertains to the link between my cousin and I, as well as all documentation you have on Logan. If you do not, I won't turn you over to the Feds. I have a select group of friends who will make your sterile lab downstairs seem like a five star palace compared to the pit in which you will end up. And you won't be alone. They will violate you in every way known to man and a few more that are not. They will keep you alive, suffering until you no longer remember who you are, only that pain is your only comfort and oblivion is denied you. That is my promise. Now give me those files."

Clare's heart thumped in her chest. The pressure Harley's intimidation put on her threatened to make her lose control and pee herself. "You make a good argument," she conceded, stepping back.

Harley stepped after, backing her into the one corner of his office where there were no windows. She had heard tales of this office and the spurious reasons Harley had never moved to better quarters more befitting his rank. If she wasn't careful, Clare was going to become one of those tales. *Just try it,* she dared him.

"The files..."

"...are not here. You honestly think I would risk myself by bringing them to your office? Your cousin is downstairs surrounded by the body parts he pillaged from the morgue. Sooner or later someone down there is going to wonder why their vaunted captain isn't making it his concern."

There it was; the killer blow. Her opponent flinched as his mind processed the information. Harley punched the wall beside her head, his fist smashing straight through the plasterboard to the bricks behind.

Clare covered her mouth from the dust. "You might want to watch that temper. The files are safe. You touch me at all, and they go where you can't. I would get used to tight quarters, Andrew."

Harley smiled, tipping his face so he could stare down her blouse. She felt the warmth of his breath, the eagerness of his hands to touch her.

"You are turning into a scrawny little wretch but I'll still make use of you." He turned to leave; her bluff had failed and the captain knew it. "Your files are exactly where you stored them, in the detachable drawer base in your office. Don't for a second think that I don't know every single thing that goes on in my precinct."

I'm counting on it.

Outside the office there was a commotion, many bodies pressed together in the narrow corridor, dark uniforms blocking the rare gap Harley had allowed in his window blinds. With a satisfied smile at her, Harley reached for the door, stepping back as it was opened for him. Satisfaction turned to confusion. "Chief Goldsmith..."

"Mr Harley," an elderly gentleman walked into the room. His stooped frame held ample sagging skin, enough to show that this man was once full of vigour and vitality in his younger days. The old chief had been big and strong, a real leader among men. He had been a legend. Even in his current state, wearing a Worcester P.D. baseball cap and a green and white polo shirt, he was still a force to be reckoned with. Keen blue eyes shone out from beneath shaggy white eyebrows, the goatee on his chin just as snowy. Behind him several officers waited. For the first time in her life, Clare saw real doubt on the face of the captain.

"Mister?"

"That's right."

"What are you doing here?"

The chief nodded at Clare, who smiled in response. He perched on the edge of the desk as if standing were too much effort and pointed at Harley. "I'm removing you from your position, Andrew. It's come to my attention that your endeavours in this department no longer align with what we stand for. I have the authority to remove you should I see fit to do so."

"Stan, you can't do this," Harley hissed.

"I *am* doing this, Andrew. Don't make it any harder than it has to be."

"I get a board of review. Due process requires that I…"

"We're leaving the board of review and your cronies out of this one, son. You're being placed under arrest."

Harley's eyes narrowed. "On what charge?"

The chief shrugged. "Larceny, corruption, homicide. Take your pick. Cuff him."

Two officers Clare had never seen before entered the room. They were outsiders; untouched by the sour taint of Harley's push for power.

With rapid jerks of his head, Harley frowned, looking like he sought an escape, but his own trap of an office held him now and the chief had positioned himself right where Harley's gun sat on the desk. There was no way out. Harley turned back to Clare, raising his hands.

"Don't, sir."

Harley paused, his head turning even as he reached for her, hands murderous, ready to squeeze the life from her. One of the officers pointed a gun at him; face calm, ready to fire if he even twitched.

It was at that point the resistance bled out. Harley shook his head, pushing at the inside of his cheek with his tongue. He'd been beaten and he knew it. The officers moved in and cuffed him. All the while he stared at her, his gaze very much like that of his cousin. The rage seethed under his mottled skin as the pair led him away.

Harley paused at the door. "It's a shame about your imminent illness. You should get that looked at. However, not everybody realizes the bloodwork is in fact yours, not your brother's. Your closest friend can be your worst nightmare. You're dead, you hear me? Dead!" He glared through the window at her as he was led away.

Clare stood alone with the chief in the office as the information sank in. "The janitor isn't the monster," she said to the chief. "He's known that all along. He knows who it really is."

"Maybe," the old man agreed. "Young lady, even this old man can see you're not well. Why don't you get that looked at?"

Clare's phone began to ring. Several people all calling at once.

Chapter Thirty-Four

Terrick, Helen, Tina. Who to answer first? "I'd better get these, sir," Clare said with respect to the chief.

"Please go ahead, my dear girl. You look like a woman with a lot on your mind."

If only you knew. "Hello, Helen? Tell me you got something."

"What else do you need from this slaughterhouse? There's enough analysis to be done down here to keep us busy 'till Judgement Day. Did you ever come across anything about your intended target being a shooter?"

"I never found anything specifically, why?"

"Are you done up there? You might want to come back down to the forensics lab, take a peek."

The old man gave the appearance of a mother hen hovering over a fledgling brood, as if reluctant or unsure as to whether to let them free. "Nothing that can't wait, young lady," he said with a smile.

"On my way," Clare said and turned the phone off.

"One thing, if I may," Chief Goldsmith said, holding his hand out to stop her. "You like this office?"

Clare stared back past the chief, at this remnant of an episode she hoped to forget. The tar stains on the walls, the grimy window, the thick, claustrophobic nature of looming walls. "No sir. I hate it. These offices should be torn down and refitted. The longer you give decay its freedom, the deeper it digs in. Sometimes a total clean out is the only way to get rid of all the vermin." Clare smiled at the old man, who nodded thoughtfully as he digested her words, and left him alone.

She descended once again into the belly of the beast, gripping the rail in the stairwell until she felt as though her hands would cramp up. The halls were still buzzing; this was a city in chaos and work remained to be done.

"There you are," Helen said as Clare pushed the glass door of the forensics lab open, the weight almost too much for the strength in her arms. "Let me show you what I've got."

Helen led her over to a counter where the team had begun to sort through the evidence. Items that had already been bagged and tagged sat in a series of evidence boxes. Helen reached into the middle of the pile and pulled out a long wrapped black object with a grunt.

"You found a rifle?"

"Not just any rifle. This is a Tango fifty-one long range rifle. One the professionals use. We are talking SWAT teams. We tested the janitor for G.S.R. and he checks out. He doesn't even want to deny it. He seems sort of proud."

"I was shot at recently," Clare mused. "That would make all sorts of sense. Why don't we know his name?"

"It's not on any record we can find, Clare. It's like he doesn't exist."

"I found a crime scene cleaner ID in his room labeled 'Juan Mendez'," Clare supplied. "We could ask his cousin if that's him." Clare took the gun, the weakness in her arms causing her to unbalance as the weight of the weapon burdened her. "However I think Harley is less than likely to talk."

She placed the rifle back amidst the bags on the desk. "There is no conclusion, it seems, only the next dead end."

"There were also these..." Helen picked out a bag and tossed it to Clare. Clare turned the bag over in her hands, the plastic pliable enough to feel the thin brown discs inside. "Are these what I think they are?"

The Eyes Have No Soul

"We've haven't done any more than bag them but they look like they've been cut from a cactus and dried."

"Look up the Peyote cactus. It's a source of natural mescaline. Our janitor was a fanboy for the real killer."

"And you're sure this is not him? It's pretty damning."

"It's meant to be. Yet this time last night, I was face to face with the real thing."

Clare walked over to the water dispenser and poured a cup, swallowing it in one go. It wasn't enough. She took another and a third. By the time she had a fourth cup in hand, Helen laid her arm over Clare's, preventing her downing the drink.

"The thirst just won't go away."

"You need to get back to hospital, love." The compassion in Helen's face was without pretence. There could be no stopping her though. It was still out there.

Hospital. Terrick.

Clare pulled her phone out. She had totally forgotten about the sheriff. He had called several times, a sequence of missed calls on the screen of her phone blotting out any sign of Tina having called. She was close by. Terrick must have wanted something real bad. Clare pressed call back.

"Where you been, girl?"

"I'm sorry, Terrick. It's gotten very busy round here. We're caught in a deluge of incident and evidence."

"Well we got information that might just prove critical, given where you are. We've finished lookin' over the security footage. One guy did come onto the ward. He didn't leave."

"It wasn't the janitor," Clare said.

"I know. This guy had a blue hoodie on but he turned just for a second. It was enough for the nurse who was watchin' with me to ID him. She described him as the guy who plays and I quote 'Awesome guitar at the Lucky Dog'."

Clare struggled to think. An innocent invitation to the open-mike night the week before gained a darker meaning. "Go on…"

"She said somethin' like Dean Ascobar. She couldn't be sure."

Everything slammed into place. Clare's mind became totally lucid. Every memory she retained; every stolen glance at him from other women as well as her own covetous looks. The recollection hit her with a pain she wasn't prepared for. Clare dropped to her knees, spilling the phone on the floor.

"Clare. Clare?" Terrick continued.

Gasping, she scooped up the phone. "Daniel. Daniel Acosador."

"Yeah, that was the name. You know him?"

"He's our M.E. here at the precinct. You sure he never came back out?"

"Been over all the footage myself. The man was the only one in before the young lady was found. Girl, you think that's him?"

Those smiling eyes and the cut of his jaw covered by that raggedy beard. The way he had spoken straight to her soul that night as he played. It couldn't be. "I'll have to look into it. Terrick, thanks for calling. Just remain there a little while longer. Those people need you."

Clare stared at the phone before finding Tina's number. As ill as she was and as weary, she just didn't feel like sleeping. Maybe it was survival instinct pushing her body beyond its limits; if she fell asleep now she might never wake up.

"Tina."

"I was about to come get you, Clare. You need to get to the morgue like right now. Bring Helen too."

Still clad in the boiler suit, Clare stumbled back to the morgue, Helen catching her several times as her legs gave way. The human remains had already been removed from the confrontation with the janitor. All that was left consisted of bloody marks and a weak iron tang in the air. The doors were wedged open, a series of Clare's fellow crime scene analysts moving about the morgue ahead of her, white clean-suits merging their outlines with the bright white of the walls.

She smiled in greeting as several acknowledged her presence. "What is it?" she asked Tina.

The detective came over and hugged her. "If only we'd known earlier."

"What? Known what?"

"I've spoken to Sheriff Heckstall. Believe me when I say his assertion as to the identity of this thing looks beyond contestation now."

Clare's stomach tightened. Deep down she had still hoped they were wrong.

"First, we have these." Tina led them over to the storage units and pulled open two. "These bodies are missing certain vital parts. I believe you found them earlier."

"That doesn't tell us anything," Clare countered.

"Look closer," Tina advised, pulling the slab all the way out.

Clare did as bidden, her eyes scanning up what was left of the headless corpse until she saw very familiar markings. Red and puckered, the upper arm scars showed evidence of recent violent conduct but the skin torn, flesh missing. "Did he do this too?"

"It would make sense if he did. He has a fixation on the creature that borders on hero-worship and would be an obvious culprit given the other mutilations. I was arriving at the same conclusion but then I had a look at the security footage."

Tina took them from the cold storage to the far side of the room, where a series of instruments and scopes surrounded by Plexiglas hoods sat alongside softly-whirring computers. "Watch this." She typed in a code and set footage to playing. The room was empty to begin with. Nothing untoward that Clare could see. She leaned forward on the desk, hot despite the chill of the room.

A man appeared on the screen, clad in a blue hoodie with the hood drawn up. He stumbled around, his head bowed. "Daniel," Clare said, "If that's the same hoodie he wore in UMASS."

Another joined him, this man wearing a blue boiler suit. "The janitor," Helen added. "We pulled his security badge and did some checking. He's been out a lot over the past few days. For hours at a time."

Clare recalled the image of the doorframe shattering next to her head as a bullet intended for her missed her by an inch. "He gets around."

Both men began to argue, the janitor waving his arms about with more animation than she'd ever seen. Acosador kept his head down but was no less passionate for it.

"Where's the sound?" Clare looked for an icon on the screen.

"There is none," Tina answered. "I've tried that already. It's been disabled. There are two other cameras in here; neither worked in months. This one isn't supposed to but it looks like it got repaired. There's a repair request in the log but it had no action against it. Watch this. It's where it gets real weird."

Daniel shoved the janitor away, storming over to the cold storage. Pulling one open, Daniel proceeded to uncover the body. Pulling his sleeves up, he grabbed the cadaver by the upper arms, leaning over them as he appeared to pulse. His whole body began to spasm in a frenetic manner. A moment later the janitor appeared with a third person to pull Daniel off of the corpse. The person was tall, bordering on corpulent.

"Harley," said Helen.

"So it appears," Clare agreed. "He's well and truly screwed now."

On the screen the two cousins wrenched Daniel off the body, marks left in the flesh of the upper arms. Daniel turned toward them, his face exposed just for a second as he argued with Harley.

Clare gasped. "Last night, the assault; it was him."

Tina hit the pause button. Acosador's face was emaciated, bereft of flesh just as Clare's own had become. What had been a proud beard now hung off his face in dense patches. His lips were drawn back, teeth bared but what stood out were his eyes. They were completely without colour, white as if he had rolled them back in his head. In the bright light of the morgue there was no luminescence but it didn't matter. The eyes in the dark shone at her. Given the frame of a face, Clare became terrified, stepping away.

She lurched over to one of the desks, supporting the weight of her body with her hands as she gasped. "Daniel is Viruñas? All this time we've been working with him and he's that... that creature?"

"A desperate creature by the looks of it," Tina observed.

Helen just stared at the picture, uncomprehending. "That's not real. It is a trick of the light? I've known him for years."

"It is real," Clare countered. "I saw him last night. He tried to feed on me; he killed another trying to feed on them. We'll fill you in soon, Helen. Harley is guilty of a great many misdemeanours but he didn't kill my parents. This did. It hunts diabetics for the sugar in their blood. Moreover he hunts undiagnosed patients because of the sky-high concentrations."

"Is that why..? Oh Clare, what are you doing?"

"I'm bait. I'm the only option they have to stop the monster before it disappears again."

"I might be able to help with that," Tina provided. She sped the film up, while the janitor and Harley fought the creature as it assaulted more corpses. After a while all three moved away, toward the very computer that they were now watching the footage on. "The camera doesn't pick up which of these computers they used but something here caused this:" On screen Acosador hurried across the camera's view, while Harley and his cousin remained behind.

Clare looked at the bank of instruments. "Three computers; take one each. There's something on here that shows where he went."

Clare took the computer on the right, next to Tina. Logging in revealed no information of use. Recent files used only pertained to recent victims and their medical reports. Before long, Clare looked away. "I've got nothing."

"I've got something here, Clare," Helen said as she squinted at the screen. "Do you have a brother called Jeff?"

Clare closed her eyes, swallowing. "I do. However I didn't submit my bloods under my name."

Helen turned the screen toward her. 'Jeff Rosser' shone out at the top of the screen. "There are some seriously elevated blood glucose levels here. Do you think Daniel knows they aren't yours?"

"Not everybody realizes the bloodwork is in fact yours, not your brother's..." Clare quoted Harley's words from their confrontation upstairs. Her stomach began to tie itself in knots. "Tina, get the car. Harley's sent it after Jeff."

Chapter Thirty-Five

The twenty minutes it took to reach Tina's car, hurtle through Worcester and out toward Holden at breakneck speed still counted among the slowest Clare had ever experienced. While she was suffering heavily from the resurgence of diabetic symptoms, these were in some way allayed by the adrenaline and unbridled levels of panic she experienced for her brother.

There had been no chance to bring anybody else. Clare hoped Helen would convince some of her newfound fan club that there was a serious emergency. None of it mattered. Not now.

They reached Holden, the street lighting guiding the way. Fortunately the roads were empty. It was a Sunday night, after all. Friendly's was still open. Nearly time to shut up for the night.

"You want me to pull in there?" Tina asked.

"I'm fine," Clare lied. "We need to get to Jeff." Tina drove slower now, more cautious. It wouldn't do to have an escort of sirens when trying to catch a monster. Or Daniel; that she had been alone with him so recently caused her to shiver with revulsion. Was he testing her? Tasting her?

Clare fingered the insulin syringe as they crept along Pleasant Street.

"You could use a little of that," Tina suggested.

Clare held the syringe up to the occasional street light, the glow refracting through the syringe, sending flashes of light across her field of vision. Or was that her brain warning her she was now on reserve power only? "No. It's for one purpose only. You heard Julian. Even if I could stick this in me, there's weeks' worth of insulin in there. How much is enough? I'd probably kill myself." She toyed with the syringe for a moment longer then replaced it in her suit. "No. It's a weapon, plain and simple."

They pulled up one house away, parking on the road in the darkness. In silence they watched her house from a distance. No lights were visible from inside, only the dim glow of a street lamp the other side of the railway crossing providing any contrast to the black of the trees. In what light there was, the vines on the walls made the house look scabrous and diseased. Appropriate. Her eyes adjusted to the darkness and Clare noticed the front door, the way moonlight glinted off the window. The angle was wrong. "It's been left ajar. He's in there." Clare began to unbuckle her belt.

"I've got to draw Daniel away from Jeff. He'll be able to detect my scent. He'll go crazy for it when he does, if what the hospital gave me hasn't ruined it all. I want you downstairs as backup. If I get a chance, I'll stab him with the syringe. If he makes it downstairs we've got no option but to fight. He's got to be away from my brother before we do that so I want you to cover the front door. Jeff's safety is paramount. If Daniel makes it downstairs first, shoot him."

As Tina joined her beside the car, Clare stood for a moment, watching her house. Late September, the air was still mild, the scent heavy with the onset of fall and the promise of rebirth, of closing down to grow anew. Clare flexed her right hand, willing blood into it. Breaking open the plastic case, she discarded it, along with the sheath from the syringe. She mouthed a silent prayer that she would have the strength to act with speed and rapid decision. That being done, she nodded at Tina and moved forward into the looming threat of her own home. Her one refuge, her one place of safety had become a potential death trap. A car was parked far along her own drive, door open, warning light pulsing steadily and making a faint 'bling-bling'. Clare prayed he hadn't been there long or it would be too late. With one glance back at where she perceived Tina to be in the darkness, Clare reached the front door. She paused, touching the area around the lock. A lance of pain shot through her hand and she recoiled, the step back nearly unbalancing her. Clare held her forefinger up, several splinters piercing the flesh. *Forced. It's in here.*

The wooden frame had been wrenched apart. Clare ran her hands around the door, finding a series of evenly-spaced scorings. Five of them, as if made by hands.

Pushing the door as slowly as possible, she prayed tonight wasn't the night the hinges rebelled. It wasn't.

Stepping into the blackness of her house, Clare waited to let her eyes adjust. Something brushed her leg. Clare clamped her teeth, holding in a scream. Kneeling down, she gathered her cat into her arms, hugging him, praying he remained silent. Although glad to see her, his body was tense. He nuzzled her then wriggled to escape. He never did that. Clare let him go, shoving the tortoiseshell cat out through the door.

There was nobody she could see in the living room, so she checked the kitchen. Dishes showed Jeff had been using the house, though there were more out than he would have needed. Touching the back door, Clare found it unlocked but closed.

She nodded in the darkness. *Where else would this trap lead me but upstairs? Take a deep breath, Clare.*

She moved by touch. With her head beginning to spin she leaned on the walls, taking slow, deliberate steps. Every memory she could recall of creaking floorboards became a mental map in the darkness.

Her right foot touched the bottom stair. She paused. There was no noise from above. That didn't mean she was alone. Clare began to climb the stairs, putting gentle pressure on each. Her thighs burned with the effort.

She turned the corner. Her heart fluttered in her mouth. A sidelight had been left on in Jeff's bedroom. A body lay there, unmoving, lying at a crooked angle.

Clare paused. Her eyes drank in what light there was. *That's not Jeff. It's too small.*

Clare crept along the landing. She knelt down beside the body. It was a woman. *So that's what he's been doing with his time.* A quick touch of the neck revealed no heartbeat yet there were no marks on the arms. Time for regret would come later, if Clare survived.

She looked up. A sibilant whispering, almost crooning, came from the bedroom, so faint she couldn't understand what was being said. Her legs tensed to run, Clare tested the syringe on the back of her hand. One fat drop, probably a day's worth of insulin, splashed her skin.

Leaning to the door, Clare tried to look in the room. Someone was in there. Daniel. He was propped over the bed, his hands pushing down on something. Jeff.

"Rest, my pretty; enjoy your final dream." The murmuring was hypnotic. "Soon you will sleep the deep sleep, as will I…"

Jeff moaned, trying to twist.

"Rest easy," Daniel encouraged his victim, leaning over to whisper in Jeff's ear. "Your lover lies well beside you, safe in your arms."

Daniel's shoulders tensed, arms pushing down on Jeff's shoulders. "What? Your blood is normal! There's nothing wrong with you. They… they lied. Harley and that bitch cousin wannabe of his." He threw his head back in anguish. "Lord Iuvart, what have you done?"

Shoulders cracked and reshaped as Daniels arms grew longer. Pale flesh surrounded by a nimbus of insipid light extended from the sleeves of the hoodie. "I'll finish him anyway…" Daniel stopped and sniffed. "Ah, I sense the truth in their plan. This house reeks of a diabetic. Welcome home, Clare."

The sniff became a deep, languorous breathing. He didn't move from Jeff, who began to convulse beneath him. "Your brother doesn't have long; if you want to do something to change his situation I suggest you act with haste."

What am I doing? Clare pushed the door wider, stepping into Jeff's bedroom. Jeff twisted and thrashed in his mescaline-induced nightmare.

Daniel turned to regard her. Bright, fevered eyes pierced through hair hanging loose and damp across his face. The skin was drawn tight across his cheekbones, making his face narrower. Lips devoid of moisture were cracked, withdrawn and showing teeth more like fangs. His skin cracked as he spoke. "I will drain him," he said, "unless you offer me an alternative. It won't be painless and agreeable. My venom only works for so long. You know. You've tasted it."

"Desperate times," Clare replied, her voice cautious. His every word beguiled her. "Leave him be, Daniel. Haven't you had enough of my family?"

Daniel grinned, teeth sticking out from withdrawn gums making his face even more skeletal. "Clever girl. You worked it out."

"I thought you were attracted to me. Am I nothing more to you than a meal?"

"I want a trade; your life for his, voluntarily. I don't move until you lay down beside him to take his place. Think quickly. Each second wasted sucks his life away and his end will be agonizing. They are normally dead when I feed but you and yours robbed me of that opportunity." Daniel's hands and forearms flexed as he drew on the fluid in Jeff's body. Jeff cried out in mescaline-laced pain.

Clare stepped fully into the room, opening the door all the way. "Okay, okay. Let him go and I'll take his place; my life for his."

Daniel grinned, his top lip rising above his teeth as if scenting the air about her. He began to drool in anticipation. The eyes glowed brighter. "Oh, you're so sweet. I've watched you for a long time, and to conclude it here, how poetic."

"How do I know you'll keep your end of the bargain?"

A slow smile crept across Daniel's face. "You don't."

Clare stepped closer. Her scent, the aroma of an untreated diabetic, appeared to be driving him to distraction. He leaned toward her, even as he kept his hands pressed on Jeff.

Exhaling in his direction, Clare hoped it would throw him off balance. It did, his head stretching toward her in a slow, deliberate motion, the bones in his neck clicking as the vertebrae fought to stay aligned. As his muscles went taught, she threw everything into launching herself at him, the syringe raised like a dagger in her left hand, ready to stab.

As quick as she was, Daniel was quicker, lashing out with his left hand and blocking her blow. Off balance, she fell to the floor, the syringe sent spinning back out onto the landing. Crashing down, she rolled to her knees only to find Daniel already above her, hands clawed.

His hair swept aside, Clare now gazed up into the withered mask of the man she once knew, the monster taking over. Luminous white eyes stared right through her as it prepared to feed. Running its hands down her neck, it came to hold her shoulders, caressing her as a lover might do. It climbed atop her, legs pinning hers to the floor as they began to extend. Clare tried to scream and he clamped a hand across her open mouth. She gagged as the fleshy sucker began to detach from its palm right inside her mouth.

"Hush now. You missed your chance," it said, his voice dripping triumph. "Now I get both of you."

Clare began to hyperventilate, rapid shallow pants coming quickly as she foresaw her own end.

The creature smiled, cracked skin dropping onto her face. It withdrew its hand from her mouth, the arm stretching, growing thinner as the bone within lengthened. The fleshy sucker, fully extended, brushed across her face, sucking at her skin. "Too late for you, now," it croaked.

Viruñas squeezed her shoulders, its unnaturally sharp nails digging into her flesh.

Clare cried out. But there was no repeat of Saint Vincent's. No drug lanced into her arm like the night before.

A confused look passed across the face of the creature above her, as if this had never happened before. "What is this?"

"Looks like you're out of juice, Dan." With bent fingers she punched the creature in the throat.

Viruñas fell back, grabbing its neck. A viscous fluid leaked from between the bony claws. Was it the creature's own, or fluid from her brother? Clare lurched to her feet, stumbling onto the landing, looking for the syringe. Viruñas reached out with one hand, attempting to grab her ankle. It missed and sprawled on the floor. If the syringe was broken it meant her life was at an end. There was no sign of it. She held onto the bannister as she descended. Clare heard the creature get to its feet, stalking her from above. Odd guttural noises came from the landing, the floorboards creaking. An appendage scraped along the top of the bannister, curved claws appearing over the edge.

Clare stumbled down the final step, tripping in the dark and landing front-first on her outstretched hands. Reaching out to try and raise herself up, her hand touched something cylindrical and cold; the syringe. It was still in one piece.

"If you want me, come get me," Clare challenged. She was met with a croaking roar as the creature lost its poise. It reached the top of the staircase and began to descend, its breath rattling in its chest.

There was only one thing for it. Get out of the house.

Tina emerged from the shadows, waving Clare into the kitchen with her gun.

The creature reached the top step, bone clicking on wood as it began to descend. Clare pointed at the doorway, urging Tina back, holding the syringe up. She wasn't finished yet.

Tina shook her head, turning and pointing the gun up the stairs. "Go," she urged, and fired.

The roar changed to a scream, the creature still descending.

"Go!" Tina shouted again, firing off more shots.

What choice did she have? The creature needed to be led away from her brother. Clare headed to the kitchen, and out the back door.

Clare stumbled through her garden, heading for the only place dark enough to hide from the monster. Two more shots were fired behind her and then silence.

Clare paused, waiting. When Tina failed to appear she pushed through bushes and out onto the abandoned railway, following the rusted metal as it led into the incomplete tunnel. Viruñas still followed her trail. Maybe in the pitch black she had a chance.

Clare climbed over the rotten, wooden boards that had once been nailed across to keep the curious out, scrambling across the dirt beyond as she lost balance and fell into the tunnel. She paused, listening for any sound or pursuit. The kitchen door creaked shut. Viruñas was in her garden. Guided forward by the glint of light reflecting from mineral specks in the wall, she pressed deeper into the tunnel. Clare held on to the image of Viruñas atop Jeff. This was all for her brother now. Pushing her hands out in front only gave rise to more aching. Her stomach pulsed, her eyes stung.

The floor was uneven. Clare stumbled, shredding her knees until she found what she wanted: A pile of rubble excavated by her and Jeff in their younger, more adventurous days. It was a marker for a hole in the wall just beyond to the right. Crouching, ignoring the pain burning in her thighs, Clare searched for the wall with her hands. *Maybe it's too dark for him too.*

The hole was only a foot square, chiselled from the rock by whoever constructed the tunnel. It should have been too small for her. She lay down and pushed forward, scraping the sides as she passed. Beyond the hole was only a couple of feet high. She curled up and waited, her senses attuned to the dark, the syringe held like a dagger across the front of her legs. She wasn't scared. If Viruñas didn't find her, she would die anyway. Her time felt close.

"More sport than your parents," croaked Viruñas from the entrance of tunnel. The remaining boards groaned as they were ripped asunder. The monster was inside. "They just lay there, like a couple of honey ants ready to be popped. Those are my favourite type. You know how I found them? Your captain; he kept me fed. Information and bodies. It's funny how someone reacts when you threaten their family. I have hunted, and hidden within the body of this being for many lifetimes. There is no way to conceal your presence from me." There was a scraping noise. It was close. She could hear the rattle of its breath as it neared. Then the breathing stopped.

Clare peered at the entrance to her hiding place, waiting for the glow. Nothing. She pushed back from the gap, flattening herself against the back wall, trying to make herself as difficult to reach as she could.

The Eyes Have No Soul

She listened as something reached through the hole, scraping the floor as it searched around. Slow at first, then with increasing frequency. Clare tried to arch herself up, bracing her feet on each side of the hole. Pain lanced through her right ankle as something sharp snagged it. She screamed.

"I know all the tricks," said a guttural voice from the other side of the wall and extracted her from the hole like a winkle from its shell. Clare thrashed about, mindless of the damage she was doing to her body, but Viruñas had her now. Blind panic overcame her and she kicked out, snapping her captor's bones. The creature paused, the sound of the broken bones resetting in a series of small clicks. She tried to sit up. Viruñas yanked on her foot, scraping against her ankle and she nearly passed out. Nearly, but not quite.

Clare was dragged deeper into the tunnel. The syringe dangled from her hand. She managed to hook her pinkie through the circular grip as she was pulled over a mound of loose rubble, the stones scoring her back as they reached the rock face where the workmen had finished digging. She was picked up and dumped onto another pile of rubble, lying prone as the creature made a rustling noise. She realized it was removing its clothing with slow deliberateness, shedding any remaining link it might have to its humanity. The eyes began to glow a sickly white and she realized it could see in the dark. There had never been any chance of concealment.

Breath rattled close to her face, the scent of strong, rotting fruit. A blinding white light lit up the tunnel, dazzling Clare. She held her right hand up, shielding her eyes. Viruñas stood above her, naked, glowing, its body wraithlike and thin, muscles tight across its shoulders, non-existent in the extremities as the limbs stretched long and thin, needle-like. Across the surface of its body, more pads like those on its hands were puckered, ready to absorb the fluid left in her body.

The creature leaned in. "I thirst. You denied me two meals now. You'll not deny me a third."

"You truly are a monster."

The soulless eyes glowed brighter with anticipation. Viruñas leaned forward and for the third time, talons pierced her skin. Clare screamed as the nails tore into her arms, the pain flaring through her without Mescaline to dull the sensation. Viruñas lowered, preparing to make full contact with her body, the puckered scars sticking out, eager to absorb.

Fur flashed by, a tail whipping the side of Clare's head. Steve the cat launched from a pile of rubble straight at Viruñas' face. Claws flashed and the tortoiseshell grabbed hold of the creature's head, digging in.

Viruñas reared back screaming, arms ripping from her shoulders, the abrasive pads taking skin with them. With a roar it ripped the cat from its face and hurled Steve down the tunnel.

Clare thrust up with the syringe. As Viruñas turned back she stabbed it where the heart should have been on a man, insulin filling the creature.

Viruñas stared down at the syringe, uncomprehending. "What have you done?"

Triumphant, Clare replied, "I've cured you, Daniel. Let's just call it vengeance."

Viruñas slammed her back down on the cold rubble. Her vision swam as unconsciousness reached for her. "What… have… you..?" The glowing face began to lose its light, the skin sagging. The creature tried to speak again but all that came out was a gurgle, incomprehensible and alien. Bubbles frothed in its mouth, liquid spilling out. White light faded to grey, the surface melting like hot wax. Viruñas collapsed atop her, the scars on its body pulling at her skin through her clothes wherever they made contact. The force lessened as the creature's body began to shut down. It let go of her arms and grabbed her face, putrefying flesh falling from its bones. The head moved closer. They were nose to nose. Clare couldn't even scream. The mask above her dissolved, the discharge running into her mouth and nose, leaving an elongated skull and two glowing eyes. The creature tried to growl but instead vomited a thick liquid onto her face. The jaw moved. Was it trying to laugh? Then the eyes faded and the skull toppled forward onto her chest. It was done. She closed her eyes, finding it harder and harder to draw breath. Oblivion awaited.

Chapter Thirty-Six

Clare stirred. The surface was no longer rocky and cold. Clare felt surrounded by soft warmth, comforting and reassuring. She drew breath. The pain was gone. The aches, the knots in her stomach, the fire in her veins. All vanished.

Aromas began to register in her mind; fresh linen, a pine scent, overtones of wood. She opened her eyes, finding herself in a panelled room, books perched high on shelves that reached up to the ceiling of the wall opposite.

"I thought I might be in Heaven," she groaned, closing her eyes again. "I'm in Ashby?"

"You're lucky you're anywhere," said Dominic.

Clare turned her head to the right, letting the pillow take the weight. She was just too cosy to try sitting up. Blue eyes under a mop of black hair regarded her with obvious relief. "Dominic. Hi."

"Welcome back," Dominic Holden said through a smile. "You're lucky to be here. You dropped into a hyperglycemic coma. Your blood sugar... well let's say your blood was more like syrup than liquid for a while there. How do you feel?"

"Numb," Clare admitted. "I don't really feel anything. How long was I out? How did I get here?"

"It's late Tuesday afternoon. You've been unconscious for a good thirty-six hours. When we found you, covered in bones and slime, you were already unconscious. You have Detective Svinsky to thank for that as well as a rather unique member of our team."

Confused by his enigmatic smile, Clare turned as he nodded in the direction of the doorway.

Tina stood there, smiling and holding on to a furry ball full of claws and purrs. "Nice to see you again," she said, depositing Steve on the bed.

In an instant Steve was up by her head, sniffing at her face. Evidently satisfied by what he found, he proceeded to rub the top of his head under her chin, nuzzling in to settle down beside her, his warmth so very welcome.

"He was outside the tunnel, yowling at the top of his voice," Tina said, taking Clare's good hand and holding it tight. When you didn't come out and no lights came on, I radioed for back up and went in myself. Your brother was…"

"No…" Clare pre-empted Tina's comment, her heart preparing to implode.

"Relax, he's fine. Just had an extended mescaline trip is all. It was out of his system by this morning. I can't say the same for his lady friend."

"She was dead when I got in there. Daniel…"

Clare closed her eyes. Twin orbs of white shone back at her in the darkness. "I guess the insulin worked."

"From what we can tell, the introduction of so much rapid-acting insulin didn't just bind blood sugar. It totally destabilised the structure of the creature. There was just bones and goo left. That's all been cleared up now, taken away for study."

Clare shifted, attempting to sit up. A drip was once again in the back of her hand. "So that's it, right? Saving untold generations in return for a lifetime of medication?"

"Would you prefer death?" Dominic's voice was edged with scorn.

"No, I guess not. Why did you choose Ashby though?"

"Coz some damn fool thought a hospital in Worcester might mean a lot of questions asked." Terrick walked in, a grin shining across his face. "I took a team of paramedics, came when Tina called, avoided all the paperwork. You go back when you're ready, girl. They got everythin' you need here."

"Including a department of Harley sympathizers, many of whom we shot recently."

Terrick frowned. "Yeah well about that..." he fell silent, looking troubled.

Clare started to panic. "What?"

"It seems there was a roundin' up of local law enforcement after your showdown with your captain," Terrick explained. "State police're runnin' the show now. Ashby police've been officially closed down as have several other departments."

"How?"

Tina leaned forward. "They tore Harley's office apart after the chief had him arrested. Turns out one of the reasons he liked that particular office is he had a private closet built into the wall. The room was full of damning documentation, a whole collection of forged Federal files. Mr. Harley was very fond of concealing information under the Federal seal. All manner of government agencies have expressed interest in talking to him."

"Where is he now?"

"He's incarcerated in a Massachusetts Correctional Institution, Cedar Junction, awaiting Federal trial," Dominic said, "at least for all the mundane crimes. He's far enough removed from the upheaval here to be safe for trial, though I wouldn't wish that place on him. Most of his bedfellows are there too. It turns out he had dealings all over the state. Corruption, larceny, bribery; more than one state judge has been picked up too. It was a right little empire. He won't see the back end of the trial, though. He's got too much information."

This scared Clare. She stroked Steve's purring body for reassurance. "They'll let him go?"

"Not quite. Andrew Harley might just disappear. He has a lot of information on a project called 'Iuvart': that mean anything to you?"

"Viruñas called that name out when it was hunting me, like it had been betrayed. I swear it was communicating with someone… or something."

"They also found detailed files on you," Tina added. "Your biological father as well."

"Viruñas said my dad… my real dad, was called Maygan."

"Bud Maygan. Is that all you know of him?"

"I never met him, but I know plenty. I have a half-sister too."

A nurse came into the room. It was Dominic's sister, Ellie, who smiled a greeting. "Time for your insulin shot," she said. "Glad to see you're awake for this one. Everybody else out. Let's give her a bit of privacy. She's been through a lot." Not willing to argue, Terrick and Dominic left quickly, Tina more reluctant to follow.

Pulling out what looked like a six-inch brightly-coloured pen, Ellie proceeded to screw a lid on it, pulling a plastic cover free to reveal the tiniest of needles. "This might be a bit of a shock to the system: do you want to do it?"

Clare took the insulin pen, turning it over in her hands, examining it. "This is my future? At least it's bright. What do I do?"

Ellie turned a dial. "That's your bolus, or amount of insulin, on the dial. Just push it into the skin on your stomach and press down on the plunger."

Clare did as instructed, feeling a nip as the needle went in and a slight chill as the insulin entered her system. It was nothing compared to the bodily abuse suffered by Viruñas. "That wasn't too bad." The realization of what she was doing hit home. "Is that what you do to Jarret Logan?"

Ellie shook her head. "No, he took his insulin through the drip."

Clare didn't miss a beat. "Took?"

"His body finally succumbed to the creature's assault, late Sunday night."

"About the time I killed it. Was there a link?"

"We'll never know," Ellie said, leaning over to tickle a very receptive Steve under the chin. The cat sauntered down to the bottom of the bed and curled up by her feet.

"Can we come back in now?" Terrick called from outside.

Ellie looked at Clare, her eyebrows raised.

"Yes Terrick, please do."

Terrick returned, carrying an enormous bunch of flowers. He placed them on the bed. "These're for you, girl. They were waitin' outside."

Clare plucked the gift tag from the wrapping and unfolded it. "Congratulations," she read aloud.

"Nothing more?" Terrick took the card from her. "Funny. You fancy some food? I was gonna bring a box of chocolates but it seemed a bit insensitive."

"Sure, I'm hungry. It'll be a while before I'm up to eating stuff like that, I think," Clare admitted. "I've got a lot of learning to do to keep this under control."

"It's not the end of the world," said Ellie as she tucked Clare back into bed. "Far from it; a little care and attention and nobody will know the difference."

"And don't forget," added Terrick, "that it's sugars that you gotta watch most. You can eat as much steak as you want!"

Ellie and her assistant left the room, closing the door behind them.

Dominic stood. "Now you're all here together there's a couple of issues we have to discuss."

The serious look on his face led Clare to worry. "Oh?"

"This needs to be kept quiet. Everybody knows Harley's a tyrant, and will expect him to go down for what he did. Some aspects of this affair have been explained away, some have been kept quiet."

This riled Clare. "How does silence make us any better than Harley?"

"Maybe it doesn't but that's how it is. The stranger elements of what you saw. The girl in UMASS, the creature people witnessed. It's being explained away. Daniel Acosador succumbed to a rare tropical disease. Flesh eating, very deadly."

"Who said…" Then Clare remembered. "ARC. Those people at the retreat have done this. Maybe they sent the flowers."

Dominic shrugged. Clare looked to her friends. Tina, Terrick, Candace. All their faces were blank, seemingly innocent with the shared secret. "What people?" They said in unison.

"Terrick, after all this can you stand that? What will you do?"

"Me? I'm carryin' on my job in Holden, as it should be."

"Detective Svinsky will carry on with her job," Dominic continued. "God knows the department needs some stability. You will need to go back of course, Clare. Who would want to lose such a proficient analytical mind as yours?"

"I feel I've changed. I don't know if I want to go back to the same job. That Vulcan badge over there on my jacket was from a time when pure logic got results. If this has taught me anything, it's to really go with my gut. Maybe there's a happy medium. Maybe I have a chance to demonstrate the best of both worlds?" She looked down at her bed, the white sheets folded with precision. "I'm just not sure. Too much has gone on here. I'll never forget those eyes, those soulless eyes. How are things like that even real?"

Chapter Thirty-Seven

It was mid-November. The leaves were falling in abundance from trees throughout Massachusetts, creating a riotous carpet of red, yellow and brown wherever Clare walked. The Worcester Police Department building loomed above, traffic roaring up the highway behind her. Clare dithered around the outside of the pitted concrete behemoth, hesitant to go in. It appeared the chief had taken her thoughts about Harley's office to heart, vast areas of the floor appeared to have been demolished under a warren of tarpaulin-covered scaffolding. Six weeks out had certainly seen a lot of changes to Clare as well as those around her.

A radiant blonde descended the steps to greet her. Clad in a new and rather snug-fitting skirt and jacket, Tina Svinsky stopped a couple of meters away from her. "Well see here. The wanderer returns and not a moment too soon either." Tina proceeded to brush mock-dust from the shoulders of Clare's brown suit. "You look great. I couldn't tell you'd ever been ill."

Clare smiled, feeling at peace more now than she had ever done in the past ten years. "Congratulations, Lieutenant."

Tina had the good grace to blush. "Aww, shucks. If it weren't for you, then this place would still be the same rotting den of corruption it always was. Harley would probably be chief and you'd be in a shallow grave, one way or another. How goes the treatment?"

"It's still a little odd. I don't think I'll ever get used to it."

The Eyes Have No Soul

Tina grinned. "Go on then, show it to me."

Very self-conscious, Clare nonetheless lifted the hem of her blouse, pulling a small black mechanism about two inches by three from a skin-coloured pouch she wore close to her skin. A wire-thin tube stuck out one end, curling in loops from the machine to a small bandage on her skin.

"That's it?" Tina seemed surprised.

"It's not exactly kidney dialysis. I take a pin prick of blood and measure my blood sugar on a small handset, then program any changes to the pump by remote. Change this canula every other day," Clare pointed to the bandage, "and the insulin cartridge every four. Simple. The rest is diet and exercise. I'm not without incidents but I'm getting there."

"It sure beats the alternative. So you ready?"

Clare closed her eyes and took a series of deep breaths. Twin orbs stared at her from within the privacy of her mind. She locked them in a box, storing the memory as a reminder that she had a responsibility to herself. Life was precious. "I'm ready."

Tina turned and led the way up to the main doors of the precinct lobby. Clare followed, pushing through the doors and coming to a stop just inside. The hallways were now free of litter.

"Like it?"

"I hardly recognize the place."

"Following Harley's rapid downfall, the whole precinct's been given a new lease of life through sudden and quite extensive funding. It seems the corruption was quite far spread and when Harley fell, all his adjuncts toppled like dominos." Clare had her suspicions about the source and these were confirmed when Tina led her into the room that had previously been Harley's office. It now held a conference table.

"I trust you find the precinct more to your liking?" Clare didn't recognize the man in a dark blue suit with his captain's badge hanging over the belt of his trousers. He was tall, with mousy-blond hair and a goatee. Perching on the edge of the table he looked quite at ease in this environment. He was quite different to the previous occupant,

298

but not the only occupant of the room. Another man in a beige suit stood staring out of the window toward the city's skyline. "It's a vast improvement," she replied.

"I'm Captain Andy Cassell, homicide, narcotics and whatever else they decide to throw at me until the new chain of command is fully established. I'm looking for new detectives, Miss Rosser, and you're top of my list. How do you fancy moving out of the lab and undergoing training?"

The offer stunned Clare. After so long stuck in the guts of the building she finally had a chance at a new beginning. Yet something nagged at her, like this was too much of a temptation. Was this a reward for her near-death experience? Maybe. Maybe not.

"That sounds wonderful," she said with genuine gratitude, "but the only case I ever really wanted to solve was the death of my parents. I've done that now. Perhaps I'll take your offer another day, if you still think I'm worthy of it."

Captain Cassell watched her for a moment, stroking his goatee. "Tina said you'd probably say something like that. Consider the offer open-ended." To Tina he said, "Lieutenant, I've got a few ideas I'd like to run by you in my office." He led the way out, Tina moving with her tiny, rapid steps behind him.

Clare found herself left alone in the conference room with the stranger, who still had not turned.

"He wasn't wrong, you know. You have great potential, more than even you perhaps realize."

"Thank you." Clare poured a glass of water for herself, then one for the stranger. Lifting hers, she took a small sip. The ice-cold water went down her throat with such exquisite pleasure she shivered. It was nectar. The stranger turned and took the glass, raising it. "To your good health," he said with a smile. "It's nice to be in control, no?"

His accent was European, though beyond that Clare couldn't pin it down. A mix of English, French, maybe some Dutch. What was recognisable was his face. The eyes were less hard, the jaw set at a softer angle. "You were stood beside Julian Strange when he argued Harley down."

He inclined his head in acknowledgement. "Some people are just so used to throwing their weight around they forget what it's like to have to back down. I don't back down, and neither do those I work with. My name is Swanson Guyomard, Clare. Your work and your resilience in the face of such a potentially devastating illness has been noted. Your willingness to go the extra mile and seek out illogical solutions; they've all brought you to the attention of my colleagues, who insisted I meet you."

It all clicked. "Those were your people at the artists' retreat. Scope. Ellen Covlioni."

"My people are everywhere. My organization… well let's say it has its fingers in lots of pies."

"Yeah but so did Harley."

"True but he was small time. You want to know what became of the man? You, Clare; you happened to him. You happened right from the very start. Your boiler suit had a camera. We saw everything."

"You could have stopped this from the very start," Clare accused. "Logan. My parents. Those children."

"We were too late for your parents, Clare. I could have stopped Harley at that point; yet what would we have learned from ending a story before it started? My people are forced to make desperate decisions every day. We wanted to see what you were made of. Besides, you wanted this. It was your plan to try and trap the creature in the city. When that didn't work you took it upon yourself to draw it out. We need people with that sort of gusto."

"Why? What could a diabetic possibly offer you?"

Swanson gave her a sly look, his eyes narrowed. "Is that how you see yourself? Is that what defines you?"

The comment gave Clare sufficient cause to doubt her words. *Don't begin this stage of your life relying on excuses, Clare.* "No. I'm a survivor."

"Damned right that's what you are. You are not a diabetic. You're a woman, a human being. You have qualities the likes of which many people would give their right arm to possess. You are defined by what you do in life, not by what you are."

"And who are you? What is your role in this?"

Swanson sat down and folded his hands together on the desk. "I am the man who is going to recruit you into my organization. You will be the first of many."

"I already turned down the captain. What makes you think I won't do the same to you?"

Swanson smiled. "We recently had a situation in Afghanistan. Another young lady from this very city showed her mettle there, too."

"I've seen the news reports. There was some great light show on top of a mountain in the Hindu Kush region. It was all out of focus."

"Would you like to know the truth behind the excuses? Would you like to see what we are really up against? You might end up understanding that Viruñas was just a sideshow, the merest of distractions."

For the first time in months she was truly intrigued. It was an invigorating feeling. "Go on."

"You rid the world of a menace. Viruñas was one of the soulless. He was part human, part supernatural being. That takes guts. That sort of thing comes to my notice. I want to recruit you. Here. Now. I think you know enough of my organization to understand this is not an open-ended offer."

Swanson waited with patience. 'Never appear too eager', Jeff often said.

"I'm in."

"Excellent. Your first task isn't far from home. Do you know West Labs?"

Clare frowned. "You mean that Biopharmaceutical facility over by Worcester State Hospital?"

"Something's amiss there and I need someone on the ground."

"For how long?"

"Until you find the answers."

Swanson was being coy but Clare knew the feel of a negotiation. "I found the answers about my parents and you want me to serve a higher purpose, right?"

"It's not without its benefits." Swanson opened a briefcase and pulled out a laptop, folding the screen open and turning it toward Clare. As the screen powered up, it revealed a picture of a woman smiling, touching close with a brown-haired man in a ponytail.

"The woman's name is Eva Ross. The man she's with is called Madden Scott."

"Eva? I have a half-sister by that name. She looks familiar."

"She should be. Eva's been in the media a lot lately. Working in Worcester State. On the run halfway across the country. That light show in Afghanistan. She's been very busy."

"No, it's more than that."

Swanson watched her for a moment. "You're most perceptive. You know the name of your biological father, yes?"

"Bud Maygan. Viruñas knew the name."

"We think Viruñas has been around a very long time. Perhaps centuries. It is only a pawn in this game. Those responsible for setting it loose on the world have been tracking Eva and her entire family for generations." Swanson leaned forward. "Your entire family."

"My..."

"Eva Ross is the daughter of Bud Maygan. She's your half-sister. So here's the deal. Get to the bottom of West Labs. Find what's festering there. Once you are done and Eva has finished her tasks, there is a top position waiting for you in Geneva if you would like it. I will arrange for the both of you to meet."

Clare felt the sting of the bargain, exhaling involuntarily through her nose. "If I get you your answers... what have I got to lose? Okay, I'm in."

Swanson let crack a little smile. "Excellent. Clare, welcome to Anges de la Résurrection des Chevaliers. Welcome to ARC."

Epilogue

Dean Bartow perched on the end of his bed, alone but for the chirping of bluebirds outside. He stared at the smeared glass of the window, not seeing the empty house beyond, not truly. Instead he imagined a time when people lived there. The woman, her brother. Even the cat. His father, on the rare occasion he had happened by, always fixated on the family that had lived there. They shared a common bond, one that excluded him from the rest of his family. He had rescued his father from Worcester Hospital, his hero a broken man. And then she had ended it, stabbing him in the dark. Dean stared at the window, hatred infusing his entire being; his only thought was one of vengeance. He had watched as men had loaded up a truck with everything from the house. He had wandered through the barren halls after they had left. She wasn't coming back.

So now Dean watched, and plotted. He would grow, he would hunt. He would find her and he would avenge his father. The world was not big enough to hide her. Behind him, on the floor a series of bodies filled one side of his tiny room. His mother, his siblings, grandparents. All twisted and empty, drained of fluid. He understood the hunger now, accepted it. He had nobody to help him. He would do this alone. Dean stared at the window. Two glowing eyes stared back.

About the Author

Matthew W. Harrill lives in the idyllic South-West of England, nestled snugly in a village in the foothills of the Cotswolds. Born in 1976, he attended school in Bristol and received a degree in Geology from Southampton University. By day he plies his trade implementing share plans. By night he spends his time with his wife and four children.

http://www.matthewharrill.com/

Printed in Poland
by Amazon Fulfillment
Poland Sp. z o.o., Wrocław